A Matter of Time

A Novel

Shannon Dill Strachan

Lulu

This book is a work of fiction. Names, characters, places, and incidents are products of the author's imagination or are used fictitiously. Any resemblance to actual events or locales or persons, living or dead, is entirely coincidental.

Copyright © 2008 by Shannon Dill Strachan

All rights reserved.

Cover design by Shannon Dill Strachan
Cover photograph © Viktor Pravdica - Fotolia.com

ISBN 978-0-557-00137-8

With profound gratitude to
my Creator, who teaches me to love,
my mother, Sandra Dill Little, who taught me to love writing,
my dearest friend, Tricia Ulch, who taught me to be brave and
all of the authors and poets who taught me to love words.

"Now faith is being sure of what we hope for and certain of what we do not see."

— Hebrews 11:1

A Matter of Time

Chapter 1
A Meeting

An offering of golden light generously spilled into the window, flooding the room with the kind of light indicative of a fading day. The sky was a peculiar shade of blue, and was particularly animated by the solitary cloud slowly drifting by, which seemed to be illuminated by the very light of hope. Though her presence was expected in less than an hour, the strangely flushed sky was a rare sight, and she was drawn to its curious glow as if it were some piper directing her steps with his romantic tune. Her long gown of silk rustled against the bare floor as her dainty steps approached the window. When she stepped into the light, she closed her eyes softly and as its warmth embraced her, whispered, "Thank you".

'How can I ever repay the kindness which has been bestowed upon me?' she pondered. The enchanting evening was perfect for the occasion before her, the kind of event which begs reflection upon one's past, an appreciation for certain blessings, and the anticipation of leaping from one stage in life to another. Less than a year ago she had known the darkest hour in her young life, a time when she had found herself completely lost upon the bleak sea of the world, with her dreams her only compass. Fate had plunged her into the depths of a lonely and forsaken existence, but he had changed everything, with one knowing look, with kind words and with a truth she had searched for all of her days.

He had touched her life, he had looked at her, and he knew her and she was alive again and far removed from her previous state of despair. The darkness which had once covered her heart seemed quite distant now, and in only a brief time, life as she knew it had been irrevocably altered. A window to her soul had been opened that snowy night long ago, opened by his courage, a courage when once reflected in her, made it possible for her to see in him what had been unnoticed by others.

He was not a fiend at all, but rather the most generous and kind person she had known, and all she had to offer him for his kindness was her devotion. She prayed it would be enough. As clear as a spring rain bathes a day in a fresh newness, so was the clarity of her place in his world. She had reached the time in her life when her life's security and future happiness was fully realized, and cognizant of this truth and resting in its peace, she remembered the night she first met Edward Withers and her long journey to Brookhaven...

Chilled to the bone and starving on a blustery winter night in the year 1887, she found herself lost in the outskirts of Asheville, North Carolina. Utterly lost, with no memory of her past and with little hope for her future. Her name, her memories were unknown to her. Who was she? From where had she come? Who loved her? Who remembered her? Who may be waiting for her to come home? These questions repeated in her mind, but answers refused to follow.

Her eyes were starving for something, someone she could recognize. When had she last eaten? She could no longer remember. Her mind was a war with taunting thoughts and questions, and as the battle raged on, she noted the tall, bare trees above her seemed to fight a battle of their own. The trees wearily stretched finger-like branches towards the night sky, as if to capture the glowing moon. Pearly shadows opened a pathway before her, leading her to the place where the answers to all of her questions would finally be revealed.

Her footsteps in the snow followed the melodic tune of her mind, and with each cold step she drew closer to her destiny. The constant crunch, crunch, crunch of her delicate steps seemed to comfort her until she heard its rhythm no more. The sudden silence brought her to the acute awareness she had stopped, and her eyes were bright and wide as she beheld the vision before her, which seemed to have been conjured from some wild and distant dream.

Unwittingly she found herself clinging to black gates of iron, cold, yet somehow protective and within the archway of those far-reaching gates, there was a carving in stone upon which contained the inscription "Brookhaven".

"Brookhaven," she whispered, as a billowy breath of air escaped her lips. 'Are these the forbidden walls of which I was warned? Is it even real?' she questioned, 'and if it is, I swear I have seen this place and known its many halls. What I would give to be inside those warm, familiar, yes, familiar walls,' she pondered as she stood clinging to the icy gates, thrusting up from the cold earth toward the sky.

Nothing would do but for her to have a closer look at the dark, castle-like estate. She eased inside the gate, glancing to her left and then shifting her eyes to the right to ensure she had not been seen or followed, but she saw nothing and no one. There was no sign of life in this abandoned edge of the world save for the warm glow from a window on the east side of the estate. As the gate closed behind her and she gingerly walked towards the window, a dark cloud cleared the face of the frozen moon illuminating the fine estate. The delicate intricacies of its design were revealed. As doleful and brooding as it was, there was something of beauty in each detail and she sensed it had been designed by gentle and loving hands. As she made her way to the window, she admired two massive and fierce stone lions guarding its doors, but not even their menacing stares could detain her steps.

Before she was aware of her position, she found herself outside the aforementioned window, intently gazing inside, and then in a sudden rush her heart warmed as soon as she saw him. No longer could she feel the throbbing pain in her icy extremities. The pain was replaced by a welcome numbness, but it was more than that. She felt a part of her waking from a deep sleep. She felt as though winter had presently melted into spring, and it seemed hope had somehow found its way back to her. The gentleman stood before a table. In front of him was an imposing mantle of marble and wood, above which an enormous portrait hung and under which a weakening fire glowed. She could almost feel its warmth and hear its crackling embers.

The man appeared to be working on something, but she could not see the object which entranced him. She continued to watch him as he momentarily abandoned his work to tend to the waning fire. He was a tall man with black hair and of dark complexion. His movements were very precise and with a certain purpose, and as he turned away from the fire she caught a glimpse of his face. He had very strong features: distinct dark brows outlined his penetrating eyes, and the bones of his cheeks were round and set high upon his face, every indication was he appeared to be a man of at least forty years, with a healthy, slim build, and his hands, his hands were beautiful and somehow elegant as he carefully stoked the fire. He allowed himself only a minute's warmth and returned once more to the strange table.

Her curiosity could not be contained as her eyes searched every inch of the spectacular room before her. If only she were a little closer. Without thought, she moved nearer the window and stood on the balls of her feet, and clinging to the edge of the window, shifted her weight to her weary arms, but in doing so, lost her footing and slipped on a small ice-laden rock just beneath her foot.

As her body made its descent to the frozen ground, she let out a harrowing shriek and found herself paralyzed on the cold, hard earth in the next instant. Stunned and alarmed by the fall, a strange echo of the weak lamentation she had uttered repeated in her mind and suddenly she realized her presence would most certainly be detected. The muscles of her stomach tightened as this knowledge dawned on her and a great, excited, anticipation consumed her as she feared to what end her curiosity had led her.

Edward wiped his brow and stood back to analyze his work. 'Just as I hoped. Perfect,' he thought and allowed a smile of self-praise. He had spent days working on this present project and he had finally completed the work. And though it was a chilling night, and when he had begun his task he had felt winter's chill deep within his bones, he had worked himself into a frenzy polishing the marble and was damp with his labor. It was a wonderful release to work again and a much needed distraction.

Looking at it now before him, he could hardly believe he had created such a thing of beauty. He would celebrate with a rare bottle of scotch.

He stood by the fire admiring his work for a moment more and noted how very still the night was. For certain there was not a sound to be heard other than his quiet breathing and the occasional pop and crackle of the smoldering fire. As he carefully covered the piece, a noise from across the room startled him.

'An intruder, at this hour?' he questioned, as he promptly walked to the window, pulled the heavy drapes aside and stared out into the night, but saw only darkness. 'Perhaps a wayward animal,' he thought, 'but no, it was too loud and quite obviously human, I must investigate.' Angrily, he reached for his boots and shoved his feet one by one into them grumbling, "I shall make him sorry before this night is through".

Edward lived almost as a hermit and employed only the necessary number of servants to sustain his sprawling estate. He had hoped he would be left alone, not only this night but for all nights to come. He was removed from the outside world and he preferred it. No one understood him, no one of the living world, at least, so it was his choice to remove himself from others. He had chosen to live in the isolation of Brookhaven and now his happy solitude had been broken, and the grounds would have to be checked for the unwanted intruder. Typically such a task would be left to a servant, but Edward was so disconcerted by the interruption, he decided to personally handle the matter.

Being a December night, he covered himself with his wool cloak and then walked down the corridor to the stately front doors, and as was customary, brought his fingers lightly to his lips and placed a gentle kiss on the corresponding lips of the sculpture, which was carefully placed on the foyer table, keeping watch of the doorway. Mindful of the task before him he withdrew his hand and opened both doors with a forceful arm, and as he did so, a bitter coldness greeted him. He walked to the edge of the verandah and noted how the moonlight revealed a fresh set of tracks in the snow before him, making his task simpler than he had expected.

Edward followed the path of dainty steps with his eyes until it ended beneath the ground floor window from where the disturbing sound had come. When he took his first step toward the window, the chilling night wind danced by him a second time and he shuddered as it seemed to pass through his wool cloak chilling him to the core. 'Peculiar,' he thought.

The young girl had composed herself and was now standing firmly and solemnly against the cold walls of the mansion as she heard his heavy footsteps approaching. A paralyzing fear seized her as she held her very breath. A voice deep within her urged, 'Do not just stand here, move, quickly before he sees you, there is still time.' But her stubborn body refused her mind's urging call. A large figure was coming towards her and its shadow appeared to be some nine feet tall. In her panic she allowed her mind to become entangled within one's most irrational fears; she thought perhaps this huge shadow looming ever nearer must be a giant and she had stumbled upon some sacred, mythological palace of another world.

Rationality soon took over and she realized the land beneath her feet was quite real and she had not drifted into a dreamland, but rather upon someone's private property and she would most likely be punished for trespassing. The long shadow would certainly find her in a matter of seconds and she would probably be sent to the authorities for her crime. As she clung to the wall of the enchanting estate she was truly sorry she had intruded here, but the estate, the grand castle, she could not resist its call to her. It had drawn her in and taken her.

As Edward approached the window, he saw a small figure, the apparent shadow of a woman. He wondered what could have possessed her to be lurking about his estate in the middle of this dismal and silent December night.

"Who is there?" he demanded. He was answered by silence. The giant's voice was as deep as his shadow was tall. 'From what sort of man did such a voice come?' fear whispered through her mind. She closed her eyes and again held her breath, pretending if she did not allow herself to see him, she would somehow be invisible. But regardless of her simple prayer, the stranger continued to come closer. Slowly. Closer. She could feel his warmth, and then he reached out to her.

His strong hands gently touched her frail arm and she opened her eyes. She exhaled cautiously and gave in to reality. His touch was almost gentle, for certain, he could have easily and with good reason grabbed her harshly, but he did not. She sensed a kind of compassion in his manner and believed she would not be harmed after all, and consequently found the courage to make herself known to the stranger. She stepped slowly into the light of the window, and upon seeing her face, the stranger took a step back, releasing her arm and slowly whispered in a raspy, feeble voice, "It is you."

She stared at him blankly for a few fleeting seconds, forcing away the smile just beginning to form on her slightly parted lips. She could have been mistaken, but had he said it? She blinked in disbelief. With moonlight reflecting in her moistened eyes, she questioned him, "Do you know me, Sir?" her teeth chattering as she spoke.

His mind raced frantically. How long had he waited for this moment, the moment when he would see her again? At last she was here, at long last. He often wondered if she had only been a dream, perhaps he had imagined her; perhaps she lived only in his heart. But now she stood before him. She was real, flesh and bone. He reached out to her and took a step forward. 'She has finally returned to me, she is here, she has found me after all of the lost years.' In his dreams she had come to him so many times before, and they had rejoiced in their happy reunion. He could not remember a time when she had not been in his heart and mind, and the constant theme of his thoughts was the moment he might see her again. Silently, internally, he repeated, 'thank you, thank you, thank you.'

Chapter 2
A Mistake and an Invitation

After a moment she repeated, "Sir?"

"Shh...just let me look at you," he said, now holding her tiny arms within each of his strong hands. His dark eyes entranced her and his obvious familiarity with her seemed so real in that instant she did not question it for a moment. Oblivious to the cold air surrounding the two, he desperately searched her every feature, and then suddenly his grip loosened and he slowly turned away from her, as if the sight of her pained him. As he turned from her, she instinctively reached for his hand and he turned to face her once more, though he would not allow her to keep his hand nor his gaze.

"But..?" she asked with her shaky voice and just as clearly with her eyes, frantically searching his stormy eyes and strained expression. He glanced upon her young face once more, but the light she had witnessed in his eyes had now vanished and though he looked at her, it was as though he looked through her, it was as though he were not allowed to look more closely upon her as he had willingly accomplished before. Not only would he not look upon her, but the softness of his face had turned as cold as the ice beneath her feet, and his peaceful expression had been replaced with a painful grimace.

Refusing to look into her eyes again, he said, "Let us speak inside. You should come in now, before you catch your death. It is predicted tonight shall be the coldest night of the winter." The warmth in his voice had vanished. His manner was altogether different now. She hesitated momentarily, but then took his hand and followed him across the verandah and up the marble steps to the grand doorway.

"Forgive me for intruding so, Sir," she offered.

"Do not bother seeking my forgiveness, I dare say I cannot imagine what has possessed you to be found here, but I trust it is not your choice, for who would choose such a thing?"

"Yes Sir, I shall explain as best as I can shortly."

"There is ample time for explaining, do not worry yourself."

She was all confusion as his words were void of any warmth, and she wondered what might become of her in this place. She followed him quietly, her eyes searching the mansion with each step. He led her to a parlor of richly painted crimson, furnished in fine European furniture, and left her unaccompanied for several minutes before leading her into the room she had seen from the window only moments before.

The curious room was as warm as she had imagined, and in the center of the room was the table the odd stranger had been standing behind. But instead of discovering what had demanded his attention, she found the table had been well covered with a draping cloth, concealing the object upon it from sight. She desperately wanted to remove the cloth and reveal the object or at least to inquire of it, but since he did not see fit to enlighten her on the subject, she allowed the desire to be squelched as she was much too nervous and too grateful for his hospitality to ask any intrusive questions just now.

"Well don't just stand there, come now, sit by the fire. This is the room of your apparent interest is it not? No matter, I shall have Charles prepare something warm for you to eat," he offered, noting the girl's embarrassment by the distinct shade of blush upon her cheeks.

"Please do not go to any trouble, I really cannot ask..." she began. But he interrupted her before she could finish, "It is clear you are cold and lost, the journey to Brookhaven from the nearest town is at least two days on foot, and I must insist you take your rest here. I shall have no argument."

"Thank you Sir, I am grateful for your kindness, indeed your assessment is quite correct, I am lost... and until this night, I feared I might never be found." Her voice weakened into a deep despair he could feel and somehow understand.

"Good, then the matter is settled," he said quietly.

She could wait no longer to ask the question which screamed inside her, and apprehensively she inquired, "Before, on the grounds, you said 'It is you,' what did you mean?"

He knew the question would come, but he wanted to pretend for just a moment more, to suspend facing the inevitable truth, and besides his reluctance, he did not know how to answer her. How could he explain to her that her face was the source of his life's bliss, the very sun around which his life revolved? How could he make her understand he had lived in some sort of distorted dream until he had seen her just a few moments before? He did not want to frighten her. What should he say? He wanted to confide in her.

He wanted to open his heart to her as he did so often in his mind. But he looked at her youthful face and said, "I am truly sorry Miss, but I was mistaken, dreadfully mistaken. I was uncertain as to whom I would find beneath that window and when I saw that it was you, a young lady, I was shocked and my imagination raced before me for a moment. I thought you were someone I once knew, in the darkness, the shadows, you reminded me of her."

"Oh," she responded with a look of disillusionment.

Feeling she deserved a more complete explanation, he continued, "Her name was Emily and I knew her many years ago, when I was a young man." He wanted to continue and explain that Emily was not just someone he knew, but she had been the source of everything good and true and kind in his world. Knowing her had been the greatest joy of his life, and the light her life had beamed into his own was entirely extinguished when she lay dying in his arms all those years ago, but he could not speak of her, of the charmed time of his life, not to a stranger, even if she did bear the resemblance of his lost bride.

Instead he said, "I suppose I have so frequently imagined her returning to me that I allowed my eyes to deceive me when first they fell upon you. Do forgive me?"

The tortured expression on his face and the pain in his voice, the reverence with which he spoke of this 'Emily' was clearly evident to her and she interrupted, "It is I who must plead your forgiveness, I see I have opened an old wound. I am in no position to ask anything of you, nor to expect any sort of explanation, it is just, I, I have searched for so long," she explained as a single tear suddenly escaped her melancholy eyes. She had held the tears back for so long now, but seeing the intensity with which this man had once felt love was the tiny crack in the dam of her soul which unleashed the multitude of tears which followed.

She began to cry, quite uncontrollably, for she could no longer speak, only tears and more tears. For a moment she forgot herself, and allowed herself to lose her composure before this compassionate man who had seemed to rescue her. She felt like a child, crying hysterically. He was so kindhearted and seemed to know her somehow, even if he did not know her from her past as she had hoped.

For the past two years she had retained a strength untold, a brave hope that she would one day find the place where she belonged, but on this night, the incessant fears chasing her for so long had backed her into a corner and descended upon her and finally overtaken her heart. The torment and sadness of the previous months ravished her body as she shook and heaved uncontrollably.

As he watched her crying, overwhelmed by the circumstances of her life, he felt compelled to go to her.

"There, there, child," he said, dropping to one knee against her chair, offering her a silk handkerchief.

"No harm shall come to you; you are safe here, upon my word. Your dear face was not created to feel the warmth of such hopeless tears." Noting his attempt at consoling the girl did not seem to alleviate her distress, he added, "Shall I leave you to your sorrows, would you prefer a moment of privacy?"

In answer she shook her head in the negative before finding these words, "Most kind sir, I would not have you go, I do not know what came over me. Please forgive my foolish tears," she said clutching the handkerchief. "I have come such a long way...on a most arduous journey. Would that I had received such kindness from others as I have from you. I cannot explain my outburst just now, I may have fallen ill, it may be the recognition you seemed to have earlier, or perhaps the strange feeling I have about your estate, a feeling so familiar and unlikely, but for some reason I feel safe here in this place."

"And safe you are, but I must ask how it is you came to find Brookhaven?"

"I am not certain of how I came to be here. You see, I am not certain of anything, really. I suffer from a condition which renders me unable to recall my past, or anyone from it, amnesia. I have traveled for days and days. A journey started two years ago and I have been unable to discover anything or anyone who can give me a clue about my past, my identity. But tonight, I found myself in front of your stunning estate and it was as though I had come home, my steps were not my own, I could no more turn away from this place than I could breathe. Some force compelled me to stop here, I cannot explain why, and when you saw me, I own I was terrified at first, but then you said 'It is you', and naturally I thought I was found. I thought I had finally found someone who could tell me who I am. But instead, I find myself lost yet again."

"I am sorry I misspoke, that I, raised your hopes only to lower them again. Amnesia, you say, for two years?" he asked.

She nodded wiping the last traces of tears away with her soiled hand.

"How very peculiar. I have heard of the condition of course, but I have never encountered someone who has experienced it 'first hand', as they say. Every memory of your life just vanished from your mind, how frightful, and yet," he continued lowering his eyes, "it could be a blessing to forget. Do you remember anything?"

"Very little really. There was an accident, it occurred on my journey to this country. I was on a ship to America which had departed from Liverpool, though I do not know why. I awoke to strange faces in the infirmary of the ship. Those eyes searching mine, I remember to this day, and the wave of questions following, none of which I could answer.

When the ship arrived in America I was no closer to remembering my past and there was no where for me to go. I met a kind, elderly lady and her daughter on the ship who waited with me in port after the ship docked. We waited there until the last passenger had departed. We hoped someone would be waiting there for me, expecting my arrival, but no one came. Being the kind souls they were, they took me to St. John's hospital in New

York City where I was given into the care of an order of the holy sisters.

I hoped my memory would return in a matter of days or weeks, but it was not to be. The sisters spent countless hours with me trying every conceivable trick to unlock my mind; one of the first was my introduction to the looking glass. We all prayed for a miracle, but each new look into the glass only revealed the same stranger staring back at me. It was like seeing myself for the first time. There was not the slightest clue as to where I had come from, my only possessions were the very clothes I wore, a hair ornament, and my necklace," she said, touching her hand to her chest where the necklace lay beneath her dress.

"The painful bruise on my head had healed completely by that time, but my disorientation of mind and the displacement of my memories were far more disturbing than the physical condition had been. After staying with the sisters for a short while, I decided to search out my past, and there were far more needy souls than I requiring a bed and the sisters' attention. I became very close to Sister Anne, and she kindly asked that a collection be made for me which afforded me with the means to make a journey to the next city and I was off, and for the next few months I simply followed my own will anywhere it would take me.

I believed if I could just recognize someone, somewhere, I would have a clue, but strangely everything seemed so foreign. There was nothing familiar to me, until tonight. This estate, I feel as though I must have seen it before, but instead of answering my questions, I am afraid it only poses new ones. I want to continue my search, but I am afraid I am beginning to lose hope. Along the way many people have told me to start over, to forget the past and perhaps they are right, but I am haunted by my absence of memories. I have no past, but who else is a person but the experiences they have had? I do not know if I was a good person or a bad person. I worry there is someone out there loving me or needing me and I worry also there is no one and I am destined to travel this weary journey alone for all time. No. I cannot deny this urging of my soul. I must regain my past, whatever the cost."

Edward listened intently, intrigued by the phenomenon of losing one's memory. While forgetting might be a way to ease the longing, it would separate him from his most precious memories, and that was worse than forgetting.

"I understand," Edward offered, "without the knowledge of your past you can never truly be at peace, and peace is something I value above most things. How very lonely and frightened you must be."

"Yes, in a world full of people to be friendless and alone seems impossible. The very worst of it is having lost my past, I have lost my family, my friends, my relationships and any hope of felicity. There is a constant longing for some little hint, no matter how small. I just need some intimation that I did not merely fall from the heavens."

Edward smiled, for he felt "the heavens" was precisely from where she had come.

"Although, I suppose I do have the dreams," said she thoughtfully.

"The dreams?" Edward questioned.

"Yes, I have been haunted by the same dream on a number of nights and I choose to believe the dream holds some connection to my past."

"Well, that is a start, Miss...?"

"Oh forgive me, Lenora, you can call me Lenora. You see, I do not know my name, even my name is borrowed. The sisters called me Lenora because I would call out for 'Lenora' in my dreams."

"Well, Lenora, I am sorry you are lost and alone in the world, but I am glad your journey has brought you here. I should like to help you find your past. My name is Edward Withers."

"Pleased to meet you Mr. Withers." she said smiling.

"Please, no formalities. You may address me as Edward."

"Well then, thank you, Edward."

"But what of your dreams and who might this Lenora be?" he asked.

"I do not know, I can only remember fragments. But each dream is the same. I am walking at a rather quick pace and I am surrounded by people, but their faces are all as a blur, reminiscent of paintings I have seen, I believe the technique is called impressionism, nothing is truly distinct, but in any event, I believe it to be a summer evening, for the wind meeting my face is warm and I hear the sound of water, as if I am near a shore. And there is a breeze, an intense wind actually, for I hear it whistling so loud and mighty as if the wind itself is chasing me. And just as the wind reaches its most thunderous, harrowing moan, there is another sound, it is a human voice. At least I think it is a voice. It seems to plead with me, but I do not understand the words, nonetheless I am drawn to them and I begin to run. I see myself running, from what or whom I know not, and then all is turned to darkness and I awaken. It rather sounds like a nightmare and no dream at all, but I find these hazy recollections comforting, for they are the only remnants of my life before this one."

"I am certain you will find the answers for which you search. Life can be a mystery to us all at times. But do not lose faith Lenora. In time, the answers will come. I believe there are no coincidences, and only when we find ourselves in our darkest hour do we begin to rise into the light."

Lenora was rejuvenated by the warm fire and it was lovely to share a quiet moment with someone, and this someone had turned out to be such a caring person. Perhaps she was not friendly after all. After a brief, wonderful silence, Edward asked Lenora if she was ready to retire for the evening. She secretly questioned her decision to spend the evening at Brookhaven, but where else was she to go? He had said himself there was no other sign of life for miles, and besides that, somehow she trusted Edward, and she knew she could finally enjoy a long awaited rest.

Though his eyes guarded a fierce intensity, she instinctively knew he was incapable of harming her in any way. Lenora followed Edward up a dark and winding staircase of beautifully hand-carved wood. She had never seen anything like it before. Brookhaven was wonderfully handsome. With each step she felt simultaneously a familiarity and a strange newness, neither of which she could understand. Edward showed her to a room at the end of the hall on the third floor of the estate.

Noticing her ragged attire he offered her the full use of the room to which he led her, explaining she would find suitable clothing in the room and she may make use of anything she desired. He promised to send a servant to her room with food and water and assured her his room was at the opposite end of the hall and he would be at her service should she have need of anything at all. She thanked him again for his generosity and closed the door behind her.

At Edward's instruction, a fire had been started in his guest's room. Lenora was embraced by its warmth immediately and welcomed the smell of the burning wood. She ignited a lamplighter and lit the lantern by the bedside table. For several moments she looked in wonderment at the room. She took a deep breath of the warm air and stood close to the fire as her eyes drank in the splendor of it all, and she wondered if she had ever been in a room so beautiful. She would have been thankful to rest her head upon a rock or a pillow of straw, but instead she placed her hand gently on the bed and mused to herself that Fate had finally smiled upon her.

The grand bed was suitable for a king. She stepped on the foot stool and fell back onto the beautiful, plush, down pillows as though she were falling upon the snow as a child to make an impression of an angel. Lying on her back, her eyes scanned every inch of the luxurious room. She had never been so weary and yet, at the same time, had never more wanted to fight fatigue's tug on her weary mind and body. She feared sleeping because in waking all the magic of this night may have ended.

And then her thoughts turned to Edward, her gratitude for his kindness, and she could not help but to sense a loneliness about him. It was a feeling only the lonely could recognize in another. She wondered why he seemed such a tortured soul, and what had happened to the young woman he had told her about, Emily. Emily had obviously been lost to him for some time now, and perhaps the loss of his young love was responsible for the painful expression in his eyes. 'Pity such a fine man has known such sadness,' she thought, but Edward's past fate escaped her mind quickly and was replaced by the overwhelming beauty of the room. 'Are you dreaming?' she asked herself.

She explored the room a few more moments before noticing a large and obviously very old armoire. It was positively lovely and when she opened its doors, she found it full of exquisite clothing. 'How strange' she thought, 'could these clothes belong to the woman Edward spoke of?' But as she examined the clothing she noted the gowns were unlike any she had seen before. The dresses, coats, bedclothes, gloves and hats appeared to be from some other time, far and away from any she knew.

Again her mind shifted from these present questions and rushed on to others, in the excitement of seeing the beautiful colors and in feeling the many rich fabrics against her skin.

[handwritten annotations at top: "research the era", "language", "Southern lango"]

"Lovely" she whispered, as she selected a beautiful silk gown, and held it against herself. 'It will be a perfect fit,' she thought. Just then she heard a faint knock upon her door. "Ah the meal" she said as she remembered, and laid the dress on the bed.

Upon answering the door, the woman behind it looked at Lenora for an almost awkward moment without saying a word. It was a look of shock, of uncertainty, indeed she looked as if she had seen a ghost.

"Is there something the matter?" Lenora asked hesitantly.

The woman knitted her brow, started to speak, but then paused, and shaking off her unformed thought responded, "Of course not. Good evening, Miss, my name is Lily. There is soup here for you, and warm water for the basin. I will see to the fire again directly, going to be a chilling night."

Lenora heard uneasiness in Lily's voice and continued to sense a peculiarity in her stare, making Lenora uncomfortable and self-conscious.

"Are you sure nothing is the matter?" Lenora asked.

"Nothing at all. I was just startled to see you here. I mean, I ..."

"Oh, I understand now, Edward told me of Emily, his past love. Mind you, he spared few words on the subject, but I could see he regarded her as the love of his life, and judging from your reaction now, I realize now he must have minimized the resemblance I have to her. For certain, he said very little of her, yet it is obvious his heart is still full. I do hope my presence here causes him no further grief. But I have said too much, and I shan't mention her again, for I see the discomfort in your eyes."

"Don't mention it Miss," said Lily, as she nodded as though in agreement with Lenora's supposition, but her manner revealed quite the opposite affect. Her face still spoke of confusion.

"It is rather frigid and I cannot remember the last time I consumed something warm. The soup smells delicious. Thank you Lily, my name is Lenora." As Lily walked passed the bed she could hardly ignore the beautiful gown that lay across it.

"Edward kindly offered the use of these fine clothes," Lenora offered nervously.

"My, that is a lovely one. Has not been worn in decades I'd say."

"Is that right? I thought they all seemed rather old."

"Yes, part of the estate, they were. Master Withers is very protective of such things, he must have taken a liking to you." she said smiling. "Please do forgive me Miss if you find my manners poor, you are the first guest we have had in years upon years, excepting Dr. Weatherly. Well, I'll leave you to your dinner now. Just make yourself at home."

Lily closed the door behind her and marveled at the young woman, 'Emily? The love of his life?' she thought, 'whatever did she mean?'

༄༅

Lenora walked over to the silver service laid out before her and placed her hands atop the welcome silver dome, and enjoyed the warmth it emitted. She uncovered it quickly and found the promised steaming soup and the aroma of chicken, carrots and spices filled the air. Accompanying the soup was a hearty loaf of bread which she broke and dipped into the creamy, aromatic pool. She had forgotten how delicious food could actually taste as she savored each morsel of nourishment more thankfully than the last. When all traces of the soup had left the bowl, she rinsed her hands in the basin of warm water, provided for that purpose, chose a simple night gown and brushed her hair with a pewter brush set she had discovered in a top dresser drawer.

Brookhaven, Edward, the room and the combination of it all made her forget her previous hopeless plight and she went to sleep smiling for the first time in her new life.

As Lenora slept peacefully, Edward sat in his room before a crackling fire in his favorite chair. He sipped his celebratory scotch and his thoughts remained intensely fixed on his guest. 'How had this come to pass? Was this *really* happening?' His mind became jumbled with all of the questions he wanted to ask her. He knew he would never find rest this night, not with her here in Brookhaven. He forced himself to attempt sleep, as he certainly did not want to be bad company in the morning, but images of his beloved began to cover his mind as they did at this hour of the evening, "Edward," he could still hear Emily's soft and knowing voice uttering his name.

Emily had entered his heart as no one else had and as a result of her untimely departure no one had entered it since. When she left him to face the world alone it was as if his spirit gave birth to wings and flew away on her dying breath. As his thoughts of her finally waned and upon drifting into a state of being half asleep and half awake, he heard a voice. It was Lenora's.

'She needs me,' he thought, 'I must go to her.'

Edward was at her door in moments. He could barely make out her words.

"No!" she murmured. Then frantically, "Stop, stop at once!" she sobbed. And then silence. Edward stood by the door and suddenly she began screaming "No. Please. No. I must go to her."

At this, Edward entered her room and ran to her side, "Lenora, Lenora, wake up, you are dreaming." He shook her softly and called her name again. "Lenora, it is all right, I am here now, do not be afraid." All at once she opened her eyes, and finding him hovering over her, she shrank from him.

"It is all right, I am Edward, remember," he assured her.

And remembering his kind face she asked in a whisper, "What happened?"

"From the sound of it you were visiting your past, but you sounded frightened, do you remember the dream?" he asked.

"A dream, yes, it was only a dream, but this time I *do* remember something. There was the warm wind as before, but before the wind came, I was in a room, a room in a very large house. I seemed at home there, I think I must have been home. Yes, it was *my* room, but Edward, it was, it was here, it was Brookhaven. But that is all wrong, it cannot be...then the wind came and the faces and an envelope, I can almost see it now. It was made of fine paper and I held it close to me, but suddenly it fell from my hands and I was desperate to catch it, to retrieve it, as though my very life depended upon it, but it was lost. That is all. I remember nothing more. Perhaps I am only confused. But it was this place, it was. Admittedly it is not much, but it is the first time I have had any feeling of a place where I belong and never have I seen the envelope, oh what must it contain?" she said with an inquisitive smile.

"You see, everything will be fine. You have been here only

hours and already your fate is changing. But are you sure that is all you can remember?"

"I am trying to remember. You said I sounded fearful, did I say something?" she asked

"Yes, you were upset and you asked "Why," and then you began to scream "No, No," and I believe you said "I must go to her.""

"I must go to her." She repeated in a whisper, "But to whom? Lenora? Yes, it must be she. What trickery my emotions play on me, one part of the dream was the most tranquil feeling, as calm and happy a feeling as I can remember, but the other borne of desperation and fear, the hopelessness I felt as I watched the wind carry my precious envelope away from my grasp. All I know for certain is I am glad I am here."

"Yes, as am I. You really should rest now, but I can be here in a moment if you should need me, just call for me, do you promise you will."

"I promise," she said smiling back at him. Edward retrieved the candle by her bedside and bid her a good night. As she watched him close the door behind him, she gave thanks for being under his care. But the warmth her heart felt for this place and for this generous man was to be overshadowed by the haunting dream. She sank back down in the warmth of the bed and thought about the events of the night.

The dream was the first new memory she had had since her past memories had been forgotten. She was convinced the dream was indeed an authentic memory from her elusive past. There were parts of the dream that did not ring true, as the notion Brookhaven had been her home, but the envelope was a far different matter, and she pledged her every waking hour to discovering what it may have contained. 'Could it be being in this estate, being with Edward has caused me to remember?' she thought. 'It could not be, yet before this night, I had lost all hope, and now my hopes have been renewed once more.' Again she fought the desire to sleep to postpone the inevitable end of the night, but her weariness soon overcame her and she drifted into a deep, dreamless sleep.

Chapter 3
A Secret

Edward walked down the hall pondering what Lenora's dream had meant. The desperation in her voice was haunting. Lenora had sounded so frightened and yet determined, and he wondered what terrible events might be lurking in the shadows of her past, and why she seemed to feel she had been in Brookhaven before this night. Was it possible? Perhaps it was simply exhaustion; he had dreamt many strange and disturbing dreams, which in reality had no connection to anything bearing reason. He had neglected to ask Lenora how long she had been in the elements, and he began to fear her journey and exposure to the frigid temperatures might result in the serious deterioration of her heath. With the thought of her falling ill or experiencing any further pain whatsoever, he decided, vowed to be more precise, to remedy those painful days she had endured. He sat at his desk and began scribbling a short note. He folded the parchment and handed it to a young servant.

"Deliver this immediately," was his only instruction. He returned to his room and as he stepped across the threshold, his thoughts drifted to another place. He quickly found a comfortable position in his chair by the fire and lingered there for hours recalling again Emily's familiar bright eyes, her perfect lips, indeed every aspect of her loveliness inundated his mind. The years that lay between them had not deterred him from searching every face in every crowd, from praying to meet her again, if even in his nightly dreams, or from imagining she may return one day.

But all he had of her now was his memory and the sculpture. All at once his pleasant expression turned dark and his brow became furrowed, "The sculpture," he faintly whispered and continued in thought, 'I must remove it from the hall at once. How could I explain it now, after our clumsy introduction, how could she possibly understand, this girl so confused and full of doubts.'

In truth, he did not understand himself. He hurried down the winding stairway, and walked toward the table whereupon a faint moonbeam was casting a minuscule ray of light directly upon the sculpture, but there was also a certain light radiating from the sculpture itself. He had carved it from the finest white marble and polished it to perfection. There she was, and her human counterpart lay sleeping only footsteps away. He walked over and stood before it in silent adoration. It was perfection. In his genius, he had captured her beauty, her youth and gracefulness. He picked up this perfect form of Emily and as he did, the moonlight disappeared and the room was left in darkness.

The sudden darkness drew his attention away from his task, and after returning the heavy sculpture to its place on the table, he walked to the closest window and looked out upon the dark, ominous clouds covering the sky. The clouds raged as a sea in a violent storm. The wind began to whisper and moan and a shower of snow began to fall over Brookhaven. The torrent of white powder raining down that night became known as the blizzard of 1887. Never since then had a snowstorm paralyzed that part of the country to such a degree. Inches upon inches of snow and ice covered Brookhaven, covered everything in sight.

What began as a clear and ordinary night had ended with a shock, and now the fleeting moon left in its wake only darkness. Edward secured the windows in the east wing of Brookhaven and decided on a temporary place to conceal his treasured sculpture during Lenora's stay. It would be an undertaking to transfer the heavy sculpture to the place he had in mind, but he was a strong man and he had no choice but to hide it in a safeguarded place, a place where Lenora could never find it.

℘℘

While Lenora slept peacefully and Edward conspired to preserve his secret, Edward's epistle found its way to Dr. Hamilton Weatherly. Hamilton had just returned from Asheville with supplies to last him for the next two months. He would postpone any interaction with the fierce winter until absolutely required. His muscles ached from forcing the horses to stay in the path on the way home. It seemed at each turn they wanted to follow their own course. Midnight, his most prized possession in all the world, would never have given him this kind of grief, but he was thankful he had saved the horse from such a journey.

Hamilton had made it home before dark and methodically placed each of his new supplies in its appropriate place, as was his custom. He ate a dinner of warm soup and retired early, but his quiet rest was interrupted by a knock. The knock was forceful, loud and urgent.

"I am coming" he shouted. "I am coming." When he opened the door a tall figure stood before him. When the man stepped closer, Hamilton recognized him, it was Edward. But he looked different. When he stepped yet closer, Hamilton's eyes fell upon the deep and bloody gash over Edward's heart. Hamilton gasped when Edward came near. Edward said nothing, but his countenance revealed a hint of madness.

"My God, Edward, what has happened?" Hamilton pled. Edward slowly raised his arm to touch the wound, and as he did his hand was instantly covered with blood. The blood from Edward's wound began to cover the floor, faster and faster, and it flowed until it was rising from the floor. Hamilton felt a fear welling up in his body and finding a way to his throat, and suddenly his resounding words rang out in the cold air.

"No, no!" Hamilton shouted and jumped from his bed. It was then he heard a heavy rap upon the door. His heart raced. 'Is this a continuation of the nightmare?' he thought, as he stared in fear at the door. But he realized he was part of the rational world now. He felt the warmth from the small fire in his room and the quickening beat of his heart in his chest. 'The horrible dream was only a nightmare, thank Heaven, but why such a ghastly dream?' As he considered the question, he hesitantly opened the door to a young man who greeted him as follows: "You Doctor Weatherly?"

"Yes," Hamilton replied.

"A message for you Sir," he offered, extending a letter to him, "Says it's urgent."

"Thank you, can I offer you a moment by the fire, the cold is shocking tonight?"

"No thank you, I best get be getting on," the young stranger replied and turned away.

Still trying to force the disturbing images of his dream from thought, he opened the letter. It read:

Hamilton,
Again, my friend, I find myself at your mercy. I need you to come at once. I shall explain later, but some inexplicable fate has brought a young girl to Brookhaven. She has traveled on foot, and I fear she may be quite ill. I believe your services will be most beneficial.
Urgently, Edward

'A young girl, on foot, on this night?' Hamilton questioned. 'Ill indeed, or mad even to be traveling alone in the countryside.' But this was Hamilton's chance. Only one other time had Edward asked anything of him and he would not let Edward down. He felt Edward's confidence in him to be a great compliment and set off for this new challenge. He abhorred the thought of facing the cold night yet again, but this time Midnight would be his companion and he would dress accordingly.

The night greeting him was fiercely cold and still, it offered no wind, not even the distant sound of animals calling out. Hamilton normally enjoyed the quiet, but on this night it made him feel he was the only living being on the face of the boundless earth. He wondered if he was destined to travel the rest of his days in cold stillness such as this night. When feeling alone and isolated such as this, his mind naturally turned to warmer days, days spent knowing there was some person in the world who loved him. But he had chosen his profession. Would there be no love for him?

Hamilton had known love once, but he had been young and foolish. The young lady had given her affection freely, but he had reserved his heart on the notion that some other one would have the power to bring light into his heart. 'But where is this perfect one?' he wondered. Her absence betrayed him. He tried to make himself forget his one love, but try as he may, he could still see himself in her eyes. He had become quite addicted to the feelings he elicited from her, he might only enter a room and for her the light of a thousand suns flooded it with light and warmth, what love there was in her eyes, but he longed to be the lover and not simply the beloved. In the end he had hurt her and it was his one regret.

The cold and soundless night was his sole companion now. The full, silver moon above was like a great glowing opal set in a velvety night sky and its brilliant glow shone upon the white ground below him. He allowed his mind to wander about in the days of his youth, for Midnight knew the way to Brookhaven. Hamilton pondered this feeling of loneliness and doom, and how he feared it. There was no way to escape these thoughts and no evidence around him to prove them false. Suddenly, a great wind began to whisper and moan as though it was formed from deep in the earth's throat, and almost at the same time he looked about him and watched an enormous, sinister cloud envelop the moon, leaving the world around him in total darkness.

The farther and faster he traveled, the wall of snow became thicker and heavier. Had he been on foot, he would have lost his way and surely frozen to his death in this remote and lonely place. But Midnight trudged on, he knew each step and he would not stop until he had delivered Hamilton to Brookhaven. Finally Hamilton spotted the welcoming iron gates. Freezing to the point of numbness, Hamilton walked Midnight to the stables, fed him and thanked him for saving his life with a quick massage of his weary muscles. With his last ounce of energy, he made it to the front doors of the mansion. He could scarcely feel his balled up hand as he placed it against the door, but the sound it made confirmed he had made contact. Shortly, Charles answered the door.

"Doctor, my heavens, come inside," Charles offered taking the bag from Hamilton and placing it on the floor.

"There is hot tea in the parlor, come sit by the fire."

"I am lucky to have made the journey Charles. What a night! It was so clear and peaceful, but then a great wind began to howl, it reached over the sky and turned it black. I have never seen such a snow storm. And the cold, the bitter cold." he shuddered.

"It was the same here, all quiet but then in an instant we became quite entombed."

"And Edward?"

"He is with the young lady now, I shall tell him you are here. You should warm yourself with my spiced tea," Charles offered as he disappeared up the steps. The spiced tea and blazing fire quickly warmed the young doctor, but his mind was full of questions about this person who had called him forth from his warm slumber and into the treacherous night. Just as Hamilton downed the last drop of steaming tea, Edward appeared in the doorway to lead him to his patient.

Edward explained to Hamilton how Lenora had appeared as if from a dream and that she could not remember why or how she came to be there. Hamilton noticed Edward seemed somehow changed this evening, but he was uncertain in what particular aspect. Edward led him to the room where the young girl was resting in a deep sleep. Lenora's golden hair lay across a white pillow and Hamilton looked upon her with curiosity. At first he was taken with her beauty, and then he looked more carefully upon her.

"Edward?" he whispered as almost a question.

"What? What is it?" Edward responded eagerly.

"Do you promise to forgive what I am about to ask, Edward?"

"But why do you ask such a thing?"

"You must know I would never ask anything personal of you...I would never..." Hamilton stumbled.

"My God man, what is it you wish to ask?"

"Is it she, Edward?" he asked in a whisper.

Edward looked at him perplexed, "You know her?"

"Forgive me Edward, but I rather think you should certainly know her?" he replied, baffled.

"But for certain, I do not," Edward retorted.

"But surely you recognize her Edward, look, it is she, the sculpture in your foyer shares her face, or do my eyes deceive me?"

"Ah yes, you see the resemblance too? But you are mistaken, Hamilton. Lenora lies here asleep and warm. But the angel who inspired the sculpture lies cold, in a deeper sleep, never to awaken."

"But Edward, it is extraordinary. And the sculpture, she was of this world then, and not simply from one's imagination, if I may ask..?" Hamilton said stumbling over each word.

"She lived, she lives yet, but only here," Edward said quietly, placing a hand over his heart, and continuing, "You must understand and trust me when I tell you I simply cannot speak of her. There are trials one endures, but may never overcome. Speaking of her now cannot bring her back to me, but your question is nothing to be pardoned, for certain, it is quite the puzzlement. I thought myself mad when first I saw this poor girl. I am certain all of us here at Brookhaven feel the presence of a ghost among us, yet she is most alive. She looks peaceful lying here, as if nothing could trouble her gentle soul, but in truth it is entirely the opposite. And Hamilton, it is I who must ask your forgiveness for placing you in danger, my friend. When I sent for you it was yet a clear evening. As the storm approached, I feared you may not make it, I am thankful you arrived safely."

"Of course, Edward, I am only happy to be of some assistance to you."

"It is good to see you, Hamilton, you have been missed." Hamilton smiled and began to attend to the mysterious sleeping beauty. It was incongruous, the way Edward had reached out to him as if they were great friends, perhaps he had finally leapt the bounds of the chasm between them and had become just that, but no matter what had occurred, he fancied he felt comforted by Edward's newfound affection toward him. He prepared herbal teas for the ghost-like girl and watched her closely. She lay so still he thought her to have left the world of the living on several occasions. But with each inspection he found she was merely in a deep sleep. After administering every remedy and action in his power he joined Edward for scotch in the music room.

As was customary he found Edward in a quiet, reserved mood. He was weary himself from the long day so he bid Edward goodnight and retired to the room which had become "his" in the many previous visits to this beloved estate. The morning came early for Hamilton, and he found the young girl still sleeping peacefully and all signs of life and health obviously restored. He longed to linger in Brookhaven for a few more days, but the Rogers' baby was due any day now and they would need his assistance. The position of their home would render them immobilized so there was nothing to do but to go to them.

Fortunately the Rogers' resided in a farm neighboring the Brookhaven estate so the journey could be made without further risk to Hamilton or his loved horse, Midnight. He would remain with the Rogers' until the bridge became passable and then return to his modest home in town. Noting the still-falling snow, he did not relish the thought of facing the storm head on, but the Rogers' were a lovely family, and he could not desert them in their hour of need. He walked down the stairs seeking one last moment of warmth by the fireside before his blustery journey. He noticed a table in the middle of the room. The table was not ordinarily in the parlor, and because a linen cloth was draped over it, hiding some tall object, his curiosity was piqued.

"Good morning." Edward said from behind.

Turning to greet him, Hamilton answered, "Morning Edward, I have tended to your young guest and she is resting comfortably. I regret to tell you I must depart this morning. I have a child to deliver and I must hasten to the Rogers' farm."

"Are you mad, have you not seen the snow is yet falling?"

"I have seen, but it is a short distance and I shall be fine."

"I shall not argue with you, but what of Lenora, do you need to examine her when she wakes?"

"She was simply exhausted Edward. I see no need to return, however I strongly recommend a steady diet of robust tea and plenty of hot soup and bread. Of course if she experiences anything out of the ordinary, please send for me. Do not worry, she will be fine. I expect I shall be at the Rogers' for several days. This blasted storm has been a rather cruel companion to one who is obliged to tend to the sick."

"For certain. I do wish you did not have to leave so suddenly. As for your journey, I must insist you take one of my sleighs."

"But it is not necessary..."

"It is useless to argue, it will only take a moment to ready it for travel. While we wait there is something I would like to show you. I see you discovered my work table."

"Yes, I own the object has stolen my attention."

"Let us uncover it." Edward offered.

"May I?" Hamilton asked. With Edward's approving nod, Hamilton walked over to the table and slowly removed the linen cloth. Under it he found something which left him speechless, he looked to Edward for explanation.

"For you, my good friend. Seldom do I find inspiration these days. I had not worked in years and then the first day we met, years ago, when I saw that fine creature of yours, with the noon day sun splashing across him, catching each perfectly defined muscle, I was mesmerized. He is the most beautiful animal I have ever seen. I often thought of memorializing him in sculpture him, but it took more than his elegance to inspire me. Over time, as we met on many occasions afterward, your affection for him, and his for you, became so apparent it prompted me to immortalize him in this way. You may take it. It is finished now."

"I do not know what to say," Hamilton answered, running his fingers over the beautiful sculpture of the likeness of Midnight. He could not take his eyes from it.

"You need not say anything Hamilton, I only regret I could not have given it to you sooner, but 'tis a long process, and the materials did not arrive for months."

Hamilton was shocked by Edward's revelation, as it offered sufficient evidence to prove Edward had planned his gift months ago, while all along Hamilton was under the false belief that his many visits to Brookhaven had been tiresome to Edward and his friendship had been unwanted and had meant nothing to Edward.

"And I thought...never mind. Edward, I shall treasure it always," he said, running his fingers against the marble figure one last time.

"Good, and do not be a stranger, it is rare I find the company of others so pleasant, you are welcome here anytime. And now I shall not keep you from your duties, farewell and safe journey."

Taking the sculpture and wrapping it safely he departed in the astonishment of having failed to realize in all the months before, that he had apparently made some sort of lasting impression upon Edward.

Chapter 4
A Warning

When Lenora awoke from her long sleep she felt completely rested, but could not resist enjoying the warmth of the plush, feather bed for a few more moments. A bright morning peeked from beneath the drawn curtains, greeting her with a feeling of security which had eluded her for some time. She felt utterly content in the grand bed, but ached with the sudden discomfort of hunger. Reluctantly she emerged from her nest of down and shivered as her feet touched the cold wooden floor. She quickly made her way to the door chest and found a small pair of slippers and grabbed the warmest garment in sight, a long, formal coat, the kind one would wear to the opera or some similar event, and then walked over to the huge window to see what kind of day God had given her.

When she pushed back the heavy curtains the brilliant light exposed was almost blinding. She blinked to adjust her eyes and focused them on a most amazing sight. The entire world beneath her was white and without blemish. Below her third floor window she could see Brookhaven and its grounds were completely covered in a beautiful blanket of freshly fallen snow. The swirling wind lifted the dusty flakes off the ground and intermingled with the new ones yet falling, creating haunting shapes upon the landscape. She watched the disappearing figures for several minutes and fancied they were ghosts, and much like herself, were trying to find their way home.

"Snow, lovely snow," she mused, "How beautiful you are. But how am I to continue my journey in this weather, how am I to impose on Edward's kindness, but the sleep, the food, the relief of a place to rest, how am I to leave this safety?" And besides, she somehow believed her journey had just begun and the answers for which she searched lay somewhere in this magical place. She was not sure what she should do next, but she knew she would have to face the day.

A pitcher of fresh water had been recently placed on the dressing table, but was cool to her touch so she moved the basin to the hearth and poured half of the water into it. Once the water was warmed to her liking she rinsed her hands and face which made her feel very much awake. Her dress lay across the dressing chair and had been laundered along with her stockings and undergarments. She blushed at the thought of anyone seeing or handling her clothing in their unsightly condition.

Ever mindful of her safety and vulnerability, she bolted the chamber door and returned the lovely coat to the wardrobe, where it hung beside the most delicate and beautiful garments she had ever seen. How she would love to wear something new, and Edward had given her permission to do so, but she could not be so bold and instead donned her newly cleansed, but somewhat stained dress and walked over to the mirror.

The mirror was tall, an antique, French by design and beautifully carved, and the reflection which it now displayed made it all the more captivating. She looked at herself for the first time in weeks. She almost gasped to find herself in this condition, and seeing this tired, worn dress against her fresh, young and vibrant skin seemed quite unreal. Her eyes strayed to the elegant room behind her in the mirror's reflection and she silently wished she may never have to leave its comforting walls. Shortly she returned her intent gaze to the woman before her.

Lenora's dress was tattered and graying, a dress which to her memory had previously been a deep and lovely shade of blue. The heavy fabric appeared clean, but was still damp from its recent washing, and from it lingered the slightest scent of perspiration. It would not do, she could not wear this distasteful dress for one moment more, and then she began to study the girl wearing the dress, and was surprised she had any color left at all, but supposed the night's sleep had restored her. Even in this shabby attire, she was a beautiful young woman. Perhaps her most stunning feature was her blue eyes, but to make such a statement is misleading, for it was not their color which made them extraordinary but rather their brightness. One could say they glistened. These glistening eyes were complimented quite nicely by her unblemished and fair complexion, soft and fair despite the harshness of the last two years.

Lenora stood brushing her long golden tresses and thought about how warm and safe she felt. With the last stroke of her brush, she began unfastening each hook and eye and allowed the old dress to fall slowly to her feet, as if shedding an old skin she would be content to leave behind her forever. In its stead, she chose from the ancient collection what would suffice for a simple day dress. With the limited materials she found in the room, she pinned her hair in the style of the day and then walked out into the hall.

It was a grand hallway with an arched ceiling rising twenty feet above her, and she admired with intense interest everything she passed on the way to the stairway. Lovely portraits of men and women were strewn along the walls and there was one of a child she particularly liked. The child was a boy of six or seven, grasping in his hand a tiny toy sailboat. There was a charmingly melancholy expression upon his face, and his eyes in some way looked familiar. She looked at it for several minutes, but then heard footsteps coming toward her and instinctively began to walk along the hall. As she reached the top of the stairs, Edward met her on the landing.

"Lenora," he said, "are you sure you are well enough to be up and about?"

"Good morning, Edward. Yes, I am quite well. I had a wonderful night's rest and I feel splendid, just splendid."

"You must be famished, what would you like, I shall have my cook prepare anything you wish."

"Please don't got to any trouble, I shall simply have whatever you are having. I've been admiring these beautiful portraits, but I must say I am quite in need of breakfast, shall we go downstairs now?"

"Of course, I was just coming to call on you. Lenora, it is

obvious you are not aware of it, but, well, I must tell you, more than one night has passed since last we met, you have been in a deep sleep for nearly two days."

"Are you entirely sure?"

"Yes, I was very concerned about you. As it happens, my closest friend is a doctor, and he was kind enough to check in on you. I sent for him the night you arrived. Apparently the journey here, together with being exposed to such extreme temperatures caused you to fall very ill. He said it was most likely exhaustion. But all is well now, and I must say you look well rested."

"I cannot thank you enough for your concern. I feel so silly. I appear on your doorstep and then fall asleep and require a physician's attention. I am rather embarrassed," she said.

"Embarrassed, now you are being silly. I am very pleased you found your way here and I am honored to be of some assistance to you," he answered.

"May I thank your friend, the doctor?" she asked.

"Perhaps another time. You see he is the only physician around for miles. He arrived just as the storm began and attended you, but he was needed elsewhere for an emergency and had to quickly depart."

"But in this weather?"

"He is young and I could not reason with him. I allowed him the use of my best sleigh, he takes his profession very seriously and if he is needed somewhere there is no stopping him."

"He sounds like a fine gentleman. I do hope to thank him one day."

"Yes, perhaps you shall. Now let us see to your ...breakfast," he replied with some hesitation and an expression hinting at a smile.

"What is it Edward?"

"If it is breakfast you desire, then you shall have breakfast, but it is nearly mid-day."

"My confusion continues, or but are you teasing me?"

"Afraid not, but not to worry, we shall have a late dinner tonight and you shall return to a normal schedule tomorrow."

Edward showed her to the informal dining room where Charles had prepared a small feast for her. It was a cozy little room and she enjoyed her rather large breakfast while sharing a pleasant conversation with Edward.

"I am quite taken aback by this most horrible snow storm. I had planned to leave for New York on the morrow, but now I shall be unable to leave for at least a week. And Lenora, I do hope you will feel comfortable here. Under the circumstances, you have no choice but to remain here, and I'll have no argument. My conscience will not allow me to cast you back out into the world without having learned of your past."

"That is very kind," she replied. "I find it most reassuring being here, I shall be glad to stay."

"Good, I am glad to hear you say so. I am very intrigued by the events which led you here, and I hope to have the pleasure of hearing the happy ending I am certain will happen upon you."

"It is what I pray for," she said.

Lenora explained to Edward the places she had been over the previous several months and the journey which led her to Brookhaven. She remembered the sea of unfamiliar faces and the expectations which had been broken one by one. There was a strange sense she did not belong in this country. The people she encountered were frightening at times and had grown increasingly so as her appearance had become more and more disheveled. There was a definite correlation between her appearance at any particular point in time and the willingness of strangers to offer their assistance. The winters were the worst. The cold, the numbing cold seemed to never end and she truly wondered if there would ever be a flame hot enough to warm her again.

Lenora was too ashamed to admit it to Edward, but there had been times on her journey when she had prayed for death. The day she reached the outskirts of Asheville, only a few days before, had been one such time. Lenora quietly passed the street vendors keeping her eyes low to the ground. As she passed one vendor, her eyes became fixed on a cart filled with the most beautiful red apples. Her mouth watered remembering the taste she had long been denied, but she had not even one nickel left to her name. The thought of taking one, stealing one, passed through her thoughts, but somehow she knew the guilt from such an act would withhold her from its simple enjoyment. If only she had something to bargain with. The only thing of value was the necklace she wore, but she could not bring herself to part with it, not even for a feast much less a few tasty apples.

As she walked passed the apple cart her hunger waned and she continued along the path before her. She longed to rest, it had been so very long, but there was no safe place to remain in the city without being noticed. The rural areas were a risk to one's health. There was no guarantee of food or water, but she preferred to take the risk in lieu of lingering in the city where one is subjected to drunkards and sneers from strangers. She reasoned perhaps there would be a cave or a stable or she would find some other safe, dry place to lay her head for a while, if she just continued to walk.

As she followed the path before her, leaving the little city behind, the distant tread of horses became audible, and she prepared herself for the worst. She feared the fate which threatened a young girl as herself had finally come upon her; that God himself had abandoned her and her life would soon be ended. With those deathly thoughts looming over her, suddenly a voice called out to her, "Miss, if you headin' my way just hop on the back of my wagon."

"No thank you Sir." She answered, without meeting the gentleman's eyes and quickening her pace.

"Suit yourself, if you prefer to walk in the snow, but it is mighty cold, even icy in spots, a young lady should not be walking in the country...where you headed?"

She looked up at him this time and he appeared to be a man of a great many years. And suddenly, somehow she seemed to have no fear at all of this country stranger. There was something in his eyes which spoke of gentleness. And she had not seen a shade of blue quite so lovely since she had stared into the summer sky some months before. Her fear faded away quickly and she began to confide in the stranger.

"To be quite honest, I am not sure where I am going, but I will know when I get there."

"Hmm?" the stranger looked puzzled.

"Tell me Sir, are there any farms or homes along this path?"

"I'm just traveling through to sell my wares, Miss. If you need it, I got it. Tonics, salves, cooking pots, all the modern conveniences right here in my carriage. Looking for a farm you say, hmm, nothing and nobody much here in the country. A few farms here and there and there is one old estate a few miles up the way. I go this route a few times a year. Are you sure you don't want to rest your legs a bit, or can I offer you a tonic, good for any sort of pains?"

"No thank you, but I suppose a rest would be nice, but just for a few miles, all right?"

"For as long as you wish Miss. Whose farm ye looking for?"

"Oh, no one in particular, but do you know if there is a Lenora living in this county?"

The old gentlemen looked up thoughtfully and seemed to concentrate on this question. But shortly answered, "No miss, can't say I've ever heard tell of such a name in these parts."

"It was worth a try I suppose, and now, if you would be so kind as to stop, I shall join you for a short ride." The kind old gentlemen brought his horse to a stop and Lenora adroitly climbed upon the back of his carriage and held onto the sides of the bench. What a relief to rest her feet, which seemed to throb rather strongly and she would have sworn that her heart had transported itself and taken residence in them. After a short while she was asleep in spite of the unsteady and jolting ride. Just before dark, the carriage stopped, rousing her. A whispering wind made its way through the sheltering trees along the path, and the trees seemed to communicate to each other in some unknown but disturbing language. The gentleman had abandoned his seat to remove a large branch, which had fallen to the ground directly in his path. She jumped off the seat feeling surprisingly rested, and startling her driver, he said…"Oh, never ye mind young lady, just had to stop for a moment, we'll be on our way in no time."

"That is quite all right. I do thank you ever so much for the ride, but I should carry on now."

"Whatever you say Miss, but there is nothing much about this wood and night is falling soon. Is there anywhere I can take ye?"

"No Sir. I shall be fine."

After a moment he said, "Don't say I told ye so, but the Rogers' farm is just up ahead. Their stables are first rate.

Otherwise there's only Brookhaven, but I'd steer clear of there if I was you," he warned as he shook his head.

"Brookhaven?" she asked.

"Yes, some say it is haunted, and the master of the place, Withers, he's an odd sort. Never met him myself, never want to. Doesn't take well to strangers. The farm is your destination, I'd say, but don't say I sent ye, ye hear."

"Thank you, yes, I understand."

"I best be getting on now," he said with a breezy smile and as the carriage pulled away he yelled, "Best of luck to ye Miss."

The silly tune the old man had been singing had found its way into Lenora's consciousness, and was relentlessly repeating through her mind as a most unwanted companion. The countryside was beautiful in the darkness and completely untouched by man. In what seemed like a short while, just as the nice old stranger had recommended, she came to the Rogers' farm, but another theme plaguing her mind was his mention of the estate, and more specifically its name, "Brookhaven." Her body chanted in a deafening voice, 'go to the farm,' but her soul's cry of 'Brookhaven, Brookhaven?' drowned the other voice as she passed the pathway leading to the entrance of the farm.

The cold had crept into her bones at this point and she was no longer in control of her actions. She lost all sense of time and it seemed hours had passed since the farm's broken promise of hay to rest her weary mind and body. She no longer felt the frigid air and her mind seemed completely void of all thought until she reached those hypnotic iron gates. Gates which held for her a kind and generous man named Edward Withers. He had been so hospitable to offer her shelter from the cold and a sense of security she had lacked for longer than she cared to remember.

As she reflected on her odd journey to Brookhaven, she remembered the stranger's warning that it might be haunted and the prospect of Edward leaving her alone there seemed more than a little frightening, but being thrust back into the empty world again was a fate she was unwilling to accept.

Curious about her tremulous fate if Edward kept his plans to travel soon, she inquired, "And what, if I may ask, takes you to New York?"

"I am drawn there each December, on a pilgrimage of

sorts. A day's travel from New York City in the county of Suffolk, is a small but flourishing city named Riverbend on eastern Long Island. There is an orphanage I support there throughout the year, most particularly during the holiday season. Ours is a cruel world Lenora, but there are things one can do to ease the suffering some of us face, and I own this is my one goal, my grand purpose. To help these lonely children, to remember them. There's is a kind of deep sadness few can understand. I find my visits there ease my own sorrows and remind me where I have been, lest I forget what is meaningful in life, lest I become unappreciative of what gifts I have been given."

"It is a wonderful, selfless thing you do, how very generous you are with your wealth and time. I can think of no greater need than to bring joy to the suffering children of this world. I cannot say I am surprised by your charity, for I have enjoyed the same generosity, but I am curious how you came to choose this particular orphanage?" As soon as she spoke Edwards countenance turned quite grave, and believing she had intruded continued, "but that is none of my concern, of course."

Edward hesitated, but replied, "It is a little known fact, but I was once a resident there." He saw his revelation had changed her cheerful manner, she appeared uncomfortable and for once she could find no words to continue or to move the conversation into another direction, so he rescued her by opening his world to her further.

"I assure you no pity is to be felt for me, dear Lenora. I was well taken care of. It was by accident I came to live there. I was a boy of seven when I lost both of my parents. My parents and I were on a trip to America on the grand S.S. Victoria II. While my father was a wealthy man, I understand he was to double his fortune in bringing his experience and knowledge to America. He had planned to assist in the development of communication systems and to plan and organize the new world's largest cities. He brought with him on the Victoria II all of his and my mother's dreams and hopes for the future. Everything we owned was stored on the ship for our adventure to the new world.

It began as a wonderful trip. My father's greatest loves were the sea and ships, and it was his first chance to experience again the excitement of the sea through the eyes of his only son.

He was very excited explaining in great detail, as I listened intently, to his explanation of each part of the ship. I was amazed and a bit frightened by our new floating home. The first few days of the trip were uneventful. I stayed by my mother's side most of the journey. She was a wonderful storyteller, and she made the trip a grand adventure for me. She told me of great adventures of the sea, pirates and bandits, and the like. I understand now it was a mother's love telling me the stories, she sensed how frightened I was when I saw the vast sea. Mother took away my fears with her simple storytelling, she had a way of doing such things. After several days at sea, the weather turned stormy. I would have hardly noticed, but the mood of the passengers changed rather drastically. I could see the fear on the faces of the men. I did not understand it at the time, but everyone, even a seven year old boy could recognize it. I have never seen such a torrential rain as in those two days. The sea began to swell and the waves grew larger and larger, and the fears of the passengers grew with them.

In the final moments, people were running, screaming, even jumping from the ship, it was utter chaos. At the worst of it, I was somehow separated from my parents in the confusion. I was terrified, but then suddenly I saw her. My mother stood on the upper deck of the ship by my father's side. I do not know what words were exchanged between them, but I could see something terrible was about to occur. I ran to her and she knelt down beside me, holding me desperately. She explained the ship would be taken by the sea and I would have to be strong and brave. She explained there was not time to save everyone. It was simply a matter of time. What she said next would change my life.

My mother tearfully explained that she and father would have to go with the ship. As she said these words, she removed her wedding ring from her finger and placed it on a golden chain. Twice she wrapped it around my neck and locked the clasp. Now, "Eddie" she said, "keep this always in remembrance of me and your father." I look back on her courage and bravery and cannot imagine her calmness in such a disaster. I later learned the captain had promised to send out two of the small boats if time permitted, but there was no time or room to save everyone. With my family's status, my mother's seat on one of the boats was secure. Her life being saved was a certainty, but in her kindness she relinquished her place to a young woman bearing an unborn child, and who had a young husband waiting for her back in the New World.

In those few seconds she gave up her seat and made me an orphan, but as it was, she made the right decision. Looking back I understand her reasons, and I love her even more for her sacrifice. I sat by the young woman on the boat and she held me tightly until finally, a ship came into sight. It was a miracle. It was like God's own hand sweeping down to save us. I was thankful to have survived, but I would spend the next few years trying to forgive and forget that terrible night. I would try to eradicate the sight of the Victoria II being swallowed by the unmerciful sea, as I watched my family disappear forever and all of our possessions with them.

My paternal grandmother promised to send for me immediately. But as you can imagine, I would not agree to set foot on another ship, not just yet, at least. My father had no friends or relatives in this country so until a decision could be reached as to my fate, I was placed in the temporary care of the state, in the orphanage. By the time I agreed to make the journey, some number of months later, though my grandmother made arrangements for me to be returned to her, her health began to fail, and she died before she could arrange for me to return to her. All of her possessions were held in trust for me until I reached the age of eighteen, at which time I would be released from the orphanage and sent to the university in London, as my father before me.

For twelve years I lived in the orphanage. I was too old to be wanted by anyone. It was the mere acceptance of my unfortunate fate, as dismal as it sounds, that gave me the strength to endure it. My last years there were spent trying to make the others feel at ease in their transitional home. It was a sad place, but knowing I was not alone made me feel comforted in a strange way. There were always children who seemed to have had a worse life than I. It was a trying time, but I must say I would not take back, were it in my power, one moment of my stay there, for I have often wondered what gloom would have befallen the other children had I not been there to protect them. It is the life I was given and I accept it, embrace it even, for one must find contentment in one's life or be doomed for misery."

Lenora's heart ached for Edward. It was so tragic she had no words but offered these anyway, "How unfortunate to have lost your parents at such an early age. I am sorry, so sorry."

"I have actually fared well. I have wanted for nothing and the solitude of Brookhaven has been a great comfort to me. But enough of me, tell me Lenora, how are you feeling and have you remembered anything new?"

He searched for a hint, an indication of how long she would remain at Brookhaven. He knew he could not bear to part with her just yet, and inwardly searched for a way to keep her there with him. His motivation was driven by two equally influential forces, his hope to become a part of her future, and the deeper need in him to assist her, to save her even, by helping her find her past.

"I believe I must have been led here somehow. Many months ago I decided I would let my senses be my guide. I prayed each day I might listen to the spirit within in me, that I might hear the voice of God which I believe is in every one of us, and allow that voice to guide me where it willed. At the slightest feeling of a sign I would follow the feeling. At times I would believe my senses failed me because every path or other would lead to nowhere at all. But all my wanderings about did lead me here, of that I feel certain. I suppose I am not certain what shall become of me just now or where I am to go, but I have to believe I am exactly where I am supposed to be at this moment. I suppose I will have to impose on your kindness until the weather is safe for traveling again. But I must tell you I cannot think of another place I would rather be stranded. I have felt a sense of peace here I feared I had lost forever."

Edward was suddenly consumed by an intense feeling of relief at these kind words from Lenora, and she could hardly ignore the obvious joy her revelation had given him as he beamed with the knowledge she would continue her at Brookhaven.

"Then it is quite settled. It has been a dark winter, indeed, and your stumbling across us has given a new light to this old estate." As they continued, Lenora spotted a beautiful piano in the adjacent room. She seemed to be entranced by it and found herself struggling to focus on what Edward was trying to tell her.

Her eyes seemed to follow along the length of it, and as they walked along she charted their course into the room which held the lovely instrument.

"May I?" she asked.

"Please do," he consented.

Chapter 5
A Melody, a Reunion and a Proposal

Lenora admired the instrument for a moment, hardly aware of the words Edward was speaking and then instinctively sat down on the bench before it and gently stroked the keys. In the next moment, she began to play the loveliest melody. The music was somber and touching and the melancholy notes reflected the very mood of the cold and dark estate. The sounds rushed over her like a wave of peace, and her thoughts and actions escaped her for several moments. Moments soon turned into an hour. As she took command of the piano, Edward quietly took a seat and watched her, quite in amazement. He listened to the magic she easily demonstrated and become so intoxicated he lost track of time and allowed his mind to drift where it pleased.

Edward's life of obscurity had imprisoned him from the simple joy of pleasures such as this private moment with Lenora and her haunting music. How long had it been since he had been entertained, indeed, his very dream had awakened into a most splendid reality. There she sat, the image of the woman he had lost many years before. 'How was it possible?' he pondered, 'perhaps God has pitied me and sent this angel to replace the void Emily left in my despairing heart, whatever the reason I am thankful for the relief.'

Edward imagined Emily, how young and beautiful she had been and with a heart heaving with love, a spirit as pure as any he had known. Years separated him from those happier days, but he was content to remember . . .

The summer of 1867 had finally arrived and it would be only a matter of days before he would see Emily again. He had completed his final examinations at the university and arrived in Brighton to meet her as he had promised, and all of their plans lay before them like a perfect puzzle. But he had always been cautioned about planning too much, about depending too much upon another to satisfy his happiness. He wondered if he would ever learn that lesson. He had invested his security with his parents and then with his grandmother and each time, at the very moment he felt safe, another person was taken from him. 'But this time it will be different,' he reasoned. Emily's brother, Bryson Talbot, had counseled Edward about God's love and Edward was so eager to believe in such a thing and once he met Emily, he began to understand that powerful Love and Mercy more fully.

The dark years in the orphanage were hard to forget, and harder still to overcome, but he could endure it all and more with her love. On the day they were to meet, a close friend of Emily's met him instead with the message that Emily's father had unfortunately accompanied her to her aunt's home and their coveted meeting would be postponed until the following day. To say he was disappointed was a grievous understatement. Disappointment soon gave way to anger, anger at Emily's father, for he had been the one source of discomfort where their relationship was concerned, and now he had found a way to interfere yet again.

'Why had he come with her?' Edward wondered. 'It makes no sense. The meddling old man, shall we never be free of him?' he thought, but then he pondered the question further and conceded that these were the expected actions of any father sending a daughter away for the summer. Getting through the day was difficult and every passing hour became more unbearable to endure, and later in the evening he decided nothing would do but for him to see her. Patiently he had waited for months and this was the night he had dreamed of, after all of the hoping, this day had finally come, and now it had been taken from them. But no, it would not, he rose and made for the door. Only a short walk separated him from the love of his life, and he would not be consoled with less than seeing her this night.

As he gazed out of his window, rain fell with a vengeance. It was a terrible night to be out and even though every indication was for him to remain in his room, he went out into the hellish night and sought the one person who could still his heart. It was a difficult walk in the rain, but Edward walked at a steady pace as if it were not raining at all. In fact, he hardly seemed to notice, knowing she was only footsteps away carried him each step. He had passed by the Chastain home many times, but this night it was different. Tonight Emily was there, she existed within its walls and the pull he felt towards her could no more be denied than the moon giving way to the sun.

Though his resolve was fixed, he was not so bold as to risk coming face to face with Emily's father. As he reached the house, he walked up to the dark porch only after ensuring he had been unseen, and to guarantee his anonymity found a large chair to hide behind. He peered into the window to gain a glimpse of her, but saw no one. He crouched by the window for several minutes, and realizing his position, became quite annoyed with himself for stooping there hiding behind a chair, sopping wet with the summer rain. He wondered what he would even say to her, if she were here before him now, and what she would think of him, and again he believed deeply she deserved so much more than this, she deserved a man who could come to her door openly and freely. As these thoughts began to ravage his mind and replace the joy he had felt just moments before, he quickly decided to abandon his position, but at the same moment he heard voices approaching from the lawn, and he froze in his dreadful spot fearing he would be discovered after all. He quickly identified one of the gentlemen as Emily's father, but the young man accompanying him was a stranger.

As the two reached the porch their conversation was discernible, "Terrible night out, I abhor traveling in such conditions, I assumed it would be a lovely summer evening. I am anxious for you to meet my Emily. She has been looking forward to meeting you."

"Yes sir, I am pleased to meet her at last. You have spoken of her so regularly I feel I already know her. I only hope our meeting meets your expectations."

"Not to worry, young Daniel, I happen to know Emily will be very fond of you, now are you ready to meet my daughter, or do you want to stand here in the rain all night?" Mr. Talbot asked with a thunderous and self gratified laugh.

"I assure you, I am ready." The young voice replied.

Emily's father knocked on the door and was answered by a woman at the height of loveliness and grace. She was Emily's Aunt Amelia, her dearly departed mother's sister.

"Mr. Talbot, please come in, were you waiting long?" she asked. Emily's Aunt Amelia always addressed Emily's father as Mr. Talbot, even though the two were on warm and informal terms.

"No, we have only just arrived. Amelia, it is lovely to see you again as always. May I present Mr. Daniel Lawson, he is the young man I wrote you of."

As she started to answer, the large door closed leaving behind only the sound of the warm, pouring summer rain. Edward, dumbfounded, attempted to process what he had just witnessed. "She has been looking forward to meeting you?" he mouthed in a mocking silence. 'What could this mean? Has she been untrue? No, impossible.' But he felt an urgent need to speak to her, to speak to her at once. 'But how? I am not even supposed to be here and if I am discovered, her father will never accept me and our chances of being together will be greatly threatened.' As his mind whirled searching for a way to speak with her, or else to resolve the fears within him if he departed without speaking to her, he noticed movement in the window.

"My angel" he whispered. He watched as Emily met the young man. She extended her hand to him. 'She is only being cordial,' he reasoned. He watched her every move. If only he could hear what they were saying, but it was no use, their words were inaudible from his strange position. As he stood there once again in the shadow of her life, on the outside, literally looking in, he was determined it would be the last time. Edward resolved he would not leave until he had spoken to Emily. He waited and he watched until her father and the young man had departed.

Edward walked to the back of the house and searched for the window which might be Emily's, and smiled when he saw a window which had been slightly open, for it was her practice to always allow the fresh night air to fill her room. His mind raced with every breath. 'Should I leave this place and never return, could she be interested in this Daniel? But her eyes, her perfect eyes, I know she loves only me. I will not turn from her, never.' With a strong resolve, he lifted himself to the second floor balcony and tapped gently on her window. He waited a moment and then tapped a little more purposefully. He saw her shadow move across the room. She walked casually to the window. The curtain swept by very slowly to reveal her beautiful face behind the glass.

"Edward," she whispered and though he could not hear her soft voice, he knew she had spoken his name. She pulled the window open a bit higher and asked, beaming: "What are you doing here?"

"I received your message and I tried to stay away, but I came here tonight only to catch a glimpse of you, but once here, I could not wait another day to see you my darling."

"My Sweetheart, my love, you are more handsome than I even remember, will you kiss me?" she asked.

"Here is your kiss." He pressed his lips to hers softly. "I have come to rescue you, my Juliet, come away with me now," he whispered with his warm breath.

"I will follow you anywhere my love," she said smiling. Then her smile softened into a sad frown "Oh that I were your Juliet, of course with a different ending. Edward, in my ending I would go away with you this very night and we would share each day in joy and in love. But we are forced to wait until the time is right. It is only a matter of time and our waiting will be over."

"From what I witnessed here tonight, your father seems to think Mr. Lawson would be a better suitor. Perhaps Bryson was right, your father plans to hand pick your husband."

"Edward, how long have you been here?"

"Long enough to fear the worst?"

"Whatever do you mean, you know my love for you is constant, unmoving. At least I thought you understood the extent of my feelings," she said with the disappointment is her voice lingering.

"Forgive me, I spoke foolishly, I trust you, I do, that is why I did not leave here in a jealous rage," he said smiling, "I remained here to speak with you about this new suitor. Why must your father insist on meddling in your affairs?"

"You must remember, Edward, he knows not that my heart is already promised."

"Of course, you are right, but we must enlighten him on this fact before he has every eligible young man in the country asking for your hand."

"I know, I know," she answered with her infectious laugh. "Darling, I know we must tell him, but not enough time has yet passed since the incident," she said, placing particular emphasis on the word "incident", "though you must know that it is rather uncomfortable for me to conceal this love I have for you. I simply fear the news given prematurely would not be accepted well and should he not approve, he will force me to return home immediately and far from you my love. And Edward, we have planned such a lovely summer, we cannot spoil that now, can we?"

"How can I refuse you when you look at me this way? You win, we shall wait until the summer's end and then we shall tell him."

"Lovely. I do have good news. The young man who was here tonight, my new suitor" she said, pausing with a laughing eyes, "is a scientist, he and Father have been working together to create a new invention, it is very exciting and they have reached a breakthrough, but they go about in whispers and will tell us nothing of it. I have never seen Father in such good spirits, he says their work will change the world. They must return to London tonight, and I am convinced he will be so occupied with his work he will give little or no thought to me. I do apologize for our plans being changed, but we can meet tomorrow, yes?"

"Yes, when can you get away?"

"Fortunately, Aunt Amelia is rather busy this week, in Father's haste he informed her I would arrive next week. It could not be a more pleasant blunder. I assured her I would call on a childhood friend, who could reacquaint me with the city so my presence here would not interfere with the other arrangements she had made. I am free all day tomorrow. Aunt Amelia will be departing at half past ten in the morning. How soon can you be here?"

"Mark my words, Emily, I shall be here at 10:31 on the very mark. I cannot wait. One more kiss for me?"

She kissed him sweetly and touched his face.

"Tomorrow," he said.

"I shall hardly be able to sleep. Edward, thank you for coming tonight."

"You owe me no gratitude, for doing only what my heart must do." He climbed down the trellis and walked home in that particular haze within which once is so enveloped when having just left the side of one's beloved. He had finally seen her again and his heart spilled over with joy. At last he could trust what his heart had longed for. Emily loved him, she loved him and they would indeed be together as they had planned and dreamed. The cool night air blew against his face and he promised himself he would never forget this feeling of hope. How could he ever be the same after his heart had been touched by the feeling of such a pure and true love. The awakening of his heart, learning the emotions of love and trust, the ability to allow another to become a part of himself was extraordinary. And though he knew not what the future held, for him it could only include a life with Emily.

The following day he woke with the sun and took his exercise in a spirited walk along the countryside, whereupon he chose the choicest summer flowers growing along the hillside. When he returned to his room he anxiously dressed and with bouquet in hand returned to the Chastain home. He stood by the corner and watched Amelia Chastain's carriage drive out of sight. Anxiously, he walked up the steps and knocked on the door. Emily kept him waiting only briefly and then opened the door to greet him.

"Good morning," she said beaming, "I.."

"Shh...no words, just allow me to look at you for a moment. Every time I close my eyes your face is what I see, even when I blink." He stared deeply into her eyes for several moments and then said, "Emily, you take my breath away, and seeing myself here in your eyes, I know I can do anything, anything with your heart entwined with mine."

She smiled at him, glowing as she did when he looked at her. "Edward, I have a surprise for you, will you follow me?"

"Anywhere you go, I shall follow," he said bowing

dramatically in the fashion of an honorable knight.

Emily laughed and kissed him on his cheek, "Then follow me, kind Sir Withers."

"But what's the surprise?"

"You shall see, be patient darling."

"I am trying. Emily, are we alone?" he asked, stealing a kiss.

"Yes, with the exception of the servants of course, but why do you ask?" she said with smiling eyes looking as though she needed to be kissed again. This love he had for her was a sort of frozen fire. Though he knew it was to blaze wildly, for now he would hold these desires at a safe distance. He understood her love had been a rare gift to him and he would not allow anything or anyone, even himself, to destroy it.

"It is difficult to stand in this room alone with you, with no one here to stop us, to stop me. We should leave at once," he warned.

"Stop you from what dear Edward?" she asked coyly.

"Emily! I am serious. You underestimate the power of your eyes."

"Edward, really, you are the strongest man I know, I do not believe your desire is stronger than your will."

"Even so, would you like to go into the country?"

"Oh, can we? There is not a more lovely place to spend the first day of our reunion and we could have a picnic."

"That is just what I was thinking. But Emily where is my surprise?"

"Just sit in this chair and I shall show you."

Edward sat comfortably in the chair as Emily took her place on the piano stool. As she sat upon the stool, her form became transformed as it did when she played. She was a professional and took her playing very seriously. Her slender arms became poised and her dainty hands rested beautifully on the ivory keys and ebony sharps, she sat completely upright and straight as the notes began very slowly, soft at first and then rolling together deeper and deeper and then turning and turning as though telling a story. There was passion in the notes but a sadness too that overwhelmed the listener and brought remembrances of the day he first met her, but stronger still was his memory of the feeling of giving in to his love for her as he kissed her for the first time in her father's home. As he remembered that feeling of love, of passion welling up in him to the point of drowning and then the fear of a life without her, the vision of her before him now became blurred in his moistened eyes. The notes she played revealed to him she shared precisely those same feelings.

Emily lingered over the last note and then turned to Edward with eyes sparkling, "Well, what do you think?"

"Magnificent, how did you put our feelings, our first kiss, into music? It is haunting. It is woeful and hopeful in one."

"Really?" she asked. He answered by taking her hand in his and kissing it softly.

"This piece is the product of my entire winter without you. And you know me so well, my darling, it is called 'The Kiss.' Maestro Von Vinsky gave me the task of writing a short piece of music. I had written music before, but after I met you, I was changed. There were feelings, I cannot explain..." she said blushing.

"I understand, do go on."

"When I finished it, I could hardly play it without coming to tears, but eventually I found my composure when playing the composition and I was ready to play it for Maestro Von Vinsky. His reaction was astonishing, straightaway he began making plans to have it published, to arrange concerts, but before he could have me performing over all of Europe, I stopped him and informed him I did not wish to share it with the world. This song was written only for you to hear. I only shared it with him so I could satisfy my need to know if I could really compose, but this, I shall keep only for us, as a testament of our love."

He held her close to him and looked at her, the sadness and longing of her music still lingering through his mind, "Emily, whatever happens, please know I love you. I have lived a difficult life. Things seem wonderful now, but life has its twists and turns, I want you to hold on to these brief moments we have. I will do everything in my power to make you happy, and know I will always love you. If we are ever parted, by war, by death or by any circumstances beyond our control I will remain faithful in my love for you."

She took him in her arms, "Poor Edward, you have had so many losses, but you cannot lose me. I promise you we will be together. I will not leave you, for there is nothing on earth or beyond that can separate us."

"Nothing except your father..."

"Not even Father wields such power, he will simply have to accept you, and if he does not, we will face that too, together, as we should. No matter what happens, I will be with you. I cannot live without you, I refuse to. Now let us spend our day in joy and not in sorrow. God brought us together. You were on the other side of the world, and then one day you came to me and I loved you instantly. As I watched you step off that train with Bryson, I knew you were the one I had waited for. There was a waking up inside my heart, a part of my spirit that had always been there, but had been hidden from all feeling, paralyzed until you and you alone told my spirit to wake up, to walk and even to run. Our love is no accident. He brought us together, don't you know that, and He will not separate us now, for to do so would be.. unconscionable."

"You are right, as always, and it is a day to celebrate this life, this time we have waited to share. Follow me?" he asked with a sly sort of grin.

"But where are you taking me?" she giggled.

"You are not the only one with surprises, my dear." Before leaving the house, he asked her to close her eyes and allow him to guide her to his secret destination. She eagerly consented and followed him several yards into her aunt Amelia's rose gardens. She played along and kept her eyes tightly closed as he led her to the tranquil spot and she was delighted with his surprise. She knew she was in the rose garden because the scent of sweet roses overwhelmed her senses. But this was not the surprise.

"Let me see, how much longer?" she pleaded.

"Patience, Emily, patience, just another few steps. . . now!" Emily's eyes flashed open and his lovely secret was revealed. Together they stood on a blanket strewn with rose petals, the cloudless sky above was an intense, bright blue, and Edward had placed a picnic basket full of delicious treats at her feet.

"Welcome to our private little island under God's blue sky!"

"It is lovely, but when did you..."

"I have many secrets for you, it is nothing, really."

"Nonsense, it is magical, wonderful. And what is in the basket?"

"Oh only your favorite cheese, fresh berries of all sorts, pastries, from the best bakery in the city, and an excellent bottle of wine, but right now I would like us to sit here on these beautiful petals and plan our perfect future together on this perfect day."

She extended her hand to him and he took it in his as she leaned nearer to him for a soft kiss on her pink cheek. He took her in his arms and held her and then cleared a spot for her to sit down. She sat atop the petals in her fine attire and looked so peaceful and happy he could not wait to ask her the question he had rehearsed in his mind a multitude of times. His resolve the night before was ever present in his mind. He would not, could not be on the outside of her life.

Edward leaned over the basket for a moment and then turned to speak to her as a fullness of heart overcame him, looking at her and kneeling before her, she instinctively drew closer to him noting his serious expression, "Emily, my life, my heart is so full at this moment. I love you, I love you with all I am and being apart from you has been the torture of my existence for the past few months. Hiding this joy I feel from others, but I have failed there, I am afraid. People everywhere stop and ask me why I am smiling, they hear my love for you in my voice, as it is somehow changed. I find myself humming cheerful songs throughout the day, I never hum! What I am trying to say is I never imagined I could feel this way, your love has changed my life. It has sent a ripple through my life and touched every part of it and being with you here, now, seeing your face so happy I know I cannot bear to be without you again. Emily it is my greatest hope that you shall be my wife, if you will honor me by accepting this ring."

Between his thumb and index finger he offered her an antique, sparkling sapphire ring.

"Edward, what are you saying?" she asked, as her tear filled eyes searched his.

"I am asking you, no, begging you rather to spare me the pain of another separation, to share all of your days, from this day until your last with me, Emily, will you marry me?"

"It seems I have waited to hear those words since the beginning of time, and now they sound more wonderful than I ever imagined. From the moment I saw you, I knew, my heart acknowledged with a deafening voice 'you are the one I have waited for.' There was a longing, an undefined longing in my heart, for you," she said, but she was so overwhelmed by his proposal she could not continue in that moment where time stood still. The beating of her heart increased and a small tear softly touched her rosy cheek. Never before had she felt the feeling of standing on the threshold of her life. Like spring, every cell in her was full of new life, her heart fluttered in the wind of his sweetness which now consumed her.

But Edward mistook her silence and knelt beside her in painful anticipation of her last words, afraid to break the silence, but unable to go on another moment he said, "Have I spoken too soon? I thought this is what you wanted, Emily, I know I am not the man your family would have chosen for you, I know it is all happening so quickly, and I cannot promise you the life to which you are accustomed. I am a wealthy man, but my path is far from one of status, power or influence, but there is something far above those things which I most certainly can pledge, and that is myself, my very self I pledge to you and with a constancy, unlike financial spoils or social status which can in moments be wholly stripped away. This feeling I have for you will not change. I can tell you I belong to you and you belong to me and nothing and no one can deny that."

"Edward, you do not understand, I am not questioning your love nor mine. What a fool I would be to even consider letting you slip away from me. I feel so much for you, I need you like I have never needed anyone else and it frightens me. If anything ever happened to you..."

"Emily, my love, nothing is going to happen to me, listen, I am here with you now and I wanted my proposal to make you happy, but I have frightened you instead. But where is my answer?"

She gazed up at him with her eyes smiling, and took his

hand in hers, "Edward, nothing could make me happier than becoming your wife, my answer is and always has been yes, with all my heart, YES."

He took her hand and placed the exquisite ring on her finger and said, "Emily, with this ring I am your husband. It was my mother's. She gave it to me in secret before she said goodbye, she told me I should have it for it was the one symbol, other than myself, of their love. The ring is the only remaining personal possession of my mother in existence. As you know everything else was lost. I hid it and kept it always. At the orphanage, and then later at the university, I have always kept it in a safe place. It has been the one thing in this world I have treasured the most, until now."

"It is beautiful, and the stone is magnificent."

"Indeed, it is beautiful, but the blue of this stone pales to the beauty of your sapphire eyes, it is their familiar deep blue my heart longs for, but when you think of my love, look upon this stone and know my heart feels a depth of love deeper than the deepest blue sea, it ranges higher than the highest blue sky and longer and farther than Time can reach." He kissed her softly and then overcome with their joy, he picked her up and twirled her several revolutions until they were both laughing and dizzy and altogether out of balance. When they stopped, they both fell to their knees on the ground and began scooping handfuls of rose petals and tossing them in the air above them. The petals fell like a fragrant rain all around them.

"Today is the most wonderful day of my life, thank you my darling, for making my most cherished dream come true," Emily said.

"And you have exceeded my dreams. I do not know if we can have a proper bridal tour just yet, there is little time with the university's schedule. . ."

"All that matters is we are together now, and not to be parted again. We have our entire lives to travel, to see the world. I will be proud to be your wife and even if I never leave this spot, I will have known the fullness of love and joy and there is no where else I would rather be. I know in my heart I could never feel more joy. No matter what happens nothing can match this day." Emily said to him comfortingly.

"Sweetheart, I do not want to spoil this happiness, but I think we should discuss how we might share the news of our engagement," Edward said.

"How is it possible my heart can hold such gladness, but be held in such fear at the same moment?" she said clutching his hand in hers.

"Obviously your father will not be pleased with our news. Perhaps we should wait to tell him or anyone else, except for Bryson, of course. He will be leaving at summer's end and I should like to take him into our confidence. But he and he alone can know of our news. I do not mean to steal your joy, and I vowed I would never again be as a shadow in your life, but for now I think it is best to keep our engagement, as we have kept our love, a secret. I just could not wait another day to prove my true intentions. I could not hold that ring any longer when it belongs to you. I want you to keep it in a safe place, it is yours now, but the time is not right to share our blessed news just yet, do you understand?"

"Yes, I know we must wait, we must hold our happiness inside, but knowing I will be your wife makes me want to be even more. I want to be your wife in every way. How much longer can I hold these feelings back. I want to show you . . ."

"Emily, I know. I can hardly sleep at night for my constant burning for you, I wonder at times if I can go on without being with you. I want to kiss you and I do not want to stop until you are mine completely. It is harder every day to limit this consuming fire. I want to wake with you each morning and sleep with you by my side." He saw the passion in her moist eyes. His heart began to race, he closed his eyes. . .

ಸಂ

Edward was suddenly aware of the silence filling the room and reality rushed back upon him as he realized Lenora had stopped playing the piano.

"Forgive me Lenora, you played so beautifully, I must have lost myself in thought." he said.

Lenora did not answer at first. He walked over to her and

watched her slender hand subtly brush her cheek. He knew not the reason for her silent tears, he only knew he wished to make them no longer appear.

"Are you all right?" he asked. She took a quiet breath and turned to him.

"Yes, Edward, I am all right, more than all right. I suppose I am a bit amazed, you see I did not even know I possessed this talent. I simply saw this beautiful instrument and was drawn to it. When I touched the keys, the music came back to me, it seemed to flow from some place deep in my very soul. My fingers danced across the keys so happily, finding each note, as though they were embracing old friends. I kept playing, searching for something. Something familiar. I did not know where my playing might lead, but the last piece I played was different. Although is was a simple tune, I feel something deeper in its notes, its familiarity. And though I cannot tell just what, I felt such a deep sorrow and longing, as though it were a memory."

"What a discovery. Lenora, your playing was exceptional, no ordinary talent. I would confidently wager you have had extensive training."

"Really? Another clue I suppose. But even if it leads me nowhere, it is a delight to play and I should like to play again should it be acceptable to you?"

"Acceptable? I rather insist upon it, you may play at any time you wish."

Chapter 6
Another's Past, Another's Sorrow

Throughout the day Lenora heard a beautiful melody in her mind. She could not stop replaying it over and over again, and each time it played in her mind, it seemed to recall to her a relationship of great importance in her life, detached completely from any memory, but nonetheless the hint of a link between her heart and that of another. The feeling was the clue to her past she had longed for, and she could concentrate on little else. Meanwhile Edward had retired to his study. Seeing Lenora play the piano made it progressively more difficult for him to distinguish between reality and what he hoped for. He sat in lonesome solitude with his thoughts of her, which eventually wandered down the pathway to his memories of Emily.

How he longed to reach out to Lenora, to comfort her at times, but he would not allow the indulgence, for in truth, he secretly wondered if she would feel the same as Emily had felt. Would her skin be as soft, would her hair smell of gardenias? If only he could find the courage to tell her all he was feeling, but he had to reign in those thoughts, to remind himself once and for all she was not Emily. Emily was lost to him forever, and no one could replace her, but the notes Lenora had played, were so beautiful, and hearing such fine playing now, how could he not think of Emily? Emily had been a pianist, a brilliant talent. And now this lovely young woman had entered his life, and she too offered him the gift of music.

Quitting his study just before dinner, he found Lenora reading in the piano room. Seeing her there seemed entirely natural, and the thought of her being an intruder never entered his mind.

"I see you have found the library," he said entering the room, and noting a few volumes on the table beside her.

"Good evening Edward. I have not had the opportunity to read in ages. I hope you do not disapprove."

"Do not be ridiculous, reading is one of the great pleasures of life, and I would never deny you such a wonderful exercise. And how content and at home you seem. What I mean to say is you seemed so afraid and out of sorts when first I met you a few days ago. I am glad you are feeling more suited to your new surroundings."

"Indeed. I am much improved and I believe being here in Brookhaven has sparked this new contentment. I must confess I have fallen in love with this mysterious place. I am curious, how is it you came to find Brookhaven in this remote land?"

"It is a long story, but an endearing one," he answered.

"Would you tell me?" she urged.

"Where shall I begin," he started, "after reaching adulthood and upon leaving the orphanage, I traveled to Oxford to continue my education, in my family's tradition. I studied many wonderful subjects and a world of knowledge and greatness was opened to me. While at the university I met a most upright and moral young man, Bryson Talbot. We became the closest of companions and he entreated me to join him and his family during the Christmas Holiday from the university. My consent resulted in a most life altering experience. You see it is there I met his sister, Emily. As I mentioned to you before, our union was not to be. The truth is she returned to heaven, from whence she came quite prematurely. I scarcely remember how the following two years at the university passed, but after graduating, my family fortune was fully restored to me. There was no end in sight to the loss of my Emily, no mercy to the void her presence had left, and seeking to escape, I found myself in Scotland, my father's homeland, in hopes my heritage would open a new door to me, that I might forget, if only for a brief time. But, as fate would have it, upon meeting my distant relatives, I shortly had a great understanding of why my father had decided to sail half way around the world to start a new life in America.

No matter how vehemently I tried, I could feel nothing for them. Instead of the security I longed for, I found only more loneliness. I loved my adventures in those ancient and exotic places, but there was something fresh and new about America which nagged at me until I finally gave in and returned to the only place I had known as home. My yearning for America could not be silenced. I had no particular destination in mind, but I had heard tales of the Blue Ridge Mountains and was intrigued by the prospect of living nearer to nature, and in solitude. I sailed to America with a few potential estates in mind. You see, with me I brought many family treasures, portraits, sculpture, furniture, china, and the like, and as such I was in desperate need of a household to hold these priceless treasures.

I arrived in Asheville quite by accident. I had come in hopes of acquiring a new steed, and Ashford Stables was known for the finest stock of horses in this country. The rolling landscape reminded me of my father's village. While testing a fine spotted gelding I explored the countryside. And upon this lengthy jaunt, I discovered Brookhaven. To be sure the location was quite remote, and far from the city, but what need did I have of city life? I cannot explain exactly why, but with one look, I knew I was home. She is strong, beautiful and mysterious and possesses the perfect combination of what I desire in a home. I could live in America where I believe I belong, and I could enjoy the European inspired estate and grounds reminiscent of my childhood, the privacy was unmatched.

It was not until I had become fully settled when I discovered her history and after learning it, I began to picture her as a bright and happy home. Sure she is darker now and her past dreams remain asleep, but before the deep sadness, there was a time when this was a place of excitement and life, a special sort of joy that one hopes for.

I suppose it begins and ends with John and Elizabeth. At the turn of the last century, a young man named John Collins had a vision of Brookhaven. He designed it to the last detail. He built this mansion as a home for him and his love, Elizabeth Brookhaven. She was to become his wife. He met her when he was a young man on a trip to England. They fell rather hard for each other, but she was quite young and accepted his proposal of marriage on her father's condition that John prove himself a worthy provider. Heartbroken but driven by an intense purpose, he returned to America, and made his fortune. Through the months and years during his apprenticeship, they faithfully wrote each other letters expressing the many dreams of their future happiness."

"How charming," Lenora said smiling at the thought of the young couple.

"Yes," Edward continued, "but destiny does not allow us the courtesy of planning our own lives, life has plans of its own. I'm afraid life had a much different plan for our John and Elizabeth. But my words fall short. Lenora, there is a way of finishing the story. You see, I happen to have the very letters they wrote to each other. When I found Brookhaven, it was in a bit of disrepair, for not a soul had passed its threshold for over half a century. Many of the original pieces were still here. During the restoration one of the carpenters found a secret hall behind the wall in the Master bedroom, quite common in an estate such as this. When we opened it, I discovered the letters, and John's personal journals. I was able to learn of their lives through their correspondence and I filled in the missing years with his journals. I've kept them all these years and I should be happy to allow you to read them if you wish."

"Would you really? I would like nothing more."

"It is a remarkable, but tragic story." he warned. "This home began with a dream, with one simple promise and ultimately became a sort of harbor for lost souls seeking to be near that same hope, however distant and far from reach it may be." Edward sounded sorrowful when he related this story, for he believed he and John were permanently linked by their inexpressible despair and their shared love for Brookhaven.

How appropriate that Edward should love this place, that he should be drawn to it so and once he had read the letters, he had understood. Edward knew what it felt like to live day after day clinging to the past. While his past was the anchor that hindered him from moving forward, it was also his only peace. To forget his past, to leave it behind would be a betrayal he could not bear. The breadth of emotions of love and of pain were completely shared by these two men, but the amazing ability of one's mind, or heart rather, in this case, to accomplish such distinctive ends when faced with virtually the same emotions was remarkable. For so similar were the peaks and valleys where their hearts rose and fell, and yet so distinct and opposite were the effects these emotions had had upon the two. John's feelings of love for Elizabeth were true and pure, yet those feelings almost turned on him as he lost her. The pain was too strong for him to endure and weighed upon him so heavily that it ultimately brought him to hopelessness, and eventually to ruin. And though Edward knew the same depths of love for Emily, his reaction to the loss of her yielded quite the reverse outcome, a triumph of hope over hopelessness. In Edward's case, love had somehow masked the sorrow and did not destroy the man at all, perhaps it was partly due to Edward's unfortunate familiarity with the notion of loss, or perhaps his faith had carried him through the valley of despair, but whatever the case, he defeated the pain before it had the opportunity to defeat him.

That is not to say Edward was not wrecked by the despair of his heart, on the contrary, it consumed him for a long while, but then one day a decision was made and whether it was a conscious decision or some internal struggle of which he had no part, Emily's love for him saved him yet again. It was as though there lay before him a large scale, shiny and beautiful, with no care for the outcome it might yield, and on the empty plate hanging to the right, Edward took all of the pain, torment, regret, and despair, and emptied it thereon. The scale quickly became over burdened and tipped far, far out of his mind's eye, so quickly that he summoned all of the love he had felt for this dear girl, all of the hope he had known when in the rest of her gentle heart, and placed it upon the opposite plate.

The plate on the left, bearing the contents of his heart, began to make a quick descent, but the scale remained in constant flux. It was not until Edward remembered what he had so foolishly forgotten to include in his second offering that the balance shifted. With his remembered thought, he called upon the love of his beloved for him and he took that love, the very love she had had for him, and placed it together with the love he had for her, and when intermingled with his own, the scales began to move at last, and the combined hearts of the two weighed down more and more until it became even with the pain and sorrow, and it seemed the scales remained there at equilibrium for such a long time, but in truth it was only a mere second, a second upon which his future clung, but suddenly his heart became lighter as the love became heavier and heavier on the plate, diminishing the power the pain had held over him for so long. And after that day, Edward could go on, he could live without her because he had lived with her, he could face tomorrow because his yesterdays had been so glorious. And so her love urged him on in the mundane day to days that followed, and with every joy he knew and in every silent happiness he experienced, he shared them with her and experienced them for her.

ಸಾಡ

After hearing Edward's brief account of the young lovers, Lenora was left with a feeling of curiosity which knew no stifling. In addition, she felt a compassionate sadness overshadowing the pain of her own plight, and she was haunted by Edward's hint that their love or perhaps lives had come to ruin and pain. Nothing would do but that she might quench her thirst for every detail of these two who had loved and lost. At her first opportunity she kindly asked Edward if she might see the letters as he had promised.

"Edward, would you be so kind as to allow me to read the letters that you spoke of? I confess I have been unable to remove the thought of them from my mind?"

"Certainly, and perhaps it may be an interesting way to pass your time in this lonely old place. As you know, I am very protective of any of John's belongings. I have kept everything as I found it, and for as long as I have been here and as long as I shall live, I shall share Brookhaven with John and Elizabeth. After reading their letters, I feel as though they are dear friends. There is so much of them here at Brookhaven. Just look above you," he said glancing toward the ceiling.

Lenora looked above and her eyes were met by four faint

cherub angles with harps hovering above them on a canvas of powder blue mixed with delicate white and pink clouds. Each angel held a symbol representing the four seasons, the spring Angel holding a cherry blossom, was her favorite.

"Edward," she said almost in a whisper, "it's lovely."

"It is rumored it was a wedding gift from his friend and mentor to celebrate their union. There are many hidden treasures in Brookhaven. John was a talented artist. I shall show you his sketches. There are a number of Elizabeth. The sketches are of a young woman in a land by a shore. In addition to the other items, I have some of her clothing. Each piece was so lovely I could not destroy or part with them. They are all in the armoire in the room in which you sleep. The dress you are wearing belonged to her, but she never wore it here, here in her home."

"Oh, Edward, I had no idea. I was unable to determine from where or when the clothes could have come. I suddenly feel strange wearing her clothing, I wonder if she would have minded a stranger some eras ahead of her borrowing them for a brief time, and are you quite sure I may wear them?"

"I would not have offered had I not been sincere. Besides, look at you. The dress suits you and a tailor could not have cut a more perfect fit."

"I suppose you are right," she said looking down at her sleeve and touching the soft fabric with a new awareness. After hearing the story of John and Elizabeth, Lenora fell into a very somber mood, a melancholy which would not pass until she walked over to the piano and began to play again, and this time she played for John and Elizabeth.

Chapter 7
Yellowed Letters and Opened Hearts

Even through dinner the relentless ill humor of the day could not be escaped. Everything seemed to remind Lenora of John and Elizabeth and as such, she had been uncommonly quiet during dinner. She appreciated Edward not breaking the silence, but eventually she summoned her good manners and began, "I apologize for being so quiet this evening, dinner is excellent."

"Yes, I was just thinking it is exceptionally good this evening. I have been most fortunate with my staff."

Edward interrupted the brief pause with a question, "I heard you playing before, it was lovely."

"Oh, thank you. I am afraid I have been bad company this evening. You must forgive my somber mood. Even the music I played earlier was a sad tune, but I cannot help but to think of the young couple, John and Elizabeth. May we look at the sketches after dinner?"

"It would give me great pleasure, I always enjoy looking at them again, and it has been several months, perhaps even years since I've seen them."

They finished dinner and without pause went to the room on the second floor wherein the precious letters and sketches had found their home. Lenora was weary of her own sad tale and she could not wait to fill her mind with the details of someone else's life. The account of John and Elizabeth was a most welcome distraction. Edward opened an aged trunk in a sort of storage room to reveal a mass of old yellowed letters and what appeared to be a writing tablet. Forgetting herself she impatiently stooped down beside Edward and picked up one parcel of the letters.

"What order are the letters in?" she asked eagerly.

"Well, I believe you have the earliest ones and there is another set of letters here. John's journals and sketches are just underneath this compartment. " he answered.

"May I see his journal?"

Edward lifted the divider in the trunk and extracted a journal as requested and handed it to his lovely guest.

"May I read from it?"

"Please do and I shall attempt to put some order to the letters." As Edward leafed through the various letters, Lenora began to read aloud a passage from John's journal:

13 March 1805

Why? Lord in heaven why did you take her from me? I suppose she was so lovely and good you wanted her by your side. But look at this world! Can you not see the darkness that covers the face of my days? Lord, help me to find a way to endure this pain. I feel as though I cannot breathe without her. I think of the countless days I spent waiting for the day she and I would be united, my entire being focused solely on her bright face. The only moments of peace I know are the seconds of each day when my day begins. All night I dream of her and when I wake, for a moment, it is as it was before. I feel her with me in those fleeting seconds until reality sweeps over me, and I remember I shall never see her again on this earth. I beg of you, to loosen this grip of pain that holds my sanity ransom. Deliver me from this sadness.

20 May 1807

I look out over the countryside surveying the rich land beneath my feet. Again spring has come and although the world is alive once more with flowers and the distant songs of birds, my heart remains dead as in the peak of winter. The budding flowers, the tune of the birds in the overhanging branches curse me as I curse them for reminding me of another spring, long ago and far removed from my present life. If one can call my empty days a life at all. I wonder if I will ever be reborn again into a bright spring. Where are you Elizabeth? Where are you? Are you watching over me? I know you asked me not to mourn you, but I cannot forget. I grew accustomed to waiting for you all those years ago and now I find I still wait, only now I will see you in heaven, if only it could come sooner and rescue me from these dreadful days. To see you again would be my rebirth. I am afraid my spring will only arrive when I see myself again in your eyes.

5 August 1808
Another year has passed away and still you are the same. Though you left me, the love we shared lives on in my heart. In my heart you remain the beautiful, young, kind and perfect Elizabeth. Each year on the date of your birth I read your letters again. They are as worn and used as I at present. I miss you. I wonder if in some way you are still waiting for me. Sometimes I feel you waiting for me, somewhere. Do you hear me when I speak to you? Or do my words mean nothing? Oh Elizabeth I do not know how I can go on without you. I can no longer work, I managed to keep our home, but it is so empty without you. Can you find a way to come for me, I need you my angel.....

"I am sorry, I cannot read further, it is terrible, Edward, terrible, that poor creature so consumed with grief."

"Indeed, love such as this is powerful and all consuming. And perhaps you should listen to your heart, it seems it may break in empathy, I would advise you not to read on just now."

"But I feel I must read the letters now. There is something in his painful words, a loss so tragic, yet the notion of a love so true, it is an overwhelming thought. I should like very much to continue, but perhaps I shall delay my curiosity for a short while."

"As you wish," Edward answered, as he handed her the bundle of letters.

"Read them at your leisure, but it is drafty in this little room. When you are finished with these I shall be more than happy to fetch the others. Lenora," he continued with a hint of gravity in his voice, "there are many items in this room I would prefer to keep untouched. Everything has its place, and I must ask you to enter this room only when I may accompany you, and besides the room was never completely finished and therefore could prove dangerous with its exposed nails and untested beams."

"I understand, and thank you. You spoke of their lives so eloquently, and I am captivated."

"You are much too kind, and I assure you my rendering of the events will not compare to your reading of their lives in their own words. There is nothing I may add to their truthful writings."

Edward escorted Lenora back to the great hall where they took tea and dessert before retiring for the evening. Lenora was rather exhausted at the long day's end and feeling sluggish after the heavy meal. In truth, she was unaccustomed to dining so regularly, as fate had borne her into a meager existence for the last two years of her life. There was not a moment when she was not full of gratitude for her new found abundance.

As she sipped the rather good tea, she asked, "Do you live here throughout the year, Edward?"

"Yes, I do not like moving from place to place. Many individuals of similar means as myself, have a summer home, a cottage in the country, and on and on, but I prefer one place to call home."

"I understand, having just one place is all I shall ever want, again."

"Sorry, how foolish of me to go on about this when you are so far from home and lost."

"You are the least foolish person I have ever met. I only

wondered how Brookhaven must look in the spring. It must be handsome."

"It is nice enough in the spring. But it is never more lovely than when it is cloaked in the garment of pure white snow as it is now. There is a serenity here I have yet to find elsewhere. And there is something about winter that matches my spirit somehow."

"Yes, I believe you are right, I rather enjoy winter myself, there is nothing more comforting than the blaze of a warm fire in the midst of such chilling cold, and yet winter seems hard on one's emotions. I had so wanted to have a real Christmas this year. This year will mark my third "lost" Christmas. I have seen families and friends gather around trees, exchanging gifts and most importantly exchanging their love for one another. This world can be very lonely." It suddenly occurred to her how hopeless she sounded each time she offered a comment. She wanted to escape from the dreariness she felt, but it haunted her, followed her as if there was no escape and she would never again be without it.

The only reprieve from her own sorrows was when she thought of John and Elizabeth, and remembering them, she promptly retired for the evening.

When Lenora was settled in the comfort of her bed, she carefully untied the small parcel of letters, tied ever so neatly with a yellow ribbon of satin, and opened the first letter.

>
> 24 September 1801
>
> My dearest Elizabeth,
>
> I have only just left your side and already my heart is flooded with sadness. My hand trembles as I write these words because I find myself lost without you. How shall I spend the days ahead without you beside me? I am dedicated more than ever to coming back for you. I ask our God to bring me safely back to you even before I reach my homeland. Each day when I rise it will be your sweet face that my mind will see, and each night as I pass into slumber I shall think of you and of the day when I will bring you to America to

live with me forever. Please be patient my love. Wait for me, as I wait for you.

Until we meet again, my love, John

ଗଙ

2 December 1801
Dearest John,

Your letter arrived today and my eyes have read its precious promises over and over again. I feel my heart should surely break if I were not certain of your return. I know your sadness too well, for my heart aches for you each day. Do not fear the endurance of my patience, my love. I shall wait for you. These three years will seem an eternity without you, but I shall wait how ever long it may take for you to come for me. Until I hear of your safe arrival, I will wear the ribbon you gave me and keep a prayer upon my lips. I will pray that God will hold you gently in His hands and keep you from all harm.
Faithfully yours, Elizabeth

ଗଙ

5 December 1801
My dearest Elizabeth,

Though the winter wind howls and chills my very bones, within my heart is a springtime of joy knowing you share my hope of our love and life together. The memory of our days together brings my heart a joyous peace. As you know, I have returned to my work and mentor, Mr. Eli Sanderson, with a vengeance. Mr. Sanderson, as I have told you is a very interesting man, and upon his very shoulders rest our future. Immediately upon my return, he promoted me and placed an apprentice under my direction. There is still much for me to learn, but teaching another my skills will

only strengthen my own knowledge as a master craftsman. I regret Mr. Sanderson is such a melancholy old fellow, and regret more the reason for his sadness. Losing his only son in such a severe battle with a deadly illness. But I suppose his loss built the bridge over which he and I developed such a fast and wonderful rapport. But how are you, my love? How are you filling your days? The days pass slowly for me, but it is a beautiful country. I cannot wait to run with you through the purple meadows and golden fields. I am here in body but I know that my heart never made the journey. It remains with you, my beloved Elizabeth. Until we meet again, my love,
John

ೀಲಿ

4 March 1802
Dearest John,

Your letters and your promises of our future keep my heart alive. I am filled with joy knowing someday our hearts will be one. I am so pleased to hear of your new appointment, but I already knew the treasure you were to Mr. Sanderson. You spoke to me on many occasions of his strong character. How sad a man such as he has suffered such a great loss, and perhaps that is why God has placed you into his life. For I know he must think of you as a son. As for me, it is rather lonely here, but I am trying to keep smiling. After our summer together nothing can compare to being with you. My days are full enough, I have been volunteering the greater part of my days in Kielderbridge. It is very sad John, we have so many poor and I cannot bear to see the children in their ragged clothing and hear their cries in the night, while I have been blessed with so much. I am helping

them as much as I can. It is not much, but I know my being there gives them a little hope. I can find no peace except in putting my hands to use. My only solace is easing the suffering I see around me. All my love goes out to you, my darling John. Your absence from my world makes it dark and lonely. But your promises keep my heart glowing eternally.
Faithfully yours, Elizabeth

ഌറ

24 March 1802
My dearest Elizabeth,

      Good morning my love. The day has yet broken and I have stolen a moment to send you these few words. I have been diligently working with Mr. Sanderson on a new project. My apprentice has proven to be quite intelligent and learns at an astonishing rate. Already he has been with me for nearly four months, our work is steady and relentless. I hardly have a moment for anything save for eating, sleeping and longing for you. Always longing for you. I have learned much about the craft and Mr. Sanderson's company. I humbly admit I have become irreplaceable to Mr. Sanderson and he has even hinted he may want me to carry on the business. It could not be a more excellent situation. Remember it is your sweet face that carries me through each day, which is another day closer to when you and I shall be together forever.
Until we meet again, my love, John

ഌറ

12 June 1802
Dearest John,

I am gazing upon a full moon tonight. It is magnificent. I only wonder if it is shining upon you. Are you looking out into the night and seeing the same sky? Do you hear my heart's constant song of love to you? I say a prayer everyday that God will watch over you. How lonely are my nights without you. Sometimes I wonder how I will endure the days, the weeks, the months without you, but then I close my eyes and I see your face. I imagine I am looking into your brown eyes and my heart says "patience". I hear your joyous laughter and I smile in silent joy. There are times I wonder if you are real or if you are an apparition my lonely heart created. Your letters and our beautiful memories are evidence of your existence, but weeks have passed and I have not heard from you. Please send word to me soon of your safety. I cannot rest until I know my beloved is safe and secure. My love and prayers go out to you.
Faithfully yours, Elizabeth

ಸಿಂ

10 June 1802
My dearest Elizabeth,

I hope this letter finds its way to you quickly. I fear my procrastination may appear as though I am not thinking of you. Thinking of you, your beautiful face, your sweet angelic voice is the only hope to which I cling. I miss you so very much, my darling. I waited until dark to compose this letter so I could look up at the moon knowing you too were gazing upon it. I wanted to share a bit of news with you my darling. I found the most beautiful plot of land today on Mr. Sanderson's estate. Seeing my enthusiasm for it, he said he will sell it to me for a fair price. You will love it as I do. There are rolling hills and meadows overrun with wild flowers and according to Mr. Sanderson the scene is even more lovely in autumn when every tree is dressed in brilliant and fiery colors. When I saw it my vivid imagination took hold of me and I could see you here with me, I could see our children in my sweetest dreams surrounded by love and full of all happiness. One day soon those dreams shall be a living truth, until then, may the stars of heaven watch over you until I have the honor of being by your side once more. Until we meet again my love, John

Enchanted by the letters, Lenora tried to picture the young lovers and she wondered what would happen next, but then she remembered they most certainly had come to some sad end, and the feeling struck a cord in Lenora's heart, forcing her to discontinue reading another word, for now at least. She almost felt she was intruding on something sacred. She could not help but to wonder at the cruelness of life. 'There is so much sadness in the world. Elizabeth vowed her love to John, however long it would take, but fate answered, leaving him lost in this world that, without her, held no meaning. Why were so many people forced to live in the immense world alone?' It seemed intrinsically unfair to her and being unable to accept the sad reality of their fate, she closed her eyes and pretended that life was as it should have been for John and Elizabeth.

She imagined John and Elizabeth's wedding. She pictured Elizabeth's angelic face as she walked into the home John had so carefully constructed for her. Her imagination ran wild as she watched their children growing up around them, filling each space of Brookhaven with love and laughter. She pictured them dancing in their old age with their love stronger than ever. She hoped their spirits at least were able to walk these halls and fill these rooms with their undying love, but even if it were not so, she believed she had kept their love alive by knowing of it, by reading their words and hearing what their hearts had pledged to one another, and as long as she lived she would remember their love, she would hold on to the hope of it, and holding tightly to her pledge, she wiped the moisture from her eyes and turned over and fell asleep.

Chapter 8
A Mutual Plan

A number of days passed quietly by and the calendar marked only three days until Christmas Eve. Lenora awoke in her customary manner, first drawing open the curtains in her room, and allowing the outside world to be exposed. The view greeting her was familiar, the heavens above had not broken their ritual of sifting sparkling flakes upon the land. Aware of the imminence of the approaching holiday, she wondered how Christmas would be celebrated at Brookhaven, might it be decorated from top to bottom and scented with pine, cinnamon and nutmeg, or would it pass as every other day without ceremony? There was no sign of a tree or any other decorations, and there had been no mention of the coming holiday. Again she would face another year without the family Christmas she had longed for. 'Perhaps next year,' she sighed. She dressed hurriedly this morning and found herself anxious to share the morning and breakfast with Edward.

Lenora was growing accustomed to the rhythm of her days at Brookhaven. She and Edward would meet for breakfast in the mornings, and afterwards he would excuse himself for some hours in his study and she would read, practice her penmanship, or sketch little copies of her favorite artwork hanging on the walls of Brookhaven. Late in the day they would meet again and take tea while discussing the news of the day on which Edward had no doubt educated himself during his solitary morning hours. And then, just before dinner, she would play the piano as Edward looked on, listening. She mused to herself about those evening moments and then thought, 'The piano, that is it. I will try to practice some old carols in secret, and this will be my Christmas gift to Edward, he seems to enjoy the music so, and who does not enjoy the familiar notes and strings of the carols? 'Perfect,' she thought. 'There is nothing like Christmas music to make one feel it is Christmastime.'

As she opened the armoire, she reflected once more upon Edward's kindness in extending her an invitation to wear Elizabeth's clothing. As she studied each beautiful garment, she admired them with a new appreciation. The young woman who had owned these beautiful gowns had lived such a short time, but oh how she lived and how she was loved. The clothes were of a different age, but timeless nonetheless. The years were of no consequence to their particular style and elegance.

As she examined each dress carefully, she came across a stunning gown. She imagined how Elizabeth must have worn this to the opera or maybe a family holiday ball. Perhaps Elizabeth had even worn it for John. The armoire was deep and wide and though it had double doors, it was difficult to reach the hangers on each of its sides, but as she looked in the very back of the right side she saw something that made the effort worthwhile. The last hanger was draped with a solid white sheet, and she wondered why she had failed to notice it in all the times she had opened these wooden doors.

'What is this?' she asked. Carefully, she slid the other garments aside and pulled the hanger closer. When she uncovered the sheet, she gasped, at the sight of loveliest wedding gown she had ever seen. Her heart seemed to drop to the very floor beneath her. The gown was the sad holder of the promises of Elizabeth and John's future, a stolen future. She imagined how many tears had been shed over the loss of their dreams of a life together. There were too many to count. She carefully covered the wedding gown and returned it to its place in the closet, but its presence there haunted her. Though it was hidden away in darkness, its image was firmly imprinted in her mind. She had lingered long over the treasured clothing and suddenly realized she might be tardy for breakfast. As she closed her door behind her, she promised she would not allow herself to waste a moment feeling gloomy, for Brookhaven had known too many sorrows.

As she entered the dining hall she chirped, "Good morning Charles."

"Good morning, Miss Lenora, Master Edward asked me to give you a message, he has gone in to the city for a few supplies, he should return in two days time. He said for you to make yourself at home."

"Thank you, Charles, I shall miss his company today. But what of the weather, is it safe for travel?"

"Not perfect conditions for traveling, but not to worry, Master Edward will be quite all right. I must say I am a bit concerned though, I wonder what I am to do if the temperature does not rise soon, the weather has taken a terrible turn for the worse and it could not have happened at a more inopportune time, with the holidays just before us."

"Do you have a family, Charles?"

"Yes, Lily is my wife, and we have two fine young girls. We live behind the main house in the guest quarters."

"Oh yes, I met Lily my first night here, but I did not know she was your wife. Charles, I have an idea. I, as everyone else in the household is, am stranded here for the holidays. I suggest we plan a nice Christmas dinner. With your family and the rest of the staff, we could have a splendid time."

Charles looked at her strangely and then said, "Miss Lenora, while your idea is lovely, Master Edward does not generally celebrate, not even for Christmas. In fact, as you can see by observing the estate that one would hardly find any evidence that we are heading straight for December 25th. To my knowledge, we have never celebrated Christmas in this house."

"What a pity, this mansion is so lovely and it begs for life, what it needs is a little spirit." Then she remembered how Edward had told her he celebrated Christmas in his own way at the orphanage. It was not true that he had no Christmas spirit. Christmas was simply a sad and lonely time for him. Thinking of this she returned, "Charles, if you will make a nice Christmas dinner, I will take full responsibility for it if Edward does not approve."

"I don't know..." Charles began.

"I'm not suggesting we deck every hall, as it were, it doesn't have to be a grand affair, but just something extra, to mark the wondrous occasion. Lily and your girls could join us for dinner and I will practice Christmas carols. We could have a special evening together. Please say you will help me?" she pleaded.

Charles thought about her wish for a few moments and then agreed to help her, for he had witnessed the change in his employer since her unexpected arrival. She asked also that they not mention it to Edward and explained she wanted the celebration to be her gift to him for his very generous hospitality over the last few days. Charles agreed to keep her secret. The remainder of the day passed quickly as Charles spent the day in the kitchen thinking of what he had available to create a Christmas feast. He was elated as he thought about his girls, and how they would have a wonderful and joyful Christmas. While Charles planned for the Christmas dinner, Lenora played carol after carol. She could not remember feeling this happy in a long time or looking forward to anything, save remembering her past. It was not the music, it was the excitement of being able to do something for Edward. He was so kind and generous. She wished she could come to understand him more fully so she might be able to comfort him, as he had comforted her over the last few days.

What she felt for him was not pity, she was aware he regarded his life as having turned out well, and judging from his kindness to her, a complete stranger, she was convinced of the same, but she could not deny he was a lonely man. He lived in isolation, with no one to share his soul, and she believed with all her heart people were meant to share their lives with others in order to reach one's fullest potential. Edward revealed to her how he had lost the only love of his life and she knew from their conversations he was a sensitive and loving man. There was a sense of protection she had for him. She wished she could show him how grand life could be, that one did not have to live one's life so removed from others. But then she laughed at herself with such a thought, remembering that the notion of sharing and love were as foreign to her as they were to him.

ಶಿ)ಲ್ಲ

Edward looked out of the horse drawn sleigh and thought about the children at the orphanage. One by one their faces came to him and he sorely wished he could be there for them this year. The holidays were always the most difficult for the children, the older ones at least, for they still remembered being with their families, they remembered their siblings, they longed for them, they felt a loss so deep, a loss Edward fully understood. He struggled to amend how he could celebrate Christmas without being there, but he knew his instructions would be precisely followed, and each of the children would receive a warm meal and a special gift. At the same time, he could not deny he was thrilled with the changing fortunes of time having granted him an opportunity he had never even imagined. An angel had fallen right into his life and he was so thankful for the snow which had kept her in his care.

"Beautiful white snow," he whispered, "you have built a fortress to keep Lenora at Brookhaven. Your soft billowy flakes may save me after all." He lingered over the thought of Lenora's sad words describing her lost Christmases. 'Such a pitiful state for so lovely and kind a girl,' he thought, and he began to wonder how he could relieve her sadness. Perhaps he would give her a Christmas gift. 'Was it appropriate to give her a gift?' He simply knew he wanted to make her feel at ease, to forget, if even for a moment, her feeling of being lost and alone. The holiday season often reminded him of the most extreme meditations of his soul, the height of happiness, candle-lit trees, sleigh bells ringing in the distance, carols, beautiful meals, Emily, in a red, silk dress....and then there were the times after Emily, changing Christmas to a time of being outside of the living world, a sad reminder of what he had lost.

Looking out at the snow and how beautifully it covered the evergreens, it occurred to him he could give Lenora a tree. He had been blessed with her presence during this snowstorm and she had said herself a Christmas celebration was what she longed for. 'And a Christmas celebration she shall have, complete with a Christmas tree,' he thought. He counted the days and noted it would be three days until Christmas Day. He planned to return to Brookhaven on the morning of the Eve of Christmas. He hastened the driver to speed the horses and hurriedly completed his other duties to avoid any delay. The two days in Asheville passed quickly, but he endured them with great agitation as he severely missed his guest and found himself, on more than one occasion, counting off the remaining firewood in his mind in the needless apprehension that she may be cold or uncomfortable or somehow need his assistance. As he had planned, he arrived at Brookhaven just before dawn on Christmas Eve. He unloaded the crates of supplies and food, led the horses to a trough for a drink and a rest and called for the horses to be secured in the stables. Charles met him on the verandah

"My lord, Withers what is all this?"

"You may think me mad, or foolish, call it 'Christmas spirit,' but I found the most wonderful new shop in the city. In these crates you will find fruits imported from all over the world and the most delicious breads and cheeses. I trust you will prepare a royal feast for us for Christmas Dinner?" he asked.

"Well," Charles paused, with a slight twinkle in his eyes, "Yes, I believe we can manage that, and Withers, I do not think you mad at all," he smiled and added, "she has had an affect on us all."

Edward started to answer but held his tongue, instead he confided that he had also brought a Christmas tree and instructed Charles to keep it out of sight for it was to be a surprise.

ଚ୍ଚର

There was a certain feeling radiating through the halls of Brookhaven Christmas Eve day. It was the spirit of Christmas come to touch all who resided within its stone walls. Lenora awoke earlier than usual and had begun her descent down the long stairway leading into the parlor. Edward was sitting in the corner of the room, and when she came into view he held his breath. What a vision she was. As she walked he watched her every step, she was so elegant and for a moment he pretended she was his Emily. He knew in that instant there was nothing she could ask that he could refuse. Edward stood allowing himself to come into her sight and her eyes lit up when she saw him.

"Good morning, Edward, I am so glad you have made a safe return."

"Thank you, my dear, I must say it was an exhausting trip. I was able to acquire many of the supplies we desperately needed. It was indeed, a productive trip. And you, mademoiselle, the dress you have chosen is stunning,"

Returning his smile, she answered, "Edward, thank you again for allowing me to wear Elizabeth's clothing. Wearing items which belonged to her makes me feel close to Elizabeth somehow. I have been reading the letters, especially last evening and you were right. The letters do tell a fascinating story. It is so intriguing, I cannot wait to read more."

"Yes, their words have a way of staying with you, not unlike a melody. Lenora, I was hoping you would play the piano for me? I am weary from the journey and I would like to rest before starting the day. Your playing is very calming, will you?"

"I would enjoy nothing more, do you have a particular request?"

"If you would be so kind as to play the one you played before, the one you 'remembered' from your past the first time you played? I should like to hear it again."

Chapter 9
Christmases Past

Lenora sat on the stool and began to play the slow somber melody remembered only in her heart, and with each chord she struck, Edward's heart fell to its deepest depths and touched him as no words could possibly do. The more she played on, the happier she felt, in spite of the sorrowful notes. Edward closed his eyes and let his mind drift, and drift into the deep memories of his past. He could see himself the first day he met Emily. . .

Edward met Bryson Talbot at the university. Bryson had just begun his final year and being a fourth year, was granted the responsibility of sponsoring an underclassman. Owing to the most sensitive events of young Edward's particular misfortunes, Edward was required to participate in the sponsorship program during his first year, and as fate would have it, he could not have been placed in more capable or perfect hands than Bryson Talbot's. Bryson proved to be a very altruistic fellow and knowing Edward had come to this foreign place from an orphanage in America, he developed what one could call a soft spot for Edward. They became fast friends and one could scarcely be seen without the other. Half a year passed and naturally as the Christmas Holiday drew near, Bryson insisted Edward join his family in their English estate in London's most beautiful countryside for the occasion. Edward resisted at first, but eventually acquiesced reasoning he would be quite left alone in the dormitory if he did not accept his friend's invitation. When they arrived in London, Bryson's sister was waiting for them at the train station. Edward was immediately smitten with her at first glance.

"There is Emily now," Bryson said pointing to her.

"Do you mean the girl wearing the blue dress?" Edward asked with an unfaltering hope, for this girl in blue had been the very vision which had captured his gaze upon the train's halting, so much so that his mind seemed to block out everything around her.

"Yes, isn't she perfect Edward?"

"Perfectly beautiful," he whispered.

"What's that?" Bryson asked.

"Nothing, nothing at all" Edward answered.

"Emily!" Bryson shouted, waving his arm "Emily, over here!"

When Emily saw them her face brightened as she smiled. All sense of propriety was discarded as she literally ran up to them.

"Bryson, I missed you terribly!" she exclaimed, embracing her beloved brother, "I have been so lonely here without my best friend, you must tell me everything!"

"Hello," she continued, turning the sunlight of her gaze in Edward's direction, "Emily Talbot," she offered, extending her hand to Edward, "but do call me Emily." If it were possible, the sound of her voice and her charming manner were as intoxicating as the light turned on in Edward's heart at the first sight of her.

Edward took her hand, as if it were some rare crowned jewel and kissed it, "I'm Edward Withers, a pleasure to meet you, your brother was kind enough to invite me to share this holiday with your family."

"The pleasure is ours Mr. Withers. We are so pleased you have joined us, we shall have a splendid time, do you ride? You will find that our stables are first rate." she answered, never leaving the gaze of Edward's dark eyes as he affirmed her question with a nod.

"Bryson, I must warn you, Father is not in the best mood. He received your letter and . . . can I speak openly?"

"Of course sister, Edward is my closest friend," Bryson answered.

"I understand you have abandoned your study of the sciences and have been studying philosophy and religion?" Emily asked.

"You understand correctly, and I know very well it is Father's wish that I take over for him one day, but I have learned so much Emily, and I have changed. There is so much to be done and I have decided to enter seminary after graduation. I will complete my studies at the university as Father requested, but I will not follow in his footsteps. I must live my own life in my own way. I feel a special calling Emily. There is a place God wants me to be, and it is not the President of Talbot Illuminations."

"I completely understand, Bryson, but I beg of you to consider Father's feelings in the matter, he will be disappointed and I fear he will never accept your decision. He does not even believe in..," but she stopped short being interrupted by her brother.

"Emily, I know very well what Father believes and does not believe, but all of his power is nothing compared to the power of a single word from God. He cannot control me. I belong to God now, I always have, I just did not know it until now. I share Father's vision for lighting the world, I really do, it is just that he wishes to light their shops and homes, while I wish to light their souls."

"Well said, Bryson," Edward assured his friend.

"Mr. Withers, forgive me for discussing such serious matters..."

"Please, its Edward, I've enough of formalities at the university," Edward interrupted as Emily continued.

"All right then, Edward, I only want to assure you that I support my brother in any dream he may have, but I felt it necessary to prepare him for my father's mood. We make him sound like a monster, but truly, he is not. He has come from a long tradition of wealthy and successful men. He only wants the best for all of us. He has always required the very best from each of us, but in the last few years he has pushed even harder. He finds our individuality makes him lose control over our lives. But I assure you he has good intentions, however futile they may be," she urged.

"Be careful how you defend Father, Emily, I suspect he will not grant you your dream of being a composer. He will have you joined in marriage, a marriage of his own choosing of course, and your music will be lost. It will be the same fate for you, you must accept the truth. You must choose to do his will or your own. Decide now before it is too late, do not deceive yourself into believing you can do as you wish and please him as well. It will be his way or yours, there is no compromising with an uncompromising man, it is that simple."

"Bryson, please, you are going to scare away our guest. Father is a driven man, I admit as much, but I believe he will eventually come around. And, Bryson, really, as for his arranging my marriage, that is utter nonsense, I will marry only for love, be assured. Enough of this talk, let us now enjoy these short weeks together God has granted us."

"I agree," Edward offered, "and I am sure your father loves you very much. Bryson if any man can convince your father you are choosing the right path, it is you."

"I wish I were as hopeful. Emily, Edward here is charmingly optimistic. Whatever life places in his path, nothing is capable of diminishing his will, I have learned much from you my friend."

"Then we have learned much from each other," Edward added.

The three boarded the Talbot's coach, which was of the finest quality Edward had ever had the fortune of riding. As they made their way to Bryson's family home along the captivating English countryside, Edward admired the scenery. He had never been to this part of the country before and he thought it very beautiful, but it paled to Emily's striking beauty. He had never met a girl like Emily. He loved her innocence, she was warm and friendly and beautiful. He was so pleased he had taken the trip with Bryson and knew he had made the right decision. After the long journey's end, they arrived safely at the Talbot estate. Bryson's description of his home had been a modest one. Edward had expected an English cottage but found an extensive estate, complete with servant's quarters, stables and a private winery. The bags were delivered inside the mansion where Bryson's father greeted them.

"Son, good evening, I hope you enjoyed a pleasant journey. Your sister has talked of little else but your return this entire month." Mr. Talbot said.

"My happiness in returning is quite equal to Emily's. The trip was uneventful, thankfully and Father I must now present Edward Withers."

"Good evening, son, we welcome you."

"Thank you sir, I am honored to be here."

"I understand you are a classmate of Bryson's, are you studying the sciences as well?" he questioned.

"Actually, Bryson and I met under more pleasant circumstances than that of studies. He has been a godsend to me. I am a first year, and I have to say he has made my transition to the life of a university man quite seamless. Your son is the most honorable man I have ever known. As for my studies, I am just starting sir, but I do share Bryson's interest in some of his endeavors, such as law and philosophy with its grand ideals, but my true love is the Arts."

"The Arts?" he inquired.

"Yes. I hope to become an artist, a sculptor. Sculpting is a gift that comes naturally to me and nothing gives me more pleasure."

"That is very interesting, but do you plan to make a living with this sculpting?" he asked incredulously.

"Father" Emily interjected brightly, "these two have had a long journey, and we have three weeks to discuss matters such as these, may we allow them a moment to retire and dress for dinner?"

"Far be it from me to cause any distress to our guests."

"Thank you Father. I'll show Edward to his room now," Bryson said, winking at his sister as soon as his father's eyes were averted, for she had rescued him from many a worse inquisition.

"I am sure you are all very tired. It is good to have you home again, son."

"It is good to be home," Bryson answered, as a dutiful son.

Edward was shown to one of the many guest rooms which would be his home for the following three weeks. Although he had been born into a family of great wealth, his later fate of want had ruled his conscience and thereby forced him to feel quite at odds in any arena of the wealthy. Dinner was to be served promptly at 8:00 and he had been left to acquaint himself with his new surroundings and to take rest from the journey. He carefully unpacked his clothes, shortly acquired upon his arrival at the university, and in fact this evening would be his first opportunity to dress for dinner in the fashion of the English. He attempted to rest, but had never been able to do so during daylight hours and decided instead to return to the novel he had recently started and as such the hours passed quite quickly. Finishing Chapter Nine, he began to dress for dinner. He stood in the mirror quite contented with his new look, for to be certain he was the vision of a dashing young man in all respects and would be considered so in anyone's opinion.

But Edward's vanity was only a thin layer of his thoughts and underneath it was a far deeper feeling of uneasiness. He had only been at the university for a few months, only months removed from his home of orphans. And seeing himself now in this splendor brought to mind their utter poverty, and he thought it would please him to no end if he should be allowed to strip away every piece of his finery and replace it with blankets and toys and little trinkets that would lighten their dark worlds. Their faces were never really far from his mind and therefore he seemed to perpetually have one foot in this world and one foot in the other. Even at night he found little peace.

Though he had longed to be far from the cold walls of his previous home, he seemed very alone in his newfound life and found himself longing to be in his tiny cot again, to be near others who truly understood his pain, but those tiny cots and cold winters and crying children and tasteless meals were things of his past and he knew he must forge ahead and find his place in this new life he had been given. The hour for dinner had not arrived, but he was restless in his chamber and decided to see if there was anyone to keep him company, of course he hoped the "anyone" would be Emily. There was no answer at Bryson's chamber and the dining room was yet empty, but Edward heard voices from the East sitting room and promptly followed them. Edward had the peculiar talent of being able to enter any room without detection, probably owing to the many years of instilled self-restraint in his days at the orphanage.

As he approached the room, he noted the doors were not quite closed and heard his name being spoken, and instinctively postponed his entrance and listened to the conversation between Bryson and his father...

"He was reared in an orphanage, in America?" Mr. Talbot asked.

"Why yes Father, I suppose I forgot to mention it."

"Quite a thing to forget, peculiar I found him of rather good character."

"And why would you not, has your finding changed?"

"I only conclude from your disclosure he has followed a far different path than you my son, and regardless of what my business companions say, I hold Americans are not to be trusted, they are a wild sort."

"Father, you say such things! And besides he is not an American at all, his family is Scottish actually," Bryson retorted, appalled.

"No matter, I suppose his presence here can do no harm."

"Clearly," Bryson spat, "Is there some question in your mind that he should be turned away?"

"Bryson, you are a kindhearted boy, and I find your . . . charity to our guest agreeable," his father started from his usual cloud of superiority.

"Charity? Charity, indeed! I am not being charitable, Father he is my closest friend in the world, and the most virtuous, humble person I have yet to meet. Charity? Really! I suppose it would better please you to know that he comes from a family far more wealthy than we, and his inheritance will be fully restored to him upon his graduation. But I want it to be clear to you that his wealth means nothing to me. Edward has suffered many losses in his life and each one has miraculously only strengthened his character, and besides we are charged with loving our fellow men and expressly not to make judgments upon them."

"Bryson, you will strain yourself from this argument. It matters little to me how much wealth a man has or has not, I am speaking of his place in society, but you are speaking of your loved disciples again."

"You surprise me yet Father, for I did not know you could recognize the words of God," Bryson snapped spitefully.

"What disrespect. I have given you every opportunity in my power and you dishonor me in my own home. You dishonor yourself. . ."

While Edward listened to this exchange between father and son, his eyes watered with painful tears, and he was once again reminded that he did not feel, and perhaps would never feel, at ease in this world where he was supposed to belong. All his life he had lived in the shadows of other men, secretly aspiring to move through their ranks as an accepted equal, though never feeling free from anxiety among them, and rightly so, for the position life assigned him would not allow it. The manner in which Mr. Talbot had spoken of him proved to be a turning point in his life and though it was a heart-piercing feeling, it made him aware of a truth that would be the key to his future contentment.

The key was forged from the notion that he would never reveal his true nature to those of exalted position in society, and the only way he could be seen as an equal in their eyes would be if he acted inapposite to his true nature. There was a choice to be made. Either to change and become like them or to accept himself, either to continue to seek approval from others or to simply accept himself and go forward with his life. When he asked himself what it would truly mean to be like them, he realized it could only mean denying the truth and accepting their beliefs, and he could do neither. Once he realized this truth, he was freed from the chains which held him, and in the same moment, for the first time, he knew the glory of peace and he rejoiced in his own particular skin, with his own particular joys and gifts. And he vowed he would never again become distracted with the useless emotions of envy and jealousy, never again waste himself on such foolish pursuits.

Edward's self acceptance and decision to abandon the opinions of others was not an attempt to allow for selfishness or permission to strive for his own whims or needs, but rather to abolish in his heart and mind the ever false desire to remove himself from truth in favor of falsity. He had survived his poverty and he made up his mind he would survive his wealth, and with a new resolve, he entered the room, rescuing his friend, and feigning ignorance of their conversation.

Edward would spend the next three weeks with the Talbot family, and he would personally learn the full extent to which Bryson knew and feared his father. Though he loathed any contact with the spiritless man, he enjoyed the break from his studies and meeting Emily had given him new inspiration, for his art, and for his life. Once his eyes beheld her, his mind held no other thoughts outside of her being, and he sensed she was fond of him as well. Unfortunately it was during this same Holiday, which ultimately came to a disastrous end, when he first confessed his love for her, but he chose to remember his confession and nothing which followed. Those anxious days of their first meeting rose in his memory like a great wave of delight as they had often done and quickly eliminated the cruel words of her father.

ಬಿಓ

Lenora finished playing and asked Edward to escort her to the dining room.

"Lenora," he said, "Thank you for playing just now, there is nothing quite like the sound of music to enrapture the mind and allow it a special place to have its most precious memories. You too will look on happier days. You will find your past, and someday all of your toils will be a distant memory," he encouraged.

"You are thoughtful Edward, I do appreciate all you have done for me. I only wish there was some way to repay your kindness. My playing is the very least I can do to recompense your hospitality."

"Lenora, I assure you, your presence here is restitution enough."

Lenora smiled, for she could think of no words to respond to his kind admission. She wanted to reach out to him, but she would not. She wanted to embrace him, but something instinctively held her at bay. He sensed he had made her uncomfortable and not knowing what to say, he seated her for breakfast. They filled the day with the normal manner of activities and upon its end, she found herself at last in bed, as she eagerly opened the next sequence of treasured letters.

> 17 September 1802
> Dearest John,
> I write this letter to you under my protective stars. I must first assure you I have received each of your letters and each one is more treasured than the last. I am so pleased your situation with Mr. Sanderson is moving along so nicely. And the property you described sounds splendid. Please sketch it for me. I wish to see some likeness of it before my eyes behold its beauty. Father sends his warmest greetings. He cares for you so, he only wants what is best for us and your efforts are proving your loyalty and love. You are winning him over. Each day is such a lonely occasion without you and I am troubled to find you seem to hardly have time to even take nourishment, I worry you are not taking care of yourself. Remember I am here and I need you to be healthy and strong so you may keep your promise to come for me. I await your next letter and send you my love.
> Faithfully yours, Elizabeth

ഇൽ

> 24 September 1802
> My dearest Elizabeth,
> I hope this letter arrives before Christmas, but in any case, Merry Christmas Elizabeth! I have been saving for our future, but I simply had to send you a small gift. Please accept it and wear it close to your heart always. It is a symbol of my loyalty to you and my faith that God gave us this love. Knowing you are wearing a cross, will comfort me and protect you. It is so unnatural to

be without you at Christmas. As the celebration of the ultimate Love draws near, I see families laughing and being merry, and all I want is to be near you. I shall most likely work through most of the holiday, it will no doubt make the time pass more quickly. Mr. Sanderson has been a little under the weather of late therefore my assistance is needed now more than ever. Do not worry for me my love, I am closer and closer to making my fortune. I will come for you as soon as I can my darling. Until we meet again, my love.   John

Chapter 10
A Discovery

Lenora folded the letters carefully and her thoughts naturally turned to the image of the wedding gown in the armoire. She could almost picture Elizabeth wearing the gown. She often imagined their young faces, and as she attempted to recall their images, she suddenly remembered the sketches which lay in the trunk in the room on the second floor. The evening had well advanced by this time, and she fought fervently against her better judgment to hold her anxious desire to visit the room until the morning. But as it often did, her desire won the battle. She remembered Edward's request that she only return to the room with his assistance, but the hour was late and she convinced herself he would not really mind, 'If I am very quiet,' she thought, 'I will not disturb him.' She found a pair of night slippers and closed the door behind her. Only a candle lit the way before her.

Though the hallway was dark and unknown there was something so familiar in these passageways, in the size of the spaces and they seemed inviting and even comforting to her. She continued in the flickering shadows until she reached the appointed door, and pressing lightly against it, pushed it open and then closed it quietly behind her. With much care for the unsteady floor beneath her, she walked to the ancient chest. Opening it carefully she began to extract from it John's sketches. The first page was of a face, the face of a beautiful young girl. Though her image was clear, it seemed yet unfinished. She imagined it had been drawn in haste and never completed. Turning the pages she discovered other sketches of this beauty. In one of them, the look on the girl's face spoke of deep contemplation. She lay amid a field of wild flowers of every sort. Her dark curls flowing against her fair shoulders under a summer sky. The face of an angel, pear shaped with captivating eyes, round, large and black and her finest feature were her shapely lips. Elizabeth was a very exotic beauty.

Lenora leafed through the other sketches and noted in most of the likenesses Elizabeth's beautiful hair was pulled back or hidden behind a hat. It seemed wrong to her somehow. She returned her attention to the second sketch. 'Yes,' she thought, this is the young woman full of love and passion she had come to know in the letters. Here, with the warm sun kissing her softly, with the scent of wild flowers on the wind, and the taste of her lover on her lips. This was Lenora's favorite. She could understand why John had loved her so deeply, so desperately.

Seeing Elizabeth's young, beautiful face brought their cherished words to life. In one sketch, Elizabeth sat upon a bench, and beside her John knelt on one knee, the only self-portrait or image of John in existence. At first glance she did not notice it, but upon a more focused study of the couple, she noticed how Elizabeth held John's hand in hers. Lenora traced John's outstretched arm to where his hand ended on the bench in Elizabeth's faithful hands. The hour had advanced and her curiosity had been satisfied. She turned to leave the room, but as she approached the door, the glow of her candle reflected upon a shelf in the back of the room.

For some reason she felt compelled to follow the light and explore the room a little further. As she walked closer to the shelf, she saw it was stacked with old papers, a few scattered books, and an old oil lamp. 'This would have been useful an hour ago,' she mused. She used the candle to light the lamp and her eyes slowly adjusted to the light. An object concealed by a draping of cloth, on the middle shelf captured her attention. 'Could it be the very object which so gripped Edward's attention, the night of I came to Brookhaven?' she wondered. "There's only one way to see," she whispered. The compelling feeling to discover what lay beneath the old lace cloth would soon be replaced by a feeling of uneasiness.

Slowly, she pulled the cloth away from the object, revealing a beautiful sculpture. As the cloth dropped to the bare floor, she suddenly realized she was looking at a marble sculpture of a woman, but not just any woman.

The woman bore Lenora's features, every feature, there was no denying this was a sculpture of Lenora. Being quite stunned with her discovery, she almost dropped the lamp, but was able to place it on a nearby table which also served as a temporary crutch to support her. She struggled to find her breath as a multitude of fearful and restless thoughts invaded her unsuspecting mind. Closing her eyes for a moment, she thought. 'I must be mistaken, now then let us try once more' and she opened her eyes, took the small candle and boldly held it to the figure, studying it intently for several minutes. Again her eyes revealed the unbelievable truth, it was definitely her, but there was something about it which made it appear different, as though it might represent her twin, for the soul and spirit of the piece exuded an aura she could not identify with herself at all.

The sculpture seemed free and its spirit vibrant, alive and unafraid, delicate but somehow bold. She could not remember feeling such joy or freedom in all of her days. Her mind raced with questions and fears. And then she remembered spying on Edward from the window that first night of their meeting, and the intensity he had placed on the table. She forced her eyes to close tightly and concentrated on every moment and movement of that fateful night. The object had been covered with a cloth, but was this the same cloth? But what did it matter, for it was an impossibility for Edward to have created it after her arrival, when could he had found the hours, days it would have required? And yet she tried to force the impending thought that the sculpture had been made before her arrival which meant the unthinkable.

From its position she could determine nothing so she attempted to pick it up to examine it closer, but it was much too heavy. The disturbing thoughts returned and suddenly Lenora felt very much afraid. She had trusted Edward implicitly and now there could be no reasonable explanation for the existence of this sculpture. What could it mean? She knelt down below the shelf and slid the sculpture to the edge of the shelf. She hoped to find a date or some inscription on it. In the dim light it was hard to make out anything, but it did appear to have a few letters carved into its base. Impatiently and with much struggling, she turned it clockwise a half turn in order to get a better look. She saw what appeared to be numbers. 'Perhaps it is a date,' she thought. She turned it to the left a bit more and the weight of it felt unbalanced on her hands. Using all her strength she pushed it to its original position. She could not make out the writing in the golden, dusky light of the lamp, and with little choice she determined she would return in the light of day to examine it further.

Thoughts of confusion, fear, dismay and uneasiness began to race again within her mind, bringing her ultimately to more focused thinking and concentration to the night of her arrival and specifically Edward's first words to her, "it is you," he had said. 'Edward does know me," she murmured. "He knows me," she repeated, as if saying it again might seem more natural, or easy to comprehend, but it was not, and again her mind spun in every possible direction with the futile hope of weaving some reasoning into his behavior. 'But why would he act as if he is a stranger to me?' she thought.

'The story of this woman he had loved and lost seemed so believable, but it must be fiction after all. And now this, no wonder he implored me to stay away from this room, but now his deception has been revealed! Why? Why?' What was she to do after having found this hidden truth, she wondered. 'What shall I do? Shall I confront him?' she thought. 'He has been so kind, but what is he hiding? Maybe he does not want me to remember. Could he be protecting me? Or fearing me? But what could he fear from me? What purpose could he have?' And it was not only Edward in this conspiracy, she considered, as she recalled the manner in which Lily had reacted to her on that same cold night.

Whom could she trust? Without answers, she lit a short pillar and extinguished the oil lamp and quietly returned to her room. She wondered what it all meant and carefully calculated how she would react, how she would break the news of her discovery to Edward. She lay in bed staring blankly at the chamber door for several agonizing minutes and realized the only escape from the frightening thoughts would be to sleep. With a mind frantic with old and new fears, she fell asleep, but even sleep offered no rest.

As she slept, she began to dream. And shortly found

herself in a house, an enormous house, it was the place she called home. There was something very familiar about the place. She could hear a man and a woman arguing, it made her very upset. She opened a door to escape their muffled voices and found herself on a ship. The steamers sounded and the smoke drifted down to her and then she was running. Running against a warm wind and footsteps could be heard behind her. There was someone chasing her. She could not get away. "Stop!" she screamed. "Stop!" she sobbed. "Lenora, I am coming. I am coming." And then she jumped from the ship and began to plummet to the bottom of the sea as she reached out to retrieve the envelope that had fallen from her hands and had been swept away on the breeze, "Noooo!" she screamed, but then she felt herself being awakened.

"Lenora, Lenora, you are dreaming," Edward said gently.

When she opened her eyes Edward was standing before her, and she gasped.

"Lenora, it is I?" he offered, confused.

"I am frightened, Edward, I .. I had a horrible dream."

"The same one?"

"No, and yes, it is all a blur . . . I am okay now. I do not wish talk about it," she said abruptly.

"Of course, dear Lenora, how I do wish to help you. I cannot bear to see you this way. I would do anything to help you."

"I am not convinced of that." she responded hastily.

Edward stared at her in disbelief for a moment "Is that so?" he asked with a haughty, defensive tone. And quickly added, "Be assured, be *completely* assured that I am your friend Lenora. And I will help you. If there is anything you need, you may only ask and it will be given if it is in my power," he offered.

And she could not deny the sincerity reflected in his eyes, but the reality of the sculpture, and the instinctual familiarity with Brookhaven combined to convince her he could not be trusted.

"I appreciate your kindness Edward, and I did not intend to offend you," she coolly responded.

"It is late, I will let you return to your rest." But as he began to walk out of her room, he turned to her and noticed something fearful in her eyes.

"Lenora," he said, "I sense a change in you and it troubles me. Am I wrong?"

"Very well," she returned, "you have pledged your desire to help me, but there are reasons, for which I cannot tell, that cause me to question whether you really want me to remember my past."

"I do not know what to say. Except, why in heaven's name would I not want you to remember? I care very much about you and want nothing more for you than that you should be content and happy. I want to know more about you. Where you came from, who you are. I want to know about your past because I have come to care for you and now you insinuate I would deliberately hinder you from uncovering what is your deepest desire. Lenora, from where has this new mistrust come? You should know by now I am your ally, and you can trust me."

She did not know how to respond. She did not want him to know she had discovered his deception. Then she said quickly, "Edward, I am sorry, I forget myself, the dream was disturbing and upsetting. I simply need to sort things out before I can talk about it any further, please understand?" she said forcing the customary sweetness in her voice to return.

"I shall leave you alone then," he said walking away. "But you must know I am a man of my word and I do not tolerate deception in others or myself. You have my word and pledge, I will help you and I will do so with all my power."

Lenora was ashamed of herself, she sensed the sadness he felt from her indifference. But she was also angry, for she believed he knew exactly who she was and was hiding the information from her and were it true, he could not be the man she thought he was, and yet somehow she could not believe he was anyone other than the generous man he seemed to be.

Lenora's sense of confusion was equally matched by Edward's sense of bewilderment as he returned to his chamber. Why had she been so harsh with him? How could she think he did not want to help her? Had he injured her in some way? What had happened? She was usually very eager to discuss any new memories, but suddenly she was shutting him out. What should he say? What should he do? As he could think of no solution, he decided to practice patience in the matter and allow her time to mull over her situation, in hopes she would come to him with her troubles in due course. What he most hoped for was that her behavior had been caused by the disturbing dream and in no way by any aversion to him. His agitation was compounded by the fact he had planned a very special surprise for her, the Christmas tree. He knew not if he should continue or abandon the plan. Perhaps it was simply an ill mood, he knew women were known to be a little temperamental and hoped the night's rest would smooth over this evening's uneasy feeling between them.

Chapter 11
A Plea

Lenora slowly awoke to the aroma of coffee and ham floating in the cool morning air. She smiled softly in those moments just before alertness, when all is quiet and the mind is free of all concerns, no burdens, no questions, no decisions to be made, but suddenly she felt a sinking feeling as she remembered the sculpture, and then the burden of her questions began to steadily build upon her mind, each a heavy layer of gray, stony indecision. Regardless of what she had discovered, it was Christmas Day and she knew Charles and his family were now depending on her, and consequently, she would do her best to give them a happy holiday. The house would be more merry than usual, there would be guests and their presence would limit the awkwardness she now felt in Edward's presence. But avoiding Edward was not a happy thought. Edward had provided her with the only moments of happiness and security she had known these last two years, and as such, she felt an enormous gratitude for his generosity and kindness, but seeing the sculpture could not be ignored.

The sculpture was real, in cold, hard marble, and the sight of it had been imprinted in her mind, as solid as the marble from which it was made. The question it begged was intrinsic to her relationship with him, and she knew the matter must soon be resolved in one way or another. There was a new feeling she had for him, a feeling of distrust, and further, fear, and she disliked the feeling and though it seemed natural in some way, it also seemed completely false to her heart. Her conscience told her to be honest with herself, to believe the quiet urgings of the spirit of truth within her. She did not quite trust him, but she trusted the truth. And even were he a liar, a deceiver of the worst sort, she could only measure herself according to her own sense of values and as such she chose the nobler path, she would be honest, she would be bold, she would face him no matter the cost, besides, if she succumbed to being dishonest in answer to his dishonesty, the whole situation could become more fearful and perhaps even dangerous.

She resolved to speak to him after breakfast. Breakfast was served at the customary hour, and the two shared pleasantries though they both sensed the other was a bit uncomfortable. After breakfast, Lenora knew she could maintain the pretense no longer, 'Christmas or not, I must resolve things or I shall go mad from these questions', she thought, and after a moment of silence, built up her courage and began,

"Edward, I realize my change of mood has not gone unnoticed. There is something I must ask you, something very important. I require your honesty, no matter what the truth may be."

"By all means, please ask."

"Edward, Do you know who I am?"

Edward was silent. He was shocked by her question. He knew who he wanted her to be. But in reality he knew nothing of her past. Here in the dark present, she was only a fair reflection of the woman, the only woman to whom he had given and lost his heart. He had opened his heart again, opened his home to this homeless girl, and this day's ingratitude was his answer.

"Again, you ask me such a question? A question which I have already answered. What must you think of me I wonder? Have I not taken you in and cared for you as if you were an old and trusted friend? And what have I asked in return? Answer me?" he demanded.

"You have asked nothing of me, and I am very grateful for your kindness, but a secret has been freshly revealed to me and ..." but he would not allow her to continue, in fact he did not even hear the words she was saying, instead he could only feel insulted by her disbelief in him, insulted and wounded. Feeling the force of such pain, his eyes flashed in full conviction of inflicting upon her a stream of cruel words. But when his eyes met hers, he was instantly reminded of the one he had lost, and he could feel nothing less than an abiding sense of protection and a desire for acceptance and understanding.

"Lenora, I wish I could tell you who you are. I own I do feel as if I have always known you, by what reason I cannot tell. But upon my word, on my honor, I can only affirm what I promised you before. Until I met you a few days ago, outside my window, I had never seen you before. And your change of heart and mistrust is as shocking as it is painful. There is nothing more I can say."

Lenora looked at him in disbelief and took a deep breath, "Edward, I want to believe you, I do, but there is something I have discovered, and I do not want to believe it, but this discovery forces my hand. Last night I was filled with the strongest of impulses to visit the room you took me to before, the storage room. I went there to look at John's sketches, I considered your warning, but my curious nature would not allow me to rest and I did not want to disturb you with such a trifle. I went to the room and before I left, I . . .I found something."

Edward turned away from her. How negligent he had been, he had meant to remove the sculpture from the room, the very room to which he had once led her. But he had not taken the time to do so. Now he understood her distrust and wondered if she would ever believe him. How could he explain the events to her now? He did not know what to do next, nor how to answer her.

While he floundered, she continued, "What I saw was a sculpture, a sculpture of myself. Which, forgive me, proves you must know who I am and more, you have been hiding it from me. What I do not know is why. Why Edward, after all this time please do not deceive me now. I have come so far and I knew this place. Brookhaven is my home, is it not? I sense you are a good person. I have seen your compassion and kindness. Please be merciful and tell me who I am," she pleaded as tears began to form in her desperate eyes.

"Dear Lenora, how I wish I could give you the answers you seek. I am going to explain what I have said, and not said, and on my honor, this is the truth. The sculpture you speak of, I own I sculpted it with my own hands, but it was created many years ago and is indeed the likeness of another. The night you first arrived was a chilling night in many ways. You must think back and remember, remember what I told you. I explained what had first appeared as recognition in my eyes was only the darkness, the shadows playing trickery on my eyes, but in truth, it was a type of recognition, but not of you.

Allow me to explain, I saw in you the ghost of my wife, standing before me, but it was you, you, Lenora, and not an apparition, and still you remind me so much of her. I alluded to a woman I had loved, but she was more than that, she was my wife. I am a widower, of many years. I have never spoken of my marriage to her to anyone, that time of my life belongs only to me, and I could not open that world to you, not then anyway. I could not admit to myself what I had witnessed.

To have allowed anyone to remind me of her, felt like a disgrace or a kind of disrespect to her memory. I know it is all nonsense now, but I hold her memory so close, so far away from everything and everyone, I cannot let the world, the tainted world touch my memories of her. How much easier it was for me to simply turn a blind eye to my reaction to seeing your face, and I quickly made an excuse for my blunder. I saw no reason or necessity in explaining my most guarded thoughts to you, and later that evening I realized that my deception, together with the reality of the sculpture, and its decided resemblance to you, would only compel me to compound the deception with another. It was foolish of me and now I am forced to tell you the truth, which I should have done in the beginning.

I see you want to believe me, but you may not be convinced. I suppose it was the intensity of my love for Emily that forced my private nature to travel to a remote and distant land, a place incapable of being explored except by me alone. I have guarded those memories for so long now, it seems a betrayal of her and of me to disclose what is held so dearly. Emily was my all, my everything, even before I met her. I had always had a vision of the perfect partner for me. A person with whom to share my hopes and dreams. I would talk to this imaginary love, and even rely on her at times, this imagined creature. I know it sounds rather strange, but she became my closest friend, as if I willed her to me. I imagined her, and somehow she did exist.

I had known her in my mind for years, and then one glorious day my vision took shape and form, and my eyes beheld her. My prayers, in that instant, were answered. But it was not to be. Emily's father was a powerful man and he demanded control over her life. In his eyes I was not worthy of his daughter. He had not groomed her for the likes of someone of my experiences, but love is not some tactile thing one can mold, nor is a heart a thing to be trained to ignore what it instinctively feels, and regardless of her father's objections, she could not deny her feelings for me and her hopes for her future in becoming my wife.

We refused to accept his disapproval and we married in secret, but when he discovered the truth, one dark and dreadful night, he took her from me. We were so frightened, there was no escape. She had not yet reached the age to be married without a guardian's consent and as I said before, he was a powerful man. We knew he would find us wherever we were, but we were young and foolish and believed we were unbreakable, invincible. Our fears were realized the day he found us and somehow, in the desperation of it all, she ran from him, she was running back to me when she suffered a mortal fall. We found her lying at the bottom of a long, icy stairway, her body was twisted and fragile.

The steps were red with her precious blood. I ran to her and held her frail and broken body in my arms. I was the last person she saw before her eyes closed forever. Under the circumstances, her father allowed me to stay with her for a few moments. But he believed I was responsible for the death of his daughter. His words of hate and pain resound in my head even now after all these years. He would not allow me to go to her memorial service, he said it would be too painful for him, he said I did not belong there. Her husband did not belong there...He would never recognize our marriage, but in my heart, and in God's eyes, she will always be my wife. He carried her body away, and left me standing there numb in the chilling air, alone with the knowledge that my love for her had ended her precious life.

I have lived with her in my heart everyday, but I wanted to have something more tangible. My love for art was second only to my love for her. I am a sculptor, I have never been anything else. I discovered the purest piece of white marble on holiday in Florence. I was on a pilgrimage of sorts to the great master sculptor himself. Ah, to walk the cobbled streets of that city, to stand in front of the great Duomo, to hear the musical Italian language, and to be where many great artists have breathed the same air, was all intoxication. I climbed the black and white Carrera mountains and quarries in search of a stone worthy of her beauty, and she was there waiting for me inside the marble. I did not sleep until I brought her from her prison of darkness. It is Emily you saw last night, Emily and not you.

I have always dreamt she would appear to me, return to me, even here. I hoped she would find me on a summer breeze or speak to me in a somber melody. And then, by some force yet unknown to me, on a bitterly cold night you appeared outside my window, by the light of the moon with this face that looks so much like my Emily's. So many times I had wished my vision would appear again, and then suddenly you were here, but you were lost. You had not found me, you were not even searching for me, you were only on a quest for your own past and I could not give it to you. I have heard it said each one of us has a twin, surely you must be Emily's.

I only know you bear a striking resemblance to her. The woman I love, whom I have never forgotten, truly since I can remember, she has filled my every waking thought, she is the very air that I breathe. I do not know what else to say to convince you of the truth. I only hope you may come to see in time that my deception was only to spare you any further confusion. I wish I could help you discover who you are, but I have no knowledge of your past. This is the truth, I swear it."

Lenora stared at him. She tried to decide if she should believe him. What kind of an explanation was this? But could he make up such a tale? He must be telling the truth. And if so, how tragic, and what manner of love was this? To still be grieving for Emily after all of these years.

"Edward, I am not sure what to say. I am too confused by all these strange events, but I do believe you, and I think I shall simply need some time to sort it through."

"Please do not think I am deranged, I assure you I am just as baffled as you must certainly be. I wish I did not sound like a madman. I admit I hid the sculpture from you, and for that I am sorry. But I had dismissed my reaction to the resemblance and then there was no turning back. Consider my position, it is all too strange for belief. You had failed to see it the night you arrived, and after you revealed to me your situation, being afraid and lost, searching for an unknown past, I feared seeing it would only increase your confusion. I moved the sculpture to the storage room the same night, for it usually holds a place of honor in my home. I keep it there in the foyer, as a sentinel of my doors, where I can see it everyday, and so it may be the last thing I see when I leave and the first when I return. There is never a good reason for deception, but I acted with your fragile condition foremost in my mind. Can you forgive my dishonesty?"

"Of course, it is understandable under the circumstances. I believe you Edward and you do not sound insane at all. It is just that even though I thought you were being dishonest, I was hopeful that my past would at last be revealed. You seemed to know me and I seemed to have known you when first we met."
There was a brief silence during which she remembered the writing on the sculpture.

"Edward, there is a way to prove what you have told me."
"What do you mean? How?"
"The sculpture bears some type of writing. I believe it may be a date, but I could not read it in the lamp light. Will you show it to me now?"

"Certainly, that is a clever idea, I assure you it was made in the winter of 1870. Two years had passed since my loss and I had just returned from Florence and was full of a sort of passion I could only express in my work. I made sketch after sketch but none to my satisfaction. One night I awoke from a dream with a shudder, and try as I may, could not return to my slumber. I walked into my studio and I just began to carve the white rock that seemed to haunt me. The marble yielded itself to me as her spirit broke free. As an artist, I have always signed my work, come with me now and I will show you," he said.

She followed him up the dark stairs once more to the dank little room. She sat up straight on the very edge of a dusty old chair, so as not to soil her dress, as she watched Edward walk over to retrieve the sculpture. As he reached the bookshelves he discovered the sketch of John and Elizabeth which Lenora had forgotten the previous night in her spiral of emotional fear and astonishment.

"Now, this is odd." he started

"What it is?"

"This sketch.."

"Oh, I must have forgotten it. I had decided to place it in my room last night, but then I found the sculpture and …"

"I see, well, here you are then, take it" he said offering it to her.

She took it from him and held it safe to her breast. Edward walked again to the shelf and uncovered the sculpture that Lenora had so neatly replaced. As the cloth was removed he instinctively brought his hand to his lips and softly pressing them against his fingers, he placed them upon his beloved Emily, undetected by Lenora.

"As promised" he said, as he held the base of the sculpture towards the light revealing its date and inscription. Indeed it was marked as he had promised, and a wave of relief washed over her.

"Oh Edward, I do apologize. . ." Lenora started.

"Please, child, all is forgotten, but may I ask something of you."

"Anything, of course" she answered.

"May I return her to her rightful place. It seems wrong to hide her away in this cold, dark room."

"Brookhaven and everything within her walls is yours, you need not ask my permission."

"I know, but your happiness is important to me and if I should do something to harm you, I could not bear it. I only want to help you."

"You have caused me no suffering. It is only my eager imagination which gives rise to my mistrust. It is I who should seek forgiveness from my harm done to you. And knowing that, I am truly ashamed to ask this of you but Edward, will you continue to help me uncover my past?" she asked

"Oh yes, Lenora, yes if you will only permit me. There is nothing I want to do more. I know you have to meditate on all I have revealed to you, but I am relieved at last that there are no secrets between us. A large part of me feels I have always known you, perhaps it is our destiny to have met. You needed to find your past and I needed to...."

"I think I understand, Edward. And I do so wish for you to help me unlock the secret to my past," she said reaching over quietly and taking his hand, "and somehow I believe you are the only one who can."

He touched her hand gently and smiled. At that moment he felt a resolve knowing she must understand how he truly felt, and with this understanding, she had reached out to him instead of shrinking with fear or mistrust in her eyes. He knew they could now begin to build something out of this desolation that had brought them together.

"You must have been terrified when you saw the sculpture last night, I cannot imagine what you must have thought. It has always been a source of peace for me and it is disturbing to find it produced feelings of shock and torment."

"I did not know what to think. I admit I was more than frightened. I wondered what role you must have played in my past. It is uncanny how it resembles my countenance, but you are right, in this light I see it is not exactly like me as I had imagined. Even last night I saw in it a wholly different spirit, but one sees what one wishes at times."

"Indeed."

"But my eyes do not deceive me when I see what a brilliant artist you are. Do you have other works here?"

"Yes, I have a few pieces I would like to show you. I have a studio on the fourth floor. I shall choose a few pieces to show you. All of the pieces are different, but the sculpture of Emily is my favorite and in my opinion, my greatest effort. I believe my talent has been a gift to me. All of my works come from the times in my life when I have been most inspired."

"She is truly lovely Edward."

"Thank you. Lenora I know there may be some faint trace of mistrust still in your heart, but please, I implore you, forgive me completely, for not being honest with you from the beginning. I value honesty, as a virtue I practice myself and expect from others. You have my promise I shall never keep anything from you again."

"All is forgotten now, I promise, but on another matter, I was wondering . . would you mind terribly if I asked the servants to join us for dinner tonight?"

"Why, I imagine it would be all right. Why do you ask?"

"I was just thinking it is Christmas Day and it should be a time of celebration and it seems silly to dine alone. You have such a lovely estate, a wonderful music room and I truly believe we would all benefit from sharing the holiday together."

"Again, you are right my dear, I had not thought of that, and I think you have a wonderful idea."

"Thank you Edward, it means so much to me. I am sure Charles can prepare a very special dinner for tonight. I will see to it right away."

"Yes we shall have a party and a lovely dinner, but this place, it just will not do for our celebration, there is little time, but perhaps much we can do, in the way of decorations, I mean."

"Oh decorating will be easy. We can take greenery from outside and candles, we can light all of them, and ribbons if you have them and..."

"I see you have given some thought to it already. But I believe there is a trunk in one of the upper east chambers, yes, we shall see what we can find."

They searched the trunk and other storage spaces for any Christmas decorations that could be found. Edward had always spent Christmases away from Brookhaven and therefore there was little in the way of decorations save for what had been left there from when John had been the master of Brookhaven. Lenora instructed one of the servants to cut some greenery from the outlying trees for the mantel and she twisted holly berries into the greenery to form a rather beautiful strand of garland. They used anything they could find that even remotely resembled a decoration. The most plentiful decorations were those that would be hung upon trees, but in order to follow his original plan Edward hesitated to bring up the subject of the Christmas tree he had brought her.

"It is a shame these lovely things will be wasted" she offered, referring to the ornaments, hoping Edward would understand her implication.

"Yes it is a pity, but perhaps I shall put them to their

proper use next year." He replied nonchalantly, but inwardly with a delightfully mischievous heart. Her disappointment at his response was obvious, and he felt a slight tinge of guilt, but it passed quickly on his imagining her certain overwhelming happiness at such a simple act. With much of the decorating being accomplished, Edward rested for a moment and was decidedly pleased with Lenora's idea. He had not spent a Christmas in Brookhaven since he could remember and now he had someone to share it with. What he was not aware of was she had already asked everyone to come to the party and Charles had been secretly planning the Christmas feast for the last two days. In order to perpetuate this understanding, she flitted around acting as if there was much to be done, fussing over every last detail, while inwardly feeling the purest joy one feels when acting on behalf of someone else's happiness. She smiled knowing the evening would be received well by Edward.

Meanwhile time seemed to be ticking away and Edward had become incredibly agitated with Lenora's constant presence, so much so that he had almost given up on the idea of surprising her with the Christmas tree, when she announced she would be retiring for a nap.

When Lenora finally left his sight he bounded to his feet and began to clear an area for the Christmas tree. He solicited the assistance of his servants for hanging the ornaments and trimming the tree and at last his task was complete.

While Edward secretly trimmed the Christmas tree, Lenora prematurely awoke from her short nap due to her inability to rest with the excitement of the evening to come. But it was much too early to join Edward now and she was not quite ready to get dressed for the party, in fact she was unsure what she would even wear, so she found herself lingering over Elizabeth and John's letters.

Chapter 12
A Hidden Journal

Lenora was so affected by the story of John and Elizabeth's devotion for each other and she could not satisfy her hunger for learning more about them. What made such fine people, what made such large and wonderful hearts, it could only be that form of love for which every human soul longs. Theirs was a love rare and boundless, the kind believed to only exist in the imagination, and yet it was real nonetheless. Her mind reflected on these thoughts as she once again lingered over the beautiful cloths in the wardrobe, in hopes of finding a special dress, something appropriate for the holiday. She looked at the beautiful dresses, studying each one until her eyes continued to return to one particular gown time and again. The gown in question was of an elegant style, a simple design, which would make it all the more beautiful on her slim young body. The gown was a rich, beautiful shade of aged red wine, and the bodice and skirt tail were trimmed in black and matching wine colored lace. The lace was sprinkled generously with tiny sequins, which sparkled ever so slightly in the candlelight.

When she saw herself in the fine gown, she believed she had never felt so glamorous or beautiful. Reflected in the mirror also was the top shelf of the wardrobe and the hat boxes thereon, which suddenly captured her attention. She had no need of a hat for the occasion, but she was in a merry mood and decided to examine the boxes for the sake of amusement. There were three boxes. In the first box there was a black and navy striped hat with the brim trimmed in the finest black tulle and a black flower of some genus for embellishment, in the second box she uncovered what appeared to be a bridal veil. Again her thoughts returned to a sadness in knowing there were for Elizabeth so many dreams, so many promises never to be kept. But in the last box she found the treasure she had already suspected. She knew the elegant dress she now wore must have been special, and the matching hat proved her theory. She removed the little hat from the box very carefully, and admired its simple and elegant design. It was designed in a way that would require the wearer to pull a portion of her hair up into a chignon and then pin the hat directly on her crown. She was so pleased with the set for its elegance and the way she felt wearing it, it made her feel beautiful for the first time since she could remember, but she removed the hat quickly knowing it would be much too extravagant.

As she returned it to its place in the satin hat box, she lifted the box and it occurred to her that the box seemed rather heavy to be empty, so she shook it gently from side to side and heard a solid thump. Upon examining the box further she found a hidden compartment in the bottom half of the box and opened it to reveal a small leather writing journal in excellent condition. Without pause she opened the first page and discovered she was holding the diary of Elizabeth Brookhaven.

She held the journal for a moment considering whether she should intrude on these private thoughts which had passed from living memory so many years ago. These words written by Elizabeth, words even John had never seen. What secrets would be revealed? she wondered. She pondered this question for a few moments, but as usual curiosity proved to be the victor, and she opened the journal to the first page.

    21 February 1801
    Again I find myself in a restless and uneasy mood. That I am a blessed person, I have no doubt, but this longing of my heart cannot be quenched by patience and I know no contentment. I ask today, as with everyday that You send me this one you have promised. I know somewhere he waits for me as I wait for him. Where is he now? Does he long

for me too? Must we wait so long? My heart longs to find this one for whom I was created. A perfect match. But we have been changed by the world and can no longer recognize each other. At one time we were so beautiful together, as a ray of light is made of many colors but none can be distinguished from the other. Together the colors blend and light the world. Such as this one and I. We too were as light is, but now we are so distinct and separate from each other. We are colored by the world. By hurt, disappointment, the limits of our minds, the fears of our hearts. I wish to find him so terribly. Please send him to me soon and in his absence send me a patient heart. Amen

Lenora quickly checked the date of the entry against the dates of the letters and discovered those words in the diary were written before she had met John, and she reflected how uncanny it was to hear in Elizabeth's words the very longing she too had hoped for, and she mused that she could have written those words herself. She knew all too well the feeling of longing and wanting to belong to someone, but not just anyone, one who was meant to be her counterpart. She leafed through the journal and read several random pages.

10 May 1804
I learned today my days on earth are to be but few. How do I accept this news? How do I 0explain the unspeakable to my dear John. He has worked so diligently to take my hand in marriage and to secure the future awaiting us, that awaited us. The future. With only a few simple words from the doctor, it is lost. Oh sweetest John, how could we have been so wrong? I am not sorry for myself, but how sorry I am for you. What would I be feeling if it were John and not I who received this news? I think I should die just the same. What would life be without him. God, I pray you give me courage to die, give me strength to say goodbye. How

many days do I have? I know not. Therefore I must live each day as though it is my last. Yet it is an impossible task with death looming all around me. I do not know how to die, but I do not know how to live. I feel so lost here without John. I suppose we all have our demons and fears. We are all sort of lost out here in the world. Each of us longing for something we cannot quite define. But the longing is there. There are times when we forget, that we allow ourselves the luxury of forgetting, but then we always come back to where we started, alone. In those times of great oneness, I remember Christ's promises. I know He walks with me, and directs my steps when I am too weak to go on. And yet still I long for some human touch to ease the pain. Though God is with me, He has left us here with no way to feel Him as we feel other things in our earthly bodies. From the beginning, we experience life through our senses. But with the most important relationship of our lives, we are denied those familiar senses. We must simply trust what we cannot feel. Hear that which cannot be heard. See that which cannot be seen. In a word, faith. Knowing He is there. Trusting in the thing we have no way of seeing, hearing or touching. And today, as with every day, it is my faith which comforts me, which gives me courage, love, compassion and strength to face what is ahead, but still it is difficult to be a spiritual being here on the cold earth. The body is overwhelming. Its hunger, its incessant pleadings and longings. What rest there will be when we are freed from these desires. What freedom and peace. But what of John's peace? He will find no such comfort. How will I rest, even in heaven, knowing of his constant and overwhelming sadness?

෨෬

6 July 1804

I am grown weaker since last I wrote. Writing seems the only way to focus my thoughts. As I linger here in these final days I appreciate the life I have lived. Can I complain? Can I stand before God and ask Why? No. Surely not. I have embraced life, I have known its power and hope. It is only for John I mourn. It is my hope he comes to find this same breed of peace to which I now cling. Somewhere inside my soul, I know he has received my letter. I feel a new cloud of darkness looming over me. I suppose it is the shadow of our aching hearts which now hovers above us in spite of our inability to find each other. Our spirits are already together. For I know there is not another soul treading this cradle of humanity who knows my heart as John does. Maybe I was wrong to forbid him to come here. But what choice was offered me? Still, the question haunts me, should he have been the one to ask me to deny him in such a horrid circumstance, could I have stayed away? Could I grant him such a wish? I know I could not. And knowing this, I watch my door, I listen for him, for I believe I shall see him again. I only pray I may linger on until he finds me. I must be near him, but greater still is his need to be near me. I am going to a grand place, a place where there is no pain, where love abides, where I may wait for him in peace. But poor John, he shall face the inconsolable days without me. God, hear my prayer, with all I have to surrender, I pray You send my John enough comfort and peace to sustain him, send your angels to guard his heart and mind, give him rest and peace. Amen.

While Lenora poured over Elizabeth's personal prayers and hopes, Edward had finished decorating the tree and had dressed for dinner. As he brushed his hair away from his face, he recalled something important he wanted to share with Lenora this evening, and retreated to his studio. The piece in question he had named the "Madonna." The figure was shrouded in a flowing robe, her face serenely and gently bowed, gazing upon the tenderly held infant savior. Edward had sculpted her when he was a young man of five and twenty years. 'How appropriate,' he thought. The grand mantle seemed yet bare, and the Madonna was indeed the missing crown. He returned to the sitting room and placed the Madonna on the mantel and waited patiently for Lenora to enter the room.

Lenora's thirsty eyes continued to scan the ancient pages of Elizabeth's journal, but she soon came to realize she had lingered there far too long and the guests would be arriving soon. She had been lost in time. Lost in another world. It was with some reluctance that she closed the journal, but at the same time she so longed to replace her melancholy thoughts with something more cheerful. Regardless of the utter sadness of the world at times, she still believed in the goodness of the world, and she still hoped for something wonderful. Being a guest in Brookhaven cemented those beliefs and had returned to her the ultimate hope of her heart, that there was still a chance she would remember her past. With this hope at its brightest glow in her memory, she pinched her cheeks until they were quite bright, and rushed down the hall to join Edward and his guests for the party.

Edward was becoming impatient and could not wait to surprise Lenora with the Christmas tree, but then he heard her footsteps above him. The once silent estate was alive with sounds and aromas which could not have been imagined only weeks before. The fire crackled and popped and the scent of pine and apples and gingerbread heavily filled the air. Lenora walked briskly to the edge of the stairway, and the wonderful aroma of Christmas greeted her. She suddenly stopped and closed her eyes and took a deep breath. "It is truly Christmas," she whispered, beaming. As she continued down the stairs, Edward watched her reaction. He had placed the tree in the most perfect spot where it could be seen from the stairway, yet it was actually situated in the sitting room. Her eyes began to shine when she beheld his gift to her. She ran like a child down the last few steps, "Edward, oh Edward, it is absolutely beautiful. Thank you so much. When did you do this, how did you..."

"Slow down," Edward said almost laughing, "I feel I should have burst if you had come down a moment later. Your gratitude is evident in your eyes, and your reaction just now is precisely why I wanted to do this for you. I remember how you spoke of wanting a Christmas tree this year, it is nothing really. Besides, how can we have a Christmas party without a Christmas tree?"

"It is wonderful, the most wonderful surprise and more, it is the nicest thing you could have done for me. I say we have done rather well in decking these magnificent halls with festivity" just as she was complimenting their efforts she looked across the room and spotted something that quite overtook her emotions.

"But what is this Edward, it is extraordinary. A most excellent piece of art."

"Thank you, she is one of my most loved pieces."

"So it was your hand who created this beauty, I cannot take my eyes off of her, look how gently she holds the child to her, so poetic. You captured the grace and the love of Mary. I adore it." She could hardly stop admiring it. She could not believe the man standing before her had carved this incredible thing, had brought to life something so touching, from a simple block of marble into this, this thing of beauty.

"I am pleased you enjoy her so. I suppose there are many reasons to be taken with this one, perhaps the greatest is notion of the love between a mother and child. A most powerful bond of abiding and unconditional love."

She remembered how Edward had lost his mother at an early age. "It is unfortunate you only had a short time with your own mother."

"Yes, but I remember still how she always encouraged me. She gave her very life to save mine, and I believe she still watches and guides me, there is nothing quite like a mother's love."

"What a charming thought. I would like to think we have loved ones watching over us, sharing our joys and delivering us through our times of despair. Edward, I think you should keep her here on the mantle, even after Christmas, as a reminder, a beacon of hope even, of the extraordinary love that may exist on earth."

"Yes, that is a fine idea. I believe the world needs more reminders of all that is good and hopeful."

The trust between them had been completely restored and Lenora stood looking at the sparkling tree in complete amazement of the life she had found herself living.

Chapter 13
A Celebration

The faint rapping on the door signaled the arrival of the first guests. As Edward answered the door, Lenora walked into the kitchen and asked Charles what she could do to assist.

"Miss Lenora," he said, "You have already helped so much by giving us all the chance to spend Christmas here."

"But Charles, I want to do more. Are those treats over there for us?"

"I suppose one could say I became a bit carried away. I made candies I have not made in years."

"I am sure everything will be delicious, they are simply lovely."

Lenora took the trays of sweets into the large sitting room now adorned by the tremendous Christmas tree, and by the time she entered the room all of the guests had arrived. Charles remained in the kitchen overseeing the final details of his Christmas dinner. Lily rose to assist Lenora with the trays of hors d'oeuvres. Lily's two daughters stood with gapping mouths before the Christmas tree. All eyes in the room were fixed on the youngest of the two whose head was tilted back so far that she began leaning back as to follow the length of the rather tall tree, which appeared even larger from her small perspective. Lily rushed to her rescue and scooped her into her arms preventing her the misfortune of falling. Everyone gasped and then applauded the young mother's quick reflexes.

Among the other guests were the assistant housekeeper, the keeper of the stables, a man of thirty odd years answering to the name of Angus MacCainsh, a Scotsman, who had been in Edward's employ for many years, Angus' father, Robert, and a boy of twelve, named Harry. Edward had taken Harry in some two years ago when his father had died of pneumonia leaving him an orphan. Edward had given Harry a few odd jobs to teach him the invaluable lesson of responsibility and had asked Lily to school him for a small increase in their family's wage which she happily agreed to undertake.

Robert MacCainsh had arrived in Asheville, to visit his son whom he had not seen in nearly a decade, some two months prior to the blizzard and planned to remain here until the weather permitted his departure. He was a delightful old gentleman who said very little and drank very much. His cheeks were as rosy as St. Nicholas' himself and his round form and short frame only added to the likeness. It was evident everyone had taken extra care in dressing for this strange and rare occasion, in part to honor Christmas and in part the prospect of any celebration in the hall of Brookhaven.

The little girls had taken to twirling around in their holiday attire and were quite lost in their own gaiety. Before long Charles had joined the rest of the guests and announced dinner would be served in an hour or so and then joined the others in various topics of polite conversation. Edward sat in the corner of the room surveying the wonderful spectacle. Lenora was all smiles as she talked gaily to everyone. Edward watched her bright smiling eyes as she spoke of Saint Nicholas to the receptive children. He watched her as she lit up the whole world and caught himself listening, listening to a sound long forgotten. It was laughter, pure joy. Lenora had brought this back to him. The sounds of happiness. Sounds that would linger long after the guests were gone, when the elegant tree would lie dead in a quiet wood, and Lenora would be far away from this sad old place. But to this place she had brought joy, and he would not forget this priceless gift she had given him. He thought at this moment there would be nothing in the world he would not do for her. He was committed now to helping her discover her past.

Edward's only sadness was in knowing Lenora would eventually leave him alone again. But she was here now and he would enjoy this evening. Lenora made her way to the piano so the party might enjoy a few Christmas tunes before dinner was served. She sat down quietly and began to play Silent Night. The sweet music was all that could be heard for the next few minutes. Even the children held their breath. She sensed the quiet mood this particular melody had inspired so she began playing Joy To The World to return everyone to a more jovial and festive mood. Everyone began to talk again and laugh again. There was a time for feeling quiet and a time for feeling joy, this was a time to be happy.

From the corner of her eye Lenora noticed a figure had appeared in the doorway of the room, and Edward was at his feet at once walking toward the stranger. The man stood approximately two inches taller than Edward and wore a striking black cloak lined with blood red satin that shimmered in the light as he removed it. She studied him for several moments and concluded from the large black bag at his feet that he must be Edward's friend, Dr. Hamilton Weatherly. As she watched Edward walking toward the stranger she stopped playing.

"Oh do go on, do not let me interrupt this most unlikely scene" the man directed to her with a hearty voice and a white smile that seemed to light his entire face, but she did not continue.

"Hamilton," Edward began, "What a welcome surprise, come and join us, Charles, a place shall have to be added for Hamilton." Charles greeted Hamilton and set off to prepare an additional seat at the table.

"I had no thought I would find such a party!" Hamilton exclaimed.

"Indeed," Edward rejoined, "it is a rare occasion, and planned rather hastily, my being found at Brookhaven during this season being a rarity, and with such a pleasant guest as Lenora, we decided to celebrate. Allow me to introduce you," Edward offered, directing their steps towards the piano, "Lenora, this is Dr. Hamilton Weatherly, and it seems you have your wish." Lenora's heart quickened as her disapproving eyes darted towards Edward's.

"Your wish?" Hamilton inquired failing to see the

embarrassment Edward's comment had effected in Lenora.

"Yes Dr. Weatherly, I had so hoped I may be able to thank you for examining me the night I arrived."

"But of course, I *am* a doctor after all, and besides it is not customary to have such a fine patient as yourself. I only regret I had to depart so suddenly before we could be properly introduced, but as a result a healthy young son has been delivered to farmer Rogers. He is the proud father! And happily it appears you are fully recovered from my last visit. Have you any concerns about your heath?"

"I have not. And I thank you again."

"I shall look forward to continuing our conversation, but do not allow me to keep you from your duties, the piano adds a lovely and lively touch to the party," he said as he looked around the room and everyone seemed to be in agreement, "you see," he continued, "I really must beg your favor in continuing?"

With this said Lenora turned the pages of the sheet music to the next tune and began to play as the doctor had so kindly requested, and she could hardly turn her eyes away from this young and alluring stranger. There was a quality about him which seemed to draw her attention his way. His lean build, his dark hair which hung loose and required his continued effort to keep it brushed aside, his hearty laugh and bright eyes combined and seemed to contrive to magnetize her towards him. At the final note of Deck the Halls, Charles announced Christmas dinner was served.

Charles had prepared the most wonderful dinner which was served on Brookhaven's finest china and over which hardly ten words were spoken save for the general pleasure it afforded.

Lenora had envisioned there would be music and dancing, but there were hardly enough partners with their small number, and the dinner Charles had so perfectly prepared had left them all feeling rather over satisfied and lethargic. Breaking the silence, Angus whispered to his father, but the exchange was inaudible to the rest of the group.

"Forgive me," Angus then began to the party, "but I was just reminding Father of an old custom of our family in gatherings such as this, we would all gather together and each taking his turn tell of favorite memories or future hopes. Shall we enter into this exercise tonight, with the subject being Christmas?"

"Angus, what a lovely idea, shall you start it for us?" Lenora offered.

"Oh yes Lenora, 'tis easy for me. My single most happy Christmas hour was many a year ago in the homeland of my father. My village had suffered long at the hands of the nobles and we had lost our crops the same year. The day of Christmas arrived without mention, and we dared not speak of it knowing the solemn faces of our fathers, but that night we feasted, the elders danced and pipes were played, a lovely sound it was. You see the neighboring clan had heard of our misfortune and had left their homes to share their bounty with us. It was the most unselfish and noble thing that has happened in my life and I would like to toast them tonight, to the MacDonell Clan and to Scotland!" he concluded, raising his glass.

Each of them raised their glasses to his toast. "Now you Father," Angus continued.

"Angus, I never knew you remembered that night so affectionately. It was a wonderful time, when I was as young as you are now and as thin too, hee hee," he giggled, rubbing his rather rotund middle and continuing, "searching my mind I'd say the Christmas memory I hold most dear is the year I married ye mother, God rest her soul. Ah, she was the most beautiful lass I had ever seen, and she stole my heart away the moment I saw her. But getting to the point of it, it was in the first year of our marriage, and Christmas was approaching soon, and much to my dismay. I could think of nothing to give her, my bride, the joy of my life. I had never been very useful with my hands except for farming, and I regretted it more and more in times of want. I had saved a small allowance for her gift and went to seek it in the township. There was little to choose from with the amount in my pocket so I let go of my pride and asked the shopkeeper what I could buy for the small sum. He offered the following: a wooden cradle, a box of tools and a box of fancy soaps. The tools were crossed off the list first, the cradle and the soaps were left. We had no need for a cradle, and my wife always made her own soap owing to the fact she was allergic to all sorts of fragrances and such, so, by default, I took the cradle. I reasoned I could modify it to the extent it would hardly rock at all and she could use it for a planter. She did love her plants. I kept the cradle or should I say planter out of sight and we shared a quiet little meal together. "Robert," she asked, "Are we going to exchange our gifts tonight like we planned?" I fidgeted in my chair knowing my gift would bring forth a quite awkward response until I had the chance to explain my idea of modifying it.

"Ay, I suppose the time has come. I will be right back." Then I retrieved the cradle from the porch and brought it in to her.

"Robert, Robert" she exclaimed, "you scoundrel, how did you know?"

"Well, you love plants don't you, you love them and I thought it would be the perfect gift," I replied, fully proud of my purchase which had caused a most favorable reaction.

"Plants?" she asked.

"Ay, I admit it needs a little work but you'll have a beautiful planter when I am done."

"Indeed. But isn't there another use for this planter?" she asked.

"Why the only other use would be for a babe, but we've no such notion the now."

"Do we not, now?" she replied.

"Unless you've been keeping a secret," I said, joking like. But she did not answer, not in words anyhow, she just looked at me and I knew my gift had been perfect, but not for a planter at all, no it would never be a planter. It was the strangest and most wonderful thing, I had given her a cradle and she had given me you Angus, the child she carried was you."

Everyone agreed the elder McCainish's memory was delightful and humorous to all. Harry spoke up next and related his memory of his final Christmas with his parents, Edward knew without question his most dear memory was collectively every moment spent with Emily, but unable to share his thoughts with his guests, he told of the first Christmas he returned to the orphanage and the happiness he shared in the gifts given to those unfortunate little children. Lenora spoke next and happily conceded this present Christmas was her most cherished one of all, she could only remember the two previous ones and each of them were painful memories but tonight's gaiety had made up for them both. Hamilton interposed next, admitting he had to agree with Lenora. Being a physician generally meant the Christmas season usually brought painful news to those who required his assistance, and therefore finding the unexpected party and meeting Lenora had both proven to lift his spirits.

"I cannot remember a more pleasant holiday in years. I am fortunate to have been allowed to share these fine hours with old friends, and new, I sincerely hope," Hamilton said, raising his glass and glancing toward Lenora.

Again Hamilton's smile brightened his face, and Lenora struggled to disguise her pleasure at his obvious attention to her. The next person spoke up with their own particular Christmas memory and so on and so on until each had had his turn. The final person to share his story was Charles and he told of how he remembered the Christmases of his youth when his own father would tell the story of the nativity. As he spoke of the cherished memory, his girls begged him to tell them the story and as he surveyed the room it was clear everyone not only approved but entreated him to share it with the entire party, so he began.

The children sat by the tree and listened intently to the beautiful tale of the birth of Christ. Charles had a creative imagination and embellished the story to everyone's delight, making it old and new at the same time. The children had fallen asleep before he was finished, but everyone agreed it was their favorite part of the evening. One by one each of the guest said their farewells and returned to their quarters, each of them thankful to have shared the evening together.

෩෬

Hamilton, Lenora and Edward returned to the sitting room and continued to enjoy each other's company, as none of them wanted the evening to end just yet.

"I know it is late Edward, but I think I will stay awake a bit longer. This evening was so delightful, I cannot bear to let it end," Lenora said, as she stood by the mantel admiring the Madonna.

"It was a capital evening, the best I have had in many years, you must accept my deepest gratitude, it is you who made it all possible," Edward answered.

"Nonsense, it is your generosity which made tonight possible Edward, and I cannot take credit belonging to you."

"Oh but you must. I cannot explain it, but you have a way of making everything...sparkle!" He continued.

"I must concur with Edward on that account Lenora!" Hamilton offered.

Edward continued, "Sure, I could have invited the guests and asked Charles to prepare a special dinner, but without you it would not have been the joyous celebration it was."

She smiled and would argue no longer and asked, "Would either of you mind if I played for a moment?" she asked.

"Mind? I should like nothing more."

"Please do." Hamilton confirmed.

She walked over to the piano and began to play. This was the time for quiet reflection. The time to lose oneself in the beautiful notes of age old songs. Familiar songs which made one feel at home. Lenora pretended she was home for a moment, and in a strange way it seemed to be true. She continued to play for several minutes and as she did, Edward became lost in his memories of Emily. He sat there remembering a time long gone by when he had shared a similar feeling of peace with his beloved Emily. And though it was true Life had been cruel to him, there was still a place in his heart to which he could turn for happiness. In spite of his losses, he was aware of the sad truth that countless sad souls lingered the earth who had never felt the soft kiss of an angel, who had never known the warm embrace of a loving mother, but he had known these feelings and even though the pain of losing those he loved so dearly still remained, he would not trade his pain for a feeling of apathy.

"Edward, Edward you seem like you are far away from here?" Lenora asked with concern in her voice.

"I suppose I was far away. This night reminded me of Christmases long ago. I was revisiting those special places, but do not mind my thoughts or allow my expression to stop your lovely music."

Lenora smiled as if she had read his thoughts. Though

Edward was thoroughly enjoying her entertainment, he suddenly excused himself from the two, remembering he had given the staff the night off, and as such there would be no one to start the fires this evening in his room, nor the rooms of his guests. He had intended to ask Charles to have this task seen to before Charles had left for the evening, but in the excitement of the uncommon evening, he had failed to ask the favor.

As Lenora returned to her playing she found herself alone with the captivating Dr. Weatherly, an occasion she had secretly hoped for during the whole of the night. In a moment he was standing beside the piano watching her, and she became so preoccupied with his presence that she missed a note, and then another and then suddenly stopped playing altogether, exclaiming that her mistake was to be attributed to her weariness.

"Lovely nonetheless," he offered, "I was just wondering what sort of spell you have cast over Brookhaven. I never expected to find such an evening at this oftentimes gloomy estate. I really must congratulate you on this feat of transforming it so."

"Congratulate? But I have done nothing," Lenora replied confused.

"On the contrary, you have done a great deal. There has never been a celebration of any sort in this dark manor. When I arrived tonight and heard the music playing and laughter I thought I was in a dream."

"You do not like Brookhaven, Dr. Weatherly?"

"Not like Brookhaven? That is almost blasphemous, I adore this estate. And I would testify there is no other like it in all the world."

"But the adjectives you use to describe it, dark, gloomy, would suggest you see it as a depressing place and one needing alteration in some way."

"Perhaps I should have chosen my words more carefully. But you must agree Brookhaven is a mysterious place, and yes, a dark and gloomy one at times in fact and the master of the estate, well...," but he stopped short of completing his thought.

"What, what about Edward?"

"I really should not continue, I am afraid I have been too casual with my comments, and it is unbecoming of me I know."

Lenora paused for a long while, deeply concentrating on

the words which had just passed between them, wondering what he had begun to say, but unwilling to inquire further. It seemed his words had some negative connotation regarding Edward, and this troubled her. And yet she could not help but agree with his assessment of Brookhaven being quite a mysterious place. Perhaps his description was not intended in a negative fashion. "Mysterious?" she whispered, though she thought the word had not escaped her lips.

"Yes, mysterious? Then you agree?" he questioned.

"Pardon?" she asked

"You said 'mysterious'"

"I suppose I did," she agreed

"I could think of other adjectives as well if it pleases you?"

Lenora had scrutinized his every word and their exchange suddenly made her overly self aware, and she could think of nothing else to say to him.

Hastily she replied, "I shall relieve you from choosing any words at all Dr. Weatherly, and bid you good night."

"Wait," he whispered, "first of all, please call me Hamilton, only my patients call me 'Dr. Weatherly.' Have I said something to offend you? Allow me to mend it if I have. I had a trying day, but finding this unexpected party, and meeting you has been delightful. My casual manner is often off putting, but I abhor pretense and I felt as though we were already friends, even thought I've only just made your acquaintance. I assure you I shall be on my best behavior if you remain here a while longer."

But the damage was done to her sensitive pride and there could be no convincing her.

"I thank you for the apology Dr. Weatherly, but none is required. The day has been long for me as well. I must assure you my retiring just now and your behavior have nothing to do with the other. I shall see you tomorrow." But in truth, his words had everything to do with her being required to quit the room. Her cheeks had turned to rose several times and it was shocking how he spoke to her with no formality at all, so frankly and so presumptuously.

Though she was not one to stand on ceremony, there were basic rules one depended on in mixed company, and he had all but accused her of dwelling on each word from his lips, presuming in her a higher interest in himself, and her embarrassment lay in the truth of that notion, though he had said it in good humor and with no knowledge of the truth in it. Nonetheless she had been mortified and just as strongly as his presence had lured her to him, his words had been the one thing which de-magnified her of his charms, for the moment at least.

"As you wish, Lenora, tomorrow then."

She said nothing further and quitted the room. As she reached the top of the stairway she met Edward.

"Lenora, you may find your chamber needs a moment more to warm, I have just started the fire."

"I shall be fine, but you should have told me, I would have helped you."

"Nonsense. Has Hamilton retired?"

"I think not. I have just left him in the parlor."

"I shall join him there then, Lenora, sleep well. And thank you again. I shall keep the memory of this night for a long time."

"As will I, thank you for giving me a real Christmas this year."

"Lenora, Merry Christmas," he said with a warm smile.

"Merry Christmas!"

Edward watched her walk out of sight, and returned to the parlor to find Hamilton warming himself by the fire.

"Edward, I am afraid I have scared Lenora away. Unfortunately it has been quite a while now since I have had the pleasure of sharing the company of a young lady in a social setting, and I must admit I have made a mess of things."

"Not you Hamilton, I am sure it was nothing. She is still recovering from the events of the long journey which brought her here, and she is a little fragile and must be treated very carefully. It is nothing more. You must understand her trust is a privilege which must be gained over time."

"But I am infuriated with myself because I know that Edward, I am a doctor for heaven's sake, and I know the fears and despair she must be experiencing, but I suppose I was not thinking of her as a patient, but rather as a lovely girl."

Edward looked at him with an uncharacteristic sort of look in his eyes and Hamilton could not easily determine if the look was that of apprehension or approval. And suddenly

Hamilton began to wonder if he had unwittingly crossed some sacred ground between the two, but it seemed impossible the more he reflected on that possibility. He considered the difference in Lenora and Edward's ages and more importantly the fact that Edward seemed incapable of letting anyone completely enter his world, not even the likes of this beautiful creature.

"Edward, might I ask you a personal question?"

"You may ask anything, but I cannot promise I shall answer."

"I'll take my chances. One cannot help but to see the change which has come about this place, even changes in you since Lenora has arrived here and seeing these changes, well… one wonders if perhaps, well, that you have come to care for her is obvious, but is there something more between you, do you, .. love.."

"Hamilton!" Edward interrupted quickly, "you are wide off the mark with this questioning. I shall answer you, but honestly I am alarmed you should ask such a question of me. How might you imagine such a thing after I have so recently brought you into my confidence concerning my past? Apparently you failed to grasp the sacred nature of my loss, you may be unequivocally certain there is only one woman who shall ever exist in my world."

"I do not know what has come over me. I have scared Lenora away and now I have offended you."

"You have not offended me as much as you have shocked me with such a thought, I care for Lenora, yes, I am indebted to her, completely, for reacquainting me with life through her hope and lightness of heart, but I could never love her, not in the way you suggest. My heart is not my own, which is all I can say on the matter of love. But trust me, friend, the changes in me are as evident to me as they must be to all. I suppose I was content with my lot before she found her way to me. I had accepted my life, but there is something about her which allows me to hope again.

Over the last few days I have once again experienced the simple pleasure of giving someone comfort and protection, and this feeling is something I very much want to continue to experience. I imagine she makes me feel needed and useful, for the first time in many years. In the beginning, I could not look at her without seeing the reflection of this one who holds my heart ransom, but now I only see a young girl, a human being who needs assistance and guidance, in many ways, and I am simply compelled to help her in any way I can."

"I see, and allow me to say that she is the fortunate one to have found herself here under your protection. I appreciate your honesty, even more so knowing I should not have asked."

"For certain," Edward remarked with a tone of 'obviously', "which makes one wonder why you felt it necessary to ask, but alas, I think I am beginning to see."

"You see nothing of the sort."

"Of what sort?"

"Edward," Hamilton answered, flashing his infectious smile, "I am suddenly quite fatigued," (feigning a wide yawn) "and I feel I must retire at once."

"Very well, but you cannot escape the subject forever." Edward warned.

They parted in the most good humored way. Hamilton feeling embarrassed for having bared his soul to Edward regarding his new-found feelings for this girl to which he had not quite harnessed or yet fully understood, and Edward feeling amused at having rendered Hamilton speechless, a state rarely known to the young man.

Chapter 14
Living Words From Lifeless Hearts

Lenora was not quite ready for her night's rest, she had so many thoughts to digest, to sort out. Though the party had been a complete success, reality had a way of creeping back over her. Her thoughts returned to the shock of finding the sculpture bearing her own likeness, and Edward's admission that it was actually a sculpture of his late wife, Emily. A question formed in her mind 'why do people who love each other have to be separated?' Lenora wished there was something she could do to comfort Edward now. Though unwillingly, Emily had left him alone to face this dark world without her. Emily had left him, but then she pondered 'What of Emily's loss? Perhaps Emily had searched for Edward and found no peace even in heaven. If only Emily could break the barrier of death, and come to Brookhaven, and Edward would have found Emily under his window instead of me!' Lenora even thought of Emily's father, and how the sad outcome was certainly not his intention, but nonetheless he had created the obstacle of death. How could a parent be so consumed with fear that his child might loose her fortune or reputation, that he causes her to loose her soul?

She thought about Edward and Emily, of John and Elizabeth. Would she ever know a love like this? Could her heart stand losing such a love? She knew not. Before going to sleep, she returned to the letters she loved so very much...

> *24 December 1802*
> *Dearest John,*
> *It is Christmas Eve and all is quiet here, a Silent Night. I have tried to call on the holiday spirit, but I am afraid my efforts are of no use. I certainly am thankful for all of my blessings, but I cannot escape this constant longing for you. My heart is calling out to you. Can you hear it? I blew you a kiss, did you feel it going out across the deep sea, above the shining stars and landing sweetly on your lips? John, it is moments as these when I feel I cannot go on without you. I think of our long walks and how we talked endlessly about nothing and about everything. There is a raging silence deep in my heart and only the whisper of your sweet voice can calm it. Come for me soon my Darling. Merry Christmas. Faithfully yours,*
> *Elizabeth.*

ഈ⊗

> 2 January 1803
> My dearest Elizabeth,
> I am so pleased to learn you received my letters. I miss you terribly my darling. It is a cold and dark winter without you. It just began to snow and it is as if diamonds are raining on the land. How I wish I could take them and make a crown for you, my queen. I was invited to share Christmas Day with the Sanderson family. They still grieve for their son and it was obvious how delighted they were to have a young person in their company again. Please do not worry about my welfare, I assure you I will be in the best of health when I come for you. When I come for you. The months are passing by and soon we will be together. That is my prayer

and the hope which pushes me onward to each tomorrow. I send you my love and pray God will watch over you and keep you.

Until we meet again, my love.   John

ಸಿಂಧ

2 March 1803
Dearest John,
As I compose these words I am wearing my lovely cross necklace. I wear it now and I shall never remove it from where it rests so close to my heart. I find myself touching it several times a day, and somehow I know in those moments you are thinking of me. Please forgive me, my love if I sometimes sound full of desperation and plagued by negative and futile emotions. I only succumb to those feelings from my abiding love for you, but I assure you I am strong in my love and I will be here waiting for you when you come for me. How are you getting along? I hope your work is progressing well. We endured a severe winter, but spring has come at last, and how lovely it is to have the color returned to this formerly darkened corner of the globe. I love Kielderbridge deeply, but I long to start our new life together in the new world. I have thrust myself into my studies and I am learning many wonderful and interesting things. Another month has passed, another day closer to when I can see you again. How I long for that day! Seeing you and being your bride is the light that brightens my every day.
Faithfully yours, Elizabeth.

ಸಿಂಧ

10 March 1803
My dearest Elizabeth,
Reading the words of despair falling from your lovely hand is heartbreaking, and though I know my pain will only add to your own I must repeat you are not alone in your sorrow. My heart longs for you each passing moment. Please trust that we shall be together soon, my love. I am busy with work but you are never far from my thoughts. When I picture your face I cannot believe I have won your love and devotion, what precious gifts they are to me. Elizabeth, you, your love, is proof to me God answers prayers. Please be patient a bit longer, I will come for you and soon our separation will be a distant memory and all our promises will be kept.
Until we meet again, my love.   John

ℰℭ

12 April 1803
My dearest Elizabeth,
Spring is here my lovely angel. I wish you could see the colors covering this beautiful land. Soon my love, soon. Though the world is new and fresh, I must report dreadful news. Mr. Sanderson has fallen quite ill and his prognosis is not hopeful. He has given me control of his business. My work has increased and I hardly have time to steal a moment for myself, but my darling, this turn of events will help me to keep my promises to you. I do not delight in Mr. Sanderson's misfortune, on the contrary, I fear for his life, for he has become as a father to me. I shall be required to increase my labor but I am working for us, for our dreams. One day soon, I will hear your sweet voice again. I cherish your letters, but nothing replaces being in your presence. Please take care and remember I have ordered the stars to watch over you.

Until we meet again, my love, John

28 June 1803
Dearest John,
I am crushed by the news of Mr. Sanderson's illness and I shall pray for a speedy recovery. How reassuring it is to learn that you are ever nearer your goals. Is there a chance you can come sooner? A silly question, I know, for if you can be here a moment sooner, I trust you will. I know you are probably working too hard so I ask you to take care of yourself. I continue to work in the village and I regret to report a terrible illness has spread itself like a curse over our city, and stolen the lives of many of our dear citizens. No one is safe from it, and it is not discriminating. Just last week an entire family was lost to death's call. Father has asked me to discontinue tending the sick children of our village, but I simply cannot allow them to die alone without hope, not when there is something I can do to ease their suffering. And besides, the more diligently I work, the more quickly the days are passing, but oh how I long for the day when you arrive and take me away from all of this sickness, the very darkness of death. When I am with you all things are possible.
Faithfully yours, Elizabeth

ഔ

24 September 1803
My dearest Elizabeth,
Today marks two years since we were parted. The hardest times are surely past us now and soon we shall be together. Elizabeth, be assured, I shall come for you as soon as time allows. I hope you can hold on for a little longer my love. I am planning a very special wedding gift for you.

Darling, your father is most prudent to encourage you to limit your assistance with the sick, and I wholeheartedly agree with his plea. I understand your need to lend assistance, but it could be dangerous. Please reconsider. Bad news. Mr. Sanderson has not improved. I fear he will not be with us much longer. I sorely regret you two shall never meet, he is fond of you already from my incessant going on about you. Please know you are my constant thought.
Until we meet again, my love. John

ഌҀ

2 October 1803
Dearest John,
I write to you today with a full heart. I shared a wonderful week with Aunt Mildred. At Father's pleading she took me to Paris earlier than originally planned to purchase my wedding attire. John it is all so lovely, I cannot wait to be your bride. With your arrival drawing near and seeing myself in a beautiful wedding gown, I believe it is really going to happen. As much as I loved you when first you departed, I feared the oceans separating us would drown our precious love. I thought all of the empty days would dilute the strength of our love. But John, my love for you has only grown. Where I was a quiet song, I am now a great symphony. Where I was a cloudy sky, I am now a brilliant sunset exploding across the night sky. The feelings I have for you have grown stronger with each passing day. I wait for you with a patient heart. I shall light a candle for Mr. Sanderson and pray that God deliver him from his suffering. Peace and love be with you always. All of my love goes out to you. Faithfully yours, Elizabeth

1 November 1803

My dearest Elizabeth,

I write this letter under the most terrible circumstance. Eli Sanderson passed away today, and with his passing, the world has suffered a great loss. To say he was a great man seems so shallow, inadequate and insufficient. And his death has left me with such sadness of heart, especially considering his feelings toward me. You see he has given me so much. I was a poor farmer's son, but he saw a fire in me, a sheer will to work, to learn, so he gave me an apprenticeship, he worked with me night and day teaching me his skill and later sent me to Europe on a most special mission for his business. What a great honor it was for me to carry out his wishes and then, while there, I met you my darling. You see, it was he who was responsible for you being in my life. So much he has given, so very much, only last month, he gave me the plot of land he had promised to sell me, only he would accept no payment for it. The very land that stands beneath my feet is ours. My life's work, my home were all given to me by his hand, and more, he has willed Sanderson Company to me. I am utterly shocked. I am three and twenty and I own a business, a business I helped create and build. I would be happy, elated if only this abundance were possible without the loss of my great friend and teacher. The days will be much more lonely. Only your gentle presence could ease this loss. I will write again soon. I count the days until we are together once more. Until we meet again, John

17 January 1804
Dearest John,
My every thought is with you in the loss of your dear, dear friend. But take rest in knowing Mr. Sanderson is at peace now, for I know his last days were very uncomfortable. I wish I could be with you, but we will be together soon. Do not be discouraged and do not lose hope, all of this waiting will be over soon. Those places you live and walk will be lived and walked with me at your side. We will be wed and all of our dreams will become a living reality. I also fight melancholy. It is probably your news, it is unbearable to know of your despair and be forced to be here unable to help you. And yet, I am overjoyed at his generosity in giving you so much, leaving his business under your care, but I cannot say I am surprised, for his love and respect for you were never hidden. Whatever happens, remember I am here loving you as always. Then and now, Faithfully yours, Elizabeth

ஓ☙

28 February 1804
My dearest Elizabeth,
Good morning to you my love. I am sorry it has been so long since last I wrote. Taking over Sanderson Company has proven to be a formidable task. I am at the helm now and everything is running smoothly, in fact, I am taking the day to make my travel arrangements. I must plan everything to the last detail so our happy reunion occurs as planned and as I promised. The day is drawing near. The day I take you as my bride. I cannot wait to see your lovely face again. My wedding gift to you is now complete but I will

not be bringing it on the journey. Once we are wed and we make the trip back to Asheville you may have it. I know it is something you will love. I plan to purchase a few gifts to bring to your family as well. I feel so fortunate to have your hand and now that our future is secure I want to share the blessings. Until we meet again my love, John.

Chapter 15
A Life Altered

Edward settled himself comfortably by the crackling fire and allowed himself to relive the party and all the joy it had brought him. Though he felt a certain loss at having been denied the company of the children of the orphanage, he had enjoyed the evening immensely. Just a day before he had feared he had lost the trust of his sweet Lenora, but the morning's conversation had settled the matter. 'Still, she must have been terrified,' he thought. 'What must she have thought when she saw the sculpture of Emily?. Oh Emily, I thought you had come back to me. I imagined you walking into my chamber so many times, and when I saw this young girl, I thought God must have sent you back to me to ease my empty days. But alas, she is not you, and no one could ever be. Your warm touch, your heart so pure. My own soul was alive only briefly. Knowing your love meant knowing life. I was alive, I was loved. To you my soul belongs, eternally. If you have sent Lenora to me to comfort me in my last days, I thank you and I promise you I shall watch over her and protect her. I wish you could have been here this night. It was a lovely Christmas. Good night my angel.'

As he said goodnight to her, he remembered how he had spent Christmases in the past. First, with his parents and then those dark years at the orphanage, but then the Christmas he shared with Emily. A Christmas he could never forget. It was remarkable to him how one event, one moment could set the course for the rest of one's life.

He remembered that day as if it were yesterday. The day he and Emily confessed their love for one another. It was Christmas Eve and he had spent a lovely December day horseback riding along the English countryside with Emily and Bryson. With each day of his vacation he felt more and more certain Emily shared his desires. Throughout the day he had caught her looking at him. He loved the look in her eyes when she glanced at him. Her eyes seemed to say, "I care for you, I would like to know you, really know you." If only he could steal a brief second alone with her, he may be able to declare his feelings for her. But what chance did he have? Her father was pleasant enough but he had plans for each of his children and somehow Edward knew he was not to be part of Emily's life. But if he could kiss her just once, if he could speak of his yearning for her and share one private moment with her it would be enough.

He promised himself he would find a time to reveal his feelings to her before he returned to the university. The knowing looks she had given him, the longing looks, she could not possibly deny. Later that evening the Talbot house was brimming with excitement, it was alive with the sights and sounds of Christmas. There was a grand dinner followed by the singing of Christmas carols and the telling of stories. And later that night the most remarkable thing happened.

Late in the evening, after everyone else had long since fallen asleep, Edward lay awake thinking of Emily and how urgently he desired to speak to her. There was only one week remaining for the Holiday and once he returned to school there would be no chance for them to meet. He must speak to her before leaving. At the same time, Emily awoke from a most disturbing dream. She did not know from where these thoughts had arisen. Deep within her soul something was crying out. She tried to stifle these thoughts tormenting her, but they kept reappearing in her mind. She tossed among the cool white sheets as they caressed her skin. But she wanted more than this. She wanted to be touched by Edward. Visions of him kissing her, touching her, telling her he loved her flooded her mind.

Emily recalled seeing him earlier in the day. The afternoon sun filtering through his hair. She studies his every move as he mounted the stallion and rode him like a prince reminiscent to her of some childhood fairytale. He was such a lovely man. She had never met a man more handsome. He spoke little, but in his eyes she saw his thoughts. She knew he must feel these feelings of attraction for her too. If only he would confess it, she would be his. She would give herself to him at this very moment if he asked it of her. His arms were so strong, and his hands, his beautiful hands, she wanted to feel them touching her. But her mind took control of her heart and reprimanded her for her thoughts and forbade her from having them again, it was simply not proper.

Restless from the delicious thoughts, she decided to go to the kitchen for a piece of apple pie, or perhaps she would go to the music room and play the piano. As she walked down the stairs, she noticed the candles in the great room had not been extinguished. When she entered the room she was a bit startled to find Edward standing by the fire. She blushed intensely at the sight of him unable to forget her passionate thoughts, and instinctively turned quietly to retreat, afraid her thoughts might be read if she met his eyes.

As she walked away she heard Edward's deep voice whisper her name, "Emily . . . please don't go."

She turned around and reentered the room. "I see I am not alone in my restlessness," she said softly clutching her robe to ensure it revealed nothing.

"You are shivering, come join me by the fire." He asked

"But I am not dressed, properly dressed" she argued.

"Please join me Emily, I promise I will close my eyes or look away," he offered, knowing it was an impossibility for him to turn away from her or to guard his eyes from her presence.

Emily did not answer, but walked timidly towards the fire. "I know why I cannot sleep," Edward said breaking the silence, "but for your part, I suppose you are excited about the Holiday?"

"Yes, but it is much more than that Edward," she said looking into the fire.

"Yes. It is much more. I had hoped..." but he could not finish his sentence as he stood there looking at her only an arm's length away. Their eyes met and she blushed once more so he turned from her again and the tension between them was so profound that the moment seemed to linger between them for an eternity. Keeping his head turned he glanced in her direction and their eyes met again, but this time he fixed his eyes on hers and challenged his sense of propriety.

"You had hoped I would find you here, alone?" she said staring into the raging fire reflecting in his eyes.

"Is it so obvious?" he answered, and as he spoke to her he moved closer and closer to her with each word. "I tried to conceal my heart, but I am afraid I have offended you, forgive me?" he pleaded with a quiet desperation in his voice.

"But Edward," she said looking deeply into him, " there is nothing to forgive."

"Do you mean. . .?" he looked at her wildly hoping to affirm that she too felt this desire.

"I do not know what I mean," she whispered looking away, "I only know it is my heart speaking words which I do not yet understand." But he reached out to her and turned her face to him most gently, "Then let your heart speak for you. It will speak the truth. Emily, yes, I *had* hoped to be alone with you. There is something I must tell you." He took her hand in his. He felt it trembling in his own, and she allowed him to keep it. "I know we have only just met, but I, I love you. I cannot go on another second without you knowing you have my heart. There, I have said it." He looked at her searching her eyes for some sign of how she had received his words.

Lost in her eyes he did not notice her beautiful smile and he feared for a moment that she did not return his love.

"Say something," he pleaded.

"Shh, listen," she answered in a whisper, "someone is coming, follow me." Taking his hand in hers, she led him into the ivory music room. They stood together in the dark, still hand in hand, in silence until the footsteps finally returned upstairs.

"I cannot see your face," he whispered. She answered by taking his hand and leading him to a window. In the starlight, he could make out her beloved face, but she had not responded to his pledge of love for her. He wished for her to break this painful silence, but again her actions spoke for her. She took his hand and brought it to her cheek and began to kiss it. His heart was on fire now. Blazing wildly. He took her face in his hands and kissed her softly, then passionately. Her sweet lips held no reluctance.

Then he held her tightly in a desperate embrace for several moments. Neither of them wanting to let go. The love inside them holding them prisoner to this most longed-for moment of confession. Edward did not want to think of the consequences of his passion for her, but he remembered his promise to himself. If he could have just one moment he would be satisfied, and then on the heels of that thought, was the imposing thought of her father and how he would never accept him into is family. He slowly broke the embrace and looked at her lovingly.

"My sweet Emily, what have I done? Now that I have confessed my feelings, my love for you is deeper still, yet how can I hope to gain your father's acceptance. I fear I have wronged you. I fear I have been selfish. I have revealed my feelings to you, but I cannot offer you love without pain. To love me would be for you to choose between me and your family and I cannot ask it of you."

"Stop it. Stop. How can you say those words to me after holding me this way. Do you not see you can give me something no one else can give? I should never forgive you if you take back your words now. I love you. I love you Edward. I loved you the first instant my eyes saw you and I prayed morning and night for these precious few sweet moments with you. Tell me you love me. Tell me again," she pleaded.

"Yes my darling, I love you, with all of my strength. And foolishly I believed if I shared one kiss with you, one precious kiss I would be content, but now my heart is drunk with you. I am not the same man who arrived here two weeks ago. I am altogether different now. I do not know how I will go on without you."

"But you will not, we will find a way to be together. I cannot be without you now. Edward, love can conquer any obstacle, as it is written in the scriptures, 'love always believes, it always endures, it always hopes; and as long as hope is alive, we can endure the parting...'"

"But your father Emily, do you really believe he will allow you to marry a man like me? You know my past, I came from a wealthy family, but everything was lost when I lost my parents. I was raised in an orphanage, and as such I have a different way of living, one which causes suspicion and isolation in the society to which you are accustomed. And though my fortune has been restored, I am not the sort of man your father would have you marry."

"It is true you have not had a storybook life, but the past does not matter to *me*, excepting only that it makes me love you all the more."

"But there is the matter of society, of what is expected of you," he reminded her.

She looked away from Edward and out into the black night. She pondered the stillness of the stars and how they prospered and thrived without the intervention of man. She watched a single star fall into the void of blackness leaving a faint sprinkle of stardust behind it. How should she answer this proposition that society's expectations were to be regarded as higher than her own?

"Edward, look there, do you see how grand our world is? God made all of this with his hand. In all its glory it exists without any assistance from man. God's world is so simple. It is full of beauty and wonder. It is only man's interpretations, neglects and manipulations which bring it to ruin. You are right, there is the matter of society to consider. But I refuse to believe any set of rules or etiquette is to be held above the feelings of one's heart. You and I belong together. Do you think I can dismiss these feelings or ever forget you because my father believes you do not meet certain standards that mere men have created? No. There is only one rule of life I follow. It is God who placed this love for you in my heart and to deny it would be to deny God. You cannot ask it of me and I certainly cannot ask it of myself."

"Dear Emily, you do not have to convince me. I too find my worth according to God's own principles instead of man's. But it is not so simple, I have known the downcast looks, I have heard the whispers among those who would shun me as soon as my back is turned, and while I can live with the exclusion, I cannot say I can live with anyone excluding you, and they would, by your association with me. And though winning your heart was effortless, your father's approval is a far different matter. He sees the world through eyes far different than our own."

"But it is not your choice, Edward, it is mine. And I would make it a thousand times the same. It must be you. I choose you, whatever it may mean. In a perfect world I could have your love and the love and respect of my father, but it is not a perfect world, and if I should be asked to choose, it would hurt me to live without my family, but to live without you would be no life at all. You are my life, and my choice."

As her words of truth poured out, Edward realized the truth in them and immediately began to formulate a plan for their future.

"How could I think of leaving of you? We are bonded now and nothing can separate our hearts, but we must proceed with our courtship very carefully. I must return to the university and finish my studies, and you, your music. We should keep our feelings a secret until the time is right. You are right, there is no denying what we feel. It is as if I have only just taken my first breath, and I know I shall never be the same. We need only to listen to our hearts and the urging of those perfect words, love can endure because 'love always hopes.' I promise you we will be together, by my life and my love, I promise you."

"I understand. We shall tell no one, not even Bryson. He has a heavy burden of his own, and I do not wish to add to his troubles. I will write to you and I will find a way to see you again soon. Edward, I have it, my aunt Amelia lives in Brighton, it is the perfect place for us to meet. There are lovely museums and a music conservatory, it is perfect, just the place for our meeting. As a child I spent my summers there with her. I could visit her in the summer and you and I could be together. But can we wait that long? It may be the only. . . I know I can be patient until then, tell me you approve." She pleaded.

"Yes, yes, Brighton will be splendid. But you cannot write me and I shall not write to you, for it is too a great a risk if our letters should be discovered and our deception. I have never been to Brighton, but I have heard much of its charms and I shall be free to do whatever I choose during the summer holiday, and I should like nothing better than to have the entire summer with you, and there, no one would discover our secret. But Emily we should return to our rooms now before we are discovered."

"If only this night could go on without end, if only we did not have to be parted. Edward, kiss me again, kiss me now."

Edward took her into his arms, he held her close to him. As he kissed her, he looked at her. He kissed her forehead and her cheek then her lips and pausing he whispered, "look at me." Her soft eyes opened to him as he kissed her, deeper and deeper, they looked into each others eyes and their very souls seemed to meet and be fused together as one whole, and in that moment, his life would be changed forever.

Edward's much-loved memories were interrupted by a harrowing voice pleading for mercy. "What is that? Lenora!" He said aloud. He rushed up the stairs to find her crying "no, no."

"Lenora," he whispered, "it is all right. Go back to sleep now, my dear, it is only another dream. You are safe here at Brookhaven." These words from his familiar voice seemed to comfort her, and she must have felt his presence there because she became quiet and went back to sleep. Edward left her alone and returned to his chamber and to his thoughts of Emily. Although he could have never forgotten Emily, his memories of her had become more dim, less intense than they had been in the past. But since Lenora had arrived, his memories of Emily had sharpened. He questioned if he had done everything he could to save her. 'Why had it ended in such disaster?' He remembered being a different person. A young man, in love, in hope.

In his later years the loss of hope had made him become disillusioned with the world. He would have given Emily anything. He loved her, but her father had taken away everything. He remembered their wedding night. A marriage in secret, one night of pure love shared before she was torn away from him forever. From a feeling of intense love to a spiral into despair he had fallen. He shuddered even now as he remembered the rage in her father's eyes. Edward was not the man Winston Talbot wanted for his daughter. He did not have the right future, nor the right past, he was an artist, and he had been raised in an American orphanage. This was his crime. That he had lost his parents and was left alone in the world. No. It would not be a proper match for his daughter. The daughter of one of the most successful and powerful men in England. And what Winston Talbot wanted, he made come to pass. And one man's power became Edward's defeat.

Edward wondered if Emily might be watching over him in this very space in time, which is why he could not let her memory die. She was not here in the physical world, but her spirit lived and it was out there somewhere loving him, waiting for him. When he saw Lenora the night of the blizzard, he believed Emily had finally found her way back to him, and in a way she had, this young lost girl had awakened those memories, and he was thankful. He wanted so much to find out who Lenora was, where she had come from, so he might help her as she had helped him. But he also wanted to keep her here with him. Lenora's presence comforted him, safeguarded him from all the sadness that had colored his world in blackness.

Chapter 16
An Unlikely Friend

As Lenora read the ancient letters and Edward reminisced with his most treasured memories of Emily, Hamilton finished his brandy while lingering by the fire imagining the moment he had walked into Brookhaven tonight and witnessed the sound of Christmas carols and the beauty who played the piano. He envied Lenora's ability to endear herself to Edward so instantly, perhaps it was her beauty. Whatever power over Edward she possessed, Hamilton was determined to come to understand it and thereby share in its wealth. Though Hamilton had proven to become Edward's closest friend of late, it had been quite different in the beginning. . .

Hamilton had settled comfortably in the mountains of Asheville long before he first heard any mention of Edward Withers. As the town physician, Hamilton had chanced to encounter many different types of people, some of whom would occasionally speak of the strange and eccentric man living in an estate called Brookhaven. Their rumors were varied and included every sort of criminal and ghastly happenings as one could possibly imagine. One such elderly woman was convinced Edward was hiding out because he had murdered someone or had committed some equally appalling act. Why else would a man settle in such an ominous estate and choose to keep oneself hidden away from all society, she reasoned.

Hamilton was not much for believing rumors, especially

those told by "well meaning" busy bodies, but because of the number of suspicious townspeople, he began to secretly create his own version of Edward Withers' mysterious past. After a tedious triumph over a deadly virus, he reached a slump in his practice, and the days began to linger and he found his mind wandering and searching for some new adventure to fill his days. On one such day he fancied he might attempt to locate the mysterious Brookhaven and for once and all uncover its secrets.

He had acquired a crude map of the central area when he first arrived in order to better serve him in locating his patient's homes. Brookhaven was marked on the map with a simple, capital "B". He estimated it would be a two hour journey so he packed a few supplies and set out for his trip. He began to whistle some ancient tune and to wonder if he would find Mr. Withers at the estate or if he would find it empty. He enjoyed a leisurely ride and took special interest in the local vegetation surrounding him. The forest was a veritable garden of Eden with flowering rhododendron growing wild and beautiful in white and bright pink, over which a hosts of butterflies fluttered about and captured the eye of the traveler.

There were trees of such grandeur lining the long and winding approach as Hamilton had never seen, and as he had calculated, he came upon a bend in the road leading to Brookhaven after nearly two hours of travel. Having reached the end of the approach, he was met by two immense and elaborate iron gates, standing open as if to invite him in. But somehow he sensed they did not invite him at all. He believed himself a fearless man, but he could not deny the intense feeling of dread which consumed him and his instinct to turn back toward home.

Hamilton quickly checked his fears and clung to the notion that he was a grown man and as such would not allow the presence of fear. He continued following the pathway before him. The sparsely traveled, overgrown road led him forward for approximately one and a quarter mile and it occurred to him the untrammeled road may yet be another sign that his company, or the company of anyone for that matter, would be completely undesirable. As he reached the entrance to Brookhaven, another set of iron gates, of the same design, appeared before him.

As he passed the gates, a most stunning estate stood

before him. It was not what he had imagined. He had pictured something darker, even fierce. 'It is magnificent,' he thought and scolded himself for not having made the trip earlier, 'and they say one man alone lives here. One man and his servants? Remarkable.' He secured Midnight and ventured toward the great set of doors and began knocking. There was no answer. He concluded if one were in some far corner of the home, it would nearly be impossible to be heard. After two attempts and two failures, Hamilton decided to walk along the property. Rumor held that Brookhaven had once had a beautiful garden, complete with reflection pools and Italian fountains and many varieties of vegetation, and he thought he should like to view it in its entirety, as he was a lover of a nature.

He walked around the vast grounds and to his delight, found the remains of the esteemed gardens. The vague outline of an extensive manicured garden was still visible. 'In its day, this must have been breathtaking,' he thought. He had not seen a more lovely estate since his travels in Europe. After lingering awhile in the now overgrown and neglected garden, he made his way back to the front of the estate. And as he approached, he saw the lean, muscular figure of a man standing by Midnight. His first response was panic. 'Wonderful,' he thought, 'Hamilton you are brilliant. What are you to say to this man when you have been discovered wandering throughout the grounds of Mr. Withers' property as if you were an invited guest? Perhaps you can charm your way out of this.' He summoned all the courage he could and yelled out, "Hello, I took the liberty of securing him there."

"I see you did. This is a fine animal. One which should not be left alone." Answered the man in a cool voice and manner.

"Do forgive me Sir, I have come to meet Mr. Withers of this extraordinary estate. I tried the door, but he is not here at present and after the long journey, I thought I might take rest in the famous gardens."

"Do you have an appointment, young man?" he asked in an even colder tone.

"Why, I cannot say I do, but I assure you I require only a small amount of his time."

"Very well then, I am Mr. Withers. What brings you to this hidden part of the world?" he queried.

"As I said before, I wished to meet you Sir. I am Dr.

Hamilton Weatherly and I have served this region for miles around, for nearly two years and have never been introduced to you. I would like to assure you that should you need my services, I would be happy to assist you or your servants for that matter."

"Is that correct?" he asked with a certain sly tone.

"Indeed."

"Young man, at my estimation, your humble dwelling lies nearly a two hour distance on horseback and even on this fine creature, and even on such a lovely summer day, I should question your, shall I say enthusiasm, to come such a great distance with only a brief introduction being your full intention. Could it be you are truly here to see if I am indeed the beast the townspeople whisper of, and somehow delight in? Better yet, maybe you are here to satisfy some uncommon preoccupation with the town curiosity. You said you are a physician. Doctors have an insatiable need to heal people. Let me assure you, I am in no need of healing. I simply prefer to live my days in solitude and to my knowledge that is as yet no crime. Since your questions here have been answered, I bid you Good Day," unleashed a very angry Edward Withers.

As Edward walked away with determination, Hamilton stood in a daze for a moment. He was unaccustomed to being dismissed as a child and Edward had accomplished his dismissal quickly and effortlessly. 'Who does he think he is?' Hamilton thought.

"I beg pardon sir, I assure you I had no such intention. You are correct in one case, you are quite the curiosity to those whom have encountered you and your temperament, no doubt is the object of their disdain. I shall take no more of your time," Hamilton retorted, but Edward paused only briefly, never looking back.

৪০০৪

Months passed and Hamilton had never forgotten Edward's callous words to him. He had sacrificed a perfectly pleasant summer morning for that journey, and never received so much as a kind word for his trouble. He reasoned that Edward must certainly be disturbed to lash out at someone completely unprovoked as he had done. Though the words still stung him, a chord of compassion struck him as well. Himself being the object of adoration and respect, he imagined how one would feel knowing himself to be feared and cursed, avoided at all cost, for he had seen grown men cowering in corners so as to avoid the man. It would be a most disturbing state he concluded. He would attribute Edward's conduct to such a state and forgive him.

Though he forgave Edward the unfortunate confrontation, it was his constant, underlying fear Edward would indeed require his services and he shrank from the thought of that imagined encounter.

Hamilton's fear was realized one wintry evening with a knock upon his door.

"Who the devil?" he mumbled, for he had just then settled himself in front of a fire and opened a new novel. He placed the book on a nearby table and answered the door. In the doorway stood a frail man he presumed to be in his late fifties.

"Can I help you, are you ill Sir?" Hamilton asked.

"Are you the doctor?" the man of slight build asked expectantly.

"Yes, please come in. What brings you here?"

The stranger made his way quickly to the blazing fire as he recounted his purpose for appearing on such a night. "My name is Paul. I was bidden here by the master of my estate. One of the servants is with child and the pain grows more intense. We have tried to help her but the master said we should call for you, he sent me to collect you, I was of no use there."

"I see, you were right to have come. I have delivered many children. Is this her first child?" he asked.

"Second," Paul replied.

"I shall gather my instruments and we'll be off, not a moment to waste in child birth. And it sounds like the woman is having a hard time of it. How long is the trip?"

"In this weather, maybe as much as three." he answered.

"Hours?" Hamilton questioned, "Is there no physician or midwife in your county?"

"Only you sir, you see the estate lies in the northern most region of the county, nothing there but land and mountains."

"The north, but there is only. . . Brookhaven?"

"You know the place, then?" he said sounding relieved.

"Oh yes, I know it," Hamilton answered. As he began to gather instruments and herbs, Paul said, "I was so pleased to find the warmth of the fire I almost forgot," and from out of his coat pocket, he offered Hamilton a folded piece of parchment. Hamilton opened the paper and stared at it for several moments, in a hastily written scribbling it read:

> Doctor Weatherly,
> Please come immediately.
> Your services are needed.
> I shall spare no expense.
> I beg of you,
> Edward Withers

Edward's short, direct sentences spoke of urgency and the closing "I beg of you" spoke of his regret. Hamilton understood. It would be the best apology he could expect and besides he had already forgiven Edward's harsh treatment. He accompanied Paul to Brookhaven and experienced a most harrowing night. Hamilton had not been untruthful when he said he had delivered many children, but of all his deliveries this one would prove to stand out in his mind.

Upon his arrival at Brookhaven he expected to be directed to the servant quarters but instead he was taken to a charming room in the main house where he found the brave young mother.

"Hello, I am Dr. Weatherly, I am here to help you. I shall prepare something to ease your pain."

Her eyes said thank you for it was obvious she could not summon the strength to utter the words. From a dark corner of the room a man's voice said, "Her name is Lily, she is my wife, please help us."

"I understand this is the second child, has your wife been ill during these last few months?"

"No sir. The baby has come early this time. I think that is why she is so afraid. Can you save her?" he whispered.

"I shall try, I shall try. What is your name sir?"

"Charles."

"Charles, it may sound unorthodox but I want you to go

to her. Take her hand and tell her you will not leave her side. She must be very frightened and she will need you to be her strength. Can you do this for me, for Lily?"

"Anything, whatever it takes," he answered.

After an examination Hamilton concluded the child was coming, but the source of Lily's pain was the unfortunate position the child had taken in moving to the birth canal.

After several hours of struggling with the surges of recurring pain, Hamilton asked Charles to take a short break while he gathered some additional supplies. In the linen closet he found what he needed and quickly returned to Lily's room. Before entering her door he heard a voice speaking to her. At first he thought it to be Charles', and stood quietly outside the door as to give them some brief moment of privacy. But upon closer examination, he realized the voice came from Edward Withers.

Hamilton continued to stand outside the door and he peered into the slight opening and listened. Edward stood by Lily's side and comforted her. Taking her hand Edward said, "Lily, I know you can fight this battle. You are a strong and brave girl. I know it is painful but all of this pain will be diminished with one look upon the face of your new little babe. Imagine that face, and with each piercing pain, remember this shall pass. Do not fret over anything. This young doctor will help you. Do as he says. Lily, Charles is the closest thing to family I have and I will do anything in my power to help you. I have never said as much to him, but it is times as these when such words are to be said. If there is anything you need, just ask and it will be yours. I will leave you to rest now."

Hamilton ducked into an adjacent room allowing Edward sufficient time to pass. Before returning to his patient, Hamilton took a long breath and continued with his duties. After two more sluggish hours passed he heard a knock upon Lily's door. He rose to answer and found Edward standing before him.

"Can you save the child?" Edward asked.

"Hours have passed already, it is the position of the child, we must wait until the baby has moved. Often in childbirth there is tragedy, but I promise to do all that is possible to save them both," he answered.

"It is just that I . . . no matter, I will leave you to attend to her."

In between the urgent moments of attending the young mother, Hamilton discovered Edward was to have left the following day for New York. Though Edward had summoned a physician, he postponed his travels until he was certain the young girl and her child were out of danger. 'It is no monster who behaves in such a way,' Hamilton thought.

The girl was frightened. Hamilton knew her first child had come so easily that she simply never expected these complications. Her fears were further heightened due to the unfortunate truth of her own mother having died giving birth to her. Hamilton had almost given up, he was weary from the stress of it all and he found himself asking for help from some higher power. 'I have done all that is humanly possible, someone, some force, some miracle please break this cycle of struggle. I fear Lily cannot go on much longer,' he thought.

In the following minutes the pain began to wash over her again. "Doctor" she whispered. He rose and began to massage her swollen abdomen again and though it was a subtle difference, he felt there had been a change. In the last few moments the baby had finally moved and was on its way into the world. As Hamilton brought the child into the cold world he felt a flood of gratitude he could not remember feeling before. Lily delivered a healthy baby girl. Hamilton laid the pink and screaming child in Lily's arms. She said nothing, but as she looked down at her new daughter, Hamilton witnessed a solitary tear trickle down her cheek and then her eyes closed completely.

Knowing her child was safe at last, Lily allowed her fatigue to overtake her and she settled into a much deserved sleep. Hamilton cleaned the child and swaddled her in a blanket and handed her to the distraught father. These miraculous moments where the reason he became a doctor. No matter what struggle had ensued before, the simple gratitude seen in the eyes of that young father absolved all of his efforts. No words could express it. No other profession could fill this space of wonder inside him. It was not the power over life, for he knew the power was not his, but to be an instrument of that glory was enough.

Hamilton packed his supplies and walked away quietly, his work having been done. When he reached the last step of the stairway, Edward met him and invited him into the rather large parlor. He followed.

"Scotch?" Edward offered.

Hamilton nodded in approval.

"It is a great thing you have done tonight," Edward said extending the glass to him.

Hamilton took a gulp of it and answered, "I have only done what I was trained to do."

"Nonsense, you have done more than perform some mundane, deliberate task. Unless they are teaching patience these days. I must commend you young man. There are many men who would have given up on that poor girl. But not you. We heard the screams, the pain which seemed to never cease, and now she lies in peace with her little daughter safe. Please accept our thanks."

"As you wish, sir," Hamilton replied.

Edward looked down at the small black bag by Dr. Weatherly's feet. "Surely you do not think I would allow you to return to your home after such a long and distressing evening. A room has been prepared for you. I took the liberty of having your dinner placed in your room and you may retire at your leisure."

"But Midnight, my horse?"

"In my stables, comfortable and fed. You needn't be troubled, but you may see him if you wish."

"That will not be necessary, thank you Mr. Withers."

"Edward, call me Edward."

"Edward, then, thank you, it is most appreciated, I assure you. It has been an exhausting evening and I think I shall retire, thanks for the drink, it was certainly needed."

Edward asked the housekeeper to show Hamilton to his room. The dinner which had been prepared for him was still warm and he devoured half of it in a moment without even tasting a single bite. His weariness from the child's birth superseded his desire to finish the meal and he crawled into the warm bed neglecting to even remove his boots.

Hamilton awoke the next day to the distant sound of a child crying. He splashed a handful of cool water on his face and went to look after the newborn. After finding mother and child in good health and explaining to the mother her various remedies, he proceeded to the main floor to say farewell to Edward. The place seemed eerily empty, but he knew the household was astir from the pleasant aroma of strong coffee. He followed the scent and it led him to a kitchen where Charles stood over a stove.

"Charles?"

"Oh good morning Doctor, would you like some breakfast before you leave?"

"Do not go to any trouble. Is it ordinarily so quiet here?"

"Somewhat, but Master Edward has left for a month or so and most of the other servants are taking holiday."

"So I have missed Mr. Withers then?"

Charles nodded as he flipped a small griddle cake.

"I say, you seem quite proficient at that, " Hamilton offered, impressed.

"And it is a good thing, it is my profession, you know," Charles responded with a smile, "Master Edward takes a yearly trip to New York and he had postponed the trip for my dear Lily. Once he was satisfied she was out of danger he took leave. He left before sunrise."

"Do you not take a break like the others when the master is away?"

"Well, now and then, but we still must eat you know."

"Right you are. I regret I was unable to speak with Mr. Withers this morning. But I shall return some day when there is more time."

"Of course, of course. And we'll look forward to seeing you again anytime, but I insist on making your breakfast. And Doctor, I thank God you were here for my Lily. Speaking of Lily, she'll be looking for her breakfast soon. I better get this tray up to her now. I'll be back to walk you out. I took the liberty of having the stable boy feed and saddle your horse."

"Many thanks. I gratefully accept your fine breakfast and will wait for you in the sitting room."

As Charles excused himself to attend to Lily, he handed Hamilton a plate covered with a cheese omelet and toast. He also placed a folded piece of parchment bearing Hamilton's on the table beside him. Hamilton noted the handwriting matched the letter he had received the previous night. Before partaking of breakfast he opened the sealed note. On the paper, in Edward's hand was written the following:

Doctor Weatherly,

I apologize for leaving so suddenly, but my appointments could no longer be ignored. I do appreciate your great efforts in bringing our Lily and her new daughter out of harm's way. If there is any way I may be of service to you in the future do not hesitate to announce your need. I have enclosed payment for your services which I believe to be sufficient. On my return to Brookhaven you must join me for dinner.
Edward

Behind the short letter Hamilton found a note made out to him for seventy-five U.S. dollars which caused him to nearly drop the note in his plate. He was utterly shocked. The payment was well over the amount he had expected, and nearly triple the amount he would normally receive for a similar service. And to add to his payment, Midnight had been fed and stalled in Brookhaven's stables, which to be sure were second only to the esteemed Ashford's stables. Edward had stated in his summons the day before he would spare no expense. Edward was a man of his word.

Hamilton folded the note carefully and placed it in his pocket. He felt a tinge of guilt in accepting such a generous offer, but he reasoned he had come a long way and the delivery had been very difficult. Upon finishing the omelet and feeling well satisfied, he went to the sitting room and began looking forward to the journey home. It was a beautiful countryside and nothing would clear his mind and return to him his most sacred sense of peace than becoming one with nature again. As he awaited Charles' return, he looked around the mansion and was still amazed that one man alone lived in the estate.

An estate of this size would require at least twenty servants to maintain its immaculate order, but Hamilton had only encountered four people during his entire stay. Just as he became comfortable in his surroundings Charles returned.

"Well now, are you quite ready to leave us Doctor? You may stay a bit longer if you wish, it has been nice having a new face in Brookhaven, it is rather uncommon for us to enjoy visitors."

"I appreciate the offer, but I have other patients I must

attend to".

"I understand, I shall show you out." Charles answered picking up Hamilton's bag and walking him to the front door. But Hamilton had spotted the sculpture of Emily and had been drawn to it and was quite immobilized.

"This is exquisite," Hamilton whispered.

"Indeed, but oh...please do not touch it," Charles warned, "Master Edward is quite protective of it."

"And I can see why. Such a beautiful work, this girl, she is beautiful. And there is something almost alive about her though she is fixed here in this marble. I shall ask Mr. Withers where he found such a wonderful piece of art.

"If I may, sir?" Charles asked.

"Yes?"

"I would not suggest asking Master Edward about the sculpture. I would not speak of it if I were you."

"You know him better than I and I have no reason to doubt you, but may I ask why?"

"Master Edward is kind man, but with a very strange and mysterious past. I oftentimes believe he is much older than he is in years, and that some unspeakable pain stole his youth. Only Lily and I and a handful of other servants have attended him for many years. We've been here for so long he treats us as his family. We know his ways. Outsiders do not understand him or his life, and so he allows us to live a good honest life here at Brookhaven. By securing us here he is assured he will not be required to expose himself further to the world. He only brought you here for Lily's sake. You are perhaps the first guest I have seen in the last two years. And this" he said, pointing to the sculpture, "this we have learned not to question".

"A few years back," Charles continued, "one our servants had to leave Master Edward's employ suddenly and another was sent in his place. He was a rather jolly sort of fellow and we all welcomed his enthusiasm and passion for life. But from the beginning, Master Edward could hardly endure his joyous personality. And one cannot blame him really, for it is true when one is sad, or angry with the world, it is quite unbearable to be in presence of a fellow who is happy with his lot, and not simply happy, but bouncing with energy and vitality while you are left brooding in your hopeless misery. It was this way for Master Edward and Henry, Henry was his name. Master Edward had long since left us all with instructions that he and he alone was to polish the sculpture. But his travels had left him away from Brookhaven for months and Henry had taken it upon himself to polish the piece.

As Henry approached the sculpture and began polishing it, it was as if Master Edward knew his most prized possession was being handled by someone other than himself, the doors of Brookhaven opened and Master Edward stormed into the hall. It is almost humorous looking back on it now, poor Master Edward had been away for months, longing to be here among his belongings, and who is to greet him, but Henry? Happy, happy Henry. And not only was Henry's smiling face a vision Master Edward had not wished to see, but even more dreaded a sight was Henry touching the object, which for Master Edward, held the utmost importance over all other possessions.

When he saw Henry he became enraged "What are you doing?" he thundered.

"But it has been months and it needed cleaning" Henry pleaded.

"Take your hands off of her" he answered back. "I made my wishes clear, you were not to touch her."

"But Master," he begged.

"Out, out of my sight!" Master Edward replied in a roar as he picked up the sculpture and stormed up the stairs to his room. Poor Henry was in tears. There was nothing to do but for him to leave us. Master Edward kept the sculpture in his room for months after the incident, and then finally without mention, returned her to her original spot. He has never spoken of it since and we know not to question his actions. So you see, it is best if you let it be. He has been most kind to me and my family, and though I am curious about his past, I have resolved it may forever be a mystery, and in truth it matters not, we live together in harmony and for that I am thankful."

"Right you are," Hamilton agreed, "What matters in life is having a kind of peace, finding contentment. I am sure his actions, like everyone's actions are a result of some past pain. I have observed his kindness for those close to him and I am more convinced than ever he is not the brute people think him to be. I only wonder how his strange view of the world came to be, but I will heed your warning and never speak of it or this beautiful sculpture. It is decidedly painful for him and for that I am most sorry. But I shall be going now."

"Thank you Doctor, for everything. And have a safe journey."

After a month or so Hamilton heard of Edward's return to Brookhaven. He hoped Edward would send for him. He had seen so little of the mansion and he wanted the opportunity to explore it with the attention it deserved. He was also curious as to how Lily and her new daughter were faring. Several weeks passed before he saw Edward again. Hamilton was attending to little Christian Faulkner, the mayor's youngest son. The child's condition required a very rare herb Hamilton had ordered from Egypt so that he might himself concoct the remedy little Christian needed. He opened the crate of bottles in the post office, and as he studied with care the numerous labeled bottles, a familiar voice called his name.

"Hamilton?"

"Good Day Edward, I see you have returned from your journey, did you enjoy the trip?"

"It was pleasant enough, I was sorry to leave so abruptly, but I trust you received my letter."

"Oh yes, I am glad I have the opportunity to thank you in person. I've been wondering how my patients are, do mother and child continue to be in good health."

"Quite good, but you can see for yourself if you like. The days are growing warmer now and the journey would be much more favorable than your last."

"I should like that, if it is no trouble, of course."

"None at all, plan to join me for dinner at Brookhaven one night next week."

"Next week then. Good day."

The following week Hamilton arrived unannounced at Brookhaven as Edward had suggested, on the fourth evening of the week. He found the sight of the estate took his breath away still, though it was his third visit. He arrived just as the sun seemed to cast a dreamy, yellow glow upon the lightly colored stone walls of Brookhaven. He shared dinner with Edward and talked on and on about his childhood and dream of becoming a doctor. He found himself sharing stories of his first experiences as a doctor, leaving his family, the day he purchased his prized Midnight and other special experiences of his life.

From the beginning, Hamilton noticed Edward did not offer much from his own past and he assumed Edward was simply one of those quiet, introspective souls who guarded oneself from others. He returned to Brookhaven several evenings but he began to feel the friendship was perhaps unwelcome. Edward had told him little, save that he had been alone in the world for most of his life. Edward never mentioned any women in his life, but Hamilton found it hard to believe Edward's stature and striking looks had not occasioned him to have had many love affairs.

Further evidence of Edward's personality were only to be gained by his taste in art and music. He had surrounded himself with beautiful things, in particular he had spied Edward giving especial admiration to the sculpture of the beautiful woman by Brookhaven's grand front doors. Edward seemed so taken with it, she seemed so personal to him, but ever mindful of Charles' warning, he dared not ask Edward about it.

Hamilton was a proud man and he had begun to feel uncomfortable with Edward's silence. He enjoyed spending time with Edward and the meals were exquisite when compared to his poor talent for cooking, but he did not want to believe he was somehow intruding on Edward's life. Edward seemed to prefer to be left alone so Hamilton decided after one final meal he would depart from the much loved place to return only upon Edward's request. As Hamilton suspected the weeks passed by and no word was heard from Edward. In the previous seven months they had shared dinner together once every two weeks and at present, five months had passed seemingly unnoticed by Edward. Hamilton had secretly hoped his absence would cause Edward alarm, but it had resulted in no such effect and Hamilton was forced to simply go on as before.

Before long another harsh winter was at hand. Already this year he had delivered three babies, set ten broken bones, healed various colds and viruses and lost four patients (one a horse), and he looked to the winter with a solemn prayer for mercy. The hardest struggle in his path was not bacteria, or any similar foe, but rather the formidable element of the bitter winter in this mountainous region. It was during this winter that he received the note from Edward regarding a young girl having found her way to Brookhaven.

Hamilton had not expected to be called back to Brookhaven, and he could not imagine a more serendipitous reason. The mysterious appearance of Lenora had allowed him to reconnect with his old friend, and he could only hope that he might connect with Lenora in a more meaningful way in the weeks to come.

Chapter 17
A Shadow of Doubt

On the morning following Christmas, Lenora awoke later than usual. Upon waking she was overwhelmed with an intense awareness that a fragment of her memory was desperately seeking to make its way into her consciousness. Perhaps it was a real memory or perhaps some lingering thought from her dreams, she could be certain of neither. Concentrating deeply on these thoughts, her gaze shifted slowly to the ceiling above, and as her eyes fell upon the circular design of the ceiling, it occurred to her that the design in the ceiling seemed strangely familiar. Her eyes followed the length of the edge of the ceiling and down the wall to the window. Almost mechanically she rose from the bed, as was her custom, and walked over to the window. She drew back the heavy drapes and turned away walking a few steps before turning back toward the window. She took a deep breath of cool air, closed her eyes, and then opened them again.

Truly it was as if she was seeing the room with new eyes, and with this altered perception, she thought, 'I have been here before. I know it. I feel I have spent hours looking out of this window.' Though the sensation was persuasive, the feeling made no sense to her practical mind so she attempted to push the feeling away. The feeling fled momentarily, but as she entered the hallway it returned. She shook her head. 'There it is again,' she thought, 'the hallway, four doors on either side and a stairway in the middle on the right.' She closed her eyes and concentrated 'behind the second door on the right is a small bedroom with a closet on the left and an oval window in the center of the room.'

When she opened her eyes she walked methodically to the aforementioned room and stood before its door, keenly aware she had never been in this particular room. Slowly she reached out and turned the knob, opening the door. She walked into the room, and there before her was a large oval window. She looked to the left and saw the small closet door. 'Could it be the dreams?' she wondered. 'What could this mean? I have not been in this room before today so how is it I remember every detail? How is it I know all the rooms of Brookhaven so intimately? As if I have lived here?' Again her thoughts turned to Edward. The sculpture. His story of Emily Talbot, there was the remote chance he could have made it all up to confuse her, but he spoke of Emily so prettily, she must have been real.

'What must I do now?' she questioned. 'All I have wanted is to remember, and now I have remembered, something, but elation is not the outcome as I had dreamed, I am only now more discontent than ever. Here is my a clue, a faint memory at best, but is it? And how can I question Edward after all he has done?' The previous few days had been so confusing to her weary mind. Her only hope had been stumbling upon Brookhaven, where memories and feelings were beginning to return to her. She did not fully understand how it had come to pass, but she believed this one event held a greater purpose and it would all eventually be revealed.

Anxious to share the news with Edward she quitted the room and went in search of her guardian. As she walked into the sitting room Edward greeted her with a hearty "Good morning!"

"I was afraid you had slipped away in the night and left us when you did not come down for breakfast," he said.

"I know you jest, for I could not be forced from this place for all the Christmas trees in the world." And she saw he appreciated her comment as she continued, "I suppose the holiday was much more exhausting than I imagined it would be, the preparations and the party, it was all so wonderful, I suppose I needed the extra rest."

Suddenly she decided against disclosing her revelation of remembering being at Brookhaven in her past. Edward had been so kind to her, and to return to a subject which had been bitter between them so recently was unwanted. She reasoned that her memories were certain to be fully restored, and at such time, when her thoughts were strong and true and not some tangled ball of yarn, she would feel comfortable sharing them. The events of the last few days were very confusing and she wanted to escape the entire matter if possible.

"Did you sleep well last night, Lenora?"

"Yes, quite."

"I only ask because I was compelled to your side again last night, another nightmare, but you were consoled in an instant."

"I knew I had dreamed last night, for its traces lingered in my mind this morning, but I remember nothing in particular, perhaps their grip is loosening."

"Perhaps."

"Would you mind terribly if I played the piano? It is too early for reading and I feel a need to play?"

Edward nodded in agreement and she took her place on the piano stool. In truth her desire to play came only to stifle her desire to speak to him about the eerie feeling consuming her with the discovery of remembering the room upstairs. She wanted to tell Edward about it, but it did not seem like the right time. She feared that he may misconstrue her questions as further misgivings on his part and nothing could be further from the truth, so she refused to act in any way which might alter the newfound trust between them. And further, she could not make a ruin of the wonderful Christmas memory they had shared together.

Her playing deferred the conversation for the present. As she played she suddenly became aware of the presence of another person in the room, and this feeling was confirmed as she heard the sound of whispers. The music stopped and she was flooded with applause from none other than Dr. Hamilton Weatherly.

"Lovely, Lenora, simply lovely. I must find a way to entertain you as you have entertained me." Hamilton offered with his applause.

"That is not necessary Dr. Weatherly, my playing was not meant for your entertainment, but I am glad you enjoyed it."

"We both enjoyed it very much" Edward offered.

"How are we to spend the day?" Hamilton asked gaily,

"We could go sleighing, or ice skating, or a book, or better, we could recite a play, do you like reading plays Lenora?" But just as she was about to answer his boisterous plea, Charles entered the room with a paper in his hand and his eyes were fixed on Hamilton.

"Dr. Weatherly, a note has just arrived for you," Charles announced, handing the message to Hamilton. Hamilton took the note from him with a raised brow and unfolded it, quickly scanned its contents, and then informed them of the bad news, "Edward, I am afraid I must take leave immediately. The Farmer Rogers' newborn son has taken a sudden turn for the worse. His birth and the first few days of his life were uneventful, and I cannot imagine what must be the source of his illness. Edward can I trouble you to borrow your sleigh once again?"

"Done."

"Must you leave at this moment?" Lenora interrupted, "Have you had any nourishment at all Dr. Weatherly?"

"You are kind to ask, but I am afraid I must take leave immediately. The snow is beautiful, but brutal and the time for the journey will be doubled as a result. I would like nothing better than to linger here with you and Edward, but I really cannot avoid a quick flight."

"I regret we will be deprived of your presence once again, but I admire your faithfulness to your work. And it is clear you are needed elsewhere," Lenora offered.

Edward affirmed Lenora's regret by adding "I do hate to see you leave so suddenly, I had hoped my two dearest friends could become better acquainted. Will you return soon?"

"I shall try, but I have not been home since the night Lenora arrived here at Brookhaven, and I feel I must make my way back to the city to obtain any correspondence which may have been left for me. As soon as the weather clears I promise to return, though it may be spring by then. I hope to have the pleasure of your company again Lenora. I should deeply regret not having the opportunity to amend our awkward conversation of last evening."

"I had hoped you had forgotten already, I have, " Lenora offered softly.

"Then I promise you it is entirely forgotten," Hamilton

answered.

Lenora held out her hand to Hamilton as a gesture of the mutual promise, and he took it in his, but instead of shaking it as she had expected, he kissed it. A wave of warmth washed over her and her heart began to beat rapidly, and though she desperately wanted to allow him to keep her hand in his, she retrieved it suddenly and looked at him with astonishment. Hamilton acknowledged her discomfort and looked at her with apologetic eyes.

"It may indeed be springtime before I return, can I expect to see you then, Lenora?" he asked, as both he and Edward waited patiently for her answer.

"I should hardly think I will remain at Brookhaven as late as the spring, though I've been assured it is a most beautiful time of year in this part of the land."

"Your sources are correct, and I would offer my own testimony, but I must be off now. May we meet again one day. And Edward, the party was a delight, thank you for receiving me so well though I was an unexpected guest, I shall call on you as soon as practicable." And then he added in whisper, "do convince her I am not as appalling as I have represented myself to be."

Edward simply smiled and walked him to the door.

૭૦౦3

The next few days passed by uneventfully and the inhabitants of Brookhaven were back to their normal routines. Brookhaven seemed so empty and dull without the Christmas tree, and the promise of the new year loomed heavily above one particular young girl. Lenora had come a long way on her emotional journey since the last New Year's Eve. The celebration of the New Year had been almost more than she could endure the previous year. She wondered if she would feel this burden if her life was restored to her. But here under the sheltering comfort of Brookhaven, she could face the night since it came without much mention.

Therefore, on the eve of the passing of the year of 1887, she lay across the bed and read the final letter from Elizabeth to John:

12 May 1804
Dearest John,
How can I tell you what I know will surely break your heart? It is as if I saw before me a beautiful angel just within my reach, but instead of embracing her and stepping into her glorious light, I was forced to tear from her head the glowing halo, and to chase away her soul-filling light. After several examinations our doctor confirms I have Consumption. John, it is a terrible sickness. The very disease that has spread so quickly across this land, and the worst of it, as you know, is there is no chance for survival. The doctors have tried everything, things you could not imagine. And they could only promise a few more months. How horrifying it must be for you to read these wicked words. At once I am in shock, in grief, but in a strange peace and state of acceptance. I do not understand why this is happening to me, to us, but I cannot question God's will. You must cancel your plans. Our future together cannot be. I love you as always, how I do love you, but I must release you from your obligation. Take solace in knowing if I had not loved you, then I would have never lived at all. Your love gave me more happiness than my heart could hold. I cannot bear to think of leaving you in a world I must soon depart. Just as you ordered the stars of heaven to protect me, I will protect you forever. I know it is difficult to face this news, but I've had many hours and days to contemplate what must be done. John, I know you cannot think about the future now, but one day you must live again with renewed hope. You are determined, loyal, successful, passionate and loving and more. I wanted more than anything to share my life with you but since I cannot, I am asking you to

find another with whom to spend your life. Please do not mourn me. You have spent so much of your life waiting for me already. In spite of this tragic news I know you are meant for greatness and you will live an extraordinary life. You have a magic surrounding you and I was a part of your spell. Our love was a dream that must wake, but you shall have other dreams my darling. You will find another love and have children and grow old together as we would have. . . I only ask you to keep a quiet place for me in your heart. Time cannot take away this love I have for you. Do not come for me John, for I cannot go with you now, and I do not want you to see me this way. Though I shall never see you again, I will keep your love close to my heart. I will not write again. This is my goodbye. I never thought I would say that word to you. You were the brightest part of my life and I shall love you beyond my days.   Elizabeth

The loving and selfless words Elizabeth offered John were painful to read and Lenora could not put a name to this feeling which came at the close of this final letter, but in truth the sad letter was not the last, for it had been answered.

2 August 1804

My Dearest Elizabeth,

I hope these words fall under your beautiful bright eyes before I arrive. Do you remember what you taught me about love? That God is the source of all love and love is best displayed in action not thought? How right you were, love is an action. It is not only a feeling, but it is so much more an action. And nothing could keep me away from you now. I understand you are only trying to protect me, but I must do what my heart demands. I am coming for you. I know I cannot bring you here, that we will not be here together, but I must see you one last time. You are

I cannot remember and he cannot forget

mine and I am yours. I am so shaken by this dreadful news and my entire life has been swept away on this black wave of death and I fear I am trapped in its fury. I am not prepared for a life without you. I am faced with the knowledge that my hope, and the future with you for which I worked so earnestly, so faithfully has vanished. Where can I go, What can I do to fill this void? Promise me you will wait for me. I should be by your side before October begins. I have revised my arrangements and it is my hope to arrive before these words reach you. I shall pray that God will keep you here on earth until I can see you one last time. All my love is sent before me. Wait for me Elizabeth, please wait for me. John

It was useless to fight the tears. Lenora's breaking heart and the steady stream of tears raised her temperature so that she stood and opened the grand window and allowed the crisp night air to embrace her. Through her moistened eyes the stars reflected even more brightly than was customary. Though she was chilled she could not stop gazing at them. The stars. Never changing. They were always the same. They had remained the constant watchers of man. They had led her to Brookhaven. They were the very stars John had offered his prayers to for the protection of Elizabeth.

As Lenora looked up at the stars, she whispered, "What I would trade for the passion of which they speak. I wonder if I shall ever know such happiness, but such pain too? Indeed, could I have already known it and simply not remember? No matter now, I am content to spend my days here with Edward. I very much want to remember, but somehow it seems less important now. Living here in this grand place has been a blessing. I am lost in my own little heaven here. I have all the books I could ever want to read and Edward's company. How I wish to reach out to him. There are times I see him, when I watch him from a distance and I can almost see Emily in his thoughts. I cannot remember and he cannot forget. We seem to be just out of reach of our dreams. Our desires lay in a constant state of waiting. Waiting for something, somewhere, someone. I wish to be contented, but this urgent need being unmet precludes me from my wish. I wonder if a time will come when I will have forgotten this present struggle. Oh Time, sweet Time, I wait for you. Only you can settle this matter. Speed your comfort to me. And stars, keep your faithful watch over me, lend your solace to me. Search you annals of wisdom and let me borrow it for a little while? Help me to find what it is I seek."

༄༅

    One by one the watchful stars faded into morning, offering the New Year's first day, but Lenora's body refused to wake. Visions of misery and of peace, intermingled with cries for help, invaded her thoughts. A dark door opened slowly as though inviting her in, but then closed as she reached out to touch its glowing light. Over the visions she could hear a somber voice repeating the words, "I'll be waiting, I'll be waiting." At present she existed in this disturbing dreamlike state, struggling to capture the fleeting dream from her memory, as it passed into nothingness, but she failed.

    Brookhaven began to stir and the aroma of freshly baked bread seeped into her room urging her to begin another day no matter how reluctant she may be. She wondered if today would pass as slowly as the previous one. But in a greater sense the days were slipping away so quickly that it was becoming exceedingly more difficult for her to accept the suspension of her life. She admired Edward's independence, his ability to carry out his daily life needing no one, but at the same time, it rendered her lost to his world. She wondered who he was, who he had once been. It was evident his current self was only a shadow of the man he had been before. But it was more than one's natural changing over time. There was something more definite about his metamorphosis. Though she felt a bond with him, he gave little of himself. Was it that there was little to give? No. Of that she was certain. Her only comfort was in saying a simple prayer for patience to endure the coming day.

    As soon as the brief words left her lips, a new confidence befell her. Days upon days had passed and she had come to love

Brookhaven, somehow it felt like home to her, as if she belonged here. As she passed the long corridor to the stairway she lingered over the large paintings along its tall, dark walls. She stood for several minutes before the painting of the child. She had since learned the child was Edward in his youth. His grandmother had commissioned the painting on his sixth birthday. With the knowledge her son and his family would be leaving their mother country, she wished to have a portrait of Edward in her home.

Many years after her estate had been settled, he had received the painting, together with the other possessions constituting his great wealth. There was something prophetic about the painting and the mature expression on the young face. It seemed to speak of a deep loneliness, but it was somehow a good sort of loneliness, as it also spoke of peace. She searched her thoughts to put a name to the strength of the countenance in the young face, but she was without words. Knowing the many losses Edward later sustained, she wondered if this child somehow knew the fate he was to endure: a life of painful losses, of poverty and then a reversal of fortune. Yet one would never know he was a wealthy man. In fact, Edward seemed to reflect more happily upon his days of poverty than any subsequent time or event.

When with him Lenora felt a certain peace and safety she hoped would remain long after she had left this beloved place. Edward's philosophy of life was simple yet granted him the freedom and peace many vainly hope to obtain. Lenora had learned much from him already and had come to admire his many commendable qualities. Loyalty. A loyalty he gave a chosen few. Loyal to consciously give his love and time for their sakes and not his own. A devotion to a fortunate few. Many have a number of acquaintances they are proud to drop the names of at important functions or in certain social circles. But to be one of the few to whom he chose to be devoted was to be cherished indeed for whom one was. Edward was loyal in his acceptance of others. Accepting peoples intentions, not their results. Not only accepting the limitations of the flawed world, but his accepting of the limits of himself as well as others. To those limits he lends gentle understanding. And his loyalty and acceptance lead to resolve. A resolve of knowing himself and the place in the world he wishes to be; being content with his resolutions, however grand or humble others may think them. His loyalty, acceptance and resolve lead to grace. A grace like the grace of God that encourages, empowers, inspires and endures.

Edward was a man of virtue, like none she had ever known. Lenora lingered by the portrait for a moment longer and then joined Edward in the library. She found him in a pensive mood, with one arm leaning against the glorious, mahogany mantle. The room was warm from the newly started fire. Edward heard the rustle of her dress across the floor and turned toward her.

"Ah Lenora, I am afraid I am at it again. I turn to these many companions for company," he offered gesturing to the thousands of books in his collection.

"Have you read them all, Edward?"

"Not entirely, but nearly. And from each I have added to my knowledge, I am constantly searching for a line from some volume or other of which I have remembered and cannot quite quote."

"I should like to choose one for today, but there are so many, can you suggest one of your favorites?"

"I shall make a list and you may read them every one!"

Edward and Lenora passed the entire day, reading and dining and resting without incidence.

Chapter 18
A Haunting Memory, an Icy Descent

Two weeks passed in much the same manner and a soft offering of morning's light began to pour over Lenora as she reluctantly awoke. She coveted these times of stillness when the world seemed fresh and new and full of hope. She tried to bring to mind the fleeting dream, but it escaped her as a delicate petal is blown about by the wind and lost in the vast sky. How strange it was that time alone had soothed her longing heart. No closer was she to the truth, but it seemed to matter less as she felt more and more a part of this strange and wonderful place. Everyone had taken her in and seemed to love her.

Brookhaven continued to cast its spell over her just as it had done from the beginning. It was hard to imagine being at home anywhere else. Still, she could not deny the nagging feeling that her presence was urgently needed elsewhere. There were times when she almost heard someone calling to her, but she had searched, she had meditated, concentrated all to no avail. It remained a mystery to her how this beautiful estate could provide her with such conflicting emotions. There was a certain overwhelming sense of security yet all the while, she also experienced the very opposite and opposing sense of the relentless pull of her past life, and the longer she remained at Brookhaven, the stronger she felt she should stay, and yet she felt compelled to leave its sheltering walls, for she knew uncovering her past would result in her ultimate return to it, wherever it may be.

Shaking the unpleasant thought from her mind and replacing it with the pleasing thought of the sun having finally broken free of the dark winter clouds, she walked towards her window and pulled the curtains aside. After adjusting her eyes to the brightness, she stared for several moments into the clear and deep blue sky. The brilliant blue seemed to enter her eyes and become a part of her as she took in the beauty and freshness it offered. Also in sight was the trickling streams of melting snow and while it would be days before she could travel, she nonetheless realized she would have to depart sometime soon. In order that she might enjoy the clear new day, she pushed the curtains aside exposing as much of the windows as possible and then began her daily ritual of dressing.

Lenora was completely comfortable here and wished with all her heart she did not have to leave Brookhaven. She was weary from all of the tireless searching. Searching for answers that never seemed to come. Day after day she struggled to regain her memories. "Maybe today I will remember," she said looking at the girl in the mirror who was becoming less and less of a stranger. Though she struggled to remain hopeful, some greater force permeated her mind and she began to wonder... 'I cannot fight this sense of dread. I feel that someone waits for me. That their very life depends upon me. Oh, what have I done? Two years I have lost and nothing. From where and whom does this voice call to me? Oh sweet urgency, be still for now. I shall listen to you, and, in time, I shall answer. Already I am closer to you. I feel your presence here in this place. Lead me. Help me to find you,' she pleaded hopefully.

As she opened her door, a stream of sunlight illuminated a small recess at the end of the hallway which she had never noticed in all her weeks at the estate. Lenora walked across the hallway to the little niche and fancied the dark little corner would be the perfect place for her to meditate or read a few lines from a favorite book of poetry. She sat down on the plush little bench in the sunlit corner and suddenly a wave of panic crashed over her. 'I have been in this very spot before,' she thought. 'From where does this sadness come and to where does my very breath escape?' Her breathing became labored. Voices. Muffled. Heartbeat. Pounding. Eyes. Searching.

"Edward!" she cried out, "Edward!" By this time she had attempted to stand, but then her knees buckled and she found herself on the floor holding tightly to the bench.

In an instant Edward was by her side, "I'm here Lenora, what is the matter?" he asked, reaching down to return her to her seated position on the bench.

"This place, this enclosure, I have been here before. I know it. I had never noticed this little recess before. There was ray of light falling upon it and I decided to spend a moment of quiet with my poetry. I walked over to the bench, took a seat, and then it happened. I began to feel very ill and I could hear voices. Oh Edward it frightens me so."

"Voices?" he asked, "But it was only my voice you heard. I was just on the stairs and speaking with Charles about our menu for this evening."

"But. . .yes, I imagine that is true, but why should this feeling appear so suddenly? Must it not mean something? I am frightened Edward, for this is not a dream, I am very much awake."

"But I am with you Lenora, and I shall not leave your side. Though I am confident there is nothing for you to fear, I am perplexed by this attack as well. Lately, I have observed your keen knowledge of Brookhaven. Though we have not discussed the matter, it is difficult to dismiss those times when you know something of her, something it would be uncommon for a stranger of her to know. Come, let us take you to your room. You must try to rest, dear. And I shall think of something to chase away these fears. Perhaps I should send for Hamilton?"

"No, no I shall be all right, I should hate to trouble him when he is needed elsewhere."

"As you wish but be assured, Hamilton would be delighted with the opportunity to see you again... I will escort you to your room."

Edward led her to her room and left her there to rest. But rest would not come. The feeling had been too strong to ignore. Days had stretched into weeks and she seemed no closer to discovering her precious past, yet this force speaking to her was stronger and stronger. She feared if she did not escape these thoughts, the weighty world upon her shoulders would smother her. Her only solace would be to join Edward in some activity that may occupy her thoughts and thereby put today's strange events behind her, if even for a few moments.

Later, when Lenora joined Edward, he asked, "I trust you found rest? And I have done as I promised, I have an idea for you to consider. Would like to join me this afternoon? You have been isolated within these walls far too long and I think a day in the sun will do us both good."

"Edward! That sounds splendid and just the remedy," she said smiling.

"I must warn you of the sun's deceit, it appears as a summer day, but it is nearly freezing so you must dress warmly, the winter wind is bitter and unforgiving. I will have the sleigh and my best horse ready in an hour and we shall take food and drink. I would like to show you the rest of the estate. Is an hour enough time for you?"

"Oh yes, I shall be ready."

When the sleigh was carefully packed and ready, Edward found Lenora in the sitting room and asked her to follow him.

"You chose your clothing well, I have blankets for the trip which shall ensure our comfort."

Edward led her through the front doors where his beautiful red and black sleigh awaited. The sleigh had been crafted in New York and would seat up to four passengers comfortably, and was a necessity in this land which was covered in snow and ice for the better part of the winter. Lenora sat on the plush velvet seat. The interior was a rich shade of red, and the frame of the sleigh was shiny and black.

"It is a winter paradise." Lenora said as she looked with wonder all around her. Everything was still covered in snow, and all was white except the sharp blue sky above and the dark green evergreens in the distance. She loved this land, but it was completely unfamiliar to her. She imagined she could spend the rest of her days here and be happy. This was a place where she could disregard the past and build a new future.

"I had forgotten how blue the sky can be," she said.

"Yes. I hardly mind the cold on such a bright day. But alas, there is still some trace of sadness in your eyes. What troubles you?" Edward asked.

"You know me too well, Edward. I so wanted to escape my thoughts, but perhaps they will weigh lighter on my mind once shared. I continue to be plagued by these sensations of some past time in my life being spent here at Brookhaven. The incident this morning was the strongest such feeling, but there was another incident which has troubled me over the last few weeks. I did not want to trouble you at the time, but I can no longer avoid disclosing these thoughts. I awoke the day after Christmas and had the most queer feeling I had been at Brookhaven before, and the feeling was confirmed by an event which followed. As I passed a certain room in the hallway, I realized I had not been in the room before. I pictured the room in my mind, and when I entered the room, it was exactly as I had remembered. The furniture was different, but otherwise, I knew the dimensions of the room, the oval window, the closet. I knew the room, as if I had been there before. And earlier today, in the hallway niche, the feeling was overwhelming. I know we discussed the possibility before, but do you think it is possible I could have been here before?"

"Lenora, I thought we settled this, I thought you believed me."

"And I do, I do, Edward. I promise I am not accusing you of hiding the truth, but I cannot deny my sense of familiarity with Brookhaven, could I have been here at some time when you were away? You did mention spending much of your time in New York."

"It is simply impossible. I have been away, but Charles, Lily, the rest of the staff have been with me for years and certainly they would have come forward. Perhaps you visited the room in these last several weeks, and have forgotten, there are so many rooms in the estate?" Edward suggested.

"That could easily be the case, except that I am certain I never entered that particular room before."

"Well, as I told you before I have lived here for nearly fifteen years. There have been times when I have traveled extensively, times when I have left Brookhaven for months at a time, but I assure you only the staff was left here to maintain the estate, cleaning, correspondence and managing the estate in general. I cannot imagine it could be possible that you were ever at Brookhaven in the past. I do wish I could explain these strange coincidences for you, but I simply cannot."

"I suppose that is just what these feelings are,

coincidences. But disturbing nonetheless."

"Come now, Lenora, let us think joyful thoughts today. I feel responsible for you since you are a guest in my home and I want to make your stay as pleasant as possible," he pled with a looked begging confirmation.

"Yes Edward, you are right. It is all simply a matter of time. The answers will come and until then I will enjoy this blessing of being under your care. You have been so kind, I shall have to leave soon and I want to enjoy these last few days."

"But why must you leave?" he asked quickly as if she had said something ridiculous.

"Edward, I cannot impose on you any longer. You have given me kindness, a place to rest, a place to ease my loneliness. I cannot continue to impose on your generous nature."

"But I have enjoyed your company. I suppose I was as lost as you are in my own way, and I was very much alone until I reached out to a stranger on a cold night and found you. And forgive me, but you have no one to go to, no place you can remember, I invite you to stay as long as you wish," he offered.

"But I fear if I stay here too long, I shall lose myself forever. If I allow myself the comfort of Brookhaven, I may never want to find my past. But it pleases me to know you would have me stay, and I agree it is for the best I should stay a bit longer," she agreed.

"Good, now that it is settled, let us take a stop here, I have a surprise for you," Edward said, stopping the sleight and quickly feeding the horse. Then he walked over to Lenora and helped her down, as he retrieved a large bag and asked her to follow him. They walked for approximately a quarter of a mile to what appeared to be a pond. The wind whipped passed them giving them a chill.

"It is so peaceful here and serene, was this a pond?" she asked.

"Yes, it is completely frozen," he replied, as she curiously watched him opening the bag. From it he removed two pairs of ice skates. Lenora smiled, she was pleased.

"How wonderful, but I do not know if I know how..."

"No matter, I shall teach you. These skates are very old but I think they will make a good fit, try them," he offered, handing a pair of skates to her. Lenora slipped the right skate on and it was a little loose but she would not mention it to him.

"Perfect fit," she said.

"Now, you will feel a bit unsteady for a few minutes. Just walk along the pond's edge until it feels more comfortable," Edward instructed as he laced his own skates.

Lenora moved very purposefully along the edge of the frozen water. She could not wait to try them out. She looked at Edward and smiled. She would have never guessed she would be spending the day with him gliding upon the ice. He was continuously surprising her.

"All right, my dear, how are you fairing?" he asked.

"Oh, I feel a bit wobbly but I want to give it a good try," she replied.

"Take my hand, I will guide you, I will not let you fall." Lenora offered her hand and Edward slowly guided her across the ice to the middle of the white, frozen pond. With each movement she felt more sure of her balance, and before long she skated away from him quite confidently, and it occurred to her that ice skating was something she most certainly had done before. The serene countryside with its boughs of snowy pines, with its symphony of winter wind, and the chilly air, the kind of air making one feel vibrant and alive, provided the perfect setting for Lenora to forget her concerns.

A childlike feeling came over her, freeing her from any thought or feeling save for joy alone. The urging voices had at last been silenced. Edward watched her expressions and was aware of her new found freedom and his heart was lifted too knowing he had eased her mind with the day's activity. They had skated for almost an hour when Edward began to become fatigued, for he was not as proficient as she on the ice, nor did he share her youth. He motioned to her his need for a short rest and she answered she would join him in a few moments.

Edward skated to the edge of the pond, removed the skates and spread a blanket over some nearby logs and sat down. He watched her gliding across the ice, 'how wonderful it would be to be young and carefree again,' he thought. Naturally his mind wandered remembering the days of his youth. He marveled at how bravely and boldly he taken Emily away in the stillness of night to marry her. How young they had been then, she underage, but Emily was what one would call a classic beauty, she walked with an air so refined, she spoke with intelligence and grace, and therefore it was no surprise the constable was easily deceived.

Their wedding was a simple ceremony, exactly what they had wanted, the two of them and God. He could almost still feel her lips pressing gently on his, and the unique feel of her long silken hair in his hands. If only he could be in her presence again, if God could grant him one wish it would be to hold her just once more. But all of those happy thoughts were mired in the agony of having lost her. Years, wasted. Years, and a deep despair for what could have been. But he strove earnestly to remember the joyful days and moments, for he would not allow her father any victory. Even though in the end Mr. Talbot took Emily from Edward, he could never take away the love still brightening Edward's heart.

Leaving those thoughts for a moment, he looked up to watch Lenora as she whizzed by smiling. "Well done!" he offered. Her gracefulness and ease on the ice persuaded him to join her before they took lunch. As he re-laced the second skate, he heard a strange noise. He looked up quickly and saw an empty sheet of white, save for one small, dark opening.

"Lenora!" he shouted frantically, "Lenora, Oh my God, No. No!" he pled. He tied a quick knot with the laces and flew madly across the ice, praying "God, please save her, God, help *me* save her!" When he reached the edge of the cracked opening in the ice, he dropped to his knees, desperately searching for a glimpse of her, but there was nothing in sight but the icy water. Panic-stricken, he thrust his right arm into the freezing water with fierce force and thrashed it about the icy waters but could feel nothing but its shocking sting.

"Lenora, I am here, I can help you, Lenora," he shouted over and over as he continued to sink his arm into the icy depths. Just then he felt something, it was her arm. Edward gripped her forearm tightly and with all his might pulled. He kept pulling her up as far as he could. Her head was extending out of the water now, she was conscious but moving very little.

"Lenora, can you hear me, can you hear me child?" he screamed.

But no answer would come, she could only look at him blankly. He looked at her squarely in the eyes and began to speak loudly and slowly, "Lenora, I can pull you up. But I need your help, just stay awake. Stay with me. When I count to three I want you to use all of your energy to lift yourself up. All right, one!, two!, three! With all of his strength, and with all of her will to live he managed to rescue her from the chilling water. He carried her swiftly as his strength would allow to the pond's edge. As Edward's arm soiled the white ground red from the gash the ice had ripped into it, he placed Lenora on the bank where he had been sitting moments before. He knew not what to do next. Should he start a fire, or should he take her to Brookhaven? They were fairly close to the estate, but it would be nearly half an hour's journey. Returning her to a place of warmth immediately was his utmost concern and he quickly elected to take her back to Brookhaven.

"Lenora, I am going to carry you to the sleight now. I will take you home to Brookhaven and I will get help for you, can you speak?" he pled, holding her head tenderly in his hands. He searched her eyes.

She looked at him and blinked, "Help me . . . I, I," she managed to whisper, but could say no more.

"I shall do all in my power to help you. I will have you safe and warm very soon. I will wrap you in these blankets and here take a drink of this hot cider, it will warm you."

He was able to get a little cider into her, but he knew he must begin the journey back to Brookhaven as soon as possible. With as much speed as he believed his horse could endure, he led them back through the path. Edward had taken the same route to the pond many times, but in this instance time seemed to linger on if it moved at all and he was filled with a matchless despair. The wind was unfaltering and he knew he must not waste a second. At last they reached the gates of Brookhaven, and when there he gently took her in his arms, as the wind spit and howled behind him, and carried her into the sitting room where Charles had recently built up the fire. The room was warm and quiet.

"Charles! Charles! I need your help." Edward summoned.

As Charles raced to greet Edward he discovered it had presently begun to snow, as witnessed by the front door having been left open by Edward.

"What the devil?" Charles muttered as he closed the door with a chill and followed the wet footsteps into the sitting room.

"Master Edward! What happened? Miss Lenora, she is soaked. And Master, you are bleeding," Charles said, with more than a little alarm.

As Edward gently placed Lenora on a chaise by the fire, he explained the terrible event, "Charles, I took her to the ice pond just beyond the oaks and we were ice skating, and she…..there was apparently a thin spot in the ice and it broke beneath her. I brought her here as soon as possible, the snow is getting stronger, but I must collect Hamilton or she may not recover. She was in the water for several minutes and she can hardly even speak, can you prepare a hot soup and have Lily get some dry clothes for her?"

"Why yes of course, but we must see to your wound."

"It is nothing, only a minor abrasion, and we must attend to her, there is no time to waste."

"Certainly, go now if you wish, what supplies shall you require, the weather, Sir, can you make it there?"

"I know not, I know not Charles, but I must go for help, I cannot let her perish, I cannot. I shall take the sleigh, but have young Harry ready the new gelding and another strong horse, I have exhausted my best horse in my attempt to return Lenora to warmth."

"I shall see to it right away. I understand, you must hurry, I shall pack a few things for you and I shall take care of our Lenora."

"Thank you Charles, I go to change into dry clothes myself and then I shall be off. I will return with Hamilton, I will find a way."

Edward changed very quickly, grabbed a bag of supplies and set out to bring Hamilton to Lenora's aid. The horses were hesitant to move forward in the slippery depth of the new fallen snow, but it was their usual path and with a little encouragement, Edward forced them to drive ahead. He rode off vowing to return, praying to return before it was too late.

Chapter 19
A Disclosure

Inside Brookhaven all was quiet. Lenora had been changed into warm clothing and was lying comfortably in her room beside a raging fire and under many heavy blankets. Lily was sitting by her side, praying for her recovery. Lenora's mind was a flood of images and thoughts as she slept quietly. Though she appeared serene as an angel, images of her past tormented her mind. She saw the face of a young woman whom appeared to be her mother, but somehow she sensed she was not her mother at all. She saw herself as a child sitting with the woman playing a beautiful old piano. The music was lovely and it was the same song Lenora had played for Edward so many times, the one she had remembered. The beautiful song hovered about the visions as a ghost.

Later she saw herself as a young woman, entering the room with the piano where she had once sat with the young woman, but there was no longer any music in the room. Suddenly her heart felt a pain she had forgotten, a pain begotten by her finding the woman had disappeared one night. Abandoning her as it were, with no goodbye. The young woman had been her governess and had showered upon Lenora all the love her heart could hold. Why had she left so suddenly? Years passed in her mind, as only a moment, and an intense memory began to take shape: she remembered hiding in a dark hallway niche listening to people talking.

The voices were those of her parents. And she was the subject of their conversation. She could not make out what they were saying. Next she found herself in her childhood bedroom. A small writing desk sat in one corner of the room and was nicely appointed with an ink well, a fine leaf collection and a variety of books. In the other corner a stately antique bookshelf was adorned by a collection of exquisite china dolls. Suddenly her attention was drawn to a brilliant light. The light blocked everything in sight except the source of the light, which was a large, oval window in the center of the room. A feeling of anxiety suddenly took hold of her, and when she blinked, the room had changed into the room on the second floor of Brookhaven. As suddenly as the light turned to darkness her attention was now drawn to the sound of a piano. Then the music began to play louder and louder, and she listened intently to find its source. She looked everywhere for where it was coming, but she could not find it. And then the voice of her sweet friend silenced the music. The voice uttered those familiar three words, "I'll be waiting" and Lenora began to weep until all the visions and all the voices went black.

ಣಲ

There was a knock on Lenora's door, "Come in," Lily whispered.

"Lily, how is Lenora, is she still sleeping?" Charles asked.

"Yes dear, I think we have her warm enough, her shivers have stopped. She has not opened her eyes, but she sleeps in a world of dreams, she was moaning only moments ago, but I could not make out her words. Poor thing, I hope Master Withers returns soon," Lily answered.

"I am keeping watch for him, remain here until I return."

"Of course. Charles, what should we do if he loses her?"

"I fear there would be nothing we *could* do, she has changed him so, and if he should lose her now, I dare say it would finish him . . . and so we must pray she returns to us."

"I have already begun to pray and I shall not cease, go now and be ready for his return."

Several hours passed with no change in Lenora's

condition. Charles began to fear the worst. He prayed Edward would return safely, he did not know what else to do. After checking on Lenora a second time, he asked Lily to keep watch over Lenora through the night. Charles checked in on his own girls and then made a pot of strong coffee so he might keep his wits when Edward returned. Just as the coffee began to wear off and Charles found himself drifting into a restless sleep, he awoke to the sound of horses driving up to the main house. He grabbed his boots and a coat and rushed towards the front door. The night air bit him as he rushed down the steps to assist Edward.

"I am so pleased to see you, Sir, Lenora is safe and warm inside, but she has yet to wake. Good Evening Dr. Weatherly, let me take your bag."

"Hello Charles," the young doctor said, handing his bag to Charles.

"Charles, can you prepare something hot for us to drink?" Edward asked.

"I shall fetch it for you as soon as we go inside."

"Thank you Charles, have the horses seen too, we've given them a rough ride."

"Immediately, Sir."

They came into the keeping room of the house and were embraced by the warmth of the fire. Charles went to the kitchen to prepare a fresh pot of tea and Edward and Hamilton warmed themselves by the fire.

"I must thank you again for joining me here so late, let me take you to her now."

"Edward, my friend, I am in the business of saving lives, you do not have to thank me, besides, I would rather enjoy seeing this young woman again. I feared I may never see her again, but I regret it must be under these circumstances. I only met her briefly, but I found her to be as charming a person as she is lovely."

"Hamilton, she is a delight. However, she is very fragile. She has apparently had a very troubled past. As you know, she suffers from some form of amnesia. She has been here for many weeks, and she still has no clearly defined memories of her past."

"Perhaps she does not want to remember."

"But, on the contrary, she is desperate to remember," Edward responded.

"I am certain she says so, but I propose that on a deeper

level, perhaps her past is something she has locked away, but no matter. What is of importance now is we restore her physical health," Hamilton suggested as they walked to Lenora's room.

Hamilton walked over to Lenora and began to examine her and Edward stood watchfully close by. After a thorough examination he looked at Edward and said, "My friend, you were right to call for me, she has suffered an intense shock. There are signs of frost bite as well, how long was she in the soaked clothing?"

"I suppose it was just under an hour, I brought her here as soon as possible. I wrapped her in blankets to keep her as warm as possible until I could return her to safety." Edward replied.

"Did she say anything, was she conscious at all?"

Edward paused, averted his eyes to the ground and said slowly, "She did say 'help me,' but her eyes seemed very glassy and distant, I do not think she could see me."

"All right, we will need to keep her warm and I will prepare a special tea for her. I shall treat her wounds with a salve and I think I shall be required to monitor her progress for the next few days."

"But will she recover?" Edward pleaded.

"I shall do all I can Edward. I must be honest with you, she is very ill and I do not know what damage has been done. From what you have told me she is a courageous young woman, and I assure you one of the best indicators of one's recovering from a situation as this is simply one's will to survive."

"Thank you for your honesty, but what can I do to help her now? Is there anything I can do?"

"You came for me Edward, which is the very best thing you could have done, she is very important to you isn't she?" Hamilton asked.

"Yes, as I confessed to you before. I have come to care for her very deeply, in a very short time she has brought a sense of happiness I had lost in my joyless life, and further, somehow I have come to feel responsible for her, and now this. It was only a few hours ago I heard her laughter and now she lies here almost lifeless and cold. Hamilton, what have I done?" Edward asked almost in a whisper. Hamilton saw the desperation in Edward's eyes.

"Edward," Hamilton said comfortingly, grasping his broad

shoulder, "you are not responsible for this unfortunate accident. As usual you torture yourself over events which are not under your control. Lenora is resting comfortably and I suggest that after I have seen to her most urgent needs, you and I share one of your best bottles of Scotch and have one of our long talks."

"You are right my friend, please continue with your examination. I shall stay out of your way."

As Hamilton assessed Lenora's needs, Edward sat down quietly in the corner of her room and prayed she might awaken.

Hamilton requested boiling water be brought to her chamber and took from his bag the various herbs and roots he needed to prepare a strong tea for when she woke. In addition he saw to the tiny cuts on her arms which her thrashing about had caused, and treated the irritated areas of her skin with a special ointment he had formulated. As he treated her wounds an overwhelming sense of sadness befell him. On first thought he assumed it was merely empathy for Edward's pain, but each time he looked upon her face, it was clear his sadness stemmed from his own pain, a very solid fear that Lenora might be taken from them both before he had the opportunity to know her as intimately as he had hoped.

Hamilton had teased her on his last visit that he might not return until springtime, which was his intention at the time, but since he had left Brookhaven that same afternoon, rarely a moment had passed in which he had not thought of her, and how he had botched their first encounter, and now he was here as he had dreamt, but uncertain if she would ever wake. He looked upon her face once more as she expressed a tiny whimper, but she would not return this night. Hamilton was satisfied there was nothing left to be done for Lenora and with compassion explained to Edward that they must simply wait.

"Very well then," Edward began, "I will meet you in the gaming room, but I would like to spend a moment alone with her."

"Of course, I shall ask Charles to fetch a bottle, take your time," Hamilton offered.

Knowing he had done all in his immediate power for Lenora, Hamilton's awareness of the rest of the world returned. And in this sudden awareness, he noted a dark stain on the sleeve of Edward's right arm, and the stain appeared to be wet.

"What's this?" he asked pointing to Edward's arm.

"It is simply a cut," Edward replied nonchalantly as if the spot were no more than an insect bite.

"A cut? Edward, let me examine it." Hamilton demanded.

Edward extended his arm revealing it to his young friend, never removing his eyes from the sleeping Lenora.

"My God man, you require stitches for this *cut*! I must clean the wound right away or you shall become infected," Hamilton ordered.

"Not now!" Edward growled impatiently, glancing at his arm for the first time, and seeing that the rags he has hastily used to cover it had become soaked through. Seeing the ugly gash again on his arm, suddenly brought forth the pain he had up until that moment managed to avoid.

"But soon, Edward, *soon*. I really must insist," Hamilton implored.

"All right, all right, I have said I shall only be a moment. There was no time, you see, to consider my own simple pain, I should have you cut off this arm if it would save her."

Hamilton did not answer, but left his friend alone as he sensed Edward's deep need to stay by her side. Once Edward was alone with Lenora, he walked over to her bedside and looked upon her face for several minutes. He had memorized every line, each beautiful feature. Even in this state she was completely beautiful. Leaning over her and whispering into her ear he began to speak, "Lenora, it is I, Edward, I am here with you, and you are safe here at Brookhaven. I do not know if you can hear these words but I must say them anyway. I am sorry this happened to you. But it has happened and you are going to be fine, just fine. You must feel very weak, but you are such a strong girl, and you have my word you will never be left alone. We will stay here with you until you come back to us. Lenora, you must know your presence here has changed me. I need to thank you, for your kindness, your gentleness. I shall be here, I shall not desert you. Only come back to me. Come back."

Edward did not want to leave her side, but he knew he must. He reluctantly went downstairs to join his friend. He found Hamilton in the gaming room as promised. He stood quietly by the fire and Edward noted a bottle of Scotch and two empty glasses had been placed on the card table.

"I'm here Hamilton."

"Ah, I've abstained from drink until I see to your *very*, minor cut, but a shot or two may very well be in order for you Edward," he offered, with his usual friendly sarcasm. Edward took a double shot of scotch as prescribed.

"Okay, Hamilton, do what you must," Edward bravely offered, as he removed his shirt.

Hamilton sat Edward in a comfortable chair and placed a lantern on a nearby table. He cleansed the wound as Edward clenched his teeth and then stitched the wound so as to not leave a hideous scar, which would have surely been the result had he not dressed the wound.

"That shall do for now. The stitches should be removed in two weeks or thereabouts. I shall do it myself if I am here, and I should think I should be," he offered, with no response from his patient. After finishing his tedious task, he made his way to the card table and poured two more glasses of scotch.

"I took the liberty of pouring a second glass for you, here have a drink with me, to Lenora's health," Hamilton offered, handing Edward a glass.

Edward took the drink in hand and held it up for a moment and then brought the glass to his lips, and took a long drink of it. But the taste of it sickened him and was poison to his senses, and with a grimace he placed the glass on the table beside him. So many nights he had sat by the fire, alone, drinking scotch of this very label, trying to chase away haunting memories. The taste that once comforted him, now revolted him, as it was only a reminder of all the wasted years.

"Is the scotch to your liking?" Hamilton asked, sensing Edward's disapproval.

Edward paused briefly, pondering whether he should be honest or simply carry on with the niceties one says and the other usually wants to hear. Frankness won the battle. "No. It is not to my liking at all. In fact, it has never really been to my liking," he said dryly.

"Forgive me Edward, but we have invariably drunk scotch together, or am I going mad?"

"I have drunk many bottles of this amber, numbing liquid, but it was not the taste of it I wanted, it was the effect. I wanted to forget, but now I find myself wanting to remember and anything that is an obstacle to my effort I dislike."

"I do not know what to say that."

"Then say nothing at all. Can two men not share a few moments of silence? Must we have to go on and on with idle chattering?" Edward said roughly.

"You are tired Edward. I will leave you to your brooding. It has been a long day, and I will join you in silence as I warm myself by the fire. I shall trouble you with my chattering no longer."

Edward nodded as if to say, "do as you will."

Chapter 20
A Life and a Death

Hamilton and Edward stared into the fire as each of them thought of their own individual concerns. Edward was spent, he knew he would not be able to sleep until he knew Lenora would recover. He had allowed Emily be taken from him, but death would not claim Lenora as well. He suddenly realized how much he had come to depend on her and how utterly empty his life had been these last few years. He surveyed his wealth, the estate and the priceless treasures which filled its halls. He considered each piece of art which he had carefully purchased, eventually comprising a collection from all parts of the world. He had the power and the wealth Emily's father had so feverishly wanted for her. He had proven himself. He had reached every goal, climbed every mountain, as it were, but nothing could fill his heart as she did.

Where was Winston Talbot now he wondered. This man who had stolen Edward's chance for a happy life. This man who had taken his future which had seemed to Edward so certain and incapable of being altered.

Edward remembered the series of event which would change the course of his life as if it were only yesterday. . .

Edward had been approved for a leave from his studies for half of the upcoming year, in preparation for his marriage. It was uncommon to marry before graduating or acquiring a position, but nothing in Edward's life was common. Edward and

Emily were to secretly marry in Oxford and begin their bridal tour a week from the ceremony in Rome. After the brief ceremony they returned to the quaint Inn Edward had arranged to be their week's home. He was afraid Emily would be nervous, but she, like him, had waited long and patiently for this night, and in truth, she had never been more prepared for anything in her life.

Upon their arrival, Emily disappeared into the washroom, leaving Edward to unpack the few items they had brought with them. Although his bride had only left his side for a few moments, he believed she was taking a rather long time, and he began to fear she may be frightened concerning what may be expected of her in the coming moments. He hastily unpacked their bags, dressed himself in a fashionable robe, and began to make the room more comfortable for her. He took a moment to turn down the bed covers, but then he suddenly drew them back not exactly knowing why. He grew more impatient by the moment, and in this restless mood decided to extinguish the candles yet burning, but once he had blown them out, the room appeared too dark for his liking, so he opened the top half of the shutters allowing a bit of moonlight to illuminate the room.

'Yes,' he thought 'this natural light makes for the perfect setting.' He stood by the bedside with his eyes fixed on the door which separated him from his bride, and then the door squeaked and she emerged from behind it. Emily walked towards him in the blue light of the moon, her hair cascading down the front of her body as if it were a fine garment, and with each step that carried her closer to him, his heart pounded stronger and more violently in his chest.

As he beheld her in this palace of shadows, she was more beautiful to him than he imagined she could have been. And at last she stood within his reach with longing in her eyes, but he was motionless, speechless before her. Her breathing became labored within those moments of silent, urging, passion and he began in a whisper, "my darling, you are so fair, as a creature too perfect for this flawed world...I...I am almost afraid to touch you."

She smiled softly in answer to his exalted thoughts of her, and then brushed her hair away from her body and over her shoulders in one adroit motion, allowing herself to be fully exposed to him as her hair tumbled down her bare back. He swallowed deeply as his eyes feasted on his new bride, but still he was unwilling to touch her delicate skin. As his eyes met hers again, he seemed to read in them her pleading "do not make me wait a moment longer," and in truth these words expressed her feeling precisely.

Emily felt a certain aching, burning feeling she was unable to resist and she took his hand in hers and placed it against her breast and said softly and soulfully, "Edward, do not be afraid to touch what is yours, what belongs to you," and as those rapturous words fell from her moist lips, he at last gave in to the burning of his desire, and kissed her with a passion which overtook him.

He touched her, he explored her and the following hours passed as in a dream, and he was overwhelmed that his reality could so far exceed his constant imaginings of this long awaited event. For months his thoughts had been consumed with her, touching her, loving her as a husband loves his wife, but never did he imagine she would be as soft, beautiful, and willing. And this being his last thought and he being fully contented and having reached a level of satisfaction he had never known before, he fell asleep with his bride in his arms.

Before dawn Emily awoke to find Edward sleeping beside her. She could hardly rest knowing he was here with her. Never again would she have to wait for him to come to her, for now they would begin each new day together. She studied his every feature. His hair was black as night and his olive skin still tanned from the summer sun. Every part of him was extraordinary. His arms were beautiful, his hands, his chest. She had only seen bodies such as his carved from stone, but he was real. He was warm and soft and he was her husband. She kissed his forehead and he smiled in his sleep, though her distraction did not wake him.

'How can he sleep?' She thought. 'We've so much to do.'

"Edward," she whispered. As Edward slowly opened his eyes to her radiant smile.

"You certainly are beaming this morning, Mrs. Withers." And her smile grew. "Why are you so excited?" he asked.

"I don't know, it is just that I cannot sleep with you here beside me. I am too happy and you are too beautiful."

"Beautiful?" he asked, "that doesn't sound very masculine."

"But you are you know, I suppose it is like the beauty in nature. When one sees a grand snow capped mountain rising up from the earth to touch the sky, one says "beautiful." Or an ancient oak tree transforming into a brilliant fiery red, it is beautiful. That is what I mean. When I look at you, I see the spirit of God in you. I always knew God. But now, He has revealed himself to me in a new way. In the greatest gift of you. Yes, you are beautiful."

"Come closer," he said. And she moved nearer to him. "I shall show you another meaning of the word, beautiful," he whispered. He kissed her deeply and she lost herself completely in him. In those precious moments, time had no boundaries. The world existed only for them, and each knew that nothing could diminish their love, but wretched time disregarded their hopes and shortly tore Emily from Edward's life. 'Oh to have that moment again. To see her as she was, to feel alive in her once more.' He thought.

The roaring fire sputtered and cracked interrupting his treasured memories. As he contemplated his past decisions, he looked over at the young doctor. He noted how Hamilton was a fine young man with exceptional character, the kind of man who still had his life before him as a blank page to be filled with living and dreams. He saw so much in Hamilton, and was particularly charmed by his astounding compassion for others. Hamilton had known privilege, and was obviously from a high upbringing, but he had chosen an obscure life in a small city administering to the sick. Not only the sick, but to the poor. He lived in a tiny home, with no servants. How did this capacity for mercy come upon him?

Edward had often wondered how the components of one's heart were distributed. Particularly he wondered how Emily's father had become so evil. How can one man be so virtuous and the other despicable. Each of them was a man. 'Do we all not have the same self-evident feeling of compassion toward one another?' he often questioned. But his answer, sadly, was always the same, no. For some individuals only felt greed, and selfish ambition. These individuals looked upon other men as branches in their paths to be picked up and cast aside or kicked out of their way. It was for this reason he chose to stay far from the world.

He often reflected on the scriptural truth that to love the world is to hate God. One cannot embrace the sins and darkness of this world, without closing out the light of it. Maybe it was foolish to hide from the world completely, for he conceded there was much of the world to love. In some cases, there did exist in man the spirit of God and all things good.

Edward chose to participate in those things celebrating truth, for maybe if he searched for those things he would somehow find Emily again. He excluded himself from the world and his exclusion covered him in peace. He read the word of God, and he studied all the great works of man and found in them a great hope. Man was indeed a study in contradiction. From man could come the most abounding love and hope. As obviously witnessed in the works of Michelangelo, the words of Shakespeare and yes, even in the simple light of a young girl's eyes. Man could be wonderful, a reflection, however slight, of God. In these shadows of truth and greatness he found hope and he pressed on. But alas, man could also be a dark reflection of evil. The darkness of the soul could demean, destroy, and devastate, thus far from this great darkness he escaped. He surrounded himself with beauty, he fed himself on the goodness of man. He poured out all the good he could find and made no concession for evil to abide in his presence.

"Hamilton," Edward offered rather abruptly, "you are right, my friend, I've been brooding, forgive my unpleasant company. I must seem like a bitter old fool to you, but you could not possibly understand the life I've lived, the losses I have suffered. I must ask you to overlook my moodiness, I am afraid life has not been kind to me. It seems it has carved deep canyons in my soul, places where no one else has ever been. These places are dark and deep. Life can bring one to this end if one is not careful. I should hate to see such a thing happen to you. Can I offer you a bit of advice?"

Sensing the importance of what was about to be revealed, Hamilton looked at Edward squarely with his undivided attention, "Edward, you are the man I most admire and respect. Of every man I know, it is your advice I would value most."

"I tell you this Hamilton, the love of a woman is a powerful thing. She will enter your heart and she will create a feeling of fullness, filling your every need, but beware of this love, and the danger which may come from the loss of it. For in its loss, the fullness and freedom you once knew becomes an empty and dark prison. With her, you can be your best and greatest. The sight of her, the touch of her, make you understand why God created all things. What was once empty, becomes filled, but if you lose this love, what was filled becomes a void of despair. And the absence of her love is not as it was before you knew her. No, once your world has been illumined by her, you understand the nature of real darkness. Before her you went along not knowing your purpose. But once you know with certainty what your purpose is, you cannot go on without her. You cannot drown her memory, you cannot work the hours, months, years away, you cannot open your heart to another. It is a restless sort of pain and there is nothing you can do to quiet its urging. Hamilton, if you find such a love as this, hold on to her with all your might. Love is the greatest feeling you will ever know, but do not let anyone or anything take her away, for with her they take your purpose, your very hope."

"I assure you if I find a love, of the sort of which you speak, I will not allow her to be taken from me," Hamilton said these words, but wondered if they had come too late for him.

"But Edward," he continued, "how will I know if I have found this love?"

"You will know. I suppose the truth of love is best revealed in the feeling shared between two spirits. Each person in the world is quite unique. I am sure you would agree that my particular personality and manner is even more removed from what one would consider typical in man, and considering this distinctness with which I find myself consumed, I often think it impossible to find any sort of harmony with another person, but then I remember how it was with Emily, and how we seemed to be made from a common thread somehow woven together. When with her, there was an absence of fear, a feeling of oneness with another person, I cannot explain it. I only know in all my life I have never met another who was quite like myself in this way. And though we were parted, I like to think myself blessed to have shared such a harmony of spirit with another human being." Edward answered.

"But what if I find this special one and she does not return my feelings, is it possible I could make her love me?"

"I am afraid not my friend. Love. Genuine love, is something that can only be given freely. One cannot earn it as one may earn respect or trust or loyalty. No, love is another creature altogether. Because love is one of those joys, a virtue that we all so desperately need, we foolishly think that we may earn it through some act or deed. But regardless of the hours of thoughtful intentions, or hundreds of countless little acts, the truth of the matter is if the person for whom the thoughts and acts are directed does not return these feelings, all the thoughts and acts in the world are in vain. The person may want to return the feelings, but the very glory of love is that it is not something that can be bought by time or earned in deeds. It is the one thing man is simply compelled to feel. In fact, it is beyond our full comprehension. It is a joyous feeling that breaks free from our imprisoned hearts and lives apart from our mere thoughts, acts or intentions."

"I see."

"How I wish someone could have warned me. I was so foolish and it cost me everything of importance."

"If I may ask, what happened to this woman you speak of?" Hamilton asked timidly.

Edward sat silent looking into the fire. He had never spoken of Emily to anyone except Lenora. Reluctant to bear his soul now, but wanting to let go of all of the pain he had been storing in his heart for so many, many years, he began to speak.

"I can still smell her perfume as it hung in the brisk air of that winter evening. It had been a blustery day and we had had a war of a snowball fight in the courtyard, her face was ruby red from the cold. We rushed up the icy steps to our little secret bridal apartment, but we were met by her father, Winston Talbot and two officers.

"Father!" she said in shock, as all the joy we had known over the previous hours vanished at the sight of him. He did not look at her though, he only glared at me and our bridal bed.

"This is he," he said, "arrest him!" The officers came toward me and she rushed to him and fell at his feet, pleading. It was horrible to see her in such a state, reduced to begging, begging to a man unworthy of her love and loyalty.

"Father, no please no, do you not see my joy, can you not feel the love all around me, is this room not lit up with my happiness? I did not wish to defy you, but you made me choose and I have made my choice. You cannot arrest him. He is my husband."

"I can do anything I wish. Officers, do as I said," Mr. Talbot ordered, "what are you waiting for?"

I attempted to come to her rescue. I lifted her to her feet and stood beside her and spoke for her.

"Mr. Talbot, I implore you to reconsider, I love your daughter. Perhaps that means nothing to you. But you cannot deny what it means to her. She is not a child."

"Not anymore," he crudely interrupted.

"As I said," I continued, "I love her and I understand your concern, but you must let her make her own choice. With all respect Sir, we came to you first, did we not? We asked for your approval. We tried to..."

"Yes you came to me. You had the audacity to come to me. Was taking Bryson from me not enough? No, you have insisted on destroying my family completely. Yes you came to me with an impossible question, come to think of it, you did not exactly ask, no I think you rather had made your decision. You had wooed my young daughter away behind my back. I do not know and I do not care to know for how long. You have already succeeded in striking a blow to my family, but you will not destroy it, you will not have my daughter!" He growled.

"Be reasonable Sir, Bryson choose the path of his life independent of my will or influence and Sir, can you not see the love we feel for each other? Do you honestly believe our feelings for each other will simply disappear because possessing such feelings pleases you not? Surely you realize human hearts are beyond human control."

"What I realize is you took my underage daughter, you, you kidnapped her and . . ."

"Father, that is preposterous!" Emily interrupted, "Gentlemen please, listen to me," she pled, I wanted to be his wife. I came with him willingly. Do I look as though I am held against my will? Do I?" she demanded.

The two men looked at her sympathetically but did not answer her.

"Seize him, I say!" her father demanded again. "Do not force me to ask you a fourth time!"

"Father, no. Wait, if I go with you, will you release him?"

"Emily! What are you saying?" I asked.

"Edward, trust me," she begged, and I did not know her plan, but my heart told me I must certainly trust her so I nodded in agreement. She continued, "Father, will you release Edward if I come with you?"

"Only if he promises to stay away from you and dissolve this so called marriage," he responded.

"Never," I said, "I promise you nothing." My anger was boiling my blood by this time, but I was being held back by his minions.

"Then I have no choice. I must have him arrested."

"Edward, darling, please, I cannot allow you to rot away in prison. I could not bear it. Father may I have one moment with him alone, to convince him."

"Very well, one moment," he said, nodding to the guards and adding, "Release him."

When he left us alone, Emily asked me to promise her father I would leave her and never return for her. A promise to a unjust man was no promise at all she reasoned. "I will go with him and you will go to, to Brighton, yes, 'our secret place, and I will find a way to come to you as soon as possible, and then we will flee to another place. A place where no one will find us, but this time we will leave no trace behind us. Please, Edward it is the only way."

Looking at her sweet face, I could not refuse her and there seemed to be no other available option for us. She called for her father's return and upon his entering our room, I spoke words which choked me, which contradicted every feeling in me.

"Mr. Talbot, Emily has convinced me it will be best for all concerned if I abandon this plan of ours. I do love her still, but my imprisonment will only bring her shame. I honor her and for this I will concede to your demands. If you agree to release me, then I shall release your daughter, forever."

"You choose wisely young man. It would serve you best to forget you ever met her," he answered victoriously.

His words stung me, but I held the venom inside and let it poison me. I remember her tear-stained face looking back at me, her eyes somehow saying, all hope is not lost. My eyes followed them as they walked away and as they passed the guards I saw her father whisper what must have been, 'Arrest him.' For as she and her father walked away from me, I noticed the officers did not follow, but in fact had turned around and were returning to me, I was struck with confusion at first, but then it became all too clear. Mr. Talbot had lied to us. He planned to arrest me to ensure I would never see her again. I began shouting her name, "Emily, Emily, the guards, their taking me, wait. Emily."

Night had fallen and darkness separated us from each other's sight, but I heard her voice calling my name and in a short while, saw her figure in the darkness coming towards me, she had broken free from her father screaming, "No. No. Edward!" But as she raced up the steps, her delicate foot grazed an icy patch of marble and down she tumbled with a horrific scream piercing the night. I saw her falling and broke free from the officers' grasp. I gasped as the sight of the steps, covered red with her precious blood, came into sight. And I knew it was too late.

"What have you done?" Mr. Talbot shouted hatefully up at me. And at a moment I was by her side.

"What have *I* done?" I asked, "It is you who are responsible." I no longer cared what he thought.

"Do you see what your selfish love has done to her?" he accused.

I touched her cold hand, and then her face, but there was no breath, no movement. There was only stillness. Her soft body had been broken. She was such a fragile flower and I had been a great wind that had plucked her up and tossed her about to die in the cold winter. Mr. Talbot's demeanor changed, he composed himself, removed my hands from her, took her in his arms and placed her in his carriage and bid me farewell. He was so distraught over her death he must have forgotten his initial zeal to have me arrested. Or maybe there was in him, after all, some small fraction of compassion.

I stayed at the inn for only one night. Part of it was an inability to be in a room that had been so full of life, you cannot imagine the stark contrast from the happy day that preceded the latter one. But another part of me, the coward, I suppose, feared he would certainly seek revenge. I fled and never returned to that place of death."

Hamilton closed his eyes for a moment and searched for the appropriate words to offer, in appreciation for Edward taking him into such a confidence.

"Edward, Certainly I have seen this pain behind your eyes.

But I never imagined from what great source it came. You have alluded to this love of your life before, but I never knew, forgive me, if ever I have been quick to judge you, for you alone are the man I admire most. And even in your suffering you have been kind to me."

"Kind?"

"Though it may have taken you a while to, shall I say, warm to me, I know what lies between us. You are my closest friend. It is no wonder to me why you have isolated yourself here in this place. To know you have invited me into your private life, I am honored, and fear not dear friend, I shall heal our dear Lenora, even if it requires the impossible, I shall do it."

Edward embraced his young friend and thought that if there was any man he could chose for a son, if God had granted him the pleasure of a son, he could not wish for a more virtuous one than Hamilton.

"If only he had left you alone," Hamilton offered, "It is sinful how cruelly you two were kept apart. And for what purpose? Some phantom notion of a man of great stature and power being better suited for her. How ironic. You have amassed a fortune, in your own right. And Edward, why did he accuse you of turning his son away?"

"He was a disturbed man. I have no other explanation to offer. And as for Bryson, I am afraid it was with the same brand of cruelty Talbot treated his daughter, that he treated his son, which caused the estrangement between them. Bryson Talbot was the most honorable man I knew and he wanted so much for his father to accept him, but it was not to be. Bryson's only love and allegiance was to God and he decided quite early on to surrender his life and all he possessed to become a disciple of the Lord.

When his father discovered his plan, he required Bryson to make a choice. He asked Bryson to choose between being Talbot's son or the son of God. Bryson made a choice, a choice which required him to abandon his father and his former life forever. I happened to be visiting the family at the time this choice was offered, and the decision was made. I suppose I was by association to be eternally hated by his father. Talbot always blamed me for his son's decision, though there is no rational reason for him to have done so. So you see, not only was I not the caliber of man he had hoped to entrust to his daughter, but I was thoroughly detested by the man.

I attempted to find Bryson, on many occasions, but his missionary works have left him quite unreachable. I am always so thankful we confided our plans to him. When he departed for his new life, he left under the impression that Emily and I were to spend our lives in joy and that he would one day return to us. For all I know he has no knowledge of Emily's death. All these years have passed and he has dedicated himself to spreading the gospel, and I gather he has found his home among strangers and in the hope of heaven to come and he has long since lost any desire to return to his previous life.

I had no way to reach him, and it seems I shall always feel there is something between us that is yet broken. I feel I failed him, worse yet I failed Emily. I promised to protect his sister and I promised her we would never be parted, and I am ever haunted by this history of broken promises."

"But Edward, you did not break those promises. You protected her to the best of your ability. Your intention never faltered. This was a tragedy, not of your doing. I believe God does not place a burden on us that we cannot endure. It is more than unfortunate to have lost her, but I am sure a weaker man could not have endured such a loss."

"I am not so strong Hamilton. And we must remember to trust in God's strength, not our own. It is not so much 'God does not place burdens on us that we cannot endure,' but rather God mercifully lends us the strength we do not possess, a well of strength which allows us to endure our hardships, if only we trust in Him. And even in my hardships I am blessed, how strange it is and a testament too how this feeling of love I have has not diminished, even without the presence of Emily for all these years. I still feel a bond with her which cannot be broken.

It is true that love endures all things and what a comfort it is to know that love's continuance does not require the constant presence of the beloved. How very remarkable, and, to me, my saving grace. I look back to those years, the first years of my loss and I know God himself was beside me always, for I know I am not strong enough to have endured such a thing. I am too fragile a being to have accepted it, to have gone on without her, but I did endure it, but not I alone, no, I must not take credit for this victory. My peace comes in knowing I shall endure this life, not because of my strength or my character, but because we were created by a being who did not abandon us. I was ushered through these calamities of my life, carried even, and I will not fear what is to come ahead, for truly with God beside me what harm can come of me?"

"Pardon me Sir," Lily said quietly as she entered the room, "I apologize for interrupting, but I thought you would want to know… Lenora seems to be delirious. I have been by her side and just a few moments ago she began to speak out in her sleep."

"Could you understand what she was saying?" Edward asked.

"I believe she said 'Lenora, I'll be back,'" Lily offered.

"Did she say anything more?" Edward inquired anxiously.

"That's all I could understand."

"Thank you Lily, you have been a great help to me tonight. You and Charles may take leave for the evening. Hamilton and I shall attend to Lenora now, but thank you, I know it has been a tireless evening."

"Yes sir, I only wish I could do more to ease her suffering, she is such a dear. I will light a candle for her, and please call on us if you should have any need at all," Lily offered as she left the room.

Chapter 21
A Truth Revealed, At Last

The two gentleman made haste to the room where Lenora rested and along the way Hamilton queried, "Edward, she is speaking, it is a good sign. But do you not find it strange how Lenora speaks of 'Lenora' as if she was another person?" Hamilton asked.

"It must sound odd to you, but she told me of her first memories. As you know she came to America by ship, but she had already lost her memory. An order of nuns in New York kindly took her in. The sisters related to her how she had repeatedly called out the name Lenora in her dreams and with the absence of any information as to her identity, they naturally began to address her as Lenora. As you may guess, I am very curious about her past. Do you think this recent trauma could unlock her mind to those lost memories?"

"It very well could Edward. From what I have studied about victims of memory loss, it is most conducive to regaining one's memory if the subject feels safe. She must be in an environment where she feels comfortable and free to open those thoughts."

"That is reassuring, she seems to feel quite at home here and before the accident she had started to recall certain memories, disjointed as there were."

"That is promising Edward, and I must admit, I too am

curious about her life." As Edward and Hamilton discussed Lenora's condition in whispers, so as not to disturb her, Lenora rested comfortably in a state of unconsciousness, but her mind began to awaken with long lost memories. . .

Lenora could see her past unfold before her as she remembered the events which had led her to this present place. While she was now a young woman of nineteen years, she recalled being a younger girl, with bright, shining eyes, curious hands, and inquisitive mind. Her name was Isabella Brookhaven. She lived in a beautiful, old English estate in the city of Kielderbridge and was the envy of every child she knew. Her room was filled with an impressive collection of china dolls from all over the world, she possessed the most beautiful and fashionable clothes to be acquired, her best friend was her pony, Sasha, and she was adored by her parents.

But secretly, the person she loved most in the world was her governess, Lenora. From the moment Isabella met Lenora there was nothing but love, graciousness and adoration between them. Lenora was a beautiful young woman, but she seemed to hide her youth and beauty beneath dull and simple attire. Isabella could not remember a time when Lenora had not been in her life, and her heart was full of gratitude and respect for her governess. Lenora had taught Isabella so many things and she loved her very much.

Lenora was a very bright young woman, she had been educated in the best schools for women so she gave Isabella a wonderful education, including the fine arts of music and dance. Isabella remembered the hours she had spent practicing her piano to please her dear friend and teacher. As Isabella's memory returned, she remembered the heartbreaking time when she found Lenora had suddenly left her family, leaving no word whatsoever. Isabella shuttered in her sleep even now recalling the feelings of pain from that unhappy day. Isabella had never understood why Lenora would have left her and her absence caused a void in Isabella's life.

Isabella's parents assured her Lenora had left so suddenly due to an illness in Lenora's family. But there was no good-bye, nor any communication at all to suggest why she had left or if she was ever to return, and this neglect left Isabella completely devastated. For the next year she would wait patiently for the mail each day in hopes of some word from her dearest friend, but day after day, no word came. Even her birthdays came and still no word. Isabella sensed something terrible had befallen Lenora and she urged her parents to inquire as to her whereabouts. Her parents insisted they had exhausted all avenues in their attempts to locate her governess, but could not find her. The loss of her friend was a constant source of pain and the uncertainty of what may have happened caused Isabella great discomfort.

A few years passed and life's ever changing cycles forced Isabella's energies elsewhere, that is, until the night she overheard her parents quarreling. Isabella had ended the day by finally finishing her reading of Shakespeare's Romeo and Juliet. She loved the rich words and thrived on the pictures her mind created when reading them, but she was a very meticulous girl in all respects, and could not delay returning the volume to its place on the hallway bookshelf. Isabella quietly walked to her favorite spot in her home, a small, hidden recess at the end of a long hallway.

As she replaced the book, she choose another of her favorites. She had read it before, but she loved it so dearly she decided to read it again. Though the little corner offered poor lighting, she sat on the bench and began to read. In moments her reading was interrupted by voices. She attempted to ignore them at first, but then the voices became louder and strained and almost pregnant with an impending explosion. Isabella had never heard these tones spoken between her parents, and her curious nature seemed to root her feet to the spot she stood and denied her the ability of respecting their privacy.

Isabella crouched in the dark hallway, motionless, straining intently to make out her parent's words.

"Charlotte, I cannot bear to keep this from Bella any longer. After these years of silence and knowing the pain we have caused her, I believe we should confess our sins," her father, Mr. Brookhaven, said.

"I simply do not agree with you Josef. The damage is done. And I am sure she has all but forgotten, why dredge up the painful past now, for what purpose? Do you remember all we endured to have a child of our own. Have you forgotten the empty years I spent longing for a child? It was not easy to find her, and the thought of losing Isabella. You accuse me of deception, when Lenora is the true deceiver, and we are the victims in this calamity," Isabella's mother, Charlotte Brookhaven, insisted.

"Charlotte, how can you look at me and say we are the only ones harmed? Lenora loved Bella. Hurting either of them in this way was not something I agreed to do. I love Bella. I would do anything to keep her love, to assure her happiness," Josef entreated.

"Exactly!" Charlotte responded, "you would do *anything*, and anything, in this case, means we must not disclose our secret. How would Isabella ever discover the truth now? Lenora is in an asylum and is no longer a threat to us. I know it was painful for her to be separated from Isabella. I am not heartless Josef! I know losing Isabella again must have been a kind of torture to Lenora, but darling, she placed herself in our home. She became a part of our lives, and unless she simply deceived herself most of all, she surely had to understand we would eventually discover her deception. I feel sorry for Lenora and for the shambles her life has become, but I will not take responsibility for it. We took her child, we gave her our hearts, our love, and have used and continue to use all of our resources to give Isabella the best life possible, I will not apologize for doing what I believe to have been just. Isabella is our daughter. We have loved her, supported her, given her a family when her own family rejected her, and there is no reason for her to ever discover the truth. You must know how the unkind truth would disappoint Isabella, how it would make her feel abandoned by her family and betrayed by us? No, I will not be responsible for bringing such pain to her."

"But Charlotte, are you ever going to admit, at least to me, that we were wrong to turn Lenora away? We forced that young girl out of our lives, out of Bella's life and now we find that by doing so we caused a great injustice. I do not know if my conscience will allow me to continue to deceive Bella, to deceive myself, are we only just protecting ourselves?"

"*I* believe we are protecting Isabella, and yes, if I am honest, I own I am protecting us as well, but what choice did we have? What choice do we have now?" she reasoned, but there was no answer to her question.

Stunned, Isabella blew out her candle and stood in the darkened shadow of the hallway niche trying to make sense of what she had overheard. Suddenly all of the reserved questions of the past broke free and became most present in her mind. 'I always looked a little different, all my aunts have a house full of children, but mother has only me and when I would beg for a brother or sister she would become quite saddened. She has never spoken of my birth, nor has anyone else in the family. True, it is not the subject ladies speak of, but not a word of it.

And Lenora, if I heard them correctly, Lenora is my mother? My sweet Lenora, but it cannot be true, she would have told me. She loved me too much to deceive me. And what must they mean by 'driving' Lenora away from here, from me? Into an asylum?' As these thoughts multiplied in her mind, Isabella was sure of one thing. Her parents were determined to keep their secret, without thought of how the deception affected Lenora.

The fragile line between peace and truth had become a fault line which had produced an earthquake of pain, and every thought in her mind had shifted to an unsettled place, and the faith she had in her parents had been shaken and could no longer be relied upon. Isabella decided straight-away to find Lenora. If confronted, Isabella believed Lenora would tell her the truth.

Knowing her father's meticulous nature, much like her own, Isabella reasoned he may have retained records pertaining to Lenora in his study or safe which might lead her to Lenora. The search for the truth became her mission. She waited for the day, the moment, when her father would be traveling, when she could search for the one clue she needed. Day after day she searched, she found herself listening intently to every word her parents said, hoping to filter some grain of hope from their words. After weeks of searching in vain, her prayers were answered.

When her father was traveling on business nearly two months after hearing the news of her adoption, Isabella entered his study, sat at his desk, and began searching for information which might lead her to Lenora. Behind the drawer where her father kept his cigars, was a concealed compartment. She removed the small drawer and behind it was a second, locked drawer. After a thorough search of the room, she finally discovered the key, and opened the drawer. The drawer contained several papers, and one of them was a letter. The letter was addressed to her father, and it was written some five years before.

It read:

Dear Mr. Brookhaven:
This letter is to inform you that Miss Lenora Lenton has been admitted to Meadowbridge Asylum. Her condition has stabilized. You were correct in bringing her to our facility. In further assurance of our arrangement, it will please you to know she seems to have taken a vow of silence. She is cooperative, but she has yet to speak a word. Your secret shall remain safe here.
Dr. Hartly B. Alms

The letter proved what Isabella had overheard, her parents were responsible for exiling Lenora to an asylum. As the full, disheartening awareness of Lenora's fate, and her parents responsibility for the same, dawned upon Isabella, her eyes filled with tears. She wiped them away as she thought 'How can it be so? How could they? My gentle, loving Lenora banished to some corner of darkness, with no hope, no prospect of love. But it must be so, why would this doctor write to Father were it not?' She felt very uneasy about the letter and as she read its words again, she pictured Lenora in silent pain in a place where people are taken and forgotten.

Isabella had never been to an asylum, but she had heard of the horrors, the hopelessness of such places. The address of the asylum was written on the top of the letter. Isabella decided she would go there to visit Lenora, and to find the answers she so desperately needed, and as for Lenora's silence, if there was anyone who could reach her it would be Isabella. Hurriedly, she scribbled down the address and quietly returned to her room.

As Isabella stood in her room looking out of the grand oval window, which dominated the back wall, she gazed down onto the grounds she had played in as a child. The home, the land she loved so deeply had all become a dark lie. Her seemingly loving parents had secretly kept her away from the person she had loved most in the world, and she knew she could not bear to remain in that house of deceit another night. She packed a small bag for the journey and she wrote a brief note to her parents. Her letter was elusive about where she was and why she would be leaving home for the following few days.

After nightfall and when the house was hushed and at rest Isabella stole away in darkness in search of Lenora. The journey was long, but she made it to Liverpool in a week's time without harm or trouble and could hardly contain her urgency to find Meadowbridge Asylum. Her first stop was to inquire as to where she could find a carriage and how far her destination lay beyond her present position. The driver assured her Meadowbridge Asylum was twenty minutes from the city, by carriage, and she could find lodging at the Geldfield Inn, not a fancy place, he cautioned, but warm and clean, which is all she required.

The helpful driver took her straightaway to Meadowbridge Asylum, and left her at the feet of its cold, stone steps. Isabella quickly scaled the many steps of the institution for the poor, outcast, and disturbed, and took several deep breaths as she rapped on the door. There was no answer. She knocked again and again. Finally, her persistence yielded an answer.

"Who is there?" a gruff voice from the other side of the door demanded.

"I am Isabella Brookhaven, I am here to see someone."

A small shutter opened inside the door revealing a set of steely eyes and the same haggard voice answered her plea.

"Visiting hours were over two hours ago."

"But I have traveled far and I must see her tonight, please sir, it is most important, won't you let me in?" she entreated.

"Come back tomorrow. We open at 8:00."

"But Sir," she began.

"That will be all, Miss," he said abruptly, quickly closing the shutter and all was silent except for the heavy footsteps moving in haste away from the door.

'I cannot believe it,' she thought, 'Poor Lenora is locked away behind those cold walls, under the care of such a miserable man. These doleful walls are all that separate us now, but tomorrow shall have to be soon enough.' As the driver had promised, the Geldfield was only a block from the asylum so she chose to walk there and attempt to sort out the uncharacteristic actions she had taken in the previous few days.

Isabella had a restless night, wondering what condition she would find Lenora in the next day. She questioned if Lenora would recognize her, it had been nearly six years since last she had seen her, and now she was a young woman and quite changed from the child she had been. There were so many unanswered questions, but she knew Lenora loved her deeply. And the notion of Lenora being her mother was still a truth she could not quite allow herself to believe. 'But if it is so,' she thought 'why after giving me away, did Lenora change her mind, why did she rearrange her entire life to be with me again? And how did my parents learn the truth? Did losing me again make her lose her mind, or is she being held as a prisoner?' These troubling thoughts left Isabella with a sadness for her mother, which words could not express. Imagining Lenora's torment, Isabella began to cry. She sobbed uncontrollably, until her heaving chest began to ache and the sobbing continued until she fell asleep.

Isabella awoke the next morning eager for the reunion with Lenora. She stood in the hallway admiring her reflection in the large foyer mirror of the Geldfield Inn, and she smiled with pleasure as she remembered that blue was Lenora's favorite color. Her dress was delightfully feminine in all its charming detail, and made from a brocade silk taffeta of the palest blue. The dress was matched by a scarf of the same material, lightly beaded with tiny pearls, worn in her hair, a style worn by only the most fashionable young ladies of England. With a final look, she stepped outside. The day before her was cold and offered no hope of the sun showing its face. She acquired a hansom cab and returned to the unkind steps of Meadowbridge.

Isabella scaled the steps to the entrance, knocked on the door, and paused awaiting an answer. The shutter door was released and she recognized the malevolent eyes appearing from behind it, and the same unwelcome greeting she had received the night before, "Who is there?"

"I am Isabella Brookhaven and I am here to see someone, I believe she is a patient here."

"Are you a relative Miss Brookhaven?"

She pondered this question for a moment then answered, "Yes, I am, I am her daughter."

The tiny shuttered was closed without response, but she heard the heavy bolts being unlocked.

"Right this way Miss," the man said as he lead her down a dark hallway into a waiting room.

"The name of your mother is?" he asked.

"Her name is Lenora Lenton."

"Wait here, I will return." The man walked away and closed the large double doors behind him. She waited patiently in the cold little room. It smelled of some ancient dampness that she could not identify. She sat upright and stiff in the small chair and felt nauseous at the anticipation of seeing Lenora. She forgot her nervousness for a moment as she heard the heavy doors squeaking as they gradually opened.

A tall and slender elderly gentleman acknowledged her presence and asked, in the most pristine English accent, "You are here to inquire of Miss Lenton?"

"Yes Sir," she responded.

"Miss, I am Dr. Greene. Lenora Lenton is indeed on our roster, but there are no relatives noted in her records, certainly no mention of a daughter," he questioned.

"And Dr. Greene, there would not be a record, I have only just discovered that Miss Lenton is my mother. I beg of you to allow me see her. I have come such a long way, and.."

"You need not beg dear, I shall take you to her," he reassured, interrupting her pleading.

"Thank you so much," she said overjoyed.

"You may wish to save your thanks, child, remember where it is you have come to see her," he warned, with a steadfast but caring expression. As they walked she asked him what to expect, "I understand she does not speak, is it at all possible she will be able to talk to me?"

"Poor soul," he answered, "I think you have been misinformed, she certainly can speak, but she says very little. Some of the patients are screamers, moaners, but this one, she stays to herself. Perhaps a visitor will do her well," he offered kindly.

As he opened the next set of doors, Isabella heard the most desperate sound she had ever heard. It was the sound of despair. Voices. Moaning. Screaming. Crying. Calling out for help. "Do not be alarmed by those voices, you will get used to them." The doctor said in a matter of fact way, but she did not believe him, and instead wondered how any living creature could become accustomed to the sadness of such a dark and horrid place.

As they passed along the hall, she caught a glimpse of a

large room filled with patients. It was obvious they were patients because they looked very disturbed. Some of them walked in unison, circling the center of the room. There was an old woman sitting in a straight chair facing a wall rocking back and forth, she seemed to be speaking to someone, though her mumblings were inaudible to anyone and had they been heard, would have been unintelligible. Others sat cowering in the corners of the room, each of them more emaciated than the next. Bella wondered if they had been given food or if they had simply been left in this place to perish. She turned her head unable to witness such sadness and depravity. They continued along the corridor for several minutes until he stopped in front of a door.

"This is Miss Lenton's room."

"A private room?" she asked

"Yes, under order of her benefactors, she is one of the fortunate ones," he said, "as fortunate as one may be with such a fate. I will leave you to your visit."

"Thank you Dr. Greene."

"You may stay as long as you wish. When your visit is finished, there is a bell at the end of this hallway to alert the desk."

"Thank you. Oh, one more thing. Can you tell me where I might find Dr. Alms?"

"Dr. Alms? I cannot say I can, he has not been in the employ of Meadowbridge for nearly three years now."

"I see."

"Did you know him? If I may ask," Dr. Greene inquired.

"No, I cannot say I did. But I know he took some part in my mother being placed here."

"If you pardon my saying so, Miss, I believe his dismissal was the best thing that could have happened to Meadowbridge. He was a true tyrant, and the fate of many souls were bought and sold upon his whims. I can tell you he did have complete authority over the facility at the time of her arrival, but as I said, there have been many changes since his dismissal."

"I understand. I shall go in now, thank you Dr. Greene, you do not know the extent of joy you have brought me," she said and Dr. Greene excused himself.

Isabella opened the door carefully to reveal a dark, dismal room. There was a small chest in one corner and a little cot at the far end of the room. There were no pictures, no sign of anything personal at all save for a few books atop the chest. Lenora was sitting on a small stool staring blankly and had not yet noticed the presence of her visitor. Isabella clenched her stomach and sat on the cot for a moment to compose herself. The sight of Lenora in this way touched Isabella's heart so deeply and painfully that she realized only then the depth of her love for Lenora. Finding courage in this love, Isabella walked over to Lenora and knelt down so Lenora could see her face.

Lenora gazed at her uncommon visitor, carefully studying each feature of her beautiful face and then whispered, "Bella? Is it really you?"

Isabella could not prevent the steady stream of warm tears falling from her eyes.

"Yes, Lenora, yes, it is I. I have come to find you, to *save* you."

"And I have waited long to see you, you are the happy answer to my prayers, but how have you come to be here, and where are your parents?"

"My parents are in Kielderbridge and do not know I am here. I am here to ask you something very important."

"There is nothing you could not ask of me dearest Bella." Lenora responding with smiling eyes.

"Before I ask anything of you, I must know you are well. You certainly do not belong here, it is only some dreadful mistake."

"Oh Bella, I am okay. I am only ashamed for you to see me in this state. My life has been a blessing and a curse. A bright warm dream and a cold frightening nightmare. I am older than my years now and my life is over, but I had my moments of joy, many of them shared with you. Moments which give me peace even in a God forsaken place such as this. I regret you must see me this way, but how I have longed to see your bright face again."

"And I you, Lenora. You left so suddenly, and you never explained, you never said good-bye. After you left my parents acquired other governesses, but no one could fill the place in my heart you had once filled. No one has ever influenced me as you did. Oh Lenora, I missed you, I missed you so. . ." with no words to express the despair Isabella's heart now knew, she allowed her warm and loving tears to speak for her.

Lenora extended her frail and trembling hands to her

daughter, and held her close to her breast and comforted her.

"Forgive me my precious Bella, forgive me. I never wanted it to end as it did. I loved you so. Always. You were my life and if I could have taken the pain from you, believe me, I would have. I never wanted to leave you, and my very heart broke the night I left your home. I will never forget that day. We had shared a lovely day on the shore, and had only returned just before dinner. As soon as I stepped into the house, I knew my life would be forever changed. There was a certain mood in the house, with your parents. I knew something grave was the matter. When I went to my room to change for dinner, two bags greeted me, packed with all my possessions. Events beyond my control forced me to leave you. I walked into your room and sat by your side as you slept in innocent blissfulness. I said a prayer over you, a prayer for God to always keep you from harm, for Him to send His angels to guard your heart and mind. I know my letter did not explain my absence, but I had to say *something*...I could not allow myself to be torn away from your life. . .not again."

"Your letter? But what do you mean? There was no letter," Bella broke in.

"But there was a letter, there was," Lenora started, but then she stopped, looking away to conceal her anger at yet another senseless act. For Lenora realized Bella's parents must had found her letter and kept it from Bella.

Then Lenora continued, "I left a letter for you on the night stand beside your bed. In it I told you I would have to go away for an extended time, but you were not to worry about me and I deeply regretted leaving so suddenly, and no matter what occurred I would love you without end and keep you close to my heart," she said pausing. As Lenora explained the contents of her letter, she understood the extent of what the interception of her letter meant. All these years Bella had been abandoned believing Lenora had not even said good-bye. 'Is there no end to their cruelty?' she thought, 'I only wanted to be near Bella, and I would have never revealed the truth. I was never a threat to them.'

"I do not understand. I knew in my heart your abrupt departure was unlike you, but there was nothing and no one to tell me differently. What could have happened to the letter, unless.... never mind. It is no longer important. What is important, is we are together now." Bella needed time to think, to take in the new little facts, each one revealing the deceitfulness of her parents. She was in shock at the thought her parents had stolen the letter, but wanted desperately to enjoy these precious hours with Lenora.

"And Bella, how is it you have come to be here now?" Lenora asked.

"As I said, it was a long journey, but one I believed to be very important. I have learned something recently which has changed everything I once believed. I overheard a conversation between my parents and it left me very confused. According to what they said, it seemed as though Mother is responsible for sending you away. It has all been very confusing. They seemed to be afraid of you. I knew from their conversation they had been dishonest with me, a grave dishonesty. When you went away I asked for you, I urged them to find you for me and they told me they had sent inquiries trying to find you, but you could not be found. Another lie, how could they see the sorrow I suffered and tell me such a complete fiction, while knowing all the while where you were? It has been deceit upon deceit, and I can no longer trust them, but I know you would never lie to me. Will you tell me the truth now?"

"I will." she answered.

"Lenora, are you," she said pausing as she looked up at her. "Are you, my . . . my mother?"

Lenora looked into Bella's eyes with the same warm, familiar look with which she had looked upon her so many times before. In the brief moment of silence which followed her pitiful question, Lenora felt all of the pain and loss from the last several years washing over her, and she turned away from her daughter in shame.

"Are you?" Isabella asked again, with a trembling voice "it matters not what circumstances have brought you here, it matters not the number of years lost, I only need to know if it is true?"

"Bella, a long time ago I made a promise to your parents, to myself, but I made a promise to you first. Bella, sweet Bella, I am your mother." Lenora confirmed as they embraced tearfully.

"Bella, I know you do not understand right now, but there is time to explain. I shall tell you the truth, all of it. I will attempt to help you to understand."

Bella did not know if she should feel relieved to know the truth, or feel betrayed by all of the adults who professed to love her. She was so very puzzled by the revelation. For though Lenora had never blatantly lied to her as her parents had done, she had contributed to their deceitfulness.

"I appreciate your honesty, it was all I expected from you. I came here full of words and questions, and now I do not know what to say. Words would fall short of expressing how I feel."

"And what could you possibly say? I can imagine only a few of your many questions. And how could I look upon your sweet face and give you any adequate explanation for these unfortunate events? Let us speak of why and how tomorrow. For today, may we fill the many spaces that have separated us? Will you tell me of the precious years I have lost?" Lenora asked.

"There is much to tell. I am fully grown now, as you can see. I have traveled to Paris and Rome. I have continued my piano lessons, though I assure you there is no better teacher than you. I have new friends I wish for you to meet. I have learned so many things since we were parted, and some have been difficult lessons. I am starting to understand life and to grow and change with its many perplexities. I struggle as we all do to find my place in the world, but I love life, and I am thankful for the gifts of peace and love I have been given. Thankful most of all that you have been returned to me, but this feeling is accompanied by such a sad feeling towards my parents. I feel I have failed them in some way, why else could they not trust me with the truth? My parents have been wonderful to me, but I have this feeling of bitterness as a consequence of their actions towards you.

My only desire now is to return you to where you belong, but I fear many obstacles shall meet us. The world can be such a challenge, with all the countless rules to follow, so many I cannot remember them all, and I do not wish to remember them. I want to chart my own life and live by my own ideals. My life has been filled with so much, but you, my dear mother, how much pain have you suffered. I shall remove you from this place as soon as possible. I have so much to ask and so much to tell."

"There is time for all of your questions Bella, but this news and our reunion has taken its toll on you, and you should rest now. I promise to rest today and build my strength for your visit tomorrow. I cannot begin to understand how confused and hurt you must feel. I assure you neither I nor your parents ever wanted you to feel this way. We all love you. You have learned something very disturbing, I only wish I could help you to understand the many losses, failures and wrong choices which have brought us all to this end. I will do my best to explain if you will allow me."

"I know you will, Mother. I will return tomorrow. But I do not wish to leave you here. I want to take you away from this dreadful place. You should not spend another minute here."

"It is not so bad Bella. I belong here now. I lived out there once, among normal people, but misery seemed to find me wherever I went. Each time I found joy it was taken away."

"Mother, it breaks my heart to hear the hopelessness in your voice. How can you say you belong here, you most certainly do not. If you insist on staying here I shall concede for tonight, and tonight only. Tomorrow you will come with me and leave this place forever."

"You are right of course, Bella. My hope *is* restored in you. I have imagined seeing you again so many times, and now I can rest. I can leave this world knowing you looked at me and knew me to be your mother."

"I must leave you now, but I shall return," Isabella said leaving the dark little room. She stood in the hallway for several minutes. She wanted to be comforted, but she could not bring herself to embrace Lenora again. Isabella knew if she allowed herself to be held in her mother's arms again, in the arms of her dearest friend, her heart would break from so much pain and joy. She knew she was not strong enough just then. She would collect her thoughts and return the following day.

Chapter 22
A Truth and a Trial

Eager to seek the promised answers from Lenora, Isabella rose before the sun the following morning. It was a midsummer day and though it was early morning, already the warm sun was an unwelcome companion. Isabella dressed and thought of what she would say to Lenora. There were so many questions, but the important one had already been answered. Her heart was heavy imagining Lenora in such a cheerless dwelling. She had been there for years. How could she have remained sane listening to the endless moans of people who had lost all reason? It was so distressing, and even more distressing was the fear that Lenora had been changed, and somehow convinced she belonged in that place of doom.

'Where is her family? Why have they forsaken her? How can they allow her to live in this condition? Do they even know she is institutionalized?' Isabella asked herself. And for the first time her mind turned to Lenora as a young woman carrying a child. Bella knew the fate of those girls whose reputations had been so ruined, how even one's family might turn them away under such circumstances. She had heard stories of cunning young men having their way with innocent girls and then abandoning them when evidence of their affair began to be revealed in the form of a swollen belly. She wondered if Lenora had suffered this unkind fate, if her father had been this type of man. But it mattered not at this moment. Bella's only concern was for her mother. Had Isabella's parents visited Lenora in her prison, she wondered. And she hoped with all she was they had not, for if they had truly understood the depth and despair of Lenora's circumstances it would be unconscionable to have left her there, forgotten. Isabella wished for her parents to see Lenora's face now. She wanted them to see the results of their deceit. She remembered Lenora's face as she knew her in the past, she was such a lovely and bright person and now the constant glow had left her eyes. The magic of her heart and been stolen away and it could never be replaced.

Isabella wiped her eyes and told herself to be strong. 'The past is over and I cannot change it. All I have is now, and what matters is I know the truth and it is in my power to correct my parents' mistakes. I can right their wrongs.'

Isabella went to the asylum once again and received the same greeting from the bizarre little man inside. He invited her in and took her straight to Lenora's room without further benefit of speech, which she neither solicited nor hoped for. As he slithered back to the detestable hole from whence he had come, Isabella entered her mother's dark room and regarded her lying on the cot. The heavy drapes were drawn blocking all light from the outside.

"Mother," Isabella called out, "It is I, Bella, I have come back as I promised," Isabella whispered.

"Is it time for lunch?" Lenora asked with a shaky voice.

"I do not know, I can ask someone." Isabella offered, surprised Lenora wasn't more pleased to see her.

"Are you new here?" Lenora asked.

Bella did not understand what Lenora meant. Bella sat beside her on the edge of the cot, and moved closer in to Lenora's view. As Lenora looked upon Isabella, she seemed almost frightened and then she asked, "Who are you? You do not look like my nurse?"

Bella's heart began to pound and a dark fear shadowed her heart as she answered, "Lenora, why are saying this to me? I am your daughter. You know me. Why would you pretend you do not? Is it my parents? Are you afraid of what they will do to you? You owe them nothing, and I promise you I would never let any harm come to you, you must believe me. Tell me the truth, tell me you know me, tell me Mother?"

Suddenly Isabella was aware that a young woman had entered Lenora's room, and was addressing her, "May I ask who you are Miss?"

"Yes, I am Isabella Brookhaven," she answered.

"I knew it was you. I am so pleased to make your acquaintance, I am Katia Thatcher and I have attended Miss Lenton for several years, what a happy reunion this must be for her. I fear she must be having a bad day. There are times when she is as alert as you or I, and then some days we lose her. She retreats to some unreachable place. But take heart, she always comes back."

"You do not know what those words mean. I have taken such risks to find her, and it has been agony not knowing where she has been. And yesterday, it was an answered prayer to see her, to see her face, to hold her small, gentle hands, to be near her. And yet today, I was right there in front of her and she did not know me. But I will trust that she will return to me again. Can you tell me more about her?" Isabella asked Katia.

"Yes, do take heart, this present state will pass. The episodes come less frequently now, but these last few years have been a desperate kind of life for her. Lenora was very disturbed when she was first admitted here. I never believed she belonged here, but I had to do my job. She was such a beautiful young woman and her courage seemed to speak to me through her eyes. In the years we spent together, we have become great friends. And you, she spoke of you always. 'Bella', she would call you. She lived for the day when she could hear word of your life, she never dreamed she would see you again. There are days when she knows everything and she is very bright and lucid, but then there are the times when she goes for days without uttering a word, and other times when she seems as a child. In those times she forgets where she is, who she is. It is very sad, I think she is too intelligent and vibrant a woman to cope with being locked away in this place. She escapes the only way she can, into a world where she cannot remember the past, nor feel the present sorrow. This must be one of those days. How did you come to find her?" Katia asked.

"It was completely by accident, I know she is my mother now, and when I discovered the truth, I set out to find her. I needed answers. I talked to her yesterday, but we postponed our more delicate questions for today, and now I fear my answers will be further postponed. I would like to talk to you more about her, the years she has spent here. Would you be so kind as to tell me about her? I think you must be my only hope now."

"Why of course, you can join me for dinner tonight if you like?"

"Thank you, thank you so much, but wait, can you tell me if it is possible for her to remember me, by tomorrow. I must return home soon."

"It is difficult to know for sure Isabella, it varies, it could be tomorrow, it could be a week. I am sorry I cannot give you a more kind answer, but we will discuss it more this evening. Are you rooming at the Geldfield? I can have my husband come for you. Shall I show you out?"

"No. I think I'll spend a few more moments here with her. I cannot bear to leave her alone just yet. And yes, I'm at the Geldfield."

"Bless you," she said, as she clutched Bella's arm, "I will see you tonight."

Bella returned to Lenora's room and sat by her side. Neither of them uttered a single word, but being near her mother was sufficient for now.

ഊ

As Katia promised, a carriage arrived later that evening to deliver Isabella to the nurse's home. Isabella was anxious to hear of the events which had transpired over the last years of her mother's life. She sensed an honesty in Katia and the fondness she obviously held for her mother, and therefore trusted she would have answers to her many questions, but she deeply regretted that Lenora would not be the one to answer them as she had hoped. The carriage arrived at a small and quaint little cottage. The night air was fresh and cool, and seemed to creep into her consciousness giving her a quite positive feeling. Katia's husband showed Isabella to the front door and escorted her inside. The nurse's home was modest, but Isabella found every inch of it was clean, and it radiated a feeling of warmth impossible to achieve in the types of homes to which Isabella was accustomed.

"Bella, may I call you Bella?" Katia asked.

"Yes, please do."

"Thank you, I am so glad you decided to join me. I have so much to tell you, and my husband will be working this evening, so you will have my full attention."

"Good-bye darling, I will return as soon as I can get away." Katia's husband said as he walked toward the front door. His dutiful wife followed closely behind him, and kissed him goodnight, closing the door behind him, leaving she and her guest alone.

"Now, are you hungry dear?"

"Yes, I must admit dinner sounds lovely right now."

"Then follow me, I prepared a simple little meal for us, and I think you will enjoy it."

"Thank you so much, you are too kind. Katia, I want you to tell me everything you know about my mother. Save nothing. I really must learn about what has happened to her since we were parted."

"As you wish, Bella, as you wish. It was six, no five years ago, your mother was brought to the Meadows. There has always been a bit of a mystery surrounding her arrival. Most of our patients share a certain intense and pervasive fragility, an outward characteristic that resonates their sense of being lost in the world, but she was not like the others. She shared a certain lost quality which brings many here, but she was markedly special. When we cleaned her up, we found behind the dirt and rags a very beautiful young woman, but she was indeed troubled. There was a man who insisted she be admitted. He met with Dr. Alms in private, the proprietor of Meadowbridge at the time, and insisted she was a threat to herself. He related that she had been found wandering lost in the city of his home, the name escapes me just now, but at any rate, he took it upon himself to be her benefactor."

"Was it Kielderbrige?" Isabella asked.

"Yes, Bella, that was the place, Kielderbridge. The man required that she have the very best of care. And he paid a small fortune to keep her here, I might add. She never spoke of this man. I did not understand their relationship, and I wondered why a man would spend so much money and effort to care for someone in her condition, especially a person who seemed to care nothing for him. Then, one day, after I had cared for her for several months, she spoke to me for the first time in the azalea garden. I had permission to take her outside periodically to give her a little fresh air, you see it has been my experience that the fresh air and sunshine make the patients feel better, not cured, but at least a little hopeful. Anyway, I suppose she was grateful for the attention, and it was the kind of blue sky day where one cannot feel sad. The sky above was uncommonly blue and one could feel the energy filling one's being as clearly as a flower blooms in the sun. Lenora began to tell me in pieces, day by day, about her life and how she had come to be here. She spoke of you so often. Your mother is a strong and beautiful woman. Do not think her insane, it is not insanity, but rather the many tragedies she endured which brought her here. With the burden of so many losses, she simply could no longer continue to survive in the normal world and there was no one she could turn to."

"But what of her family?" Bella asked.

"Ah, it is an unkind truth that her family led her to this end. Hearing such a thought must be disturbing to you, and forgive me for such an accusation, but I will explain. Like you, your mother was a beautiful young girl. And as is the fate with girls of beauty, she caught the eye of a young man rather early and fell in love when quite young. I am not absolutely certain of what happened, but I know she was deeply in love with this young man, but pity for her, her family had promised her hand in marriage to another and forbade her to marry him. Being an obedient daughter it broke her heart to betray her family's wishes, but it would have broken her spirit to have forsaken her love of this man. Love won out in the end and she planned to marry her young man.

I am not sure what events led her to this tragic end, but she lost her young man and was forced to return to the family she had left behind. Soon after her return she discovered she was with child. Considering her family's position in society, she was sent away to have the child, and little did she know what else was planned for her. All she had left of the man she had loved was the hope of their child, and knowing she would have his child was her only happiness, but all along her family planned to take the child and give it away.

When she explained the day of your birth to me, she cried for hours, even at the memory of it. For you see, she never even held you. After the difficult delivery, she awoke to find that you had been given away. Lenora lost the man she loved, and then their child was taken from her as well. Her family expected her to maintain her position in the family, her father assured her he would find a suitable man who would forgive her "unpleasant past" and marry her. Her family found the situation an embarrassment, but she would have nothing of it. Not our Lenora, she could not live a lie and there was only one thing to satisfy the longing of her heart. She needed to be with you, so she made a decision which changed her life.

Lenora denounced her family and made a covenant to God to seek and care for you. The one theme to her daily efforts was to discover where you were, and eventually her diligence came to fruition. She placed herself in the right position to be hired as a governess for you. Given her background, she was educated to the full degree a woman is allowed, and given her charm, she quickly discovered all she could about your family. Through diligent inquiries, she determined which subjects were the favorites of the Brookhavens and which arts they preferred you learn, she even learned of Mrs. Brookhaven's most prized thing in all the world, her flower garden, only it lacked a rare variety of some sort of lily which Mrs. Brookhaven highly coveted.

Lenora is a clever one, she spent a small fortune of her father's tainted riches to obtain the prized lily, and she presented it to your mother the day of her interview. Knowing her as I do, I am sure she would have easily acquired the position without it, but she could leave nothing to chance where you were concerned. Oh no, she planned each detail, she would live in your home, be by your side and watch you grow up with a loving family. And I would swear upon my own mother's grave it was never her intention to remove you from your family, she only wanted to be near you. I will never forget the glow of her face as she recalled the first time she saw you. I suppose your parents thought she simply had a love for children. She cared for you and educated you hoping her knowledge would benefit you as it would never be able to benefit her.

You see, Lenora completely abandoned her former identity and disappeared leaving no word with her family, for it was too great a risk. I do not know what efforts were spent to find her, but one day her family indeed discovered the name and location of your parents. Her father suspected she might have attempted to find you, but he did not act on his thought until years later. Lenora confided that her father would have thought it impossible for her to have obtained the privileged information of your whereabouts. But in later years, it became a more urgent matter because his health began to fail, and perhaps he wished for forgiveness. After discovering your whereabouts, her father called upon your parents. He described his daughter, but your parents denied having ever seen Lenora.

You see, your mother, Mrs. Brookhaven, was unceasingly afraid of losing you so you can imagine her horror when Lenora's father arrived upon her doorstep. Lenora abhorred being deceitful to your parents, but she was given little choice and given her current status, would have been unable to reclaim her rights as your mother, even if it had been her desire. Once the Brookhavens learned the truth, they turned her away from your home, perhaps out of equal parts of being hurt and devastated at her deception, and being terrified you would learn the truth. They insisted upon her immediate departure, urging her to think of your welfare.

With Lenora's father making inquiries, it would only be a matter of time before the truth was discovered. Lenora pleaded with them to allow her stay if only for a few days, for she had no other life outside of your world, but they would not consent to her pleadings, and instead turned her away with instructions never to return. I suspect that is when the breakdown occurred. I do not know how long she suffered or what happened to her in the following days, but your father found her walking the streets weeks later, cold and hungry. She did not even recognize him at first, but he delivered her from her poverty. Lenora had become a part of your family and I suppose his sense of decency dictated he place her here where she could be looked after. It took her many weeks to respond, but I believe she recovers a little more each day. Her world has been a dark one. Losing your father, then you, not once but a second time, but take heart Bella. You are here now, and I believe your presence is the solitary cure for her, it is all she has ever really required."

"You are kind to have been so honest with me. I only wish I knew more, but I know only Lenora can answer these questions. And yet how can I ask anything of her. She has been forced to live in that miserable place, oh I am sorry, I do not mean to offend."

"Not to worry, Bella, it *is* a miserable place. I find it hard to be there, and I am able to leave each day. It must be a terrible burden to have a loved one there."

"Could I take her away from there?" Isabella asked.

"If it were up to me, I would release her this very night, for she is troubled, but she certainly does not belong there. But the decision is not mine to make, and I honestly do not believe Dr. Greene would consent to her release. Her files are kept under lock and key and to be honest, Doctor Greene only allowed you to see her because he cannot resist a pretty young girl. But Bella, are you forgetting about your parents?"

"No, of course not. I simply have not worked it all out yet, but I shall. I shall find a way. I am angry with them right now. How could they? Whether they were afraid of losing me or not, this was a woman's life, her mind, her hope destroyed by their actions. I cannot forgive them. Not yet. There is much to be done before amends may be made. I do not relish the idea of returning home, but I know I must return and explain my plans to them, plea my case, as they say. Their appalling secret has been revealed now, and I know the truth, so what is to stop me?"

"What do you propose to do, Bella?"

"I wish to have them release her from this place and bring her home. You spoke of her past, but you did not know her before she was exiled to Meadowbridge Asylum, and she has changed so within those tiny, bleak walls. I wish to bring the luster back into her life, return the brightness to her eyes. You said I am beautiful, but I am ordinary and plain compared to her, to how she was, and I know there remains in her a vibrant, selfless and wonderful woman. It will be my mission to return her to her natural state. I am her daughter and I love her. I will do all in my power to help her recover. As for my parents, in time, I will be able to forgive them, but first they must agree to allow me to bring my mother home, not as a guest, but as my mother. She will take her place in my life, where she has always belonged."

"You are her child, I can see her courage in you. I will do all in my power to help you."

"Thank you Katia, and thank you for opening a door to her past to me. It has meant more to me than I can express. I shall try to see her again tomorrow and tell her my plans, and then I will return home. Promise me you will take care of her until I can return?"

"You needn't ask, but you have my promise."

Isabella left Katia's home that night with her spirits lifted in spite of the tragic events Katia had uncovered. She was exhilarated with the hope of knowing it wasn't too late, having the opportunity to mend this unthinkable mistake and bringing Lenora the happiness she had long suffered. All her life Isabella wanted to somehow make a difference, to do something truly meaningful, and this was her chance. She cared not who might find out about her parents. All that mattered was her mother had been returned to her. A wonderfully perfect mother, one who had truly loved her. Isabella's only desire was to rescue Lenora from her misery and return her to the kind of life she deserved.

Isabella was not naïve, she understood it would be difficult to face her parents again. She had always been an obedient daughter, and her recent actions must have shocked them, but she would not apologize for seeking the truth. The truth was there before her now, right or wrong, she knew the truth and she would embrace it. If her parents could not be honest with her, she had no choice but to seek the truth from others. 'I have never asked anything of them, how can they refuse me this?' she reasoned.

The day had been draining and far from what she had expected. Foolishly she had dreamed that Lenora would be with her by now and together they would return to her home where they would all live together as one happy family. But, alas, she found herself alone once more in this foreign city with her mother only blocks away, and there were far greater obstacles than stone walls separating them. If only there was a way to convince Lenora her fears were over, and her loneliness had passed. Finding rest became a struggle. Bella murmured prayers throughout the night for her mother's fragile mind to be restored the next day, for tomorrow was her last chance to speak with her before Isabella would have to return home. 'Home?' she whispered thoughtfully. The notion of home seemed strange to Isabella now, and she lingered over her thoughts of what the word meant and came to the conclusion that home had been a place she had never quite been before. Void of any feeling but weariness, she fell asleep at last.

Chapter 23
A Promise

The dark walls holding Leonora captive stood before Isabella one last time. She took a deep breath before entering the great doors, and prayed today would offer her the promise for which she hoped. She walked the long halls without escort and stood for a moment at the door she would later call the 'door of despair.' When she had first encountered the door two days before, she did not allow herself to see them, the sound of their voices was evidence enough of their pain. Her eyes had scanned the patients quickly, but she was too afraid to face them.

Presently, she stood unnoticed by the door and watched the same scene as before. It was as though a heavy cloud of mist veiled this forgotten room and ignored the natural lapse of time. Though it was painful to see their faces, this time she really saw them, each of them as a forgotten soul. Without hope. Without love. 'How alone they must be and forgotten,' she thought. Involuntarily she became focused on one solitary man. He stood only five feet, five inches and was as thin as a body could be. His thin hair was white as snow. For several minutes he stood with slouched shoulders looking out of the tiny, iron-barred window. She wondered what object had captured his attention. Or was he hoping to find someone coming to rescue him from this bleak place. Suddenly the clouds shifted and the sun illuminated the room and the patients all turned toward the light. But the man. The white haired man, turned away. She was able to see him more fully now. His snow white hair was matched by an exuberant beard. He seemed ancient, and she wondered how many of his days had been wasted in this place. How sad and desperate a creature he was. But wait. His eyes. Had she ever seen such piercing blue eyes? He scanned the room as if searching for a friendly soul, and then looked again upon the freedom just beyond reach, beyond the barred window. Though he had turned, she could still see his beautiful, clear eyes. It was as if they were the eyes of Christ Himself, and somehow she knew the man was not alone at all. He was very much in God's care, as were they all.

Isabella continued down the hall until she came to Lenora's room, and offered a silent prayer just before entering. Lenora sat in the same chair, with the same blank stare. Isabella's heart sank and once again she walked over to her mother, knelt down before her, and looked into her eyes.

Lenora looked at Isabella as she had done yesterday, and quietly uttered, "It was not a dream, you are *really* here?"

"Oh Mother, yes I am here. And you know me again?" Isabella said tearfully.

"Yes my precious girl, but I could not trust my own mind. I feared I had only dreamt your return."

"I was here yesterday, but you did not recognize me."

"I am sorry, it is the medicine, it dulls my senses. As you can imagine, one would be thankful for such an escape, but now I only wish to remember. To remember you, to be fully aware of the world around me because you are in it again."

"Yes, all that matters is you are with me today. I must return to Kielderbridge today. I tried to convince Dr. Greene to release you under my care, but he is under strict orders to only release you after notifying my parents. But I shall go to them and demand your immediate release."

"So you are my champion now? Dear Bella, you must proceed carefully. I admire your determination. You remind me of myself in so many ways. But Bella you must realize the complexity of the situation."

"But it is rather simple in my eyes."

"On the contrary, it is decidedly complicated. You cannot look upon your parents as enemies. They love you and they will do everything in their power to ensure your allegiance to them. They do not yet understand how your heart can hold enough love for us all."

"But you understand?"

"Of course, yes. I only caution you because I know the extremes to which people can go when motivated by fear. Your parents believe I betrayed them, and it is no longer a secret that they have kept us apart. I know your parents well enough to realize how delicate a situation this truly is," Lenora cautioned.

"But I will *make* them understand. And I will come back for you. If they refuse to help me, to release you from this place, then they are no longer my parents."

"Oh Bella do not forget what they have done for you."

"I have not forgotten, but all of their good deeds are overshadowed by what they have done to you. And, in causing this unnatural separation between us, they have forfeited what rights they once had over my heart and my loyalties. The sooner I leave, the sooner I shall return to deliver you from this place, I really must go now but I will return shortly, and we'll be together again," Isabella promised, embracing Lenora one final time and kissing her soft cheek.

Lenora broke their embrace and looked at her daughter. A glimmer of restored hope radiated from her eyes as she smiled with joy at her daughter, and promised, "I'll be waiting for you my precious girl. I'll be waiting."

ഗ‍ര

It was a long and dreadful journey back to Isabella's home in Kielderbridge. She fidgeted in her seat, silently urging the carriage to move faster, as if the miles that lay ahead could simply vanish at her will. It was uncommonly warm on this day and the carriage stopped every so often to give the horses a rest. At one such stop, she stepped out of the carriage and walked along the dusty roadside until she came to an enormous oak tree which seemed to have formed at the world's creation. She took rest under it's welcoming branches and enjoyed the breeze fluttering by. She took a seat on one of the great roots emerging from the earth, and glanced up at the melodious movements of its grand limbs. Each of its movements seemed to linger into the next, and it spoke to her of some lost wisdom of simplicity for which she longed.

From the corner of her eye a tiny fluttering creature swept down just above her head. She recognized the remarkable creature as a ruby-throated hummingbird. His desire to spend a passing moment with her returned the sweet smile to her lips and she noted how free he was. As the tiny hummingbird leapt up, buzzing all the while and disappeared into the summer sky, she realized how chained she was to this cold land and this new found mission, and she sorely wished to have but a taste of his freedom. For even with his tiny frame, he was capable of flying hundreds of miles away from here, and she took seeing the incredible creature as a sign that all things were indeed possible.

Isabella spent the remainder of the journey planning every word she would say to convince her parents to help her, and she waited patiently for time to pass as she watched the familiar path bring her closer home. When she reached the gates of her home, she walked slowly into the house.

"Mother," Isabella called out, "Mother, are you here?" Her words were followed by the sounds of footsteps, running.

"Isabella?" her mother asked. When Isabella came into sight, her mother looked relieved and as though she might cry, "Isabella? I am grateful to have you home, but you must understand you acted very irresponsibly. You have caused us immeasurable worry, immeasurable! You must never, never leave this house again without our permission."

Fully expecting these punishing words, Isabella responded, "Mother, I am truly sorry for leaving so suddenly, but there was something I had to do. Can we speak privately?"

"Certainly, there is no one here."

"And Father?"

"He's in London, returning tomorrow."

"Good, I wanted to speak to you first. I want you to know I know the truth. I know everything."

Mrs. Brookhaven's eyes widened at this revelation, and then searched for something other than her daughter to fall upon, as Isabella continued. "I love you. You have been the most wonderful parents anyone could hope for and I trust your intentions have been pure, but Mother, I have seen Lenora. She is in an institution." Tears began to streak Isabella's face, "I assure you I am returned quite changed. How could not I not be changed now that I know? I know the sad truth, and I have many questions for you, but nothing is more important, nothing matters except that we bring Lenora home. She does not belong there, she belongs with me. Everyone in her life has been taken from her, and she is the kindest, most gentle soul I have ever known. By circumstances beyond her control, she was forced to be apart from me, but now, it is over. There is no longer a reason to keep her hidden away like some terrible secret. Will you help me Mother, it is all I ask of you."

Mrs. Brookhaven remained silent for several minutes, having been shocked that her most protected secret had been unlocked, and knowing full well there was little she could say to explain these events to her daughter's satisfaction. How could anything she might say ease her daughter's pain?

Nonetheless, she began, "Isabella, I want you to know above all, your father and I love you. You are the greatest joy we have ever known. I am sorry you learned the truth this way. Saddened you were forced to search Lenora out in secret, it is heartbreaking. We love you so. How can I explain our actions to you?

You see your father and I had everything, except a child. But then a miracle happened, on summer holiday we met a man whose daughter was with child. He spoke lovingly of the girl and revealed it was their wish to give the child to a home with loving parents. We were so elated and I wanted you so desperately. We never thought to ask any questions. We took the man at his word. He prepared the legal papers for us and the exchange was made. You were brought to us when you were only days old. I could hardly stop your tears, but soon you warmed to me as I was continuously at your side. There was not a thing you wanted or needed I would not give you, we were so happy. I have to say I felt present in my own life for the first time.

I had never known such joy and it was then I decided I would never tell you we were not your biological parents. How could I take that joy from you? It was nearly four years later when Lenora came to call on us. She was a bright and charming young girl and schooled in languages and arts. We believed she would teach you much and she had the energy, and vitality you needed. You loved her at once, and her love for you was apparent as well. We lived in happiness together for seven years, but it all changed in one afternoon.

Lenora had taken you to the shore for a sketching exercise, you were fascinated with sketching in those days, and while you two were out, an old gentleman called upon us. I did not recognize him at first, but then I knew him. He was the man we had met all those years before, your grandfather. He had aged much and it was evident he suffered from some sort of illness. He said he was searching for his daughter, he showed us a likeness of her and indeed it was Lenora. I sent him away and told him I had never seen the girl. I acted in haste, but you knew nothing of the truth, and I was not going to be forced to tell you.

Panic and fear swept over this house. This girl whom we had trusted, whom had ingratiated herself to us, had been deceiving us for years, and naturally we began to wonder what else she could be hiding and too, she was your mother, and it was inevitable that she would one day try to take her rightful place in your life. She was growing closer to you each day and it would only become more difficult to separate you. It pained me to hurt you in such a way, but I could not allow her to take you away from us. You must believe me, I am not without feelings, I felt sorrow for her, I truly did, but it was she who had caused this situation. If she had not given you away." Isabella's eyes flashed. Mrs. Brookhaven, sensing she had overstepped, continued, "I know it is painful, but you really must try to understand our position."

"Only if you promise to try to understand my position, and Lenora's. You believe you know the truth, but *do* you know the truth, do you know everything? Have you seen this place of exile? What I understand is even now you are trying to escape blame, but is it really so difficult to admit you were wrong?"

"How can it be wrong to love you?"

"Oh Mother please don't try to diminish your deceit by saying it is only out of love, if this is your notion of love, then I would be happier without it."

"You don't mean that Isabella."

"No. I don't, of course. But what I mean is I know you are my mother. I am not confused about that in the least, and though I now know Lenora is my natural mother, this knowledge cannot change my feelings for you. If my feelings for you have changed at all, the source of the change lies in your deception not in the truth. I love Lenora as I always have, as my dearest friend, and there is a rightful place in my life for her and that place is not an asylum. It is disgraceful that she has lived in misery while we live here in this opulence, this abundance. It sickens me. I cannot sleep in this house another night until she is released."

"But Isabella, you forget, she is there for a reason."

"Yes, because you placed her there." Isabella retorted, inflamed by her mother's reluctance to admit fault and to help her even now.

"I will not have you speak to me this way. We are your parents, you will not forget that. There are things you do not know, after she left us, your father found her lingering in the streets and out of her mind. We did put her there, you are right, but it was for her safety."

Isabella glared at her and thought, 'You mean for *your* safety.'

"Isabella, I cannot bear to see you looking at me this way. She has the best care there and . . . "

"Did you not hear me Mother, I have seen her? I have been there. Have *you* been there? Have you heard the sound of despair? It is a sound I shall never forget. But that is no matter now, what is your answer? Will you have her released?"

"Isabella, we cannot just bring her here and live together in harmony as you wish. Do you really think it possible? Think of the consequences. How will you introduce her, how will we explain this situation to our friends? It is not as simple as you wish."

Ah, Isabella thought, now we are getting somewhere, the heart of her mother's reluctance always revolved around what others might think. Isabella never understood the logic of pretending to be someone she was not.

After a pause Isabella began, "If the world was as it should be, it would be possible. But the world is what it is. I hazard to say there would be too many questions. There would be embarrassment, shame to our family. I see why you are concerned."

"Good," Mrs. Brookhaven answered with relief, "I know it will not be easy, but you can visit Lenora anytime you wish. Life must go on as before, there is no stopping it. It is a social world we live in and Isabella your pain will diminish. It is part of growing into adulthood that we must let go, we all must give in to the way of the world."

"But I do not want to let go. I do not want to give in, to give up. This is not some insurmountable dream or some fancy of a silly girl. This is a matter of doing what is right. Do you really imagine I could visit her in her asylum once a year and spend the rest of my year in this sickening luxury without a care, without a thought for her? Do you think my heart could manage that? If I am such a person, then I am not a person at all. I will be with her, or I will not be at all."

"What are you saying? Bella you must give it time. It is all too real right now."

"Don't you see, time will only dull this pain, but it will not make it less real. Do you really think if I fill my days with idle pleasures and force my deepest beliefs and feelings aside that my beliefs and feelings are not real? It is a dangerous game you play with our hearts, Mother. Feelings ignored are not feelings which do not exist. The feelings are there, under your skin, like a caged bird whose only dream is to break free and fly. Because you ignore his fluttering does not mean he does not exist in his prison. And God help you when he opens his wings."

"I do not suggest you forget her. I am only pointing out it is not a simple matter."

"But Mother, it *is* a simple matter, it is we who make it complicated. We will discuss it with Father, but know this, my mind will not be changed."

∽∞∝

Isabella waited silently and took her dinner in her room that evening. Upon her father's return the following morning, he embraced her happily though reprimanded her for her sudden departure. Before a word was spoken between them on the subject of Lenora, her mother entered the room.

"Charlotte, what is the matter, we have our daughter back, I thought you would be all smiles?"

"Shall I begin, Isabella?" Mrs. Brookhaven asked.

"May *I* Mother?" Isabella responded.

Mrs. Brookhaven nodded yes and looked at her husband with the same desperate look in her eyes.

"You two are frightening me, what on earth is the matter?"

"Father, I have learned the truth. I heard you and Mother arguing about Lenora and her sad fate several nights ago, and I have just returned from Meadowbridge. I have seen Lenora and I wish to have her released at once."

Isabella's father appeared as though his life's very breath had escaped him. The shame he felt for his actions was obvious to Isabella.

"Bella," he started, "I do not know what to say. I have failed you, and miserably. We did not want you to discover you were adopted, and we certainly did not want you to discover the truth in this way. Please know we love you. Have we ever shown you any other emotion?"

"Father, I know you love me. It is all right. I do not question your love for me. I come to you not of my own pain, but of Lenora's. She has been treated wrongly."

Mr. Brookhaven glanced at his wife, partly for instruction and partly to affirm his daughter's accusations.

"I have already spoken to Mother and ..."

"Josef, it is Isabella's wish to bring Lenora here to live with us. She believes we can simply bring her back into our home and act as if nothing happened. Darling, please help me convince her that this is impossible," Mrs. Brookhaven implored of her husband.

"Bella, is this what you want?" her father asked.

"Father, it is all I want in the world. You know how much I have always loved her. And it is not as you think. Lenora never wanted to give me away, it was her family's decision. They deceived her and I was taken from her against her will. And now she is being kept from me against mine. She never planned to tell me the truth, it was enough for her to be near me. And now she is far away and in the worst of conditions. If you really love me as you say, please help me," Isabella begged, tears streaming.

He was silent for several moments and then began, "We must think this through. What has happened over many years cannot be mended overnight. You must realize we do not want to lose you now."

"But you cannot lose me Father."

"But we will," Mrs. Brookhaven interjected, "this love

you have for Lenora will overpower you. Already you look at us differently, as if all we have given you has been wiped away."

"Your mother is right you know. We have loved and protected you all of your life, and we never knew it was not Lenora's choice to abandon you. How were we to know? Your mother is right, we cannot simply go on as though nothing has changed. Everything has changed."

"But surely you don't expect me to do nothing Father?"

"Bella, we expect you to honor and respect our choices. To trust our opinion over your own. You believe you see the world very clearly, but your eyes are not yet matured enough to span the entire picture. Something must be done, I agree, but let us proceed slowly, do not act in foolhardiness."

"Of course I trust your opinion, and forgive me for saying so, but your actions in this most crucial matter in my life have not been the most prudent. There are things I am trying to forgive, things which are perhaps small to *you*. For instance the letter Lenora left me. I never saw the letter because it was taken from me. It was harmless and in taking it from me you caused a world of pain to be brought upon me. But I can easily forgive you, if I should only know she could be free from harm now. And more, I do not for a moment believe this has been easy for you. I understand you too have suffered. I love and trust you both, but I am not a child. And I will rely on my own opinions in matters which concern *my* life, my very future peace and happiness and I promise you I will not rest until she is released."

"All in good time Bella," her father reassured.

"As for the letter," Mrs. Brookhaven started, "I admit it was I who disposed of the letter. I only thought it would cause you to miss her more, and I hope you can forgive me, if not now, perhaps some day in the future. But for now, I can only promise we will find a solution if we work together."

"And who will speak for Lenora? The odds are surely against her."

"Bella," her father answered, "we are all in this together now. For today, please give your mother and me time to sort things out. These events were years in the making and we cannot resolve them in one day."

Her father was right, she was exhausted and empty of words. With nothing more to say, Isabella retired to her room.

The hours passed slowly and no resolution was made or offered, bringing a restless sleep. Even Isabella's dreams haunted her. She would wake and feel chilled to the bone as she remembered the sad place Lenora resided. Days after her return home, she paced, she read, she mulled over the conversations with her parents, but she could not deny the burning wish to return to Lenora's side. Those days passed excruciatingly slow and it seemed with every moment the same voice spoke to her, "I'll be waiting." Over and over she heard Lenora's voice, those words, words spoken with a soft and trusting voice, until she could endure it no longer.

Nothing would loosen the grip of despair seizing Isabella's heart in suspension. How could she reason with her parents? What else was there to say that she had not already said? Her instinct was to flee, but if only her parents would consent, how much more wonderful would their reunion be. She prayed for guidance, she waited, and she tried to read the many signs placed before her in her mind's eye, but the signs were hazy and blurred and pointing in so many directions. She stood at this crossroad hoping for clarity, wanting to be certain of her choices. The more she pondered the possibilities, the more unclear her direction seemed, and she realized if she did not force herself to move in some direction, whether right or wrong, she would remain forever in that place of ill content. 'Yes,' she thought, 'perhaps that is the key. Just moving, just deciding to go in some direction, and then to keep moving on and on toward something. Something, anything. I shall try to do this. I cannot keep waiting for a sign, I cannot wait for anything…Precious time is ticking away and away and I must fill it up with life, with living, not the hope of what is to come, but the joy of now.'

There was nothing to do, but act and there was no better time than the present. She loved her parents, but she knew being with Lenora was the just and righteous thing for her to do. Perhaps one day her parents would understand, but until they did, they left her little choice. Once she had decided to leave, the path before her became increasingly more clear. Her closet was full of beautiful clothing, fine and wonderful things and she methodically concentrated on each one, for she could not take these things with her, and she was uncertain if she would see them again. She packed lightly but carefully, being mindful of the long journey ahead. She would need money.

Reluctant, but out of necessity, she entered her father's study, and with eyes turned toward heaven, quietly asked forgiveness before opening her father's safe. In her heart she knew he would forgive her, and she secretly believed if not for her mother's influence, he would do as his daughter wished. The only task remaining would be the letter. The letter she believed her parents deserved. Regardless of their recent behavior, they had always treated her with respect and love, and out of respect and love for them she would offer an explanation for her actions.

The letter was short and to the point. There was no need for details, no need to repeat her earlier pleadings. She waited until the night of the Hollingsworth Ball, knowing her parents would be late returning. She had offered the excuse of illness for her absence, but just as darkness fell and her parents were safely out of sight, she stepped out of her old life and into the carriage that would take her away forever. As she passed the gates of her home and reached the end of the adjacent road, a strong sense of guilt rose in spirit and she asked the driver to stop. Through the veil of her tears she took a final look at the only home she had ever known, and repeated in her mind 'there is no other way.'

Just as she asked the driver to continue, she noticed her father's carriage returning. Suddenly her guilt was substituted by fear.

"Onward, quickly!" She demanded, and as the horses raced away, she frantically searched for a reason why her father would have returned so quickly. Had they discovered her plan? Had she mistakenly left some clue behind which had betrayed her? Or perhaps, he had simply left something behind. Whatever the reason, her absence would be detected and he would come for her. Suddenly she regretted the closeness she had with her father, for it would be in his nature to check in on his ill daughter, and this kindness would uncover her deception and foil her desperate plan.

Chapter 24
A Journey

Hamilton remained at Brookhaven attending his young patient for several days. Isabella slipped in and out of consciousness, but never uttered a discernable word. Once certain her physical heath was generally restored, Hamilton returned home to the city he had neglected for so long, and assured Edward she would wake soon. Hamilton was confident Isabella would make a fully recovery and assured Edward he would return in a month's time if not sooner.

Edward waited by her side patiently, and it tormented him to see her struggling. He waited and he watched. Anxious for her to awaken he found himself praying for her recovery, "God, you know my heart, I ask this of you not for my sake but for hers. Please watch over her and lead her back to us. You alone can save her now."

Unaware of Edward's presence beside her, reflections of the icy descent made her shudder even now, regardless of the warmth of her chamber. Never before had she felt so close to death. The chilling water had rushed to her lungs as she gasped and struggled to reach the opening her clumsy plunge had left on the otherwise peaceful pond. As she thrashed about in the water, time seemed to advance so sluggishly that when she recalled the incident now, she could again feel each painful moment. She remembered praying in those few moments. With her spirit pleading, she fixed her eyes toward the misty blue opening in the ice. The sting of the chilling water felt to her like a million tiny needles piercing her skin. After the first few seconds, she became numb to the stinging pain and her attention became focused firmly on the strange sounds and sights surrounding her. Nothing in particular could be identified. It was all a bluish, green blur, but in the distance she could hear the faint muffled sound of a voice. From what direction it came she could not be certain. She knew it must be Edward and if she could just make her way to him he would save her. If only she could reach out and feel his warm hand, she would be delivered from certain death, but instead, she could feel only the hard, frigid ceiling of ice above her. 'I cannot die like this' she thought.

Over and over her spirit demanded 'save me, save me.' Though it only lasted merely two minutes, it had seemed an eternity before she felt Edward's hands pull her from her icy struggle with death. When delivered from the icy liquid to the precious, solid ground, she was free to yield to the weariness which consumed her.

Edward's desperate measures to save her, the long, snowy return to Brookhaven, the steady stream of caring friends watching over her bedside, and the countless prayers and wishes hovering over her, had all eluded her. Her days of unconsciousness had instead opened for her a long forgotten world which she could at last remember.

In Edward's quiet meditation, Isabella began to arouse from her long-enduring slumber and the first word falling from her lips was "Lenora."

"Lenora!" Edward answered, drawing nearer to her, "Lenora, my dear girl, the good Lord has brought you back to us."

"Edward," she whispered, trying to find her voice, "a. . . glass...water?" she asked with a strain of her gentle voice.

"Certainly!" Edward quickly poured a small glass of water and offered it to her. "Drink slowly," he instructed as he placed the glass to her lips. "Lenora, you must take things very slowly. How sorry I am, it was all my fault, I hope you can forgive me."

"Forgive?" she questioned.

"Do you remember ice skating? It was a beautiful day, you were gliding across the ice one moment, and the next you had fallen into the freezing water. I pulled you out and hurried you back to Brookhaven. I fetched Hamilton immediately. We have been on watch night and day for these seven days. But thank God, you are back."

"Edward," she started again shakily, "I . . . remember."

"I know it was frightening. I thought we had lost you, but it is over now and you are safe."

"No, no, you don't understand," she interrupted, "I mean, I remember...*everything*."

"My dear, dear girl, it is a miracle!" he exclaimed, clutching her hand in his.

"Yes, the mystery is solved. No longer do I linger on Time's empty shore. I finally have my past, but I'm afraid it is very troubling. There is someone I need to see, I must go to her right away," she said feebly, attempting to sit up, but failing.

"Lenora, please do not test your strength just now. You must rest, and besides I cannot allow it, you cannot go anywhere until you have fully recovered, whom is it you wish to see?"

"Oh Edward, my urging heart would not be still. And now I find its truth. And that truth is an astounding light, which has penetrated all the miseries of my past uncertainties. I heard a voice calling to me. I knew not from whence it came. Night and day I fretted its longing call, and now I find it was the most precious sort of love. The love of my dearest mother. The yearning to find her was the ghost who haunted my every day. I suppose her brave love has been a well of strength for me. It was her calling to me from a dark and frightening place. This voice kept repeating, 'I'll be waiting,' and it was her voice. And now my heart answers "I shall come for you." My mother is the 'Lenora' of my dreams and she is waiting for me Edward," she continued, but was growing weaker.

"And you shall go to her, but not today Lenora. You are too weak just now," Edward urged, fearing she was took weak to relay the whole of her past just now.

"I believe you, but it has been so long now. And Edward, my name is Isabella. I had the accident on the ship because I was on my way back to Lenora. That was two years ago, she must be so frightened and alone. I promised, I promised her Edward," she said desperately. "I must go to her immediately," she pled attempting to sit again, but Edward reached out for her hand, and gently touched her forehead with the other, as she dropped her head back on the pillow.

"Please calm down, dear, you know I shall do all in my power to help you find her. But, now is not the time, you must calm yourself, it is imperative you rest."

"I know you are right, I *do* understand, and though my spirit is strong, my body is so very weak. There is much to explain. I just cannot bear to imagine her in that awful scene of misery, waiting for me...wondering what must have happened to me, and I have been lost for so long. She has no one and she needs me desperately. I had finally found her and she must think I have abandoned her. I pray she will understand."

As she spoke to him her breaths became increasingly labored thereby affirming his admonition that she was presently in no condition for further exertion.

"Of course she will understand Isabella, you are her daughter, and though your delay has most certainly been cause for alarm, it has been nonetheless beyond your control. It will only take a moment to explain, to erase the years that have separated you. Please rest now, is there anything I can get for you?"

"Your presence is all I require for now. Thank you Edward, it seems you keep saving me. How shall I ever repay you."

"I only want your well being. And I am afraid I cannot take credit for your recovery. As soon as I returned you to Brookhaven, I went straightaway to collect Hamilton. He was at your side for days. Only when he was certain your wounds were healed would he leave Brookhaven and see to his obligations in Asheville. But I shall tell him you are with us once more and I know that he will be as pleased as I."

"Dr. Weatherly was here?" she asked, almost in disbelief, but as soon as she asked the question somehow she remembered his presence there, and the thought of it made her forget the urgency of her news for a brief moment.

"Yes, he is the faithful doctor. You are fortunate to have had his care. I am anxious to hear of your news, yet I could not forgive myself if I allowed my curiosity to strain you in your delicate condition. Rest now and I'll return in a few hours to hear more. For now please know you have my promise that I shall unite you with your mother, if it be the last thing I do."

Edward left Isabella to rest and retired to his study to

ponder the news of her enlightenment. 'Poor child, she must be so distraught, and her mother, I can only imagine the fear she must be feeling. I shall bring the two of them together. As soon as Isabella is well, we will go to Lenora.' Edward sent the following message to Hamilton informing him of Isabella's recovery:

> Hamilton,
> It will please you to know your favorite patient has finally emerged from the darkness, in more ways than one. Her memory is restored. I do not have the full account as of yet, but I wish to uncover it shortly. Please join us at your earliest convenience to examine her progress.
> Warmest Regards, Edward.

Edward waited tirelessly for the following two hours to pass, and could not remember feeling so anxious in years. The thought of loosing Isabella had monopolized his thoughts for the last several days, and the weight of those thoughts having been lifted from his mind was a great relief. And with her recovery, her full recovery of mind and body, he would now be able to learn about her past and what events had brought her to him.

Edward entered her room quietly and sat by her side patiently while she continued to sleep. He wanted to protect her from any pain. He struggled to understand why it was that kind people such as Isabella had to suffer. Seeing her so helpless and pale, his mind reached back to thoughts of Emily. . .

Emily had been such a bright and wonderful woman. He could still see her tear streaked face as her father took her away from him. He had never felt such pain as in that moment. One moment they shared a beautiful day of beginning and the next he would face the days ahead alone, a continuous ending of their life together. The day had begun so happily. He had left his bride briefly to purchase a fresh loaf of bread and a small jar of honey. He returned carrying the small parcel in his hand, and little did he know she had taken a position behind a grand old tree in hopes of bombarding him with icy snowballs. As he drew near, Emily crept up behind him and began to shower him with pelts of snow. In seconds he had chased her around the tree and gotten the best of her. Edward smiled remembering Emily's laughing eyes and the sounding of her laughter. Then like death sweeping over him, she was taken away. There was no time to say good-bye. There was no time to hold her one last time. He had kissed her and made love to her that day, but as they lay in each others arms, they knew not it would be the last time.

Edward still struggled to accept how suddenly she was taken from him, and he often wondered what might have been had he been given one last day with her, one more hour to tell her what he felt. Perhaps he could have made it through the days without her, without so much despair. But there was no such time, there were no such words of parting. There was only silence, there was only her absence.

"Edward," Isabella suddenly whispered, "are you alright, you seem very melancholy?"

"Just old memories. And the question is are *you* alright?"

"Much improved. You were right, I needed more rest. I am feeling much stronger after my nap, and I'm anxious to tell you of my past."

"And I am eager to listen, but I do not want you to strain yourself. You can begin now and we can finish when you regain your strength," Edward said comfortingly, but with authority.

"I should begin at the very beginning, and I warn you, it is quite extraordinary! My name is Isabella, Isabella *Brookhaven*."

Edward stared at her in disbelief as she continued, "It seems Elizabeth was my great aunt. And this house, Brookhaven, I think I was lured here because it reminded me of my family's home. Brookhaven is almost identical to my home in Kielderbridge. I never knew much about Elizabeth. I only knew she had died very young from a fatal disease. I am so pleased to have been introduced to her here. I feel I really know her now. But, more importantly, I must tell you of my mother, of Lenora."

Isabella explained the painful events of learning the governess she loved was indeed her mother, and how her own parents had cruelly separated them, and failed to help Lenora even after Isabella had discovered the truth. She recounted her visit to Meadowbridge and the precious last moments with Lenora, and the information she had gained from Lenora's nurse, Katia.

"Lenora is not insane, she is only so heart sick she could

no longer go on in the world. After losing everything, first the man she loved, my father. He died before I was born. Though I am not certain of the circumstances, I understand it was her family who arranged the adoption. She said knowing a part of him would always be with her was her only solace. But when I was born, I was taken from her and given to the Brookhavens."

Isabella explained Lenora's devastation and how her heart could only be healed by finding and being near her daughter.

"The only thing her wealth and privilege had ever brought her was sorrow, so she renounced it. She hoped her grieving heart would heal, but each day it seemed to grow more intense. She resolved to find me. She left her family home and took nothing with her, not even her name, for she wanted nothing from them. Being from a prominent family, she knew her name would be recognized, so she assumed the name of a family chamber maid, Lenora Lenton."

Isabella also explained how Lenora came to be in the asylum and how ardently she implored her parents to intercede.

"I could see the effects of the years and losses, and I decided I must convince my father to allow me to bring her back home. You know, even in that place of doom, Lenora possessed a certain magic over me. Somehow when with her my whole world is full of light."

Isabella then described the events of the night she left home to save Lenora, and how she ended up on a ship to America.

"I endured all the patience I could, and then the time for action came. I wrote a note in my father's hand releasing Lenora from the asylum and sealed it with our family seal. I must confess I borrowed a small sum of money from my father's safe, an act I am not proud of, but I could find no other solution. Though the carriage raced me quickly to the railway station, as I stepped onto the platform I spotted my father's carriage close behind me, and I knew I would have to elude him before boarding the train.

I opened my bag and retrieved the letter of release and the money. I left all else behind. I had no time to waste and I would be more anonymous if I boarded the train alone. All the while I was looking over my shoulder full of fear I would be discovered. And of course, my destination would be obvious to my parents. I would simply have to get there first. I was safely on the train and found a seat near a window where I watched, cloaked in shadows, as my father spoke with the station master, who nodded to him and in moments, to my horror, my father was allowed to board the train. I locked myself in a private car and answered to no one. Hours later we arrived in Liverpool and it would be only a short carriage ride to the Meadowbridge Asylum.

As I left the train, still wary of being discovered, I saw my father. I had stepped off the train only moments before and hid myself behind a massive column in order to view the other passengers departing. My father quickly became engaged in conversation with a man dressed in a military uniform. The officer soon led him away, thankfully in the opposite direction from which I stood. I had eluded him, but I knew my father's diligence would not go unchecked. I walked behind the station which opened directly to the port of Liverpool. There was no where to turn at this point. I was certain my father had given the officers instructions to alert every man with a carriage of my possible destination, and if a girl of my description sought such a destination she must be detained.

As I sat alone in the darkness, I pondered what I would do as I saw a figure approaching me. Almost without thought I began walking toward one of the large ships along the port. There had been talk among the passengers on the train of the S.S. Lucreta's voyage to America the next morning. The Lucreta's passengers would board in the morning, and I decided the ship would make a fine place to conceal myself for a few hours. I observed two stewards, neglecting their nightly watch, as they flirted with two young ladies aboard the ship, and I realized their distraction would afford my shelter.

I only had a moment to board the ship. I found the perfect hiding place and decided to stay there a few hours to allow myself time to think and my father time to give up his search. It had been a long day and night and I was so exhausted from my escape. You can probably guess what happened, I fell asleep. It was not until I heard the loud steamers sounding the following morning, that I realized I was still aboard the ship.

I jumped to my feet and found my way to the deck. Frantically I walked towards the pier, but the boarding ramps were being withdrawn. All around me passengers were waving good-bye and I began to scream "No, No! I must get off this ship!" I held the letter of release tightly in my grasp. Two stewards assured me there was no way to stop the ship.

As my eyes searched through the crowd, I saw that the last ramp was just being withdrawn. I started running to the edge of the ship. I could hear footsteps closely behind mine, but I only moved faster and faster until I felt the wind striking me boldly and warmly against my face. I was almost to the ramp when I turned to look behind me, and as I turned my gaze forward again, I suddenly felt the air beneath my feet. I had come to a second level of the deck and lost my balance. And with it, the letter was released from my hand. The last thing I saw was the letter, the very key to Lenora's liberty, sailing over the side of the ship, and then all was black.

I was on my way to America and without one recollection of anything which had come before. And then, two years later, I came upon the only thing that seemed familiar to me, a place where I found rest and friendship, Brookhaven, and of course, you know the rest."

"You have experienced quite an ordeal. I wish there was something I could say to ease your mind. Your parents must be more than alarmed about what has happened to you. And Lenora, your courageous mother, who has already suffered too much and to lose you again. You have been missing for quite a long time. What can I do to help you?"

"I hardly know what to do. I could send a message to my parents, but I must confess I fear I should not alert them of my whereabouts until I have found Lenora and assured her safety. Lenora's well being and state of mind must be my first priority. I only hope I can make it there in time."

"But your parents, Isabella, should you not let them know you are safe, at the very minimum?"

"I suppose I should. Do not think me lacking in compassion for them, I love them, I do, but, at any rate, you are right Edward. But only if I can find a way to let them know of my safety without revealing where I am," she proposed.

"If you write a letter, I will have it delivered to them. I shall instruct the messenger to deliver the message under strict orders not to disclose your whereabouts. Will you write this letter?"

"If I can find the words."

"Very good then. Isabella, I have thought the matter over and I really must agree with you. Time is of the essence in this matter. Your health does not permit the long journey, but I, I could make the journey and bring Lenora here to you."

"Oh Edward, I could not ask such a favor of you."

"But, Isabella, you didn't ask, I am offering. I will set out tonight to find her. I want to do this for you and I will have no argument."

"As you wish. Edward you have my eternal gratitude. I only pray we are not too late."

"Too late?" Edward questioned, "Was your mother ill?"

"It is not her health, but rather her heart for which I have concern. I wonder if her fragile mind has endured losing me for a third time. I fear also that my parents may have moved her. They were so against my being with her and my destination was undoubtedly no secret. Ample time has passed, enough to have her placed in another institution. But I must find her. I must."

"Isabella, concentrate on regaining your health, I promise you will need it when you are reunited with your mother. I will bring her to you. You have my word. I've already sent for Hamilton and he will attend to you while I am away. Do not worry, I will return as soon as I can and keep you posted on any progress."

"I believe you Edward, I know you will bring her to me."

"Yes, yes, and now you must rest."

Isabella smiled at him and she was comforted knowing she was closer to easing her mother's pain. After all the countless hours of searching and wondering, now her past was a fresh, raw memory. She knew everything, every detail and the memories of the last moments with her mother were the most vivid. She was very pleased to finally know her past, but it was also painful to learn it was colored black with so much despair. She remembered the argument with her parents and reflected how they too had known the pain of her absence.

'Why do we say such things to those we love. If only we could cast out this darkness within us. Will I ever reconcile this pain within me. How can I love them and despise them at the same time? It seems impossible, but it is true. I am simply not their little girl anymore. I am still their daughter, but I have changed. They see me as eternally the same silly girl and they cannot appreciate how I have grown and matured. I *was* that girl. But life does not allow us to remain the same. We cannot pass through the pain, even the happiness and not be changed.'

There was so much to be done, but she knew she must quiet her troubled mind. Edward was right, she needed to gain her strength in order that she might be restored to health before seeing her mother again.

Chapter 25
A Mission

Upon receiving Edward's note, Hamilton packed various instruments and remedies and set out for Brookhaven on his trusted stallion, Midnight, just before dawn. Midnight had been Hamilton's companion since he first arrived in Asheville. After his appointment there, he purchased Midnight from a breeder of fine stock in the outlying eastern farmland of the county bordering Asheville. Knowing the countryside was so densely populated, he knew he may be needed at a moment's notice to attend his patients.

To the extent one can fall in love with an animal, Hamilton had done just that. At first sight of him, he was taken in by Midnight's stature. He exemplified all the qualities he had never seemed to find in mankind. His confidence and strength were obvious to all, as he was at the top form of his line and had been bred from champion stock. Every muscle was visible as his lustrous coat and mane were solid black.

The cool fresh air pressed against Hamilton as Midnight marked a path in the new fallen snow. Without a doubt, this was the most beautiful day he had encountered in months. The forest seemed as a fairy land with all its misty snow yet lingering, glistening flakes sparkling along the evergreens, for spring comes late in this mountainous region. It was remarkable to him how the world around him could suddenly change and seem new and fresh. He had traversed this path countless mornings before but today it was as he were a child and Midnight were a winged horse from some magical land. His short journey was so invigorating he almost passed the gates of Brookhaven. He noticed a glow in the second window on the ground floor and he saw a figure on the verandah, though he could not make out whom it was. After securing Midnight, he walked onto the porch and was greeted by his friend.

"I see you received my note good man, thank you for responding so quickly Hamilton."

"Yes, I arrived last evening from the city. Supplies and the like, you know. But you appear to be departing, are you?"

"I am afraid so" Edward said pausing, "there is little time to explain, but I am off to Liverpool."

"Liverpool, but why on God's earth?"

"It is for her I must go, but I would leave here without a backward glance if I would only have your promise to stay here until my return. You may have full use of the estate, stables, all that is mine, of course."

"But how long do you propose..."

"I must say I know not. The short of it is she remembered her past. Her name is Isabella and her mother is being kept in a dreadful place and awaits her return. Isabella has been lost for over two years and she is her mother's one hope. I promised to intercede on her behalf, the poor girl is too weak for such a matter, as you will soon see. I fear the worst, but I shall hope for the best. Do I have your promise then?"

"This bleak winter has rendered me few patients, and in any case for you my friend, of course, you have my word."

"Isabella is expecting you, do forgive my sudden departure, but I think it best to allow her to rest and I feel it most prudent in this case to act as expeditiously as possible."

"Of course, may your journey be safe and fruitful."

With a final check of his bags, Edward was off to find Isabella's mother, and Hamilton watched him as his carriage sped away. He watched him with great admiration. Like the layers of sand and stone left behind by years of erosion, Edward was composed of many deep and colorful layers, each representing an age of pain or happiness, and as each one was revealed, Hamilton's respect for him grew deeper. Today's mission was a perfect example, without notice, he was departing to a remote land to right some unknown wrong of a poor creature whom appeared upon his doorstep. Though Edward had no responsibility for Isabella, he had taken up her cause as his own and it was just this sort of behavior Hamilton aspired to gain from his treasured association with Edward.

Hamilton searched his mind, his memories, his dreams, and failed to find a man among them he admired or respected more. Edward's past was shrouded in mystery, and it was a greater mystery how in his manner he seemed to hold the very secret to achieving contentment in this life. There was something in the way Edward saw the world which made it hopeful, and something about his self-reliance which was remarkable, and yet he seemed to gather his strength and confidence from some other force. Whether it was from deep within or from high above he knew not. Hamilton believed life itself had bestowed this gift to Edward.

Whatever had occurred, Edward appeared to be content with his lot, and he seemed to have all the answers to life's many questions. And though others thought him to be a maniacal and selfish fiend, he was as far from their suspicions as a man could be, and his present undertaking to return Isabella's mother to her was yet another proof of that truth. Hamilton took particular delight in the notion that he may take some part in Edward's mission. Edward's friendship was invaluable to Hamilton and doing this one favor for Edward would be an honor.

ഔര

Upon Edward's arrival in New York he learned a ship would be leaving for Liverpool in three days. He acquired a ticket for the journey and then set himself up in one of New York's finest hotels. As he was occasioned to be so near his former home, the orphanage, he planned to spend two of the 'days in waiting' making himself useful. He arrived in Riverbend the following day by mid-morning and visited with the children until early afternoon. He spent the rest of his afternoon, into the evening hours, pouring over the children's files assuring each of them had received their yearly checkup and made notes to the headmaster to provide new shoes to this child or that, a book for Angiolena, and so on and so on until each child's particular interest or need had been met.

The following day he met with young Hollis Beecher, an aspiring student of the Riverbend seminary with whom Edward had arranged an assistant's position at the orphanage, as it was Edward's wish to have a greater spiritual presence among the children. The seminary had long been associated with the orphanage and Edward thought it the perfect place to find a compassionate and energetic youth to instruct, and more importantly, to befriend the needy children. Hollis was the first young man to take the position and he proved to learn much from the experience while giving a large portion of his time and love to the children who so desperately needed him.

As Edward and Hollis took lunch, Edward noted the pureness of Hollis' gratitude, and the theme to Hollis' comments was the idea there was never enough time for all the children. Hollis had a genuine desire to do more for them than was in his power. With this interview in mind, Edward made a point of it to consult with the headmaster, whereupon he related his pleasure in Hollis' progress and the splendid effects of his labors. Edward made arrangements to sponsor the addition of another assistant immediately. The hours passed quickly and Edward would return to New York the following morning for his departure, but he decided upon a final visit of the dear little ones who had drawn him there.

All was quiet in the orphanage and everyone had been put to bed in neat little rows. There was a stillness about the place and a familiar scent in the air which transported him to years ago when he was just a boy and lay sleeping beside them in his own little cot. He fought the tears as he studied each face and listened to the silent breathing of these present little homeless souls, but as he contemplated all he had been able to give them, he realized each was warm in his bed, with a full stomach, and more importantly, under the care of people who truly loved and cared for them.

One of the children had kicked his blanket to the floor and Edward crept silently in the darkness to retrieve it. He picked up the blanket and placed it over little Johnny and noting the chill in the room closed a window which had been left slightly open and then returned to his room.

Before leaving for Liverpool Edward sent word to Isabella of his progress. As he boarded the ship, he observed the other passengers as he took in the stunning vessel. It reminded him of the great Victoria II which had taken the lives of his parents. Despite its power over men's lives, he shared his father's love of the ocean and of ships. He felt the same excitement each time he beheld the splendor of the sea or the striking beauty and power of a grand ship. Being out to sea, under the stars, with no land in sight made him feel free. He took a long breath of salty air and continued to his stateroom.

Edward was anxious to find Lenora, to be the instrument of peace for which Isabella has so longed. Isabella had brought him hope again, rescued him from his loneliness and thus he felt a certain delight welling up in his heart in having found a way to repay her. As he reflected on the previous few months, his life now seemed almost unrecognizable to him. In only a short matter of time so much had happened, so many feelings had surfaced and new ones had touched him in the furthermost regions of his soul. To unite Isabella with her mother would be to him the perfect recompense for his awakening.

After he was settled, he took a stroll along the deck to be once again alone at sea. As he stared out into the darkness a sound disturbed his silence. It was laughter, and it was so infectious he felt compelled to follow it. He looked about and then found the objects of the sounds. There was a young couple standing alone, only their shadows were visible in the darkness, but he could see they were very much in love. They appeared to be dancing, and lost in a beautiful world of their creation.

'It is these precious little blessings which give us a reason to live.' He reflected. 'Throughout my life I've experienced countless joyous moments, and now they exist only as memories. Some would say I have created a prison, but upon these walls I've erected are beautiful images and flashes of the greatest moments of my life, and they all share the same face, Emily's.'

The evening and the remaining journey was uneventful. Edward took his meals in his stateroom and only ventured out in the evenings when he was assured of solitude. He enjoyed the peaceful movements of the ship and kept his mind busy with reading books from the ship's rather extensive library. When the ship had completed its journey, Edward was more eager than ever and quite beside himself with the urging command to find Lenora.

"The distance to the Geldfield Inn?" Edward asked a passerby, obviously a native.

"Thirty minutes by carriage, depending on the weather."

"Fine, thank you, can you tell me where I can acquire a driver for the journey?"

"Certainly, follow this young man and he will take care of you."

Edward acquired a carriage and driver, and started out for the Geldfield Inn, more particularly, for Meadowbridge Asylum. Carriages in this small town had been scarce of late which required Edward to share part of his trip with a gentleman on route to Chesterfield North, an hour's distance north of Liverpool.

"Begging your pardon Sir, but I could not help hearing you are on your way to the Geldfield. I must warn you Sir that you may have been misled, the inn is not the sort of accommodation I would imagine a gentleman of your means to require," the passenger offered.

"I appreciate the information, but I have just arrived from the States, on a urgent errand. The accommodations at the Geldfield are of no concern to me, I assure you my presence here is quite from necessity."

"Forgive the intrusion, I only thought perhaps you would be disappointed. Your manner revealed you were unfamiliar with Liverpool and I assure you the Geldfield lies in its bleakest corner. It is only a few minutes away, but it as though it were a continent away. It is as removed from city life as a town can be. My business has occasioned me to visit there once or twice. It is a damp sort of land. A bit gloomy for my taste. But, America, now it is a lovely country, so much variety, fiery deserts, sandy shores and mountains of ice, you should count yourself lucky. I was there as a boy, in the state of Virginia, lovely place, as I recalled my first kiss happened there, something a lad does not quickly forget."

"Indeed," Edward answered.

They continued to keep each other company through the long and bumpy ride. Liverpool had been inundated with heavy rainfall during the previous two months making the roads muddy and therefore either one or the other of the wheels of the carriage would become mired in the softened earth every few moments, but after an hour the carriage stopped and Edward bid his companion farewell as he came to the door of the Geldfield Inn.

Edward's companion had been correct. The fog on this dark night was the thickest he had ever encountered, and it seemed as though an invisible line separated this little town from sunlight and any form of happiness. It was not like London, or even Liverpool, it was a new sort of city and it was horrid. The melancholy mood of the town was coupled by an unsettling feeling of déjà vu. From the moment his feet touched the ground, he experienced the strange and quite overwhelming sensation he had lived these moments before. Though he knew the feeling to be false, the sense of it remained with him as a tune might linger in one's mind. He found his accommodations to be adequate, and he was eager to take rest after the long journey. As exhausted as he was this evening he could not seem to relax.

Thoughts from his past haunted him. He could not remember feeling this way before. It had started when he first arrived in this strange little town. What could possibly be happening? "Emily," he whispered, "I wish you were here with me now. I am uneasy. Come to me and take these mad thoughts from my mind," he pleaded. With these words he began to feel calm. Thoughts of her came sweeping down over him and hushed away his fears. All he could see now was her face, her sweet, lovely face. And at last he was asleep.

ಸಿಂಧ

The morning came quickly, but with little change in the gloomy atmosphere. It was a dark and gray day, the clouds above hung low and menacing. The task at hand was to find Lenora and bring her to Brookhaven. Edward continued his struggle to escape the grip of the strange feeling which held him captive. He arrived at the Meadowbridge Asylum and was greeted by the same cranky fellow Isabella had encountered two years before. The shutter door opened revealing his bloodshot eyes, and the following gruff greeting:

"What do you want?" his voice and manner were as repulsive as the strange look in his eyes.

"Pardon me, but I am here to see one of your patients, and you will open this door at once!" Edward replied with a stormy confidence in his voice. The attendant obviously took this tone for authority and began to unlock the heavily bolted doors. Edward did not give him an opportunity for a response and continued, "Where might I find a patient named Lenora Lenton."

A smirk came over the strange little man's face, "right this way Sir." He led him to what appeared to be a waiting area and handed Edward over to Dr. Greene.

"Dr. Greene, this is.." the foul little man began.

"Edward Withers," Edward interrupted.

"He's here to see one of the patients."

"Thank you, Frederick." With the doctor's dismissal, Frederick slithered away with the same odd expression on his face. And though Edward was not a violent man a vision of striking this ghoulish creature could not be avoided.

"You are here to see a patient?" Dr. Greene repeated.

"Yes, Lenora Lenton. Can you show me to her room?"

"I am afraid that is not possible," the doctor replied.

"Forgive me, I must explain, I am here under rather strange circumstances, but it is imperative I see her at once," Edward pleaded.

"Are you a family member?"

"No, I am not, but I understand Lenora has been held here against her will for years and I am here to intervene on behalf of her daughter."

The doctor held up his hand, interrupting, "I am not refusing to let you see her. She is no longer here. I am sorry Mr. Withers, but you are too late."

"But this will not do. I must find her. Under whose authority was she released? And when?" Edward demanded.

"I understand you are disturbed by this news, but I must ask you to be reasonable. There was always a certain mystery surrounding Lenora. You said you are a friend of her daughter... Isabella, as I recall?" he asked.

"You remember Isabella?"

"Yes, beautiful girl, she was here to visit Lenora. After she left, her mother's demeanor changed drastically. I had never seen such a transformation. It was as if the years melted away. But then she waited for Isabella to return for her, and until now I have heard no word from her. I never understood what could have kept her away. When Isabella was here, she promised her mother, she would be returning shortly to have Lenora released. I suppose it was about three or four weeks later when Isabella's father arrived and demanded Lenora be moved. He arranged for her departure so suddenly that he failed to take her belongings," Dr. Greene offered with a tone of nostalgia remembering Lenora.

"But you must tell me where they have taken her Dr. Greene?"

"I was sworn to silence, and besides that, they did not tell me. I only tell you what I know now because I cared for Lenora and her daughter. I wish I understood why there is such a mystery about her."

"You mean you do not know?" Edward asked. The doctor gave him a puzzled look so Edward continued, "Isabella is not Mr. Brookhaven's daughter. It seems Isabella was taken from Lenora at birth without her consent. Subsequently, Lenora discovered the identity of her daughter's parents and cunningly took a position as Isabella's governess. When the Brookhavens discovered the truth and had her exiled to this Godforsaken place." Edward stopped short and the look on the doctor's face betrayed he had been too honest with this stranger, but Dr. Greene completely understood.

"I know what you mean, it is a brutal life here in the asylum. Forgotten children, lost years, lost opportunities, it would seem God *has* forgotten these poor creatures. I do wish I could help you, but Mr. Brookhaven is not a trusting man. He did not disclose her new location. I was simply ordered to release her records, and I have no idea where she may be. I am truly sorry."

"Surely she must be in another facility such as this one, and to my knowledge there are not many in this area. Could you make some inquiries? I shall cover any expenses in the matter?"

The doctor saw the desperation in Edward's eyes and remembering how happy Lenora was with her daughter he agreed to help, "Yes, I have associates who may be able to investigate her whereabouts for me. I will do all in my power to help you, to help Lenora. Would you like to see her room? As we are not accustomed to having wealthy patients, her room has not been filled, and as I mentioned earlier, there are still a few items she left behind. Maybe you could take them to Isabella, to ease her grief." he offered.

"Yes, and thank you, any item of her mother's would be a

comfort to Isabella, but she will not have to settle for a substitute. I will find Lenora. Even if I have to move heaven and earth, I will find her."

Moments later Edward was alone in Lenora's room. It was just as Isabella described. He looked through her meager belongings, a few clothes, a silver comb and a couple of books. He picked up an old gown, removed one of the books from the tiny corner bookshelf and walked over to the little cot. He sat down and held the gown to his face, he had not held anything this fragile since he had held Emily's small hand in his own. He could hardly believe how at peace he felt in this prison of a room.

As he held the material in his fingers and closed his eyes, Emily visited his mind. He remembered the feel of her fine hair in his hands. He saw brief flashes of their days together. The gown was worn and yellowed, but how soft it felt against his skin and it had reminded him of Emily. 'I will find you, Lenora, take heart, you will be with your daughter again,' he thought. He looked around the small room and imagined how brave Lenora must have been to have existed here for one day, and it was unimaginable to him that she had endured this horrid place for five years of her life. Edward could hardly bear the injustice and since she needed to be rescued from her terrible fate, he accepted the position with great satisfaction. He needed to be the one to save her.

The day was advancing and he had no reason to linger any longer in this place now absent of Lenora. Before leaving, he leafed through one of the books he had taken from Lenora's shelf. It was a very old book of sketches of the great castles of Europe. 'Excellent,' he thought. Edward loved medieval architecture, and he looked forward to lingering over this volume when he returned to the Geldfield. As he gathered the other personal items Lenora had left behind, he dropped one of the books, and a sheet of parchment fell to the ground.

The paper was rather old, and upon closer examination, he saw the document was a page of sheet music. He remembered Isabella explaining how Lenora had taught her to play the piano and he was pleased he could send the music to Isabella in remembrance of her mother. He would return to the Geldfield with unfulfilled aims, and attempt to find soft words to cushion the unfortunate news he must break to Isabella. He planned to remain at the Geldfield until Dr. Greene could offer him some clue as to where he might find Lenora.

Edward spent the next few days exploring the little town and looking at the books he had found in Lenora's room. He wanted to learn more about her, but the simple possessions she had left behind offered little information to ease his active mind. Lenora seemed to be a very determined woman, and he admired her already. She had been treated so unfairly and it was a painful thought to imagine how powerless she must feel, and to imagine a woman who had once known such strength, as evidenced by the lengths she had stretched to be with her daughter, being reduced to such a state, to such a place, made him shiver with the coldness of which the world was capable. He would meet her soon and deliver her from that fate and he looked forward to that day with great anticipation.

Chapter 26
A Stranger and a Friend

Hamilton loyally sat by Isabella's side throughout the day. He was a man of his word and had promised Edward he would watch over her carefully and besides it was an easy promise to keep. In the hours which passed before evening, he had concentrated intently on her delicate features. He was enchanted by her beauty and intrigued by her mysterious past. How had she become separated from her mother? What had brought her here so far from home? What would she say when she awoke? He imagined her soft voice whispering his name.

He wondered if he whispered her sweet name, if she might awaken, and hear in his words the longing he felt for her, but he did not wish to disturb her quiet rest or reveal his most guarded thoughts, not yet. He was aware more than ever he had reached the point in his years when he lacked a certain lust for life. Medicine had been his passion. All other relationships and principles had been cast aside. There had been an urgent need to fill himself with each minute fact. All of his energy and drive pursued his dream with such fervor there was little room for anything or anyone else. He could not say he regretted his choice. His occupation had left him alone in the world, but his purpose had been fulfilled in medicine. All of the tireless efforts of study, the limits of mind and body he had endured, had brought him to the sublime moment when he felt the power of life and death in his hands. In one brief second, his training and skill presented itself and a life was saved at his hands. It was his duty to follow his calling and he had answered it with a resounding yes. No, he could not say he regretted his choice, but there did exist in him a sadness, a oneness he now longed to abandon.

As Hamilton considered the choices of his past, he became weary of waiting for Isabella to awaken and involuntarily joined her in slumber. Just before the sun sank into night, Isabella stirred to find a sleeping stranger by her bedside. But as her eyes adjusted, she realized he was no stranger at all, it was Dr. Weatherly, and it was a pleasing discovery. In her previous meetings with him she had forced herself to avoid looking into his eyes, but now in his slumber she could gaze upon him without fear of the consequences. She was so taken with the look of him she was speechless and quite satisfied to remain in the quiet of dusk watching his broad chest rise and fall. Before she realized it, she was mimicking each of his breaths with her own.

Hamilton sat in a lounging manner against a chair which had been moved to her bedside. As her eyes admired his healing hands so large and without blemish, she did not see his eyes were now beginning to open. The room was nearly dark now and he began to sense her eyes upon him. He allowed his eyes to adjust to the light and secretly relished how admiringly Isabella looked upon him. With a fear of embarrassing her, he shortly closed his eyes and pretended to be wakening from a deep sleep. His deliberate movements startled her, and her heart began to flutter rapidly beneath her gown as she averted her eyes from his. However uncomfortable she felt, she disguised it with grace and confidence.

"Good evening Dr. Weatherly," she said, with sparkling eyes despite the darkness of the room.

"Good evening. Contrary to what you may think, Edward has left you in very capable hands. You must forgive my napping, I hope my presence here did not alarm you," Hamilton said with some agitation as he awaited a response which did not come. With the silence between them thickly filling the air and without knowing what to say, Hamilton removed himself from his comfortable position and walked over to her beside table. Isabella's eyes grew wide as he came toward her and she strained to make out the features of his face. He opened the table drawer and placed a single match between his fingers and looked to her for approval. She nodded in agreement, and he lit the oil lantern, which instantly brought an amber glow to the room and revealed his visage to her in full. Hamilton's striking looks were somewhat overwhelming, and made her slightly gasp as she exhaled.

"Pardon?" he asked quickly, thinking she had said something.

"Nothing," She whispered, embarrassed and reddening.

"Very well then, tell me, how are you feeling?" But Isabella responded with a question of her own.

"Where is Edward?"

"He has left for Europe in search of your mother, do you remember?" he asked cautiously.

"Yes, of course I remember, but my mind seems to be a jumble now."

"And it is to be expected, the fever has finally broken and you have lost many hours. But I am here now for as long as you should need me, and I shall remain until you are quite well. Edward will have my head if I don't have you at optimum health when he returns!" Hamilton said smiling.

Isabella returned his smile, and felt a certain peace in Hamilton's confirmation that Edward would keep his promise. The silence returned and she searched her troubled mind to find a word or two to offer, but could think of none, and then he softly touched her forehead and cheek, but she resisted his touch, turning her head slightly and furrowing her delicate brow. She could not imagine his boldness.

"I was checking for fever," he admonished in his defense.

"Yes, of course," she said with a stricken look, "I apologize. I am not quite myself and recent events have left me feeling thoroughly out of sorts, and I must own I have quite forgotten how to interact with others. You mustn't hold it against me."

"Never mind all that, in my estimation your demeanor seems quite extraordinary considering. . . well, Edward took the liberty of . . ."

"Oh," Isabella interrupted, "I see, Edward explained the story of my unfortunate past. Details, so many painful ones. . .and my mother, I…hope. . ." she began as she cast her eyes away, but could not find the words to finish her thought.

"You mustn't worry now, not on my account. Edward has departed in search of your mother, and I, I am here as your doctor, but I hope you will allow me to become your friend."

"I should like that very much."

"Then it is settled, my first duty shall be to prescribe a day without worry. I forbid you to worry!"

Isabella laughed, "If only it were so easy as that. But being the fine doctor I am confident you are, I suppose you will administer your prescription for a completely care free day in the form of some delicious potion?"

"Oh, I am sorry Edward must have misspoke, you see I may be a mountain doctor, but a witch doctor I am not!" Hamilton said as they both laughed, "But," he continued more seriously, "if I could make your worries disappear I would. I'm afraid it is simply mind over matter."

"Yes, but as the scriptures say, the mind is willing but the flesh is weak. I so want to trust that all will be well, but I keep remembering my mother in that place of despair, I see her eyes void of all hope and knowing I am responsible. . ."

"Isabella," Hamilton started, "if I may, from what Edward explained to me, you cannot blame yourself. You did all in your power to save your mother, and she will know this, it is unfair and unfortunate, yes, but it is not too late. Edward will bring her to you, and all will be well, count on it."

Hamilton's confidence was inspiring.

"Okay then Dr. Weatherly, I will trust you, all will be well," she repeated, smiling.

"That's it, now you are getting the idea Lenora, sorry, I mean. . . Isabella."

"I am honored to be called my mother's name, but now that I know my name, I can tell you my friends call me Bella, and you may as well."

"Bella, I like that, but friendship is to be earned and mark my words, I intend to earn yours. And now we need to discuss your health?"

"I am going to be alright, yes?"

"I do not foresee any sustained physical injury, but one must remember we humans are not simply body alone. There are those in my profession who seek to heal the body with no concern for the spirit or mind, but for many reasons I understand the harmony of mind and body, and it is your mind which disturbs me. I wish to watch you closely and help you, if you allow me, of course, to face these frightening thoughts, these dreams which chased you here."

"Yes, it is no small matter what I have suffered. And I honestly wonder if I didn't will myself to forget the painful memories of my past. My life had been the perfect package all wrapped in fancy papers and tied with bright strings and bows, but then I found the strings were binding and the package was empty. Empty of love and of truth. Having to relive the betrayal has been a challenge, but the worst of it was seeing my mother, seeing Lenora in that most wretched place, so sad and lost. I keep imagining her in that loathsome place. I see her looking toward the door expectantly each time she hears a knock. I see her gazing out of her window through the iron bars as summer turned to spring and then to autumn, to cold, bare winter, and then summer again with no sign of my return. Had she known the extent of my love and devotion for her? Did she worry I may have fallen upon some tribulation which kept me from her? I wonder if she knows I love her. I wonder if my absence has stolen the last bit of light from her eyes and extinguished the fire which once warmed her heart. But here am I, with only these questions, and time and distance my enemies. It is almost more than one can bear, but I shall bear it, I am ready to take up this challenge. And with Edward's help, I know all of my questions will be answered."

"Your resolve is amazing Bella. You have been through much, but I assure you, Edward will do all in his power to rescue your dear mother. If it is in his power, you can rest easy knowing she will be here by your side. You have your hope. It has brought you here, has it not? And Bella, do not look upon time as your enemy. Sometimes time is our only friend. It is the one thing on which you may depend. This suffering will pass and time, while it keeps you apart, it shall most certainly bring you together again," he assured her.

"Thank you, I had not thought of it that way," she said smiling.

Hamilton excused himself to the sitting room and left Isabella to rest. Her dinner would be served in her room and he would not see her until the following morning. As he seated himself comfortably upon Edward's favorite leather chair in the gaming room, resting his feet idly on the matching ottoman, he reflected on their conversation, and looked forward to many more. Throughout the previous months he had hardly been able to stop thinking about Bella. Part of it was her beauty, but it was something far greater than that. He was intrigued by her. This beautiful young girl without a past. And with every new encounter with her, his belief that she was unlike anyone else he had ever met only strengthened. There was a genuineness about her which refreshed him and a light about her which filled any room she happened to wander into. Though she had been lost, though her world seemed utterly shattered, she was more at peace than anyone he had known before. He sensed her fondness for Edward and knew instinctively it had nothing to do with his great wealth. She, like himself, had decided to leave behind the security of her family's wealth, seeking a greater security in the peace of one's clear conscience. Hamilton's feelings for Bella were noble. He reasoned that to become her friend would be his only need, but his desire was a far different matter. Could he stop his heart from placing her image alone in his mind? Each time he managed to force her image away, he would suddenly recall how she had admiringly looked upon him when she had assumed he was asleep.

ℰℭ

    The next day Isabella was anxious for a change when Hamilton came to greet her, "And how is my patient this morning?"

    "Good morning Dr. Weatherly, I assure you she is feeling much improved, but quite tired of being an invalid."

    "Are you questioning my competence as a doctor, Bella?"

    "I should be a wonderful reference for your astute and capable abilities and say you were the best doctor whom ever lived, conditioned of course, upon your allowing me to leave this room today."

    "Hmm, you propose a bargain, what to do?" he said placing his index finger upon the side of his chin.

    "Please?" she pled, with a charming smile.

"All right, all right, you have won, but I will allow you this only as a man, and not as a doctor, for what man could not resist your smile? But truly you are too weak to walk. I shall have Charles prepare a chaise for you. In which room would you prefer to spend the day?

"The music room, no the library, or...it is too difficult to choose, I love all the rooms of Brookhaven and I should be happy in any of them."

"Shall I choose for you?"

"Yes, please do."

"I say we place you in the east sitting room. I shall push the drapery aside and you may lounge by the window on this lovely day."

"Excellent. The perfect place, and can you bring me a book to read, from the library?"

"I shall do more, I shall read to you myself!"

"Would you, really?"

"It shall be my pleasure, but I must be Dr. Weatherly again, it is time for an examination, it will be painless, I promise."

After a quick examination he had the sitting room prepared for her and retrieved the two books from Edward's book list Bella requested, and then returned to her room and carried her down the stairs and into the sitting room, an act which would be repeated over the next several days. And from this chaise she would recline in complete comfort as he transported her to the castles of England, to the cold and noble city of St. Petersburg, and into a forest of enchanted woods, in his lusty and rich voice as he read from the cherished pages of Edward's ancient books.

As the days advanced so did her strength and eventually instead of being carried, Hamilton would act as her crutch until finally she could move about Brookhaven on her own, though she missed the feeling of being in his arms. In these days of independence, Hamilton's constant doting and care were not misplaced, for she maintained a deep cough from her icy fall which caused him many hours of reflection and concern. This remnant of her fall was a source of great irritation to her as well, for it and it alone was the obstacle to her joining Hamilton on his garden walks in the afternoons. Bella's constant desire was to join him inside the fragrant paths of Brookhaven's gardens. At the commencement of each day she prayed she might make it through the day without an unpleasant episode, and with this answered prayer that she be granted the right to join her sweet doctor.

Isabella could hardly manage to rest her weary mind from all its imaginings. She felt both relief and panic at Edward's departure. How blessed she was to have found herself under his gracious care, and now she was twice blessed in his extravagant kindness to find and return her mother. Her heart went out to him, but she could not deny the uneasiness she felt in his absence. And there was the matter of Hamilton. She had not imagined he would be so wonderful. There was a deepness of soul to this man. When he spoke she could hear a tenderness and a strength she had longed for. Though he did not have the look of the men she normally admired, she was certainly attracted to him.

Hamilton was unlike the beaus she had known in her former life. For they had been boys and Hamilton was a man. The time for schoolgirl crushes had passed. She had always been fascinated by the notion of love. But never had she come close to giving her heart to another. Many of her friends had become engaged and she longed for the happiness it seemed to bring them, but she had never felt compelled to entrust her heart to someone, not until now. 'But does he think me a child? I am only nineteen. He must be at least thirty. And is now the right time with all that is yet broken in my life?' she questioned. So many changes lay ahead, so much left to be resolved. Where would she and her mother turn? Edward had been kind enough to offer them an invitation for a continued respite at Brookhaven until her mother fully recovered from the ordeal of being institutionalized, but they could not remain there forever.

Underlying the uncertainty of her future was the sadness she felt for the loss of her old self. The person she had been before she learned of Lenora's banishment would never return. A part of her was lost forever. The part of her who knew the Brookhavens as her parents. She ached for the loss of her mother, not Lenora, but Charlotte Brookhaven, the woman she had known as mother since she was a child. Isabella loved her and wanted to believe in her again, but how to resolve these feelings? Charlotte Brookhaven had been responsible for tearing Lenora's life apart. Could such a selfish act be forgiven? Bella's feelings and loyalties were divided. Her parents had given her much, but at the same time they had taken from her something irreplaceable.

Isabella fought the tendency to compare the two women. For it would not be fair with such a soft heart as hers. And besides who could not feel sympathetic toward Lenora? Since Bella's earliest years, only when with Lenora, did she feel that brand of serene peace which only one who knows contentment is allowed to feel. She believed her parents loved her, but Lenora had showered her with such addictive affection. When with her she felt a sense of home, a sense of belonging that had been nonexistent with her own mother. However alienated Isabella was from her mother now, she felt a deep longing to resolve her feelings toward her. She attempted to understand her, to put herself in her mother's position when faced with such unfortunate circumstances, but it was a feat she could not accomplish.

Isabella reflected that she and her mother, Charlotte Brookhaven, were like two separate forces which existed together, but would never truly understand one another. It was like the relationship of night and day. They each have their charms, but never can they exist in harmony together. Night is intrigued by the bright light, but at the same time, it harbors a certain jealousy for what it cannot understand. The darkness is content with its fate, and thereby the light cast a threatening shadow over it. Night says, this is who I am, I cannot change, the light is too bright and it will shut me away. But there is a time for light and a time for darkness. Neither of them is right or wrong, each of them simply exist. But just as darkness fears the light, the light knows of darkness and holds its own fears. The light wants to touch and illuminate everything, but understands that before light there was darkness. Day must honor Night, it must appreciate it, but the strength of its light is much too strong to be contained. Each one must remain separate however, together they create the whole. For who can fully understand darkness without light or light without darkness? They compliment each other. If only they knew.

Maybe one day she and her mother would realize their respective places within each other's world, and she would at last find the resolution for which she prayed. Until then she was content with her present company and had not the strength to suppress the emerging feelings which rose in her heart for

Hamilton. A week had passed since her last coughing attack and Hamilton had promised to allow her a day in his cherished gardens, and remembering this thought quieted any previous feelings of distress.

Chapter 27
A Letter of Her Own

From her window Isabella watched Hamilton below in the gardens. He would spend hours there, and tomorrow she would join him. She often wondered what he thought of when in the gardens, and wished he might give even one thought to her. Even if he never knew how she adored him, she would be happy to know this feeling had existed in her heart. Suddenly, his movement caught her eye and she noticed he was leaving the solace of the gardens to return to Brookhaven. She rushed over to the mirror, pinched her cheeks and picked up the novel by her bedside. In moments, there was knock upon the door.

"Come in," she almost sang.

"Bella, I've spent the last hour in the gardens, procrastinating, delaying something unpleasant and contemplating how I might tell you."

Isabella looked at him puzzled

"I must leave Brookhaven."

"Leave? But why, why must you leave me, I mean, leave Brookhaven?"

"Believe me I do not wish to leave, and I made a promise to Edward, but a ghastly sickness is sweeping through Asheville and reaching even to the farthest outlying counties of its borders, and my presence is required immediately. Regretfully, I must go right away and face the task before me. But I do so only knowing with great assurance that you are coming along splendidly, and I see no need for my presence here."

"I see. You are needed. Of course you must go. But when must you leave?"

"At first light tomorrow."

Isabella could hardly hide her disappointment, but his kindness and sense of duty were why she cared for him so and she would not allow herself to pout.

"I only wish we could share our day in the gardens, when might you return?"

"I know not how long I shall be needed, but not to worry, I shall return as soon as practicable, I assure you. And now, I must examine you," he said glancing toward her bed.

Dutifully, she walked to the bed and sat down. He walked towards her and her heart began to pound. He would be leaving tomorrow, but he was here now. He was right here and in seconds he would be touching her, in seconds she would feel his warm breath against her skin as he checked her heart. As he looked into her eyes, she prayed he would not read her thoughts. He examined her hands. They trembled. He touched her throat with his warm fingers. His hands touching her now made her breath quicken.

"Are you feeling well?" he asked

"Yes, much better actually. I suppose I am nervous. . . about being here, alone, I mean," she stumbled over her words.

He took her small hands in his own and stared squarely into her eyes, "Oh Bella, do not worry, no harm will come to you, and I shall return soon. I know just the remedy for you, it may be a day early, but a promise is a promise!"

"What do you mean?"

"You had my word I would introduce you to Brookhaven's gardens, and tonight, after dinner, I shall keep my word. I shall take you to the most enchanting spot, it is on the east side by an enormous willow tree."

"I know," she said without thinking.

"But I didn't think you had been in the gardens?"

She took his hand and led him to her window. When he looked out of her window he understood she must have seen him there. He wondered to himself how many times she had watched him from her window. After dinner, as promised, Hamilton led her to the gardens.

"Dr. Weatherly, look there, we can see every star, isn't this a most beautiful evening?"

He looked at her as she spoke with such innocence and joy, and responded, "Indeed, and even more lovely than usual. Brookhaven is an enchanting estate. Were it mine, I would give new birth to these gardens. This is my favorite spot in all the world."

"What do you like about it?" she asked gaily.

"What is there *not* to like? Sure, you must overlook the neglect of countless years, But if you disregard that and imagine how beautiful it once was. It is so natural and quiet. So far removed from everything else. I only wonder what sort of man could envision such a place of beauty?"

"One who has known love," Bella answered.

"Really?" Hamilton questioned with curiosity.

"Has Edward not told you of the history of this wonderful place?"

"I'm afraid not. You see we share a unique sort of friendship. It is only recently he has confided in me anything personal at all."

"Then allow me! Love built this magnificent place. There was a young man named John Collins who fell in love with a girl named Elizabeth Brookhaven, she was my father's great aunt. John built this home as an exact replica of the home Elizabeth grew up in. He was to give it to her as a wedding gift. They were to marry after he fulfilled his obligations to his employer and secured their future. They wrote to each other from across the sea. You should hear their declarations of love. When I'm not playing the piano, I've spent hours pouring over their sweet letters. But, oh how dark fate was cruel to them. Elizabeth died before they could wed, and John lived here without her until his own death. All these weeks I have read Elizabeth's words over and over and then I learn she is my ancestor. As we stand here this night, a portrait of her hangs in the home of my youth."

"Extraordinary. You stumbled upon this great mansion and you find it is indeed part of your past? Quite, incredible. You see it is altogether right you found us."

"Yes, and now Edward will find Mother and all will be

mended. It is as if Brookhaven lured me here to help me find my way home, my way back to Lenora."

"Yes, there is a grand design to all things, I am certain of it. And Brookhaven has quite the history! I really cannot believe Edward has never enlightened me of the story of John Collins and his Elizabeth."

"I was intrigued by Brookhaven, possessed almost by a feeling I'd been here before, and the reason now is obvious. Edward seemed reluctant to share all the details of the story, but even his brief mention sparked my imagination, and I became haunted by it, I suppose he tired of my questions and decided to allow me to learn of their lives first hand."

"And did it satisfy your curiosity?"

"Is that not obvious Dr. Weatherly, what about you, would you like to hear more?"

"Absolutely."

"Very well then, it was a dark age in which they lived, and disease spread itself thickly, poisoning their plans. Elizabeth's only joy in John's absence was visiting the village children everyday, offering them sustenance and care. She was gifted with an innate sense of what was truly important and she knew what she expected of herself and wanted from life. What she wanted most was to journey to America to be with John. It was her dream that together they would somehow make a difference in this world. The time for their reunion was drawing near, but their reunion was sooner than they had even expected.

While she waited patiently for the days to pass, each day a day closer to seeing him, he prepared a new home for them. Only the best for Elizabeth. He promised her he would take care of her and he kept his promise. The beautiful words of love she said to him he kept close to his heart. Clearly from the worn state of the letters each one was read and re-read. But the last letter spoke of regret and pain, for it would truly be her last. In it she revealed she contracted consumption, as you know, a fatal lung disease, most likely from her close associations with the sick children she had attended.

Elizabeth urged John to cancel his trip. I imagine she did not want him to see her in her condition. She was dying and so must their future together. She wanted him to remember her as he had known her before. Without the prospect of their life together, all was lost. Their dreams had dissolved like a summer storm in a dessert leaving only death and isolation. But our hero would hear nothing of it, when he received her final letter he would not accept the truth, nor her admonitions. He trusted God would save her and not only refused to cancel his trip, but made arrangements to return to her at once.

Her last letter had been written weeks before, and he prayed he would not be too late. At once he departed for the long journey back to Northumberland (England). The Brookhavens owned the largest estate in the county and it can be seen from every point in the city of Kielderbridge, a charming little village by the shore. The devastating disease which would claim his loved one's life, was clearly indicated by the "X"s painted in black upon the doors of many of the shops and homes, and the other undeniable indication was the solemn quietness which seemed to haunt this once jubilant town. To his delight his favorite bakery remained open and the family that owned it had been untouched by the life-taking disease. From the baker's window the imposing estate stood slightly veiled in a light mist which came from the sea just beyond its walls. He had come to love the little village years before and viewed it as a place he belonged, as it was a part of the person he loved most.

John believed God would not let him go through this life without Elizabeth, not after he had waited so long and worked so hard to make a home for her, but God's will is not always what one expects or hopes. John rushed to her side and remained there until her last breath. Peacefully she vanished from him in the night and for days he stayed with the Brookhavens. John asked that some of her belongings be sent with him to back to the loneliness of Brookhaven. Once the crates arrived, he went through each box and gave every item a special place. He spent little time here at Brookhaven, I imagine it was too painful a reminder of the lost opportunities.

He worked and he came home and he worked and he came home, again and again. Everyday was the same. Every night was the same. After many years of despair for his Elizabeth, he was found dead, clutching one of her letters. There was no medical explanation for his death, but Edward said it is rumored grief itself claimed his soul, and I believe it did," Isabella finished.

Hamilton's heart seemed to awaken from a long repose as she finished her account and looked upon the stars with her hair sparkling in the moonlight.

"Such a tragic story, but perhaps they are finally at peace, finally together."

"Yes, at last, it is what I imagine," Isabella answered.

"Bella, I shall miss these days I've spent here at Brookhaven. I shall miss you and being here in this special place."

"And you will be missed Dr. Weatherly. I promise to come here each day until you return and I will think of you when I am here, and thus you will be here also."

"I would like that very much, but my dear, you should return to your room now. You have had enough excitement for one day. You are not yet quite as well as I would wish you to be. Let us say good night here, in my favorite place in world," he said smiling.

"Good night Dr. Weatherly, and God speed, I shall pray for your prompt return," she said as she left him alone and returned to her room.

ଽଚଓ

Hamilton stood in the gardens for several moments in solitude and pondered, 'Has Bella watched me in the gardens every day? Must I allow her to slip away from me?' His heart answered for him 'No!' But how? The burning desire of his heart was to confess his feelings, but were those feelings revealed, he knew he would not be able to remove himself from her. He pondered how her eyes had gleamed as she spoke of John and Elizabeth's letters, and in that moment he knew what he would do. 'Bella will have her own letter of love,' he thought with pleasure.

Hamilton returned to the mansion in search of paper and pen to set down the words of his heart. As he had lingered long in his cherished garden, the small number of inhabitants of Brookhaven had retired to their chambers for the evening, and he found it still and quiet. He searched the parlor, and the gaming room but found no paper. He was certain he would find writing materials in Edward's study. Though he had never entered the study he proceeded to the door without pause, but much to his disappointment found the doors to be bolted. He lay against the locked door in defeat, but then decided he may try one last place.

The door to Edward's bedchamber stood before him, and to his delight opened as he turned its knob. Entering the chamber, he closed the door behind him quietly. H understood well that no person other than Edward was allowed to pass its threshold. But Hamilton reasoned his presence would never be detected, and as Edward's desk came into view any anxiety he had experienced vanished.

Hamilton opened the top drawer and found a stock of parchment and various seals, and as he removed the box of seals and a sheet of the paper, he spotted a folded piece of the same parchment standing on its side against the drawer. He removed the paper and found it was a poem, written in Edward's hand. Out of his deeply rooted sense of honor and value of privacy, he closed the poem at once, and returned it to its original position in the drawer. But then curiosity trumped integrity and he could not continue his current task without removing the poem and reading it...

> Come into my chamber my love,
> for the darkness of night is falling.
> I am here alone and all day I have waited
> for the sound of your gentle voice calling.
>
> When deep in my dreamy slumber,
> I awaken to your blissful embrace,
> where I am yours and you are mine
> In my heart's most sacred place.
>
> At last, am I, again in your arms,
> and all the spaces between us are gone.
> And I am lost in your gaze and the sound of your voice,
> a sound I have missed far too long.
>
> What sweet words and soft touch you offer,
> as my spirit calls out, "I am home!"
> And far from me now are the lost days and nights
> in this place where my soul has flown.

Here in your arms I am home once more,
and feelings of contentment and rest,
surround and sustain me as though I were never
removed from your precious breast.

And for a fleeting moment, I am yours again,
and the sadness and tears are erased.
What joy I have found in the hope of your love.
What rest in your blissful embrace.

And your heart beats as true as ever.
And your eyes shine just as bright.
And my love grows ever stronger
in these moments before Morning's light.

Oh hated light, why must you come now?
When I feel my true love's heart?
I beg of you, "Just one moment more,
Let me hold her before I depart."

But Morning and Time wait for no one.
Not even for love, like our own.
And so begins another morning,
as I face the empty world, alone.

  Once again another layer of Edward's character was revealed to Hamilton, and he suffered from its revelation, realizing the intensity and scope of Edward's loss. The thought of his friend spending his days longing only for sleep in hopes he may be united with his wife, if only for a brief and illusory moment, struck Hamilton's heart with such a heavy burden that the thought of it was too strong and heartbreaking to face.
  The only vision which could console him was his mind's ever present vision of his dear Bella, and his original mission on entering Edward's chamber. After entering the shadow of pain which reading Edward's poem had introduced, Hamilton was more determined than ever to further his bond with Bella. For what a lonely and tortured existence awaited him if he did not confess his love for her, and ensure his days be spent with her at

his side. He returned the poem to its proper place, and borrowed a piece of parchment and wrote the words he longed to shout from the very rooftops of Brookhaven. The letter would settle the matter once and for all.

Isabella had promised she would visit the gardens each day and tomorrow when he would be returning to Asheville, she would find his confession of love for her there. He lingered over this writing a few moments more and then promptly sealed it with a green seal, which he knew to be her favorite color, and which contained a representation of a hummingbird, incidentally the only suitable seal in the collection. He returned the paper, seals and pen as though they had never been touched, placed the letter in his coat pocket and retired to his own bedchamber.

Just before dawn the following morning, he positioned the envelope upon the bench by the willow tree where they had stood regarding the stars the previous night. He placed a small pebble atop the note and with much displeasure departed for Asheville. The letter read:

> My dear Bella,
> Do not think me a coward for leaving this letter in place of my facing you with these thoughts. It is simply when you spoke of the cherished letters you have come to love, though I dare not compete with those precious writings, I observed your fondness for them, and I thought it fitting to reach you in this way. I am aware of the difference in our age, but nonetheless I am constantly struck by your maturity in spirit. I have grown fond of you and pray you may consider me in the same way. That you are beautiful is obvious, but the kindness and compassion which radiate from you are intoxicating, and I boldly confess that you are all I can think of. I say this to you now because I know not how long I should be honored by your presence at Brookhaven. Someone told me once that when pure love existed in one's heart, one knew it unmistakably, and it would be a detriment and a great peril to one's soul to let such feeling go

unclaimed. Upon my return, if you should share these feelings you may simply leave a corresponding note in this spot and I shall know. If my feelings for you are unwanted, we need not ever mention this letter. In either case, in my absence, may you read my words and know the meditations of my heart, trusting that then, now and forever more, I shall hold these feelings of love for only you.
With all my heart, Hamilton

On the same spring morning, the welcome morning air cooled Bella's face as she opened the door to the verandah. Hamilton had left Brookhaven before she had had the opportunity to tell him goodbye, but last night's memory was wonderful, and she was pleased she could hold on to it until his return. It had been a calm morning, but just after breakfast, the mid morning day raged with howling, chaotic winds. There was a shower and then finally the cool rain left behind a clear and beautiful afternoon. So thrilled to be out of doors she hardly noticed the wind swept branches and broken petals strewn across the grounds of the garden. Slowly she made her way through the flowers, under the gazebo dripping with fragrant boughs of wisteria, until she reached Hamilton's favorite willow tree.

The warming sun had dried the bench so she sat down with her thoughts of him and took a deep breath of the fresh air. The sweet scent of flowers perfumed the air and the glorious greens and blues of the landscape filled her eyes and heart. 'No wonder he loves this place,' she thought. 'One can hardly be exposed to such beauty and not be positively effected by its generous offerings of serenity.' Before returning indoors she decided she would entreat Charles to see to having the grounds surrounding the gardens somewhat cleared, as the thought of Hamilton finding his magical garden in such a state of ruin much distressed her.

Chapter 28
A Gift

Day after day passed without variation as she awaited some news from Edward. It was her constant prayer he might bring Lenora to her and that Lenora would find it in her heart to forgive Isabella for abandoning her for such a long time. Patience proved to be hard to master and she struggled to be maintain positive thoughts, to be stronger than her fears, finding success at times, but then the old patterns of thought would haunt her and she would be filled with questions again. Hamilton had left Brookhaven abruptly to attend to more pressing needs of other patients, and besides, she had fully recovered now. There was no need to inconvenience him. She had monopolized his time to a fault already, though she had to admit his company was sorely missed. On this particular day, the relentless rainfall had finally ceased and the sun had made brief appearances, which was sufficient to improve her mood.

The mouths of the gargoyles upon the crest of Brookhaven's parapets spewed continuously and profusely, forming muddy pools on the ground. The steady sound of the pounding earth interrupted Isabella's concentration. She was reading a volume of literature containing poetry from the great poets of Western Europe, but found herself reading a passage and then turning a page without the slightest notion of what she had just read. She repositioned herself in her chair in hopes of gaining a new perspective when she heard distant footsteps. She jumped to her feet and ran to the door. She pulled it open with both hands, but instead of finding Hamilton as she had hoped, she found Charles, "Oh, good afternoon Charles," she said deflated.

"No doubting you were expecting someone... else?"

"I imagine I was thrilled at the thought of having a little company," she answered.

"As soon as my journey is ended, the sun decides to make its late appearance." Charles said shaking his head, "I left for town early this morning for supplies. I stopped at the postmaster and there is a letter for you," he said reaching into his coat and offering it to her.

"A letter. Oh it must be from Edward."

"It is in his hand," Charles confirmed.

"Thank you, Charles. Thank you so much. I shall go to the parlor and read it at once. There is piping hot tea in the kitchen. I suppose you would welcome it after your trip," she said as Charles turned to gather a load of supplies.

Isabella walked methodically to the music room, staring down at the letter within her hands. She sat by the window and looked at if for a moment almost afraid to read its words. There was only one way to find out whether he spoke of good or bad news. Tentatively, she broke the seal, lifted the flap and unveiled its contents. There was a small note and a larger piece of yellowed parchment sealed in an inner envelope of very thick paper for its apparent protection. The note read:

> Dear Isabella,
> I pray this letter finds you restored and in good health. I regret your fears have been realized. I arrived at Meadowbridge to find Lenora's room vacant. Dr. Greene has been most helpful and though Lenora was mysteriously moved to another facility, I have called for confidential inquiries as to her present location. I shall remain here until there is news. I remain most hopeful. I discovered the enclosed piece of music within a volume belonging to your mother. May it bring you some comfort until we find her. I shall return as soon as possible, and together we will mend what is yet broken. Rest peacefully for now, Edward

'Sweet Edward,' she thought. 'He *will* find her. I shall not think otherwise. It would be too cruel now, now when I have my memory. Now when I know she awaits my return. I will be united with her. And what of this music?' She opened the parchment and studied it carefully. The music had been hand written so meticulously one would hardly notice it was not produced in type if not for a closer examination. She tried to recall the tune in her mind, but it was too difficult to accomplish.

Curious, she stepped to the piano and placed the sheet of music on the stand and then with a deep breath attempted the soft notes, but found it to be a tedious exercise. She endeavored again and then the melody was suddenly familiar.

"Mother, oh Mother, I have found you," she whispered, as tears of joy formed in her eyes. She realized she could not quite play the piece the way she remembered it, but it was lovely as it was. She resolved to practice it again and again until she mastered it, and then she would play it for her mother. Edward would keep his promise and bring Lenora to Brookhaven.

The rolling melody was deep and full of passion. The notes spoke of a feeling Isabella had never known, perhaps that was the crux of her incapacity to play the notes as they had been intended. Her inability to master the song as she had heard Lenora once play it became a matter of contention within herself, as she could not be content to do anything less than what she considered to be her best. However her attempts detracted from her mother's rendition of the music, the solemn notes comforted her now. After a final attempt, she returned to her room for her afternoon bath and nap.

Her room smelled of honeysuckle as she had left her window open, and the breeze had carried the lovely scent from the wildly flourishing vine into her chamber. The spring flowers sparked an idea. Bella returned to the garden wall and picked several buds of honeysuckle and a handful of other sweet flowers and returned to her room. She dropped a handful of flowers in the rinsing basin, proceeded with her bath as usual, but rinsed her hair in the flower scented water.

She had discontinued dressing formally for dinner since Hamilton's departure, but this night had brought with it a strangely uncharacteristic feeling, and she decided to indulge herself by wearing Elizabeth's ivory evening gown, a gown she had never worn before, but had imagined herself wearing on many occasions.

The fabric was heavy with an overlay of flowing organza. The gown had an empire waistline embellished with pearled diamond shaped buttons. The same buttons adorned the short capped sleeves and neckline which exposed the greater portion of her décolleté. The organza met in a point on her back between her shoulder blades and flowed in abundance to the ground and beyond forming a small train behind her. The dress was to be worn with long, buttoned gloves, but she imagined the household would think her mad if she indulged to that extent. The dress was enough.

Two hours remained before dinner and she had resolved to read the final chapters of the novel she had begun with Dr. Weatherly before he left. She had put it off far too long. She would miss his hearty, warm voice reading to her. For when he read to her, she would close her eyes and picture that he and she were the characters of the novel. It had become an exercise she enjoyed. They would take turns, she reading one chapter and he the next. They had fallen into the practice of stopping to discuss the writer's intentions and then offering their own idea and philosophies of life. Whenever she came upon an interesting caption in any volume whatsoever, she would mark it down and they would discuss it. She had come to know him very well through this practice, and she looked forward to their meetings.

But tonight, she would finish the book alone. It was clear another day would not bring Dr. Weatherly back to her no matter how much she longed for his return.

As she stood before the mirror in her lovely borrowed gown. She regarded herself as a new creation. She was no longer Bella Brookhaven of Kielderbridge. She was no longer the wandering nameless stranger she had been. But from both of those identities she had taken what gifts of wisdom they offered. The woman before her was more than either one she had been before. The last two years had changed her and she felt as though her life up until this moment had been a race, that she had been running towards this moment, that her life, in all its happiness and pain, had led her here, and she was almost at the finish line.

"I belong here," she said to herself. "The only thing I lack is seeing Lenora's face and knowing she is safe. For tonight I will be happy with things as they are! I will enjoy this evening and the promise of what is to be. Edward is doing all in his power to help me and I believe he will find Lenora."

Moments later she found herself in front of the piano again. "Once more," she said.

Chapter 29
A Misunderstanding

Hamilton worked tirelessly for two solid weeks in attempts to stifle the virus which had spread through Asheville. No one was safe, but he was thankful he had reached the townspeople he could in time. He had been unable to save two unfortunate patients to the rancid plague. Two is bad enough, but it was rumored the neighboring city had lost thirty-one. Thirty one souls lost. Being so near death was troubling. It was life he loved, but such was the fate of a physician. Only because he had taken every precaution was he saved from the relentless virus.

Once he was certain everyone was safe, he had his clothing and even certain instruments burned. He had worked day and night, night and day, time had run together and he was unsure how much time had actually passed. But even in the fury of his work, never was he without the notion that Bella now knew of his love for her. And now with only hours separating them, he would perhaps find her letter to him and they would be together. No more unanswered questions. No more unmet desires.

Edward had been right, Hamilton had instinctively known Isabella was the one he had hoped for, and nothing could keep him away from her. Even surrounded by death and struggling to fight it, his heart was light with the very thought of her. He returned to his humble dwelling and dressed for the occasion of meeting the woman he loved. He packed his medical bag and a couple of changes of cloths, offered Midnight a hearty serving of oats and placed a heavy winter coat over his shoulders. Although it was springtime, nightfall in the mountains proved to be rather chilly and one never knew what could happen along the winding pathway to Brookhaven.

As always, Midnight delivered him to Brookhaven safely and unharmed. It was just before sunset, Hamilton's favorite time of the evening. He secured Midnight in the stables and brushed him quickly before rushing to the gardens, assuming he might find Bella there waiting for him. He quickly walked through the path to his willow tree and admired the new born blooming flowers of spring, the lush greens had been transformed to a tapestry of vibrant colors. As he reached the little stone bench he noted it was almost overgrown by daffodils of bright yellows and rich creams. But he found no letter, the bench was bare. He looked all around, 'where is it?' he questioned. Never contemplating Isabella had not responded to his letter.

Frantically he looked under the bench and all around the grounds, rustling through the grass and daffodils, but there was no letter to be found. Suddenly he noted the marshy grounds and considered what rains had probably visited there, making it impossible for her to leave a letter out of doors, and too, he had been away for quite a while. For certain, it was foolish to have imagined she would leave her response to the random powers of the winds and weather.

'Of course,' he reasoned 'I've been away for nearly three weeks. And she had no warning of my return. What am I doing here, I must go find her, and hear her tell me she loves me!'

He walked around the grounds of Brookhaven, through the pools of mud which had formed on the once manicured lawn. He passed between the stone lions and opened the door. A most hypnotizing melody greeted him. It was unlike anything he had heard before, and he followed the sound into the music room from which it resonated, and discovered Bella seated at the piano playing the enchanting melody. He stood in the shadows for a moment, unable to break these moving notes.

The tune was so haunting that even when she had finished he stood there in silence, feeling its weight as he beheld the person who had dominated his every thought. Just as he was about to speak, Bella realized she was not alone.

"Bella, forgive me if I startled you, but the music seemed to enchant me," he offered.

"Dr. Weatherly, you are here!" She exclaimed, as her countenance brightened.

"Yes, forgive the late hour and date. I returned as soon as I could, I assure you."

"I am only happy for your safe return. Look," she said pointing to the cherished sheet of music, "Edward found it among Lenora's things and sent it to me. And I know it. I played it and I remembered her playing it for me when I was only a child. Oh it is just wonderful," she said with her excitement radiating through her voice.

"But does that mean?" he asked with a regretful tone.

"What?" she asked searching his eyes.

"You said he found it. . . among her belongings, I do not understand, did he not make it there in time?"

"No. Heavens, no. If I had heard such news I could hardly be so happy. It is as we suspected, foul play. When Edward arrived at the asylum he learned that my mother had been moved. My parents relocated Lenora so hastily they failed to take her belongings. Edward discovered the few things left behind, and sent the music to me. He has promised to remain there a while longer, until he receives word of her present location. Isn't it wonderful?"

"Yes, Bella, it is the most wonderful news. We shall celebrate. Are you expecting company tonight?"

"No, why do you ask?"

"It is just I have never seen you quite so lovely. That is quite a gown."

As she fumbled for a reply her entire chest became flushed with his kind compliment and appeared more so against the ivory fabric of the gown.

"Oh, this," Bella said realizing she was dressed as if for a ball, "I suppose I did feel like celebrating. And I've been rather bored and lonely without you, but Dr. Weatherly, how are you? You were away so long. I missed you terribly."

"And I you. . . it was dreadful Bella. Simply dreadful. I lost two patients. There was much to be done, but I dare say I stopped the life stealing virus, and it will harm no one else if I can help it. I am only thankful to be in your company once more. Tell me, have you been to the gardens as you promised?" he asked, hoping to she would take his hint and tell him what he had waited so long to hear.

"Yes, I understand now why you spent so many hours there. It is lovely. I have returned each day, if only for a moment." He expected her to go on, but she did not, and he looked at her expectantly.

"You're staring Dr. Weatherly," she said, blushing.

"I suppose I am. It is this gown, it is gorgeous." He offered clumsily, but she sensed he was covering.

"Dr. Weatherly, is there something else?"

"No. Nothing," he said. The words he had written Bella repeated in his mind, and it was suddenly clear to him that the absence of her response letter on the bench, and now the absence of her confession of love could only mean one thing. 'I understand,' he thought, 'she has refused me.' And all the lightness of heart he had felt was now matched by a hollow sensation in the pit of his gut. The pain was intense and sudden, as if a every joy he had ever known had been drained from memory, and he shuddered in the void of nothingness that now comprised his heart. As he looked upon her now, he could only feel pain.

Casting his eyes downward, he said abruptly, as he turned from her, "It has been a long journey. I should like to rest now."

The light in his eyes had suddenly vanished. Only a moment before he had admired her and seemed pleased to see her and yet now, something had stolen his happiness. It was undeniable. Isabella was quite taken aback at his changed attitude and begged, "But Dr. Weatherly, have I said something? I don't understand?"

"I am simply tired. Nothing more."

"But our reading and dinner, did you not promise me?"

"Bella, I've experienced a succession of many trying days, as for my promise, I suggest you do your reading without me. And please inform Charles I am not to be disturbed."

Sensing his strange mood and not quite knowing what to say, Isabella felt it best to allow him his privacy. But she was injured by his dismissing her so and pained that he had not seemed more pleased to see her.

"As you wish, but shall you join me for dinner, at least?"

she called out, but he walked out of sight without a word.

He could not remember walking to his room, yet he found himself sitting on his bed. A great sense of pain washed over him. "She does not love me," he said aloud. "Dr. Weatherly, she insists on calling me, Dr. Weatherly as though we have never shared those hours and weeks together, as though I did not think of her every moment I was away." And the words from his very mouth pierced his ears as the shot of gun might when fired at close range.

'But I never expected her to be cruel. Perhaps it is her age which makes her less compassionate,' he wondered. She had asked "have I said something?" It was not what she said, it was what she had not said. It was the absence of the letter. The empty bench he had returned to. And her heart, emptier still. He had opened his heart to her. Poured out every word of love, and she wanted to play childish games with him. She insisted on asking him painful questions. Did she not understand how it felt to bare one's self? He had misjudged her, and he would not stay here another day with her. He would stay the night, but decided he could not join her for dinner, it was an impossibility to even imagine such an affair, what with the utter humiliation of having exposed his heart to her, and with every thought of her, his words of love rang out like an imposing bell. They rang in his head until his head ached with their hopelessness. 'then, now and forever more I shall hold these feelings of love for only you.'

ෂංශ

Bella postponed dinner for over an hour expecting Hamilton to appear at any moment, but soon abandoned those thoughts with his increased absence and now found herself alone before a steaming bowl of soup. And though the aroma rose to greet her she could not smell it. Nor could she see or feel or taste anything around her. She could feel nothing save for the deep loneliness she felt in Hamilton's curt words. She sat motionless and felt somehow frightened. Why had Hamilton treated her in such a way? Perhaps he noted her affection for him and it was unwanted. She had never been able to hide her emotions. But she sensed there had been an understanding between them. Had she mistook the emotion in his eyes the night in the garden? But how was she to misunderstand the compliments he had given her? In those last days he had been so kind, was kindness, charity his only feelings toward her?

'That is it' she reasoned, 'his kindness has been just that, kindness only and not feelings of love as I imagined, as I hoped. I am only a girl to him, an obligation.' But in the preceding weeks he had become more than her doctor, more than her friend. And only through realizing what she perceived to be Hamilton's feelings for her, namely the obligatory feelings a doctor has for his patient and an obligation to keep his promise to Edward, did her heart reveal her own feelings for him.

'But how must I turn these feelings into friendship now?' she questioned. 'It is impossible,' she thought. 'I love him. And my heart will know no contentment without him, and I have only just this moment realized it! But I must disguise these unreturned feelings. Sad heart, will this love destroy me? Will it ferment in me with no way of escape? Love must be expressed, but he does not love me. Even so, my love is no less strong. I wondered that it will not remain trapped in me forever. And why does this happen now? Now, when the rest of my life is finally mended? Shall I ever be satisfied? Why must I torment myself this way? I have read of true love. But only now do I understand the pureness of one's heart in the matter of loving. He is my friend. And I must be a friend to him. For it is not for me to be angered by something beyond his control. He has returned here to care for me. He has lost two patients, he has fought with death to return here, and still I ask for more. God forgive me, I do not intend to ungrateful and greedy. Give me strength to love him as a friend. To console him in whatever grief he is feeling in spite of my own grief.'

With a repentant prayer expressed, she walked to Hamilton's room, and knocked gently on the door. Hamilton still sat on his bed holding their favorite novel, his fingers tracing the passages Bella had once read to him. He rose to answer the door.

"I do not wish to be disturbed," he called through the door.

"And I do not wish to disturb you. Will you please open the door?" she asked.

Reluctantly, Hamilton opened the door. In the awkward moment between them which followed, she spotted his bag beside his bed.

"Dr. Weatherly, your bag, have you not unpacked, let me help you?"

"No, there is no need," he said, clutching her outstretched arm. She looked at him and then at his hand touching her, and she felt the blood rush to her face as it warmed and turned her cheeks a deeper red. Hamilton noticed her blushing at his touch, but did not understand why. He looked away from her in unreserved misery, realizing even now, her beauty was undeniable.

"I am leaving in the morning," he continued.

"But you have only just arrived, I had hoped," she began, but was interrupted.

"I was charged with ensuring your health, and you have obviously recovered. I am no longer needed here."

His painful words inflamed her. "I see, I am only an obligation to you, and if that is all, then yes, I am perfectly well now!" she said harshly. He stared at her in disbelief, but did not answer.

The conflicting emotions she felt consumed her as small pools formed in her eyes, but she refused to cry. She had imagined his return with such joy and hope and now she stood before him in sadness and in the grip of a great fear. She did not know how to continue, but she knew she could no longer suffer this distance between them. As she turned to leave, she suddenly turned back to question his strange behavior.

"Dr. Weatherly, really, I do not understand why your manner has changed so. You seem so very…angry."

At this accusation, he began to clap his hands rather dramatically, "Brava, Brava, you have guessed it. Indeed, I am quite angry. And since you insist on this line I must confess I am angry with myself, for being so foolish, for misjudging you so, but now I know you are not the person I thought you to be."

Stunned, Bella replied, "Of what do you speak? I have done nothing, but be your friend."

"Yes, my friend and my companion. Sharer of stories, but there is no truth between us." Again he lashed out at her for no apparent reason.

"Must you speak in riddles? I cannot bear this, tell me now what I have done to you, and by my heart, I shall repair it."

"Must *I* speak in riddles? Must you torture me this way? You say you are my friend. What sort of friend delights in another's anguish? I have said enough already. It was never my intention to speak of these things. And I shall not speak of them again. I have accepted your answer and I shall not embarrass myself further, I shall leave Brookhaven at once."

A steady, faint stream of tears began to fall against Bella's warm cheek. She looked at him as if he was a madman. She struggled to make sense of his accusations. Of what answer did he refer? It was all too confusing, and it would never be resolved if he left without an explanation. She wiped the tears from her face and resolved to press the matter until an adequate clarification had been made.

"Hamilton!" she began, and he turned to her as she said his name for the first time, "Hamilton, please do not leave here this way. You say these things which do not make sense to me. I came to you just now to try to reach you. I *am* your friend. I was your friend before I knew, I, I ..."

"Before you knew *what*!" he demanded heatedly.

"I denied my deeper feelings for you, in favor of our friendship. I sensed there was something troubling you and I came to you, but now it is far worse than I imagined, it is I who am the source of your distress. And I assure you I am feeling no delight at this moment, only sadness and perplexity. You say you have accepted my answer, but Hamilton what was the question?"

"Bella, must you insist? Do you know how painful it was, how disheartening to find you had not responded. I admit, I was foolish, never allowing the possibility you would not share my feelings. But no matter, the short of it is the bench was empty. No less empty than your heart. You greeted me as always, you acted as if nothing had changed. But everything has changed, for me at least. I believed I could ignore it. But you see, I cannot. It is too painful, and more painful than the truth, is your lack of compassion. I do not know your reasons and in the end the reasons do not matter, it only matters that you and I are not to be. And I can never act as if the words were not proposed. I have said things to you, things which hover above us now like an apocalyptic cloud and we can never be together again without this strain on my soul, so I must leave here. I must leave you. And if you do not understand just now, perhaps in time you will."

"I fear I will not! It is as though we had some other conversation when I was not present. You speak of an empty bench? Was I to be there? But I did not know when you would return. But you must trust what I say now. Each day I was there. Each day I said a prayer for you and your safe return. Whenever I heard the slightest sound I would jump to my feet and race to the door hoping for your return. But you never came. And then suddenly tonight, you were here and I was thrilled to see you. You were so kind and then this present sadness and anger came upon you, to the point of you walking away from me, without a word. I could not imagine the source of your indifference.

As I reflected on our conversation, I realized something, perhaps something I have always known. The sadness I felt when you left my side came from such a deep place. There is only one place from which pain such as this can come. For one cannot feel such pain in loss unless one first knows a deep and rooted love. And though I have never spoken of my feelings, of this love I have for you, you say we are not to be, and I see a grave disappointment in your eyes, as though it breaks your heart to even look at me. Why? Hamilton, what am I missing? What did I do to make a ruin of us before we even began?" she plead with stormy eyes.

"It is not with pain that I look upon you. It is only bewilderment. I thought you denied me, that you read my letter and rejected me."

"But I never received your letter. When did you send it?"

"I never *sent* it at all. I left it for you on the bench by the willow tree, the morning I left. I knew you were to return there as promised, and I wanted it to be there to greet you in my absence. Are you saying you never read my letter?"

"Read it? I never saw it, I have no idea what you are talking about."

By this time Hamilton was pacing, and when he realized Bella had never seen the letter, an inexplicable feeling of relief and yet guilt consumed him. Suddenly he sat down severely, placing his head between his hands, embarrassed and appalled at how he had treated the woman he so loved. Isabella stood by him silently half afraid and half anxious to rush to him, but she did not have to choose. Hamilton looked up with an anxious smile and stood to face her. He reached out to her, and she stepped forward and took his hand.

Breaking the silence, he said, "Bella, forgive me for

tormenting you so. How shall I explain? I'm afraid I have made a mess of things. Do you remember our evening in the garden together before we last parted?"

"Yes, of course I do, how could I forget?"

"Well, that night, as I stood in the place where moments before you had stood beside me, I had a revelation. I noted how charmed you were by the love letters between John and Elizabeth, and I sensed in you a reciprocation of my feelings. Before leaving Brookhaven, I wrote you a letter, a very intimate letter, expressing my deepest feelings for you, and in it I required that you simply leave a corresponding letter for me upon the same bench should you feel anything for me at all. In the event my feelings for you were not shared, I asked that we merely never mention the letter. A brilliant plan, as you have surmised. God, how abhorrently I have treated you. I only hope ..."

"So you are not angry with me?" she asked.

"Angry? I am angry only with my own foolish pride. Forgive me?"

"All is forgiven, but tell me about the letter?"

"My dear Bella, the letter simply said what I should have said long ago," he said, pushing her hair away from her face and tracing her cheek with his hand, "I love you. No matter what happens to me in the future, where I am or where I go, I will always love you. I had given up on love such as this, but your love is the discovery of a new continent of my soul, a place I never could have imagined. It is frightening and magical. It is wholly uncharted and full of promise. I discovered my best self in my discovery of you. You are all that matters to me in the world, and were I to spend the rest of eternity in your presence I should be the happiest person alive."

Bella simply took his hand and said, "The second happiest."

Hamilton held her close to him and thought if he died this very moment he would have experienced the greatest gift of life and he would be forever fulfilled, and in the same moment any remembrance of Hamilton's previous love ceased to exist, and had he been asked to recall her name or even one simple feature of her face, he would have failed to do so, for in his heart there existed no feelings of love outside the person of Isabella Brookhaven.

As her head rested against his chest, he kissed and stroked

her hair, and its scent of honeysuckle and wildflowers made him love and want her all the more. After her joyful tears were sufficiently spent, she broke their embrace and looked at him.

"Hamilton, will you promise me something?"

"Anything," he answered holding her face softly in his hands.

"Don't ever write me another letter," she responded, and they burst into laughter.

Chapter 30
A Reprieve

Edward spent several days awaiting some news from Dr. Greene, but again he returned to the Geldfield Inn full of disappointment, as no news had yet to be delivered. He had spent the day in Liverpool at a museum and took in a traveling exhibition of the work of the premier artists of the nineteenth century (as the world was underway to face a new century in the upcoming decade, and in a time of deep reflection and celebration of the one to pass). It had been a long day and it would be a longer night for him. He longed to be near Isabella, but he was confident Hamilton would protect her in his absence. Should he give up or press on? Weary of this question, he began to leaf through the large architectural volume from Lenora's room. Behind the page of one of his favorite castles he found a piece of parchment, it read:

> From deep within these iron bars am I
> So far away from love now must I stay?
> How ever distant is my love's sweet kiss
> before his silent grave I come to pray.

> Promises, sweet and forever
> you gave but life tide crushed them away
> But fear not, my Love, eternal
> my love grows stronger yet each day
>
> I imagine one bright day you still might find me
> on a hillside painted red with flowers wild
> on a summer breeze, or in the promise of a morning
> or from behind the gleaming eyes of our dear child.

Edward scanned the words over and over. The tone of the poem produced in him a great sadness. A piercing loneliness. For he could understand her loss. How many times had he felt these sentiments before? Abandonment, hopelessness, but perpetually in the midst of love. True love cannot die. He read the words, he felt them as though they came from his own mind. Sure he had his freedom, but he lived behind his own walls. Walls which separated him from everyone. And though Lenora had lost her lover, she would find happiness once more with the return of her daughter. To her pain he could offer some relief. For inasmuch as Isabella had saved him, how much more could she save her own mother from this existence of pain? He continued reading of the far away castles and of the legends built around them. It was a welcome escape. When he turned to the last page he found another poem of the same gentle hand, but this one had a different tone.

> Oh heart so heavy laden with desire,
> I ask of Fate what I most need to know
> How long must I wait for love to find me?
> Is my raging heart of love to ebb or flow?
>
> And where is my sweet answer?
> On whose lips my eyes doth rest?
> I should gaze expectant and forlorn
> Until at last his love he doth confess
>
> Cruel black sky, you cloak me now
> Come not again unless you bring
> love's light which holds and covers me
> and a morning's song to sing.

> Alas, Tomorrow then, I shall seek again
> I shall pray my constant prayer
> to You who hold the heart of him
> that where he is, I may also be there.

The longing and passion of which Lenora wrote was familiar to him. How urgent were her words. She seemed to hang on the hope of a love to be. The poem was dated March of 1866 and he surmised by his quick calculation she could not have been older than a girl of sixteen when the desperate words had been written. "Eighteen-sixty-six," he whispered. This had been the same year he had met Emily, and his own constant longing had dissipated in the same instant.

He reasoned Lenora's 'constant prayer' had certainly been answered, for Isabella had come from Lenora's love of this man in her later poem, her 'Love eternal.' Love is the saving force of us all, he thought. From out of nothingness it appears and fills us with a light so bright that from it we are warmed, sustained, and given direction in this oftentimes overwhelming world. 'Where is my direction now?' He pondered. 'Sweet Isabella, if not for you I should have surely withered from all life. I had held on far too long. I have known the comfort of a good friend or two, but not one of them knows me as Emily. Not one. Not even you, dear Isabella, and you shall never know me as she did.' 'Where is my sweet answer?' he repeated the words from Lenora's poem, and added 'wherever Emily may be.'

As the words left his lips, the bells of a nearby church chimed, and he was transported with their distant ringing to another place many years before...

The voices were like angels rising to the top of the cathedral, and the air was thick with incense. Emily closed her eyes and could almost feel Edward's hand touching hers. It seemed so real. He had seen her sitting alone in the darkened corner of the cathedral. It was time to say good-bye. Christmas holiday was over and he would return with Bryson to the university today. He sat beside her in the darkness, but she did not open her eyes, even when he had touched her hand.

"Emily," he whispered, "it is time."

At once she opened her eyes. "Did you hear my heart summoning you?" she asked and he smiled at her.

They sat quietly together for the next few moments. They listened to the soft and touching notes from the choir. They allowed their minds to roam free under the spell of the music, in this ancient place where for years, prayers and pleadings had been offered. Emily imagined her future with Edward. She marveled at how he had found her and she questioned what she had done to deserve such happiness. She felt so unworthy of such a pure emotion. To Edward this new found hope was both empowering and frightening. The grand Talbot estate, meeting Emily, even this cathedral was surreal. And Emily, his beloved Emily, was it his hand who held this angel's hand? And if he had to leave her, he could only do so in this sacred place, for she was his sacred place, the place he was indeed saved.

"It is all too terrible…that our lovely holiday has come to this end," she whispered.

"I know. I have just left Bryson and he is devastated that your father took such drastic measures. Is there any chance he might change his mind?" Edward asked.

"I am afraid this end was unavoidable. Once Father has spoken there is no turning back. I only wish it could have been delayed until after the holiday. This is both the best and worst week of my life. Only two nights ago I began to live and then after their dreadful argument…Father forcing Bryson and you to leave our home. It is appalling, appalling. I have never seen him so furious. No sooner had the carriage departed before he instructed the servants to remove any remembrance of Bryson from our home. There has been a decree to never mention his name again, I do not know what I shall do, how I shall endure it?" she asked with desperation.

"There, there, Emily, you will be all right, if it were not so, I would not leave you. The wound is fresh now, but in time I am convinced your father will come around. I will be here for Bryson, and certainly for you, you must know that. Bryson is strong, but I know he must be terribly injured by this turn of events. But I have come to you now to tell you we are packed and prepared to return to the university at once.

"Must we say farewell now?" she whispered.

"Were it in my power, I would never leave you again, but it is not. You and I are locked in this moment, in this time where we must dig in our heals and stand firm trusting that time will soon bring us to a new day, a day where we shall not have to say goodbye. I shall return and then we will never hide our love from anyone again. Emily, darling, your tears pierce me, how can I leave you this way...?"

"But they are tears of joy Edward, and of sorrow. Joy for having known love and sorrow for having known the loss of it."

"But our love is not lost. It is only suspended for a short while. Take heart my darling. For if we had never met, then should we be lost and empty, but not now, not now Emily when we have been given to each other. Though the world is a dark, dark place, you are my lantern. I am your yours. And we shall never stumble in the darkness again. Even though I must leave you now, your light will shine wherever I go. We will be together, you may be certain of it. It is my prayer, and as you have taught me, our prayers are answered by Him who never rests. Listen to their voices. Listen to the love and praise for Him who saved us. God will help us bear our separation, and He will bring us back to each other."

"Oh Edward, it is fitting we should say farewell here. For it is God who planted this seed of love in our hearts and with His light and hope it will grow in us. You are the object of my heart's deepest hope. And remember what I told you the night we first confessed our love, love always hopes. Just as it is alive and growing in our hearts, it will find a way to bring us together again."

"Love always hopes, I promise, I will remember. I shall think of you every moment and withstand the distance between us only in the thought of our reunion."

With these final words, he kissed her cheek and released her warm hand. His footsteps were heavy as he walked away from her. He turned to look back at her, head bowed and shoulders trembling. She had been brave long enough, he understood her tears, for it was all he could do to walk out of her light and back into the cold world without her, but he had found her and that would make his days brighter, his burdens lighter. How hopeful he had been in those days.

And even now after having lost her, the same hopefulness remained, and continued to guide him. At first he was angry, but he did not let his anger give way to bitterness. What others thought was cruelty in him, was simply a demeanor which turned to armor protecting him from further pain. He believed if he allowed the world to touch him, if he allowed himself to embrace it, he would somehow lose her. And the mere thought of such a loss was more painful than he could bear. So he chose the pain of remembering and living with her loss over the numbness of the empty world without her. It was the only way he could exist.

The bells chimed the half hour and Edward regained his composure and returned his thoughts to the present moment. Before dinner he reviewed his correspondence in hopes some news would come today, and his hopes were realized upon opening the first letter. The letter was from Dr. Greene, and its message contained the miracle for which he had hoped. One of Dr. Greene's colleagues had discovered Lenora's location. Of all the places she could be, she was in America, in New York City. He had been there only a few short weeks before, possibly steps away from Lenora. The Brookhavens had taken every precaution to keep their daughter from Lenora, so much so they spared no expense and had placed on another continent. The irony was poetic.

Edward's first response to the news was a fierce determination to arrive in New York as soon as possible and to return Lenora to Isabella. After further consideration, he reasoned more likely than not, that Lenora would be strictly guarded from any visitors. He must proceed with caution. There may be only one chance to rescue her, and it might be prudent to put some distance between his arrival and his inquiries, which he had been assured had been kept in strict confidence. Still, he had learned to trust only himself with matters of such grave importance. And even better he thought was that his plan would allow him to return to Brookhaven so Isabella could accompany him to New York. He smiled triumphantly, realizing it had all worked out as is should have.

The waiting had allowed Isabella to recover and now they would make the journey together, which was more than he had promised. He folded the letter, wrote a brief response of gratitude, and then packed at once. He considered sending word of his news to Isabella, but he decided instead to take leave immediately and give her the good news in person.

The spring sky was shadowed by the enormous and formidable estate. Edward smiled at the sight of Brookhaven and offered a prayer of thanks to be home. Many times he had returned to Brookhaven, but never before had there been anyone to return to. He had been alone for so long and now this day there was someone waiting for him beyond those iron gates. The peaceful feeling comforted him. In a few moments he would see Isabella and bring her the news, which would change her life. A part of him wished he could stop the everlasting turning of the earth. Edward had spent all his life searching, looking forward, looking back. All he wanted at this moment was to remain in the blissful feeling of being the holder of glad tidings, of being the one whom Isabella needed most.

But time does go on and on, and the present joy Edward felt would also pass. Isabella and her mother would unite, and eventually they would leave him alone again. The thought of losing Isabella was almost intolerable. How could he return to his empty life after the joy she had brought him? But he knew he must allow her to go on. She belonged with her mother and he could only truly be at peace if he allowed her to be returned to her rightful place. But he would never forget how Isabella had brought his memories of Emily so clearly into focus.

Isabella heard the carriage driving towards the estate. Before Edward had secured the horses, she appeared from behind the door, and ran down the steps to greet him.

"Edward, I did not expect you so soon."

"I come with glad news. I have found her! Your mother is safe and sound right here America, she was moved to an asylum in Riverbend."

"Oh Edward," she said taking his hand, "How can I ever thank you? But, Riverbend, why does that sound familiar?"

"You would have heard me mention it, I go there every year," he hinted.

"The orphanage is there?" she whispered, drawing her hands to her mouth, "But it is too incredible, too much to believe. And what word of her, is she well?"

"I have it on the best authority she is well taken care of. I have often seen the Riverbend Lunatic Asylum, on my annual trips and it, like the orphanage, is controlled by the Riverbend Seminary. As such, it is a clean and humane facility. You may rest easy knowing she is far safer and in much better hands than she ever was at Meadowbridge. I would have gone straight there, but I thought you would want to make the journey with me? I propose we take leave tomorrow if you are able, but are you well child?"

"Perfectly well. Hamilton has been a dear. He has taken wonderful care of me. We've so much to talk about Edward. I am thrilled to see you again."

"And it is good to be home. Shall I find Hamilton inside?"

"I am afraid you will not, and he was terribly wounded he would miss your homecoming, but just yesterday a messenger was sent for him with instructions he was to return to Asheville. He's promised to return as soon as time permits. He is quite anxious to meet my mother."

"As am I, so I take it you did not mind his company, then?"

"Mind? I rather enjoyed it, actually. In the weeks you were away, Hamilton and I became the best of friends."

"Glad to hear it, and you look well, better than ever." Edward could not help but notice the marked change in Isabella. The heightened pitch of her voice, the ease of her laughter and the perpetual smile adorning her lovely face, he naturally attributed it to her thoughts of the imminent reunion with her mother. And he was correct, in part. Isabella was very anxious to see her mother again, but the changes in her were attributable to the fullness of love she felt for Hamilton Weatherly, a feeling she had never experienced before. Keeping this feeling a secret from Edward was torture to her, but she had promised Hamilton they would disclose their happy news to Edward together, and she dutifully kept her promise.

"And did you receive my package Isabella?"

"I certainly did, and I must say it was the best remedy I could have hoped for. It was Lenora's music, and it is the most wonderful melody. Lenora played it for me only a few times, but I remember it and now it is I who shall play it for her."

"And she will be pleased. Did you know your mother is a poet? I found some of her poetry in an architecture book left in her room. Her writings are quite lovely. I shall give them to you as soon as I have unpacked. I should like to rest here for a few hours and then we will set out at day break."

"As you wish Edward. I'm really going to see her. I cannot believe it, thank you. Thank you so much Edward."

Chapter 31
A Haunting of Sorts

Isabella lay awake in the stillness of the night imagining seeing Lenora's face again. She and Edward would depart from Brookhaven in the morning and only a handful of days separated her from her mother. Her room was not quite dark. A pearly moonlight lit up the fanciful shadows dancing delightfully across the ceiling and on the surfaces of the furniture. Given the full and bright moon this night, she had been invited to witness the strange, tribal dance of the willowy branches and leaves on the stage of her room. Their movements suited her state of mind as it raced from thought to thought, and then she began to wonder if Lenora would be angry. To be angry would be understandable, but she knew once she explained what happened, everything would be settled at long, long last.

The melody began to play in her mind over and over again. And the dancers seemed to extend their arms and bodies to the rolling notes of her mind. The music gave her a sense of her mother which nothing else possibly could. Edward could not have given her anything more special. It was different than a piece of jewelry or the scent of perfume or anything else Isabella could imagine. The music was like a part of Lenora's soul. The part that was young and lovely and courageous. There was nothing more special than having this part of her mother. She fluffed her pillow again, and turned around in the bed, wondering how she would get through this long and seemingly endless night. She wondered if Edward was sleeping. He had become such a close friend, but it was more than that somehow. He had been the one truly honest person in her life. When she arrived at Brookhaven, he had taken her in, with no questions. She felt indebted to him and wondered if she could ever really repay him. It occurred to her that after she was united with her mother everything would change. Would she have to say good-bye to Edward? She chased the disturbing thought from her mind as suddenly as it had appeared.

Isabella was not ready to leave Brookhaven. It reminded her of her home, but it was much more complicated than that. This strange and luring place had sent her on the odyssey of her life. On this journey she had learned so much about herself, she had become a new Bella and she liked herself. Brookhaven had led her to her memories, and eventually to the realization of her identity, and Brookhaven had also given her the courage to leave that her former self behind, and this time with her full consent.

'How can I leave here now?' She questioned. 'I belong here. I belong with Hamilton. And as soon we return from New York and Hamilton is back, we'll share our news with Edward. We'll marry in the gardens. Her mother would be there, and Edward...I'll ask him to...one thing at a time, Bella,' she cautioned, 'none of this will come to pass before our trip is complete, now sleep, sleep.' She closed her eyes and tried to clear her mind of everything and she succeeded. She saw nothing, at last her mind was clear, but then the music came sweeping over her again, and her eyes opened to the still fluttering shadows.

"Blast it all!" she whispered, "It is no use, I'm not going to go to sleep anyway. I may as well practice one more time."

She covered herself with Elizabeth's satin robe, lighted a taper and descended the long stairway to the piano room. The house was completely silent and still except for the rustling whisper of her robe brushing across each step of the staircase. It was a remarkable night, and it reminded her somehow of the first night she came to Brookhaven. The moon was so bright on this cloudless night it illuminated the rooms of the estate with a haunting, glowing, light. So much so that she did not require a candelabra, and preferring the moonlight, with a quiet breath, blew out the flame, extinguishing her candle.

She sat down comfortably on the stool, but then remembered she had already packed the sheet music in the bags in her room. 'Think, Bella, think, you have played this over and over, you do not need the music. Just listen to the sound in your heart, listen and remember. . .' she willed, in complete concentration.

Ever so delicately her fingers touched the ivory keys, and a smile found its way to her lips. The music flowed so beautifully from her, and she sensed this was how it was meant to be played. It was so easy, there was no obstacle to overcome, and she continued to play.

The notes had been set free at last. They had lain silent for countless years waiting to be freed from the yellowed pages. They were lifted one by precious one, and they now filled every empty space in the estate. They floated on wings into every corner of the mansion. They attacked some rooms and sang a gentler song to others. When they reached Edward's room, they hovered above him like some ancient ghosts, and they remained with him for several moments, until Edward somehow felt their urging call. Edward was in the midst of his nightly world of dreams and in this particular dream, he was with Emily and she was holding his gaze, smiling, then laughing as he kissed her neck. He could hear the music even in his dream, and he felt himself being returned to the world of reality and away from Emily, but she called for him, "don't leave me Edward."

He opened his eyes in a sudden start and listened. "Am I dreaming?" he asked. 'This melody?' He had certainly heard it before. 'Yes, yes. I know this music,' he thought. From the depths of his memory, his mind raced to find the time when he had heard this tune before, and then suddenly he knew. A griping feeling seemed to take hold of his heart, and he looked all around the room as if he were trying to see the notes. And they did not hide from him, they stayed with him revealing themselves to him one note and one memory at a time, until the sound was like a thick, warm liquid covering his body and filling his heart.

He felt the piercing stabs of each note and cried out for mercy, "Where are you? Emily, Emily? Am I going mad?" He began to take deep breaths to try to calm himself, but the notes had completely filled his heart, and he felt the music inside him, and he felt her there with him. Tearing the covers aside, he bolted from the bed and jerked opened the door to the hall. The hopeful sound covered over him even more thickly now as he rushed to the stairway, and with each step he allowed himself to be consumed in the rapturous anguish of believing Emily had returned. It seemed an eternity before he passed the bottom step. Frantically he followed the rushing notes, and they led him right to her. The vision before him paralyzed him and he could no longer move or speak, he could only see her. There she sat with the moonlight spilling over her, playing his song.

ഈ൪

A tall shadow swept across the room, and the music suddenly stopped. Isabella turned slowly to see what had caused the image. She was relieved to see it was only Edward.

"Edward, you scared me, did I wake you, I'm sorry I just couldn't sleep." She said, almost in a whisper.

But Edward did not hear or answer her. He just stood there in the darkness. His mind was racing with questions, so many questions he could not choose one to ask. How could this be? Was he mistaken? Before he realized what he was doing, he was on his knees at her side and had taken Isabella's arm. He heard himself saying, "Isabella, what is this song you were playing?"

Bella saw the desperation in Edward's dark eyes, and it frightened her. She did not understand what he meant or why he would be so disturbed.

"It is the music you sent me from Mother, I am going to play it for her, remember."

"But I have never heard you play this before. Where did she get it, tell me, tell me now, if you know," he demanded with a strong voice.

"Edward, you are frightening me. What is the matter?" Isabella asked, slightly pulling away from him. Edward saw the fear come over her, so he loosened his grip on her arm and her tenseness faded.

"I don't know what has come over me, I cannot explain it to you at present, but this song has a great significance for me and I suppose I lost my senses. Did I hurt you?"

Isabella saw a vulnerability she had never seen in Edward, which alarmed her. And while she felt the skin beneath his grasp throb from where he had held her much too tightly, she responded, "Of course you didn't hurt me, you would never do such a thing."

He looked away from her, but remained at her feet. She wondered if he was crying and searched for the right thing to say. But the silence lay between them like a great wall she knew not how to climb. She reached down and touched his face with her hands and held him there in her eyes. All he could see was Emily's face. All he could do was hope the moment would not end, and he prayed she would remain silent. He allowed himself to see Emily and denied it was Isabella looking into his eyes.

"Will you play it again?" he asked.

Isabella could not refuse him. She moved her trembling hands from his face and placed them again on the keys. He remained on the floor and she felt his eyes on her for several minutes. Eyes which were now pools, filled with waters of regret. Overflowing regret. But then he looked away, covering his face with his hands in anguish and clasped them together. As much as he wanted to remain in this moment forever, he knew the truth of the matter, that the girl before him was not his Emily. He found the strength to remove himself from the floor and he stood over her as she continued to play, wanting only to please him. He placed his warm, tear stained hands over hers gently to silence the notes once again. She looked up at him with eyes full of questions. Without pause, he began to speak, but with a new calmness.

"The first time I heard it was twenty years ago, if it was a day. My Emily wrote it for me and played it for me the day I proposed to her." He could still feel the warm summer breeze and see the bold blue of the vast sky which covered them on that joyous day.

"But, Edward how can that be?"

"I do not know how Lenora came to have it," he continued, "but it is Emily's. She only played it for me once, but I would know it anywhere. I was shocked to hear it again. I was asleep and it awakened me, and I fought the truth, but I could not deny it was 'The Kiss,' that is what she named it," he said smiling, remembering why.

"I rushed down the stairs and then I saw you. It was as if I had stepped through a doorway to my past. The music, and you. Here in the moonlight, sitting at the piano, as she did. I was overcome by it all and still I am bewildered. Nothing makes sense. I feel as though I am living in a dream, nothing seems clear to me."

Bella was stunned and she allowed his words to settle in her mind, as she wondered what it could all possibly mean. She had seen the same desperation in his eyes the night she had stumbled upon the grounds of Brookhaven. It was an expression not soon forgotten, a searching, fearful but fearless look, and then it became clear to her he had finally abandoned all sense of reason and given in to those initial feelings which had flooded his fragile mind upon her arrival at Brookhaven.

He said he had only heard the music once. Once, twenty years ago, it was impossible that he could remember, it was simply he had returned from a long and burdensome journey, and her playing had awakened him unexpectedly, and in his dreamlike state, he had seen her cloaked in moonlight and his imagination had taken over. His dreamlike thoughts had invaded his reality and he could no longer distinguish the two. She had so hoped to remain with him here, but tonight's outburst had proven her presence could only cause him pain and confusion. And because she had come to care for him so deeply and to respect him in every way, she knew she must remove herself from him as soon as she was united with her mother. He had invited them to stay at Brookhaven indefinitely, and she had happily consented, but it was clear now she must alter the arrangement, and she decided as soon as she and Hamilton married, she would leave this loved place and this loved man, never to return.

"Oh Edward the last few weeks have been such a trying time for us both. I know my presence here has caused you equal parts of pain and joy. I have seen the care in your eyes, but to see you this way is so very difficult. I know you have so many questions but there is so little I know to answer them. This music is obviously very special to you, as it is to me, I only know when I was a child, my mother played it for me."

"Tell me more?"

"When I was a child, she was often in a very reflective mood. Many thought her demeanor puzzling, but she simply preferred her own company to others, and thus spent hours alone.

One day I found her playing this song when she thought I was napping. I thought it beautiful and asked her to teach it to me, but she refused. She said she would play it for me on occasion, but it was not meant to be shared with the world, not even me, wasn't that a strange thing to say? I did not remember it until just this moment."

"What did you say?"

"She would not teach me the song. I gather she thought it was too complicated for a child, and she was right, I never could have played it until now."

"No Isabella, I mean what exactly did she say?"

Isabella smiled realizing she had not answered his question, "she said it had been given to her by someone very special and she had promised not to play it. To keep it a secret between them."

"What else did she say?"

"That is all I remember, although I do remember she was very cautious about many things. I always thought her so mysterious, of course, now I have learned she was not allowed the luxury of being honest with me."

Edward seemed lost in thought and his expressions kept changing from light to dark, in one of the moments of light he said "Isabella," pensively, but then his face grew dark again just as suddenly and he continued, ". . . never mind."

"No, please tell me, what were you going to say?" she urged.

He could not answer. He was trying to make sense of it all. Had Emily shared her work so easily? But why? Why? And when? How had she known Lenora? Maybe she gave Lenora the sheet music to keep it in a safe place, yes perhaps. But still, he could find no reason for these strange events. And suddenly another possibility came to mind. But could he even allow the thought? Could God be so kind? It was beginning to come clear to him. Could he let himself believe it? 'Edward, you fool,' he thought, 'you felt her lifeless body in your hands. It simply cannot be.'

And yet Edward was certain it was the same song Emily had written for him. Isabella had explained the events of Lenora's life, and suddenly it occurred to him that if his fantasy could be true, if Lenora *was* Emily, then Isabella could be his own daughter.

With this unbelievable thought, he managed to finally answer her.

"Isabella, is there anything you remember about Lenora that you have not told me? You see, I am trying to make sense of everything and I wonder if there is something you have failed to mention. Try to remember, even if it is something seemingly small and insignificant."

Isabella thought for several minutes, recalling every detail of her conversations with her mother and the conversations with the kind nurse who had helped her at the asylum. He asked her to start from the beginning and tell him everything. Though the hour was late, neither of them could postpone this discussion until the morning. She started from the beginning and told him everything she could remember about Lenora, with no omissions. Edward listened more intently this time trying to see through the elusive past of this woman whom he only knew of through pieced together memories. It was too simple to be true. Too simple to imagine. He remembered Emily's father and how he had not allowed him to go to the memorial service. Maybe there was no memorial. 'But Lenora told Bella her lover is dead. So it cannot be, can it?' he questioned.

Edward realized he was only hoping for the impossible dream he had promised his heart. Now the thought of it all was beginning to become a tangled, complicated fantasy. It was too impossible to believe and the thought of it both delighted and sickened him. For if it were true, the possibility she was still alive, the tragedy that they had been separated, the powerlessness to gain those lost years, the victimization of them both, made him shudder. Victims, they had been victims and perhaps no one was more a victim than this beautiful young girl who had lost two years of her young life. The morning would be coming soon and he would know the truth.

Edward did not want to alarm Isabella with what he suspected so he suggested they both try get at least a little sleep before the journey tomorrow. Isabella happily conceded with her mind full of questions of her own. She would at last be united with her mother, but that joy would be decreased with the knowledge she would have to say farewell to the one who had saved her, who had given so much of himself that she might find true happiness and peace. How could she say goodbye to Edward? Only a few short days separated her from the answer.

The following morning Edward sat patiently in the library awaiting Isabella's arrival. He clutched the architectural book he had taken from Lenora's room, with plans to offer her something of her past. As he waited, the music he heard last night played over and over in his mind. When he closed his eyes, he saw the image of Isabella in the moonlight. It would be a vision forever etched in his memory. It seemed the vision of her, the repeating melody and the events which had brought him to this day had all conspired to drive him mad.

He opened his eyes again to stop the images. 'I will finally meet Lenora,' he thought. He wondered if she would remember Emily, or if she was Emily. 'Stop it, stop!' he thought shaking his head. And then turned his mind to more rational thoughts. How wonderful it will be to speak to someone who had known Emily. But Emily never mentioned Lenora? No matter how diligently he scrutinized each word from Emily had ever uttered to him, there was no recollection of a friend named Lenora. Again his thoughts came from his heart and not his mind and again, he fought to banish the thoughts, for it was too wonderful and too painful to hope for. Uncertainty, questions, so many questions, questions which must wait, for he knew the journey ahead of them was for Isabella. And only the answers to her questions mattered.

There would come a time when he could ask Lenora the questions haunting him, and until then he would attempt to be patient. Suddenly a peculiar wave of vanity washed over him. He walked to the mirror at the opposite end of the room and gazed into it expectantly. The reflection somehow shocked him. 'From where have these lines come?' he questioned. It was rare that he occasioned to look upon himself and the image before him was staggering. Though his spirit was encased in this tired, aging body, he had never ceased to imagine himself as the man of his youth. The man he was when with Emily. The memories so present in his mind made it easy to forget the passing of time, but the mirror was a bastion of honesty. He traced the wrinkles with his fingers and then laughed at himself for being so foolish.

"Good morning, Edward." Isabella offered as she entered the room.

"Good morning, are you ready for the trip?"

"Yes, quite, and you?"

"We are all set. I have checked the carriage and packed our bags for the journey, but before we leave, I must apologize for my behavior last evening. I find no excuse for my actions, the last thing I wanted was to."

But he was silenced by her delicate hand.

"Edward, I understand your painful position in all of this, please do not apologize, it is I who am sorry for causing you to feel such sadness. You were at peace when I found you here, and now I have somehow brought your Emily back to life, to the very front of your thoughts, but I can give you no way to find her."

"Do not apologize for your presence here. I shall not hear of it. You have not brought Emily back to life, it is I you have brought to life. My days were peaceful because they were so very empty. But your presence has brought a new peace. A peace I could not have found without you. Come dear, let me now repay you for your kindness. Let us go to your mother, are you ready?"

She took his hand and followed him to the carriage.

"Charles, we shall return with Isabella's mother as quickly as possible, and until then I leave Brookhaven in your capable hands, and trust you will take special care of her, and I trust you will prepare the guest room as I have requested."

"Of course Master Withers, and may you have a safe journey."

"Good-bye Charles!"

"Good-bye Isabella, Godspeed."

As they drove away from Brookhaven, Isabella stared back at the mansion, it was hard to take her eyes away from it and she did not until the carriage had driven her out of its sight. She had not said a word since the beginning of their journey. She was unsure what to say, and her silence may have revealed her feelings, but Edward was lost in his own distractions. He fought the urge to imagine meeting Lenora. He held back the flooding emotions of his heart. His resolve was as a great stone dam holding back the strongest tide and as those waters crashed against him, he stood firm. Too many times before he had let those waters engulf him and was nearly lost forever.

"Edward, I am frightened," Isabella whispered quietly. But he was so lost in the war of possibilities advancing against his mind he did not hear her, but then the soft touch of her hand on his brought him back to reality.

"Is something the matter?" he asked.

"Edward, I am afraid. I don't know how to explain it."

"I know," Edward interrupted, "we are so close to what you have most longed for that it is almost frightening. But everything will be all right. You will be with your mother again. And as for today, no matter what it brings, it is my solemn promise you will never be alone again. Whatever comes to pass, I will be your protector and your friend," he promised.

As always Edward knew what her heart needed to hear, and with his kind words her fears seemed to vanish in the trail of dust they left behind them.

Chapter 32
A Revelation and a Hope Renewed

From a small opening in the window, a cool spring breeze found its way into Lenora's room. She sat up straight in her cot with her back against the wall, holding her knees tightly to her chest. On the night air came the whirlwind of her nightly ritual of questions. Another long day had passed with no word from her daughter. 'How long must I be hidden here? Where have they taken me? What shall become of me now? Why has life turned out this way? Have I committed some grave injustice of which I am unaware? She searched her memories, but found no action in her past deserving of this miserable fate. 'Honor thy father?' she mused. But was she to honor a man so possessed of ill will toward her, so consumed with selfishness and greed? It did not seem possible she could be punished for failing to honor such a cruel and heartless man. And there was no calendar, no clock, nor any other record of time in her drafty, modest room.

The only indication that life continued at all was from the passing of the seasons outside the small window in her room. The hope she had felt two years before, the joy of seeing her daughter again, continued to sustain her even now, yet she also felt the cruel heartbreak of the night the men had come and brought her to this present place of exile. Dare she place her only hope on the small shoulders of her daughter? The likelihood of her rescue was doubtful, but she reasoned Bella had found her after all those years, so why was it impossible to believe Bella might find her a second time? How else would she endure the days to come?

Lenora had spent her life in a state of longing for those whom she had been created to love, and yet for some unknown reason she had not been allowed to be near them. Their precious hearts had been stolen from her. It began with the news of her young lover's death. For months she could hardly find the strength to face another day. Time appeared to have stopped so abruptly. The nights would creep on and on and she could hardly endure them, and worse still was the cruel morning which greeted her with only the prospect of another day without him. There was nothing to live for, no dream that mattered without him, until she discovered she was carrying their child.

The veil of pain and the coat of armor imprisoning her were released, and she could feel again, not pain, but love. Love was alive in her heart again. The pregnancy was difficult, but her father appeared to be supportive. She could hardly wait to hold their child in her arms. She hoped the child would have its father's eyes or any trace of him for that matter. But she would not look into the eyes of her child for years to come. Even now her eyes filled with tears as she remembered that crushing night…

When the child came, she was so overcome with pain and weariness after the birth, she lay unconscious. When she awoke several hours later and asked for the baby, she realized the full extent of her father's capacity for cruelty.

"Father, where is the baby?" she whispered softly.

"Hush now, you need your rest."

"But, I want to see my child, to hold…."

"Please, you will only make this harder on yourself."

"What? What do you mean? The baby is healthy?"

"Yes, of course. Safe and sound I assure you."

"Then Father, please call the nurse, I need to hold my child." She said, but this time with more concern.

"I am sorry, but you must rest for now. It will be easier this way," he responded. As she looked at him, he refused to meet her eyes, and she sensed something horrible, irreversible had occurred.

"Father, what have you done? Bring me my baby," she asked more forcefully now.

"The truth is I cannot. You are but a child yourself. Think of the child, dear. It is for the best. We have found a most suitable home. The child will want for nothing."

"You have given my baby away? No. Please tell me you did not do this to me. Tell me it is not too late, Father, I beg you. I beg you. Please." She urged clutching the sleeve of his coat.

"She is with her new family now."

"She? A girl? How is it you have seen this precious one, and I, I who am her mother, I, who love her with all I am have not been allowed to hold her, not even for a moment? You have taken everything from me. There is nothing left. Why are you still standing here? I cannot bear to look at you. Leave me, leave me!" she shouted.

"I forgive your harshness now. You are young and have the whole of your life before you, and one day you will thank me for what I have done. I am giving you another chance. No one knows of your marriage, nor the child. Everyone believes you are simply on holiday. When you are sufficiently recovered, you will be introduced into society, we will find the proper match for you and. . ."

"Stop it, stop! Not one more word from you," she exclaimed, wiping the hot tears from her face. "I will not listen to your vile words. You tear from my heart the only hope I had left to live for, and somehow you believe I will one day thank you for murdering my hope. Even now when you look at me all you can see is something to be molded into your idea of perfection. You truly believe I will go home with you, and pretend that my life has not been destroyed, that my heart has not crumbled into a million jagged pieces which prick and scrape and tear me asunder? Do you really think I can go on without my child, it was hard enough losing ..."

"Do not speak his name in my presence!" he shouted, looking fiercely at her.

"You are a heartless old man, and there is not another life for me, there is no returning, there will be no parties, no balls, no husband, no love, not for me. There is nothing in all the world to fill this gaping hole in my life. There is nothing in the world, but there is more than this world, and God will empower me to endure what you have done."

"I repeat, everything I have arranged has been for your protection. You must accept what cannot be undone. You sound hopeless now, but you will see in time. The world is not always fair, and I wanted to save you from the shame you would have known."

"Shame? I think not. I think the person you were saving was yourself, you are destroying me to hide what you believe is my shameful secret. You are the one who is afraid, afraid of the embarrassment you would feel if others knew you could not control me. You lost your son, and then your daughter marries a man you and your comrades believed was beneath her, and then, for you, the worst possible thing occurred, the man you despised would be the father of your grandchild. This is not about my future. This is about your present. Your life. Your reputation. Your lies. Your scheming. But none of it matters without him anyway. None of it matters if I am to ripped apart from my own child."

"Understandably the pain is quite fresh now, and therefore I will forgive your accusations. Trust me, one day you will learn to accept the world as it is and then you will understand."

"But this pain I suffer is not a product of the world as it is, it is the product of the world as you have created it. No. I shall not face, nor ever accept or understand this truth of yours. Now leave me. I have nothing else to say to you. Leave me I say, leave me, get out of my sight!"

He walked over to wipe the tears from her eyes, but she pulled away from him, glaring, never feeling such strong animosity. When he left the room, she screamed out in agony. The loss was unbearable. In the distance she could hear the hushed cries of babies, babies who were not hers. And for every cry she shed a tear of her own in response. There was a certain boiling of her blood. A certain aching in her heart. A wrenching pain. She did not understand this new emotion. She had heard the word hate. And now she had experienced it. She refused to return home with her father, and elected to live with her aunt instead.

She could confide in no one, and she experienced a rare brand of loneliness only few know. How she longed for her dear brother to help her through her sadness. He had been the only one whom she could trust. But months stood between them and there was no way to reach him in his remote travels. If only he had been there to comfort her, but he was elsewhere, soothing other ailing hearts. Little did he know his sister faced such hardship. She remained with her aunt for months, until she resolved to find her daughter. Her father would disown her and never accept her if she attempted to claim her daughter. And she understood she had no means to support her daughter on her own, but she realized there was one way to be near her daughter without revealing the truth. She remembered how much she had loved her governess when she was a child. It was the perfect plan. She could live with the adoptive family, and become her daughter's closest friend.

Expecting her father would have placed the child in a wealthy family, she knew also the family would require a governess. The one person who might assist her in learning the identity of this family was her father. Though it was detestable to her, it was necessary for her to fall once again under her father's good graces. He was an astute business man, and kept meticulous records of all of his business dealings, and she knew if she searched diligently enough, there would be some trace, some clue which would point her in the direction of her daughter. It took her nearly three years to discover the identity of the family. The day after she found the papers concerning the adoption, she packed a small bag and left her father's home never to return.

One would assume she might miss the opulence to which she had grown accustomed, but on the contrary, she abhorred it. To her, all the finery was only a decoration to cover the emptiness of her family's home. Where there was pain, utter selfishness, pride and greed, there was not enough money to hide it. She purchased three plain dresses and one simple formal one to take to her new home.

The Brookhavens were a fine family, much like the one she had left behind. They loved her instantly, her grace and charm were infectious, and upon their first meeting her, their search for a governess was discontinued.

Bella was a happy child, and was nearly four years old when she first saw her. Her footsteps and laughter preceded her, as she bounced into the room and came right up to her.

"Isabella, darling this is Lenora," Charlotte Brookhaven,

offered.

"Are you my new gov'ness?" Isabella interrupted, with bright eyes and a smiling face which filled the room with joy.

Lenora knelt down, face to face with her beloved daughter. It was difficult to hold back the tears, to hold back her impulse to pick Isabella up and hold her and never let her go. She could see Isabella had inherited her father's eyes and she was so very pleased.

"Yes. I am here now and we shall have the most grand time. There is so much I wish to teach you. Is this your piano?"

"Yes Miss Lenora, but I cannot play it, will you teach me?"

"Of course I shall."

The moments she shared with Isabella were the most meaningful moments of her life. She was thankful for the years she had been given, and now thankful to know her daughter knew her, not as Lenora, but as her mother. It was all she could have hoped for. She suddenly realized she was most fortunate to have been called mother. She would hold on to that precious word. She would repeat it in her mind over and over until Bella's sweet face came to mind. Once she could imagine Bella's face, she would allow herself to nap, but the loud squeaking of the door interrupted her quiet slumber.

"Lenora, it seems your benefactor has sent a package to you."

"My benefactor?" she queried, but thought to herself 'Don't you mean my captors?'

"Yes, I thought you would want to see it right away."

"Thank you Dr. Peterson."

The doctor laid the package at the foot of her cot and left the room. She examined the envelope before opening it. Oddly it was dated some three years ago. She took the large envelope, opened it and was startled to see her family's crest embossed on the package. She carefully opened the letter and noted it had been written on the eve of Christmas and in her father's hand.

She hesitated before reading the letter. 'What could he possibly wish to say to me, more lies and excuses?' It seemed an insult to her daughter to dignify her father's letter by having read it, but she was lonely. And this missive was the first offering from home she had known in years, so she could not resist.

He wrote:

To my beloved daughter,

I do not know if you will ever see your daughter, but it is my hope you will somehow find her, and in turn that these few words reach your eyes and heart. I am an old man now, an old man with many regrets. The pain you have suffered at my hand is the constant battle I fight within myself. This letter is my attempt to right the grave injustices which I have committed against you. I understand you may never forgive me for the things I did, but perhaps my admissions will bring you comfort. If you have received this letter, then you have found Isabella, but there is one final truth I must offer. There remains one deception which I must remedy. Death did not separate you from your young husband, but rather my foolishness and deceit. He did not die as I told you. He lives. May you find your way back to him. I hope my belated honesty provides some comfort to you now. My days are not long for this earth and I seek your forgiveness, though I deserve it not. Foolishly I tried to control the world, to tame it, master it, but you taught me we must not see the world as it is, but as it should be. Nothing in life is more precious than my children, and I robbed you of such joy. It is my dying hope that you are united with your family, the family of which I deprived you by my misjudgment. Search your heart. And if in it, there is only one small remaining happy thought of me, hold on to it and in that memory forgive me. Please forgive me.

    She read the letter over and over through moistened eyes. Could it be true? Only two words from the letter mattered to her. "He lives. He lives," she repeated. Not only had her father kept her from Bella and her husband, but he had kept Bella from her father. But if it were true, she would forgive all, for all that mattered was this one truth. She wondered if there had ever been one so full of love and yet unable to share it. The weight of this new knowledge seemed to bear down on her, and she felt as though she might break under its force. These feelings in her overflowed.

The need to break free from these dingy four walls overwhelmed her, but there was no escape. 'I will find a way to leave this place. But how? Somehow, that is how, someway. I must find him. We will be together again. Thank heaven, but wait,' she thought, 'although the love in my heart is as fresh as ever, many years have passed between us, surely he has married another. He must have his own family and look at me, what would he think of me now?' This news did not bring her joy, in fact it was almost more painful knowing they had been kept apart. The pain was too much for her to bear. And then another thought plagued her mind, if he lived, 'Why did he not find me, how is it he has allowed me to pass through the misery which has been my life, alone? Unless Father imprisoned him, as he promised to do, as I am imprisoned now?'

She wanted to die, but she needed to live. Her daughter was looking for her and she would eventually find her. She must think of her daughter. She would place Bella's heart and well being above her own. She would somehow find patience, and if God were truly kind, she would once again see herself in his beautiful, loved-filled eyes.

Chapter 33
A Homecoming

"Isabella" Edward prompted softly, "Today is the day!"

Bella smiled and replied, "Can this day really be here?"

"Yes, at long last. And your mother awaits, are you ready to see her?"

She nodded affirming his question. There was nothing she was more ready to do.

"Are you sure they will let us in?" she questioned, again.

"Worry not, it has all been arranged, come now follow me." She followed along behind him. Edward's kindness was so abundant she had no words to express her thankfulness, her indebtedness to him. Even if she had remembered her past, whether sooner or later, she would have never found her mother on her own. It was his kindness, his resolve, his connections which had led her back to her mother.

As they reached the entrance to the facility, just as Edward promised, the attendant led them to Lenora's room without the least hesitation.

"Well now, all our planning and hoping has led us to this moment. Your mother is just behind this door and you are about to make her the happiest woman in the world. This is your moment, her moment, so I shall leave it to you. Go in and know that I am here waiting for you both. This is all I have wished for you since I first met you." Edward offered.

"Thank you, dear, dear friend." She said embracing him, "I understand you are anxious to meet her also, and I shall come for you shortly."

"I will be right here, and Isabella, everything will be fine, I promise," he said, clutching her small hand, and believing him, she opened the door.

At least this place was nicer. It seemed more like a hospital than a sanitarium. She walked over to her mother, who lay sleeping, and for a moment Isabella just looked at her, allowed the joy to wash over her and then, she whispered, "Lenora, Mother, Mother, I have come back for you."

Bella held her breath as she watched Lenora stirring.

"Mother," she repeated, " it is Isabella, I am here now."

"Bella, is it really you? Or am I dreaming?" Lenora whispered.

"No Mother, you are not dreaming, here," she said extending her hand, "touch your daughter's hand and know I am here with you."

Lenora's trembling hand reached out and touched the soft hand of her daughter. Tears filled her weary and hopeless eyes. For over two years she had waited for this day, two years which had come and gone, and now Bella had kept her promise. She had come back to save her.

"Mother, before you speak, I must explain. Too much time has been lost since last I saw you. I left you that cheerless day and went home to confront my parents, I pleaded with them to allow me to bring you back to us. I told them I knew their secret, and the only way I could forgive them would be for them to grant you mercy at long last, but obviously they would not hear of it. They promised to allow me to see you again, but the days kept passing by, and if I even mentioned your name it would all end in argument. I realized they would never allow me to see you again. I resolved to rescue you. I left their house soon after, vowing never to return, but Father, chased after me when I ran away. Looking back I believe I was probably safe, but I seemed to hear him, someone in the distance bearing down on me. I found escape by hiding aboard a ship, but tired from my journey I fell asleep, and the next morning, the ship began to set sail. I panicked and attempted to jump off the ship at the last moment, but I lost my footing and had a terrible fall. When I finally woke up, all of these tragic moments had disappeared. The world as I had known it died, completely vanished. For the last two years I have been wandering about the dark paths of this world, alone and a stranger, most of all to myself. It was only a few short weeks ago that I remembered everything, that I remembered you. My past, you, my parents, but mostly you, and it all came rushing over me, but I was too ill to find you, until now."

"Oh darling I am so sorry, but you are here now, you have found me again."

"You are not angry, you understand?" Bella asked.

"Angry? Bella, how could I possibly be angry with you. You are the person I love most in the world. You have been a victim, a victim of a crime which began many years ago." Bella was thrilled her mother was not upset with her and she was pleasantly surprised by her coherence. She had feared she might find her as she had two years ago, unresponsive and lost. But Lenora was not locked away in the prison of her mind, she was indeed right here in this room.

"Mother, I am so pleased to see your health is much improved, much better than I expected."

"I am recovering at last. Your promise to return has given me a well of hope to draw from. And this place has been a blessing, there is a doctor here who has worked closely with me, with new techniques and I have learned much about myself over the last few months. Being here has meant a great deal to my health and well being, and I have received other news of late, very hopeful news," Lenora offered.

"I am so relieved to be here. I was consumed with worry when I remembered you and my promise, but I am here to keep it, I am here to save you," Bella said smiling.

"I do not understand, have your parents changed their minds?" she asked.

"No. I have been lost to them too, and they have nothing to do with my finding you. I have met the most wonderful gentleman. I have spent the last four months at his estate. He has been so kind to me, and it was he who brought me here. It was he who discovered where you were being hidden away from me. He has graciously invited us to come and live with him at Brookhaven until you and I can make other arrangements."

"Brookhaven? But. . ." Lenora asked looking perplexed.

"I am sorry to flood you with so many details, for certain, it is a long story. The estate is named for the Brookhavens, but not my parents, it is here in America and I shall tell you about it later at length, but for now I would like to help you gather your belongings for we shall leave here this very day."

"So soon?" Lenora asked.

"Yes, it is well beyond the time for you to join me, you do want to leave?"

"Of course. There is no where I belong but with you Bella, but I suppose I am still quite shocked by your presence here. So much has happened," she said, remembering her father's confession. "Today is the miracle for which I have long prayed. Thank you for keeping your promise, I knew you come for me."

"It is a miracle! But do not thank me at all, it is Edward you should thank," Bella returned, beaming with the joy of being once again in Lenora's presence.

"Edward?" Lenora said softly with the corner of her lips beginning to form a subtle smile.

"Yes, Edward is the gentleman I spoke of. He is the most wonderful man. I had traveled for nearly two years with no hope of finding my past, and then one night I came upon his estate, Brookhaven. It seemed to call to me and I made my way to a lighted window. Edward discovered me on the grounds of his estate and kindly invited me in from the cold. I knew then what a generous man he was. I must admit the days I spent there began with a certain mystery. The estate seemed somehow tied to my past, and in truth it is the mirror image of my parent's home. It was foreign, yet so familiar. I did not really trust those feelings or him in the beginning, but he has turned out to be a most wonderful friend. I gather that it is his childhood, and his most tortured past which have molded him into the creature he is today. You see he was orphaned at an early age, and..."

"Bella, darling, Edward, his name, what is his name?" Lenora asked interrupting Bella's excited recounting of events.

"Edward Withers," Bella answered.

"And Bella, where is this gentleman now?"

"He is just outside the door, and he is so anxious to meet you. Shall I tell him to come in now?" Bella asked walking toward the door.

"No. Wait, not yet, just a moment darling," she said, taking Bella's frail hand in her own, "I know you will not understand, but I must ask this of you. I very much want to meet this kind gentleman, but I want you to send him in alone. All right? I want to properly thank him for taking such wonderful care of you."

"Of course Mother, but don't I need to introduce you?"

"That will not be necessary. Go now, all right, but please wait a few moments before sending him in," she urged. Isabella kissed her mother softly on the cheek and assured her she would send Edward in alone, as requested.

'Edward is just outside this very door,' Lenora thought. She walked over to the door and pressed her hand against it gently. For a brief moment she questioned the possibility it could be a coincidence, but the thought darted away before it fully formed in her mind, 'No,' she hoped, 'who else could he be but *my* Edward? Oh sweet Destiny, sweet Hope of all hopes, at last my prayer is answered!'

She wondered why he had not found her before, but it mattered not, he was here now. He was alive and he was here. And did he know she was here as well? Bella had said he lived at Brookhaven alone. Alone! Had he never married? Where had he been all these years? Why had he not come for her? Had her Father had some hand in the matter, had he deceived her husband as he had deceived her? She had grieved the loss of him every day. And so many tears had been shed. When she had watched Bella growing up, when she faced the darkness of her imprisonment, when she blocked out the screams in the night, it was his memory who kept her spirit renewed, it was his calm and loving voice she heard. And now Bella, sweet Bella had returned for her and she had a father, a living father. A father she already knew and loved, but as a dear friend.

As her mind sorted all of these rapturous thoughts, she took a small hand mirror and gave herself a quick look. The pride and vanity in her hated for him to see her this way. She was in an asylum, it was the best institution of its kind, but nonetheless it was what it was. Though the pain of the last few years was etched on her face, she was still a strikingly beautiful woman. The years had rolled by, some quickly and others seemed as an eternity and now she was here again, at the beginning.

She had lost everything and everyone, but her spirit remained strong. The silent lost years at the institutions were behind her now. Returning the mirror to the bedside table, she walked towards the light of the window, where she had offered so many prayers of freedom and of love. There, she stood, facing the light of her window and all her fears and the faint traces of insanity hanging over her vanished as a ghost leaving the earth for Heaven. In quiet solitude she waited for the door to open.

Slowly the door opened, and this time she welcomed the terrible screeching noise. She did not mind its shrill because it brought her one moment closer to her dearest dream. Her spirit rose within her as she heard the door close. She wanted to turn away from the light rush towards the promise, rush into Edward's arms, but something in her froze, and all she could manage was a silent prayer. 'Please let it be true, let it be true, let it be true.'

When Edward entered the room, he found her standing beside a small chair. She was facing the window with her back to him, and the morning sunlight was pouring over her.

The mystery was over.

The blinding sunlight bathed her in such a warm light and there was something about the tilt of her head. Even though he could not see her face, he knew. 'It is true. My God, it is true,' his heart cheered.

The door closed softly behind him and in only a few steps, he was standing right beside her, barely breathing, afraid to make even the slightest sound. She could feel the warmth of his presence, and she wanted to embrace him, but the fear she might be dreaming stopped her, and she was content to stand there with only the hope that this man who stood so close to her was her husband. He was so close now, that he could smell her hair and it was familiar. Again his senses confirmed him.

Unable to wait another moment, he whispered, "Emily?"

Tears filled her eyes as she lowered them and found the courage to turn and face him. As she raised her eyes to look upon him, tears fell in streams as she let out a gasp, "Edward!"

When he saw the face he loved so dearly, he too struggled for breath, and quickly caught her in his arms as she attempted to maintain her balance. Feeling her in his arms again, he finally felt free and safe and loved, really loved. He wanted to speak, but he could think of nothing, his eyes raced, searching her face and as he tried to utter something, she saw his eyes fill with tears, and she smiled at him and took his hand and brought it to her face. He stroked her hair softly and then took her hands in his and kissed them.

"Emily, what have they done to you, my darling? I have come to save you."

He still looked upon her with the same urgency, a kind of desperation which only their love could evoke. Seeing herself again in his moist eyes she responded, "You saved me years ago. I thought you were dead Edward, I thought I had lost you."

"No. No, not for one moment have you lost me." And they embraced for several moments, first with tears and then with smiles as the pieces of their hearts slowly regenerated and once again became whole.

"Edward, it was my father, he told me you had lost your life in an accident. When I awoke at the hospital, I asked about you, if he had had his guards arrest you. He appeared appalled by my question and assured me he had not, but he said he wished he had, for if so, your life may have been spared. He said he dismissed the guards after my accident and that he told you I would be taken to the nearest physician and you were to follow if you desired. You did of course, but in your urgency, your carriage overturned and you were sent over a ravine and to your certain death. If his words would have been true, you would have shuddered in your very grave to the lamentations of my mind and heart. Foolishly I believed him, for how could a person unleash such a horrific pain upon their own flesh and blood? If only I had known, nothing could have kept me from you."

"Nor I from you. It was a terrible night, after your fall, I held you in my arms. It seemed all life had escaped you. Your love was alive in my heart, but your body was broken and without breath. Your father forbade me to come anywhere near your family. He called me a murderer, and I accepted the title. And now, so much has happened, so many lives have been touched by this tragic deception."

"I know, I know," she said, the warm tears streaking her face again, "But, Edward . . . you are here. I can see you, I can feel you. It is not a dream this time, so I can forget the rest. But I do not understand how you found me. How you found Bella."

"Love always hopes. . . you taught me how to love and in

your love all my life's hope existed. In my darkest moments I would remember those words you said so often. You cannot imagine my astonishment the night I first saw Isabella. She appeared outside my home. There under the moonlight was she, with your face. I was elated, then devastated. I hated the world for making me see you so closely again, and I hated myself for dishonoring you by languishing in the crushing pain of the loss. I had lived a simple life until I saw her and though it has been a joy to know her, it meant having to lose you all over again."

"But I am here Edward, I am here with you now," she said, squeezing his hand tightly.

"Even now you try to comfort me, but my pain is nothing compared to yours. Isabella is your daughter and you have been kept from her all of this time. The loss, frustration and pain you must have endured. Your daughter was taken from you, time and again."

"It has been my cross for certain. But Edward there is more, she wasn't only taken from me, but from you. Bella is yours, Edward, she is *your* daughter. Not long after the accident I realized I was with child. Father kept me under the delusion I would carry on with my life and become a mother, but he took her from me as soon as she entered the world. I never even held her. Those years are painful to remember, but the pain was overpowered by my love for her. I allowed my love to direct my steps until I discovered where our daughter was. I did what was necessary, it was not a decision at all, there was no other path to take. I left Emily Talbot behind completely. I buried her, with you my darling, and chose another name, another life. I knew I could be content just to be near her, and I was until my father interceded yet again. I was taken from her again, and I could not even say goodbye to her, or explain my reason for leaving her. It was difficult enough to be forced from her life, but to think she thought I had abandoned her, or that I never cared or loved her sent me into such despair I quite lost myself. But now I am found."

"Each of us has suffered long my angel, but you, you have suffered most of all."

"But all my suffering has only increased my joy. When Bella said it was you who brought her here, I could hardly contain myself. And Bella loves you so. She feels indebted to you."

"Indeed, she believes I have saved her, little does she know it is she who has saved me."

"Saved us, you mean."

"Yes, shall we tell her together?"

"She will be so pleased. I see she loves you already. And how could she not?" she said tightening her grip on his strong hand and then kissing it softly.

They embraced again with hearts overflowing. Now that they were in each other's presence again, all of the pain and loneliness disappeared. Emily had been rescued from a lie, from life, from death. She knew at this moment nothing would keep her from him, unless..

"Edward, you never married?" she whispered.

"Only once. And it was forever. I stand before you now, battered by life, but my heart remembers you. How it *does* remember you. Though all these years have passed, my love for you has only grown, it is the one thing which has not aged or weakened. Emily, before I bring our daughter into this room, there is something I must ask of you."

Her eyes looked upon him expectantly, for there was nothing he could not ask of her.

"Will you keep your vow of love to me? Tell me you are still my wife."

She was so overwhelmed she could hardly speak but a triumphant tear rolled down her rosy cheek as she found the strength to say, "I am your wife. It is all I have ever been. Your wife and the mother of your beautiful daughter."

He kissed her softly and held her face in his hands.

"Oh Emily, I suppose I could describe our time together as a dream. When we were together it was as if the world stopped and everything around me was more beautiful, and at the same time everything was hazy and out of focus, everything outside of you. How fortunate are we that our minds are selective, and the sands of pain and despair are sifted out of time's sieve. You see I never think of those darker times, and in all these years which have separated us, I have only thought of that dreamlike state and wondered if I would ever be inside the dream again, and here am I at last, and with a daughter, my daughter, shall I bring her in, are you ready?"

Emily smiled at him and nodded with approval.

Edward opened the door and invited Isabella inside. As he looked at her with the fresh knowledge that she was his daughter, the sense of care and love and protection he had felt for her multiplied in him, and he felt a sense of pride the likes of which he had never known. When Bella entered the room she immediately sensed the closeness between her mother and Edward. Edward took Bella's hand and led her closer to her mother.

"Isabella, your mother and I have quite a surprise for you."

"What is it?" she asked searching their eyes, but finding no answer.

"First of all, we both owe you our deepest gratitude. It was your brave hope that brought us all here together. You will never know how much we love you," Emily started.

"Isabella, you and your mother have waited for this day so long, but what you do not know is I too have waited for this day. When I found you playing the piano a few nights ago, I dared to dream it might be true, but I could not even speak of it…"

"What Edward is saying, sweetheart, is he and I have been separated for many years by a horrible lie, an elaborate deception which parted us, and because of you, we are now finally where we have always longed to be."

"But what do you mean? Edward, I do not understand."

"Isabella, your mother's name is not Lenora Lenton, it is Emily Talbot Withers."

Bella was stunned. Could it be true? She looked at them and she knew it must be.

"Bella darling, I know it is incredible to hear after all that has happened. But it is true. My name is Emily and I married Edward many years ago. My father's lies kept us apart. We both believed each other to be dead, for he knew only death would separate us. But he did not plan on you Bella. And neither did we. You see, Edward did not know this until a moment ago, but he is your father."

Bella turned to Edward for assurance, and he smiled at her and simply opened his arms. She ran to him and fell softly into his outstretched arms, and finding comfort there, she realized there was no place she had ever felt more safe or at home. These two extraordinary people were her parents. She belonged to them, she belonged with them. It was not her hope, it was not her strength, but rather their hope and their strength which had manifested itself in her to bring them together again. Now she realized from where her inner strength and faith had come. Tears of sorrow and of happiness touched their cheeks that day, each trusting that no matter what lay ahead, they would face it with a new strength, and with the awareness their reunion was only the beginning of the new life which was promised each of them. Hand in hand, with Bella leading the way, they walked out into the sunlight and Emily took a long, deep breath of freedom. And in many ways the lives of each of them had only just begun.

ಸಂಬಂಧ

The days were growing longer now and the long shadows spoke of warmer nights to come. This day alone could surpass the joy she had felt on that glorious day, a month before, when her parents were united. This day alone could fill her soul with such exceptional joy.

Bella found herself sheltered under the fiery sky of Brookhaven and under the spell of Love and all its hope and potential to change lives. It was evident in the love she witnessed between her parents, and in the love she felt in her heart for Hamilton. But she had lingered by her window for some time now, and the guests would be arriving soon.

The bronze glow which had lured her to the grand window of her room had also elicited her utter amazement, as she looked left, then right, then up and left again. As she reflected on the long journey which had brought her to her present joy, the scene before her was constantly changing, as the sun and clouds continually shifted and flowed together in perfect harmony. The sun setting in the distance reflected strange and wonderful colors on the clouds, emitting a strong hue which covered everything under the heavens. She regarded the scene as one from a land of dreams. The world was so changed in this light that fashioned everything it fell upon softer and more beautiful. But perhaps the fullness of heart which overwhelmed her was more accurately attributable to the ceremony which would take place in only a few moments.

Throughout the day delightful aromas flooded Brookhaven as Charles prepared the wedding feast, stringed instruments could be heard rehearsing various strains of music, and chattering voices and hasty footsteps were heard, all in preparation for the evening's long awaited ceremony.

Through her bridal veil, she could see her reflection in the window pane. Though the exquisite wedding gown had been meant for Elizabeth's wedding, it seemed to have been made for Bella and it symbolized a powerful love which she carried with her. By wearing the cherished gown, she believed somewhere, somehow Elizabeth was sharing this day with her. There was never a question in her mind she would not honor Elizabeth's memory in this way.

As soon as Edward had given Hamilton his blessing and the announcement of their engagement had been made, certain decisions were involuntary determined in her mind: one, her mother would stand beside her as she made her promises to Hamilton; two, her father would give her away in marriage; three, the wedding would take place in Brookhaven's gardens, by the willow tree; and four, she would wear Elizabeth's wedding gown. As she took a final look at herself in the reflection of the window, there was a gentle knock upon her door, and a voice from behind it whispered happily, "Bella, we are almost ready for you dear, are you ready?"

"In a moment Lily," she answered softly, "I shall be only a moment longer."

As Isabella returned her gaze to the window, she could hardly stop smiling from the blissful feeling, and then she saw them. Edward and Emily were walking along the rose garden, now in full bloom, as if they had never been parted. The sight of them together would forever be a testament to her of unfailing hope. And that she, just one lost girl, had brought the two people she loved most in the world such happiness, was overwhelming. She was home at last. She watched them as the warm, pinkish glow of the departing sun fused into darkness giving way to the world of the stars. The candles in the garden were lighted, and the strings had begun their lovely music. She smiled, gave a final prayer of thanksgiving, and opened her chamber door, in thrilling anticipation of boldly claiming the new and exciting life that lay before her.